SHADOWS

OF THE

PAST

* * * * * *

BOOK FOUR

* * * * * *

D.W. Neuman

ALSO BY D.W. NEUMAN

FICTION

<u>Shadow Series</u>
Shadows of the Mind – Book 1
Shadows of the Soul – Book 2
Shadows of the Service – Book 3
Shadows of the Past – Book 4

ISBN (978-0-9839446-6-9)

Connie,
You and your huge heart continue
to amaze me.
I'm not sure how I got so lucky.

Carol,
Thank you for your tireless
'I need to know attitude'
to what happens to these characters
you've grown to love.

The Cold War isn't thawing;
it is burning with a deadly heat.
Communism isn't sleeping; it is, as always, plotting,
scheming, working, fighting.

Richard M. Nixon

Prologue
Saturday September 27, 1997 12:17pm

The first explosive they placed in the concrete trash receptacle just outside Johnny Rockets. That bin was next to the escalators and it provided access to and from the ground floor at one end of the Sun Valley Mall in Concord, California. Sears, McDonalds and a variety of other stores were in close proximity when the primary device exploded suddenly during a crowded weekend lunch hour.

The force of the detonation disintegrated the concrete enclosure it was housed in. It redirected the tremendous blast throughout the upper level of the mall, down the escalator and sent people sprawling from its awesome power. Numerous patrons were blown backwards down the steep and narrow escalators to the ground floor.

The majority of the people who were eating at Johnny Rockets were dead before their brains had them know otherwise. The lucky ones who survived were primarily the employees who worked behind the counter and in the kitchen. However, due to the large number of ball bearings and nails that were wrapped around the bomb, a few of them weren't so fortunate.

Men, women and children that milled around the outside of Sears, a jewelry store, the GAP and other fine establishments were perforated by metal objects. The ball bearings acquired chunks of flesh during their flight, while the nails firmly embedded themselves in the soft tissue, often at weird and disturbing angles.

The sound of the explosion had been earth shattering and undeniable while store windows shattered up and down the upper concourse.

Thick dust hung in the air.

1

A faint sound of ringing could be heard from some of the survivors that were close by. Their ear drums had been pummeled.

Everyone seemed to move in slow motion.

The ceiling sprinklers popped on and began to drench the scene of carnage.

The origin of the explosion left a discernible pattern, along with a clear trail of destruction that led away from its epicenter.

Bodies were scattered everywhere. Some of them moved and some of them didn't. Anyone else had become only portions of who they once were.

And then the panic set in. The raw panic as they realized what had just happened.

Screaming; from people that had witnessed the event as well as from many of the injured.

Moans were heard from all directions along with urgent cries for help.

Cries for help seem to come from everywhere.

What had once been a safe place to bring a family had been transformed into a hellish nightmare in just a few seconds.

* * *

Hundreds of shoppers rushed the middle and north side exits to escape to safety. Within minutes the poorly thought-out mall entrances were flooded with hundreds of panicked people caught up in a flash flood of vehicles going absolutely nowhere.

Police and news choppers began to soar overheard.

The first responders arrived on the scene five minutes later and joined Sun Valley Mall's security officers who were desperately trying to do whatever they could to help people. Firefighters and EMT's flooded into the south mall entrance while the police and their tactical units attempted to establish a perimeter.

Shadows of the Past

Turning off the sprinklers had been the first priority. The floor was covered with water, debris, body parts, ball bearings, nails and blood.

The first EMT's went to work immediately accessing any person they came too and assigned a priority to each of them. The follow-up group of paramedics began transporting the wounded on gurney's, weaving around the dead bodies that they ignored for now.

Police quickly took pictures to preserve the scene. With so many emergency response crews doing their job the scene would soon look nothing like it did moments after the explosion.

The police redirected all cars still in the area towards the north exit of the mall to make room for the emergency vehicles. Quite a few people, that had been in the mall, decided they were safe and parked their cars rather than sit in the bumper-to-bumper traffic jam.

Twenty minutes after the devastating explosion a system had been established to expedite the wounded from the building to awaiting ambulances and or helicopters. They had begun to be transported to John Muir Hospital in Walnut Creek, the neighboring city. Pagers chirped on surgeon's hips all over Contra Costa County. Blood storage levels were scrutinized and surgical bays were prepped. Doctors and nurses alike, at John Muir, knew it was going to be a very long night.

The aftermath at the mall was nothing short of complete devastation and destruction. White sheets covered many of the dead and littered the area. However, many of the dead bodies were still displayed where they had come to rest after being blown through the air. Some of them were missing fingers, hands, limbs or portions thereof; and those missing body parts were scattered all over. Flesh was embedded in the walls and the ceilings. Blood splatter covered the walls where the sprinklers weren't able to reach. A bloody stump from a right arm, from the elbow down, had come to rest by a manikin's arm that had been torn off. It might have looked artistic if it wasn't for the surrounding macabre.

Twenty-five minutes after the explosion the system of expediting the wounded out the south exit was still in process. The gravely injured had been transported first. The people that remained, although wounded, were being treated at the scene. There weren't enough ambulances in the area, not to mention staff, to take everyone. A make shift triage area has been setup by the south exit to facilitate the wounded's eventual transportation. More of the wounded were being added to it every minute. Police, firefighters and EMT were in heavy attendance.

The second explosion, timed to detonate twenty-six minutes after the first, originated from a similar trash bin. This receptacle, however, was located at the south exit doors a mere two feet away from the triage area. The survivors of the first horrific event, along with a large number of emergency personnel at the scene, ceased to exist as the bomb went off.

The news choppers caught the thunderous second explosion as it blew out the south exit. Shards of glass from the entrance, ball bearings and nails found new homes in police cars, ambulances and the personnel that manned them. Many heroes lost their lives unselfishly helping people in need.

The destruction was readily visible and once the smoke cleared the entire exit had completely changed. People, which had once run to and fro, lay everywhere. Blood began to flow along the broken concrete pathway. Vehicles had been pushed back and flipped over. Fires broke out. As the news channels replayed the video for the world, later that evening, the lack of respect for human life was clearly obvious. Many of the stations apologized for the graphic content but continued to replay the video anyway.

Shadows of the Past

* * *

During the week that followed these horrific events no one had taken credit for them, which both surprised and baffled the federal investigators.

D.W. Neuman

Chapter 1
October 2, 1997

A bright light cut a swath through the dark and moonless Idaho night. A man dressed as a security guard slowly appeared around the edge of a building. He held a large flashlight. Even in the darkness his large round belly cast a shadow. The guard's breath vaporized with each exhale and hung in the cold air behind him as he made his rounds.

What was that?

He stopped his patrol and swept his beam towards a chain link fence twenty feet away. The beam danced over the fence for a moment and then moved on.

Probably just some coyotes.

He shivered in the cold as he attempted to pull his jacket tighter around his overstretched belly. He took a left and continued his patrol along the same route he'd taken the previous five years of his graveyard shift. He shivered again as he thought of the warmth of the security booth and his thermos of hot coffee.

Winter isn't even here yet and it's cold as hell. At least they pay me pretty well.

He quickened his pace to finish his round and get back to his shack.

Three men, who wore dark clothes and black face paint, raised their heads off the frozen ground just on the other side of the fence. They watched in silence as the construction company's security guard waddled back towards the other side of the property. The illumination from his flashlight vanished into the darkness.

"Just like clockwork. We've got thirty minutes until he makes another round," said one of the men in charge of the other two with him.

7

"Da. At least thirty, but I bet we won't see him again for forty minutes. Did you see how fat he was?" said one of the other two as he removed wire cutters from his backpack.

Their leader bristled in the darkness. "I won't tell you again goddammit. English only. Do I make myself clear?" The other two nodded in compliance. "Good. Now let's keep the talking to a minimum, get through this fence and get what we came for before our *Amerikan* friend begins his next round."

They all smiled as the second man went to work cutting a hole in the fence. Soon half of it was cut away. He peeled it back so they could all scramble inside the perimeter of the construction yard.

"Take point," the leader said to the third man who immediately crept off towards their destination using the darkness, and the buildings, to his advantage. The other two followed behind. They all knew the plan and their target. However, getting caught had been specifically, and very loudly, spelled out for them not to occur under any circumstances.

A few minutes later they had all made their way to the locked reinforced door. Next to it was an alarm panel. The bright red light on it lit up the area.

"Get it done," whispered their leader. The third, and up to this point, quiet thief took a look at the security system that blocked their path.

"Piece of cake," he mumbled to no one in particular. He produced a LED tool from one of his belt pouches. The two wires on the tool ended in alligator clips and he began to fiddle with the alarm panel. Twenty seconds later the red light changed to green. The third man stepped back while the second man stepped up and pulled a large tool from his backpack to tackle the door's padlock. He depressed the tool as quietly as he could and the lock snapped open. The men pushed open the reinforced door. It opened with an extremely loud screech along its unoiled hinges.

They instantly froze. They saw the security guard's flashlight frantically draw closer between the buildings in the distance.

Their leader changed tactics. "Fuck. Load the packs as quickly as possible. Move it!"

* * *

"CRREEAAAKK!"

"Oh fuck me!" Over the past five years the security guard had become very familiar with the property and that particular door. He immediately abandoned the warmth of his security booth, pulled his sidearm, and ran as fast as his large body would allow him towards the back end of the company's property. His flashlight swung widely back and forth in front of him which created a variety of elongated shadows along his path.

A minute later he arrived panting, sweating heavily and had a hard time catching his breath. The gun in his hand felt heavier than usual. However, his worst fears had come true. The door marked CAUTION: EXPLOSIVES stood wide open. The broken lock lay on the ground and the alarm panel was bright green rather than the traditional red he knew it should be. As he directed his light into the room he heard the distinctive rattling of a chain link fence in the distance. For the second time tonight he forced himself to run.

As he reached the property's edge he caught a glimpse of someone in black slip through a makeshift hole in the fence.

He tried to scream out for the intruder to stop but he hadn't caught his breath. Instead, the guard collapsed to the ground and lay there panting. Two questions came to mind. The first was who broke in to steal the explosives. The second was that he

9

hoped his years of service to this company wouldn't be coming to an end sooner rather than later.

Chapter 2
Saturday October 11, 1997

Benjamin Winters, along with his wife Maria and their son Jonathan, drove north on Interstate 15 towards Las Vegas. They had started their journey early that morning from their home in Los Angeles. As they exited the town of Barstow his thirteen year old son piped up from the backseat.

"Dad!"

Benjamin glanced in the rearview mirror. "What's up, kiddo?"

"Dad, the sign we just passed said we have one hundred and fifty miles to go until we get there. How far is that?"

"It's at least a couple hours out."

Jonathan slumped back down in his seat. His mother spoke up.

"Don't worry. We'll be there before you know it."

Thirty-eight year old Benjamin ran his own plumbing business. He'd taken it over from his father, whom he had learned everything he knew about the business. Four years ago, on a job together, his father had suddenly clutched his chest and collapsed to the floor. It had started and ended before Benjamin could begin to react and his father died of a massive coronary right in front of him. In the months that followed the business stagnated as he mourned. Then one morning he woke up and made a decision to honor his father's memory by running the business himself. In the four years since Benjamin had built up his customer base and was well known in the local community where they lived. His wife, Maria, began to work with her husband while Jonathan was at school during the day. She took care of the appointments, inventory and the financial books before heading home to meet her son getting off the bus.

This weekend Benjamin was attending a Builder & Construction show at the Las Vegas Convention Center. He wanted to expand their family business to a new market. In the meantime he also thought it'd be a great opportunity for his family to get away for a quick weekend retreat. His wife and son could enjoy Las Vegas while he was at the Convention Center and then join them for dinner, stay the night and then drive back to Los Angeles in the morning.

Benjamin glanced in the rearview again and saw Jonathan looking out the window at the vast desert they were driving through. He took his right hand off the wheel, found his wife's hand and gently squeezed it. She responded in turn as they looked at each other and smiled. They had a great life, a great son and it was going to be a great day.

* * *

Two and a half hours later they passed the "Welcome to Las Vegas" sign as they drove north into the city. Benjamin took the Las Vegas Blvd exit. Jonathan struggled against his seat belt as he pressed his face against the window to take it all in. They passed the Luxor and the MGM Grand, both only four years old, and still as imposing as ever. New York New York looked absolutely stunning and was the latest addition to Las Vegas having just been completed a few months prior. The Monte Carlo came into view and soon afterward they read a large sign that proclaimed the Bellagio would be ready, on-time in 1998, the very next year.

"Where are we staying?" asked the awestruck voice from the backseat.

"I reserved us a room at the Circus Circus."

"We're staying at a circus?"

"Not exactly, but trust me son, its right up your alley. Also, it's within walking distance to the Convention Center so I can get back and spend some time with you and your mother this evening."

"Cool. Thanks Dad."

"Don't thank me, thank your mother. She thinks you're old enough now, but I'm not so sure…"

"I am. I'm totally old enough," Jonathan blurted out. "Thanks mom!" he said as an afterthought.

"You're welcome sweetie," she replied.

Benjamin spoke back up. "What I do want you to do is look after her for me. Can you do that?"

"You got it," was their son's auto reply. A second later he said, "I hope they have an arcade."

In the front seat his parents began to chuckle as Circus Circus appeared in the distance.

* * *

After checking in to the hotel he told Maria that he'd be back around 6pm to meet up with them for dinner. Jonathan was antsy to walk around. The constant noise of the slot machines buzzing and clanking had captured his full attention. Maria told him to scoot off to the show and that they'd be just fine. He kissed her goodbye as his son dragged his mother by the arm to head off on their own adventure. He watched them get swallowed up in the crowd before he turned around and walked out the front of the hotel. An hour later Benjamin found himself in the middle of the Builder & Construction show amongst a throng of other patrons, contractors and businessmen like him. He was overwhelmed and almost became claustrophobic due to the sheer number of individuals in attendance.

All around him, in the extremely large convention hall, were booths from various companies that displayed their wares. Men, in various booths, proudly talked about their products. Scantily clad women tried to entice potential buyers to visit them from the main walkway. It was so loud that everyone had to shout to each other to have a conversation.

Benjamin turned his attention back to his goal. He was here to research how other small businesses successfully expanded and broadened their customer base. He needed to talk to people, just like him, that would help him on his way with ideas and maybe even a game plan.

The sky's the limit.

He turned against the swarm of people and, like a salmon, worked his way against the current towards his destination.

It happened without warning. Benjamin was forcibly pushed forwards to the ground, from someone with great strength, from behind. He coughed and tried to stand up but he found that he didn't have the energy. He coughed again from all the dust.

A *sandstorm...here?*

He slowly rolled over, got his arms underneath him and pushed himself to his knees. Grit was in his mouth and he spat some of it out onto the floor. His eyes hurt and his head felt wet. He wiped his hand across his face and painfully, but slowly, cracked open his eyes. He tried to focus on his hand and eventually noticed it was covered in blood. Time stopped as Benjamin's brain attempted to comprehend what had happened.

The first thing he noticed was just how quiet it was. He didn't hear anything. Images filtered in as shadows, then became clearer the more he took in. Water began to fall from the ceiling. He turned his head upwards and let it wash over his face. He blinked his irritated eyes a few more times as the grit washed away and down his face. Benjamin slowly stood up and took everything in.

A large portion of the convention center hall he was in no longer existed. It was as if he'd been transported someplace else, but that place was a thousand times scarier. Rubble, tattered clothing, body parts and blood were scattered everywhere.

This can't be real!

His mind refused to believe the carnage all around him. There were people, alive like he was, but obviously screaming in anguish from missing limbs...but he couldn't hear them. Benjamin stumbled forward and tripped over something. He clumsily caught his fall with an outstretched arm and looked back at a severed head that still had the majority of its shoulder attached to it.

He reeled back in horror and averted his gaze. His eyes suddenly focused on a very nice pair of breasts, their nipples still hard. Apparently one of the scantily clad women's bikini tops had been torn off and a trickle of blood ran down between them. Benjamin's confused mind explained to him that what he saw could be from any number of erotic Vegas night shows. That might have been true if half her face hadn't been missing. He let out a bloodcurdling scream but nothing happened. He'd felt his lungs fill with air and he expelled it. He had felt himself scream but he just hadn't heard it.

As the water from the emergency sprinklers continued to fall down upon both the living and the dead, Benjamin didn't know what else to do but sit down. He was tired; groggy. As he sat there, seemingly oblivious to the severed head and the body of the surgically enhanced model in the distance, he suddenly seemed at peace with the world. As he slumped over on his side he realized he'd forgotten to tell his wife that he loved her before they got swallowed up by the casino crowd. He didn't like how that felt and vowed to never miss a chance to tell her again. He closed his eyes and drifted off.

Later that night he woke up in the hospital with his wife and son by his side. Benjamin would be counted as one of the lucky ones that would return to their families. He would never hear again, but he was alive.

3

Sunday October 12, 1997 1:30PM

Nikolay Dmitriev stood quietly by as the priest completed the ceremony. The priest looked up and Nikolay nodded slightly in his direction. The casket lowered into the ground. Nikolay looked over the edge of the grave as the first shovel of dirt hit and scattered over the top of the coffin.

Rest in peace my friend.

Nikolay turned away, headed to his limousine and the door closed behind him as he sat down. His security detail collapsed in and took positions in both their chase and lead vehicles.

"Home," he commanded.

The driver repeated the command over his headset and all three vehicles drove out of the cemetery and made their way north on the A1 towards Florence.

Nikolay had moved from Moscow to a large villa, just south of Florence, Italy in early 1992 after the fall of the Soviet Union.

Nearly six years. It's been six years since my power was taken away from me.

Nikolay made a face as he seethed.

Where did everything go wrong?

He closed his eyes.

The Soviet Union used to be a force to be reckoned with. In 1965 it began a large military build-up of both conventional and nuclear weapons. Nikolay, and others, believed that their strong military gave them significant leverage when they negotiated with foreign countries. Their collective thought was that such a strong showing would be a natural deterrent to invasion. As the 1970's rolled around, the Politburo concluded that a war with any capitalist country might not be a nuclear conflict. Playing to

Nikolay's greed, the Soviet Union began to rapidly expand their conventional forces. And soldiers need weapons.

My specialty.

Soon afterward, on December 24, 1979, the Soviet Union invaded Afghanistan. The tensions between the world's superpowers, and the USSR, increased during this time. President Carter placed trade embargos on the Soviet Union and publically stated that the Soviet invasion of Afghanistan was "the most serious threat to the peace since the Second World War." That war lasted nine years.

Then the ridiculous Americans thought that electing the actor Ronald Reagan in 1981 would have the answer.

However, the Cold War was still very much in place and the CIA and KGB tussled all over the globe.

Of course, it's always been nice having Yuri in my pocket.

Gorbachev came into power in March of 1985, and Arms Control talks began between the US and the Soviet Union much to Nikolay's dismay. He'd salted away more money than he could ever spend by this point but his ideology is what kept him focused and driven.

The war against the Americans must be fought and won. We are a super power and the world will relent under out might.

But then things began to fall apart. The Chernobyl Nuclear Power Plant in the Ukraine had a meltdown on April 26, 1986 which was categorized as the worst nuclear accident of all time. The fall of Communism continued with the fall of the Berlin Wall that started on November 9, 1989. Two years later the dissolution of the Soviet Union began. It was a systematic disintegration of the economy, social and political structure. It resulted in the abolition of the Soviet Federal Government and independence of the USSR's fourteen countries by December 25, 1991.

Shadows of the Past

Nikolay's rise in the Politburo, the Central Committee of the Communist Party of the Soviet Union, had been legendary. When his father, Mikhail, was found assassinated in an alley Nikolay was voted in as his replacement; as the youngest member in the history of the Politburo. And from that moment on Nikolay, along with his late friend Igor Ivanov, gathered and retained vast power until the fall of the Soviet Union in 1991.

But then it all slipped away when he was banished from Russia. Certain documents had been leaked to other members of the Politburo about the hundreds of millions of dollars Nikolay had diverted from the Soviet coffers over his four decades of service.

And that betrayer has now paid the price.

Nikolay smiled as the caravan continued to safely whisk him back home.

I should write a book.

The trio of vehicles pulled off the main thoroughfare and wove through a small village before arriving at the outer gate of his estate. The ex-KGB men he employed not only enjoyed the generous income Nikolay provided them, but were all of the same mindset; that their way of life was the right way. The money helped solidify their loyalty to Nikolay but they'd all follow him regardless, as they had for years before under the Communist regime. It was a different world now. The Cold War heroes were no longer a necessity, but more importantly they were even frowned upon. The KGB has been dispersed but they each silently thanked Nikolay because he alone continued the fight against the enemies of the Soviet Union. And he did so from the safety and security his numerous land holdings afforded him, obtained from the funds he sequestered over the last forty years. Here, in a large estate south of Florence, his primary residence, Nikolay could tightly hold on to his anonymity. That privacy was made possible by heavily bribing a few high ranking officials of the Italian government to keep his anonymity safe.

Let someone think about money for a few seconds and greed will always win them over.

His front iron-gate slid open and his armed guards waved the three vehicles through. They meandered through a small vineyard on the way to the main house. Four smaller houses, keeping with the area's architecture, had been built one hundred feet off each corner of the main house that contained a combination of five ex-KGB and ex-Spetsnaz men each. Nikolay employed twenty of them at this location and no less than four traveled with him at all times off the property. His wealth alone made him a target. However, in reality it was his enemies, he'd made over the years, that kept him looking over his shoulders.

Nikolay's door was opened for him and he slowly exited the limousine. At seventy-seven he wasn't a young man anymore. He made his way to his front door, which was also held open for him, and entered his house. He headed for his office when he was intercepted by Sasha, his butler.

"Sir, I do hope Igor's ceremony was everything you hoped it would be. Once again, my condolences on your loss."

Nikolay grunted.

"There's one other thing, sir. Your doctor called as you were driving up. I've placed him on hold for you."

"Spasiba Sasha. Thank you. See to it that I'm not disturbed for the next hour."

"Of course, sir. Is there anything you require?"

"Just my privacy." Nikolay closed the door hard in Sasha's face.

Now I have to deal with this idiot.

Nikolay crossed the large room to his desk, picked up the phone and punched the illuminated line one button.

"And what do I owe this pleasure, doctor?" he said sarcastically.

"Mr. Dmitriev, so good of you to take the time to converse with me," the doctor replied tersely on the other end of the line.

Nikolay stiffened. "Your tone is unusual for a family whose welfare I hold in my hands."

The doctor paused. "There's no need to threaten me or my family, Mr. Dmitriev. I'm quite aware of the situation I've gotten myself and my family in to. Rest assured I meant no disrespect. My tone comes from you plainly ignoring my medical advice."

Nikolay smiled. "Doctor, your opinion in this matter means next to nothing to me."

"Regardless sir, believing what you want won't change the outcome."

"Enough doctor," Nikolay shot back. "I have other pressing matters to attend to than listening to your incessant prattling. You will not call me again, is that understood."

The line was silent for a few seconds. "I understand. You...you won't hurt my family?"

Nikolay chuckled. "Dear doctor, aside from your impetuousness, I like you. Rest assured that you and your family are quite safe. However, that doesn't mean I'll stop keeping tabs on you. If you breathe a word, just one word, then believe me when I say you'll watch your family suffer in front of you."

"I believe you Mr. Dmitriev. You won't have to worry about me." The doctor paused before continuing. "Are you quite positive you won't change your mind?"

"Persistence I like, but pestering I do not. Goodbye doctor." Nikolay hung up the phone.

Idiot.

He turned and removed two shot glasses from the cabinet and filled them both with his favorite brand of Vodka.

21

At least I can still feel like I'm back in Mother Russia.

"To Igor," Nikolay said as he raised one of the glasses high up in the air. He downed the clear liquid and the familiar warmth coursed down his throat and filled his belly. He put the empty glass down, picked up the second one and paused in contemplation.

What happened to my friend over the years? I grew harder while he only grew softer. He gave in to the rest of the world, aligned himself with its evolution rather than holding the true course of the USSR. I'll never be able to ask him about it. It'd been six years since I'd seen Igor. Asking him to meet me here in Florence was easy enough but I was surprised when he agreed to visit.

Nikolay grunted.

The guilt he felt must have been eating away at him. I wonder if he knew he was going to die?

Nikolay downed the second glass and then looked at it closely.

It was so easy to share our love of vodka, watch him toss it back and then watch him. His face contorted and his eyes locked on mine as the life drained out of him.

Nikolay slammed the glass down on his desk.

That idiot! He betrayed me! But Igor has paid the price of his betrayal!

He picked up the remote on his desk.

The world has changed but I can't believe people are this naïve.

The television clicked on and he changed the channel to CNN.

"...a huge section of the Las Vegas Convention Center. This is the second such attack in the past month that has taken place on American soil and currently no terrorist group has taken responsibility. As you might recall last month, there was a tremendous loss of life at a mall in northern California. Federal law officials have stated that these acts are truly barbaric and those responsible will be hunted down and prosecuted. Once again, there's been a devastating explosion at the Las…"

Nikolay turned off the television and grinned.

"The game isn't over yet," and refilled his glass. "In fact, it's just beginning."

D.W. Neuman

4
Saturday October 18, 1997 8:55pm

"Kim. Julie. These really are my parents," said Thomas.

"Hello," said Betsy, Thomas' mother.

"Nice to meet you," added Michael, Thomas' father.

"Um..hi." Julie shifted her attention back to Thomas. "Correct me if I'm wrong but when you told us your parents had died when you were young you appeared pretty broken up about it."

Thomas nodded. "I was."

"So what am I missing?"

"My parents are dead."

Julie stood up. "Alright. Ha ha. Very funny. Great joke everyone." She turned to her sister Kim. "Let's go sis." Kim stood up as well.

"Julie. There's more," said Thomas.

"Jules, you might want to sit down," Sam offered.

Julie was mad again. "I don't know what kind of game you're all playing but it's not funny."

"Em. It's time," said her mother.

Emily sat up from between her grandparent's legs. "Okay mom. Thank you. I couldn't do it any longer."

"I'll see you later dad. You too mom."

"Thanks for letting us spend the day with you," said Betsy. "It was delightful."

Michael turned to Sam. "We'll be talking again, won't we?"

"We'll see sir."

Michael and Betsy stood up.

"Bye grandpa. Bye grandma," said Emily from the floor.

"Goodbye pumpkin."

"What are you all talking about? Has everyone gone mad? This is cra-" Julie cried out. A split second later Michael and Betsy disappeared in to thin air. "-zy." She stopped dead in her tracks.

Sam spoke up again. "You sure you don't want to sit down sweetie?"

Kim let out a quick shriek and immediately put her hands over her mouth. Julie continued to stand there as the word "crazy" hung in the air.

Laura picked her daughter, Emily, off the floor. "I'm going to put her to bed and check on Gavin."

Thomas walked over to his wife and kissed Emily on the head. "Thank you sweetheart."

"You're welcome daddy." She yawned. "I'm sleepy."

"Sleep all you want Em, you really helped us out today. I can't believe how strong your powers are getting. I'm really proud of you."

His daughter beamed.

Laura spoke up as Emily laid her head on her mother's shoulder. "Why don't you calm them down and I'll be back in a bit."

"Good idea," he replied as Laura headed off towards Emily's room.

Bill came up behind Kim. "Everything's fine." He touched Kim on her shoulder and she jumped.

"What in the hell is going on around here!? That," she said pointing at where Michael and Betsy had been before they disappeared, "did not just happen. It isn't normal."

"No, it's not," Sam agreed, "but it's nothing to be afraid of either." He turned to Julie. "I know it's a lot to take in but…"

"No shit!"

"Please sweetie, keep your voice down. It's not the end of the world."

Julie put her hands on her hips in defiance. "You have got to be shitting me. Sam, what the hell is going on?"

* * *

Laura spoke up as Emily laid her head on her mother's shoulder. "Why don't you calm them down and I'll be back in a bit."

"Good idea," Thomas replied as Laura headed off towards Emily's room. Behind her she could hear Julie and Kim raise their voices. *Give them time.*

She carried her daughter into her room, pulled back her sheets and gently placed her down on the bed.

"How're you feeling sweetie?"

"Sweep-pea," she replied with a lopsided grin.

"Very funny little lady," Laura said as she pretended to grab her daughter's nose.

"Gimme!" she said reaching for her mother's hand.

"Okay…here you go," Laura said as she placed the nose back on her daughter's face. Emily giggled and Laura smiled. "But you're okay?" Emily nodded. "Good." She pulled the sheets up to Emily's neck and tucked her in. "Get some sleep."

"Zzzzz."

"Amazing. Out already."

She kissed her daughter on the head and tiptoed out of the room but left the door slightly ajar. Gavin's room was across the hall and she slowly pushed open the door to check on their four year old. Two red eyes stared back at her from the darkness on top of Gavin's bed.

"Hello Stir."

The red eyes blinked and she heard a soft thumpthumpthump as his tail whapped the bed repeatedly.

Laura approached her son's bed and tucked some loose covers in. "Thank you for guarding him and looking out for us as well." She swore she could see Stir smile in the darkness. This small animal was a manifestation of her son's thoughts. At first it had scared Gavin to death but then he learned, as they all did, that it was there to protect them. Stir, as Gavin called him, was short for 'monster' and was still as much of a mystery to her as Emily's powers were. Their daughter could not only talk to the dead but bring them back into this reality. Their children had developed these abilities as a direct result of Thomas being the center of a revenge plot of his childhood bully's twin brother. It was just too much to think about sometimes.

Laura petted Stir, who began to purr, and then kissed the top of Gavin's head.

"Tomorrow is going to be a very interesting day." Stir cocked his head to one side as she talked. "Anyway, guard him well, you've been doing one hell of a job already Stir. Thank you."

Laura left the room and eased the door back so just a little light spilled in to Gavin's room. She headed back down the hall towards the family room. As she turned the corner she saw that everyone was sitting down and was relatively calm. Julie and Kim focused in on Laura as she walked in. *Here we go.*

"Laura," said Julie, "what's going on?"

Laura sat down and took a deep breath. "It's complicated."

"We're beginning to see that," Kim interjected. "And we just thought it was our husbands that kept secrets."

Bill piped up. "Kim, that's not..."

Laura waved him off. "It's okay Bill, really." Thomas got up from his seat and joined his wife. Laura took his hand and held on to it as she began. "It's complicated but it's time you both knew everything." She looked over at Thomas. "Where do we begin?" He grinned. "Well, it's been a wild ride, that's for sure."

"You might as well start with grade school…and Nigel," said Sam.

"That's not a bad idea. But, just to give you an idea of my childhood, my mother was killed the day of my fifth birthday. It wasn't until later on that Sam and I became friends. Bill joined us later and we became inseparable. During the third or fourth grade, when the three of us were kids," Thomas said as he included Sam and Bill in his hand gesture, "there was a bully named Nigel who tormented us. He loved to make our lives a living hell. There were a few times he came along, as we played in the sandbox, and destroyed our creations and our toys."

"Is that why the company is called SANDBOX?" Julie asked. Sam and Bill nodded.

Thomas continued. "Anyway, long story short, Nigel tossed me into traffic one afternoon and I wound up in the hospital. That Christmas my father killed himself. I was only ten. Anyway, after my father died I was raised by my grandparents, on my father's side, until I went to college. At eighteen I inherited a large sum of money, from my father, when I graduated high school."

"That's a lot to take in," said Julie. "Your childhood sounds full of heartbreak."

"It wasn't the best, but Sam and Bill really were there for me. But back to Nigel. Apparently he and his father moved away and we never heard from him again. Low and behold that is the farthest thing from the truth."

"Yeah," said Bill, "Thomas was living in Running Springs, in the mountains above San Bernardino, for a number of years writing his children's books. Sam and I had tried, on numerous occasions, to get this thick headed sonofabitch to move off that damn mountain but he wouldn't hear of it."

"Then I met Thomas," Laura added, "when his publisher referred him to me. Thomas had been having horrible nightmares."

"Bad ones," said Thomas. "Nightmares about my childhood that involved Nigel. Hell, I was even led to believe that I'd killed people."

"That's horrible," said Julie.

"With Laura's help, and a number of hypnotic regression sessions later, the truth came out. Nigel, or rather this twin brother, Albert, had been injecting me with a mind controlling drug with the hopes of it driving me crazy."

"I don't understand," said Kim.

Thomas turned to her. "I didn't either until Sam, Bill and I took the fight to him. We got trapped, knocked unconscious from gas trap and awoke strapped to medical tables."

Julie and Kim reacted immediately. "What! Where? How? When?" they nearly said in unison.

"Relax," said Bill. "It was a long time ago."

"And," added Sam, "if you think about it, you wouldn't have believed us even if we'd told you."

Julie pointed her finger at Sam. "I want full disclosure from now on." She then shifted her attention to Thomas and Laura. "And as for you two, it's starting to feel as if we've never really known you at all."

Laura nodded. "Point taken, which is why you have a right to know everything."

"Should I continue?" asked Thomas.

Julie nodded.

"So there we were, at the mercy of our childhood bully, when he makes his big revelation. Apparently he's not Nigel, but his twin brother, Albert, that had been kept in the family basement. My father, Michael, who you met earlier, entered their house to kill Nigel Christmas night and couldn't do it."

"But how…"

"I'll get to that in good time. Anyway, my father can't bring himself to do it but apparently Albert kills his brother instead. Albert then comes to my house and knocks my father unconscious." Thomas paused as Laura squeezed his hand. Sam and Bill shifted uncomfortably. "Albert then takes my father's shotgun off the wall and kills him in such a way as to make it appear like a suicide."

"Dear God Thomas," said Julie softly as she glanced over at her sister. "I…um…we had no idea. I'm so sorry."

Thomas nodded. "As you can imagine it's not something I typically like to talk about, but it's a lot easier to swallow now that I have the ability to talk to my parents again."

Julie and Kim leaned forward. They wanted to ask a number of questions but they knew there would be a time for that.

"And that brings us to our two children," said Laura. "Earlier this year our family became a target. Initially the men responsible wanted Thomas."

"A target? Why?" asked Kim, unable to contain herself.

"The project Albert created was heavily funded by the United States Government, specifically the military side of it. Mind control would be a game changer. Anyway, while performing surveillance on our family they observed Emily utilizing her gift."

"Talking to dead people?" asked Julie.

Laura nodded. "Yes, as strange as it sounds, our little Em can bring dead people back. But there's more to it than that. They were out there watching us. They knew what we'd been up to and how we'd lived our lives."

"How?"

"I don't know," continued Laura, "but we'll get to that later."

Thomas continued. "When they realized our daughter was special they expanded their plan to kidnapping. They faked our children's deaths."

"Oh my God," exclaimed Julie.

Laura grimaced. "Yeah, you could say that. Visiting the morgue to identify their bodies is something I never want to go through again."

"But it couldn't have been them."

"No, thankfully." Laura turned to Thomas. "Keep going."

Thomas paused and he tried to ignore that painful memory before he continued the story. "We were left with little choice but to assault their base of operations to rescue Emily and Gavin. During the ensuing firefight Bill was shot and I thought he was dead. This psychopath, by the name of Joshua, held my kids and forced me to enter their base alone or he'd kill them. It was then that I experienced both my daughter, and my son's, powers in action."

"Both?" Julie asked inquisitively.

"Yeah. Stir saved my life."

"What's a Stir?" Kim asked.

Thomas and Laura looked at each other.

Bill spoke up instead. "Stir takes some getting used to. He's a little creature, kind of like a dog, that has red eyes and a wispy body."

Julie rolled her eyes. "Okay, that's enough. I'm trying, and I mean really trying, to take this all in."

"Easy sweetie," said Sam. "You wanted full disclosure, right? You're getting exactly what you asked for. If you think we're going to bullshit the two of you at this point then you have another thing coming. We couldn't make this shit up if I wanted to."

"It's okay Sam," said Thomas. "Julie and Kim have every right to be skeptical. What we've been saying sounds pretty far-fetched and even we lived it."

"I didn't mean..." Julie started to say before Laura interjected.

"You didn't offend us. I'm actually glad we can talk about this now. Keeping these secrets from the two of you has been very difficult."

"Then why did you? Why did our husbands? Why didn't you trust us?" Julie countered.

"I'm ashamed to say that we didn't trust you. We were protecting our children. If anyone knew about their abilities then our family would be torn apart. We...I...didn't want to take that chance. I'm sorry Julie. I'm sorry Kim."

"And what if we hadn't walked in on you this evening?"

"Let it go Jules," Sam said. "You have no idea what they've been through. Hell, Bill and I are still processing the information dump that Thomas' father read us in on today. It's a hell of a lot to take in." He paused. "It's the first time I've seen my father since he passed..."

"You...you saw your father?" asked Julie as she cooled off.

"Saw, touched and spoke to him." Sam's eyes got a little watery. "I still can't believe that it's possible. But you know what Jules, it is, and I'm extremely grateful. This is the second time that Thomas has provided me with something that I fear I can never repay, the first with how he helped Bill and I finance SANDBOX."

"Exactly," Bill added.

"I'm proud to be his friend. Quite frankly as pissed off as you might be about being out of the loop you should be thankful that you didn't know about any of this. You now hold the Clark family...Thomas, Laura, Emily and Gavin...and their lives in your hands. The information, that the two of you now possess, is not just a secret...it's the ultimate secret and can never be shared with anyone outside of our families. Even our kids are too young and innocent to be trusted with this information." Sam leaned forward. "And without trying to sound condescending, I can't begin to stress how easy you and Kim have had it until tonight. Bill and I have our secrets from our military days, but those pale in comparison to what Thomas and Laura have had to go through. Am I glad that you know now? Absolutely. But when we talk about any part of this we have to be incredibly careful. One slip up…just one…and everything comes crashing down." Sam paused. "I would give anything to help them out. We're all a family and we need to look out for each other. So please Jules…please…just trust what they're saying is true and that all of our lives are in the balance now. Can you do that for me? Please?" Sam sat back.

The silence that emanated from the room was deafening. A few seconds ticked by.

"Sooo…that's how you got shot," said Kim to break the tension.

"And I'm sure you won't let me forget it anytime soon," Bill teased.

"Never," she replied while smiling.

"Lucky me."

Sam spoke back up. "From that event Bill, Thomas and I realized that our families come first. We wanted everyone to be safe, and together, so the idea of moving to Hawaii came together."

"I guess you're right," said Julie. "My feelings are hurt. If what you're telling us is true then it sounds like you've been on quite the rollercoaster ride. I'm a big girl and have grown accustomed to living with secrets. But it doesn't mean I like them. With that being said I want to apologize for my tone. I love you guys. It just hurt to feel left out is all."

"It's okay Julie," said Laura. "What we've been telling you must sound insane."

"Truth be told, just a little," Kim commented. "But correct me if I'm wrong, now that I'm starting to believe all of this, but didn't Julie and I walk in as your father..."

"Michael," said Thomas.

"...Michael told Sam that they'd be talking again? What was that all about?"

Sam shifted uncomfortably in his seat.

"Good point sis." She turned to her husband. "What was that all about Sam?"

"It's hard to explain," said Sam lamely.

"Try me. I want to know everything."

"Okay, okay. You're right." He took a deep breath. "For the entire day Michael Clark has been telling us his story. It's been one hell of a history lesson."

Thomas jumped in. "My mother and I never knew what my father did for a living. He died when I was ten and I went to live with my grandparents, who I forgot to mention before, were also killed by Nigel...I mean Albert."

"Jesus Christ," whispered Julie.

"Anyway, my father finally revealed to us today that he actually worked for the CIA."

Julie looked around the room and then back at Thomas. "You're not kidding are you?"

Thomas smiled. "I know, right? You can ask him yourself at some point. So, as it turns out, Michael participated in ferreting out a Russian mole in the Agency with the codename, Yuri. During that process he prevented the assassination of JFK, prior to his actual assassination; put his boss in jail for espionage and theft; and discovered that his partner Kevin also worked for Yuri and a high ranking Russian Central Committee member named Nikolay

Dmitriev. Nikolay had been siphoning money from various arms deals over the years. Anyway, Nikolay ordered my father killed because he'd taken millions of dollars from him. But, more importantly, my father obtained some microfilm from Kevin, his partner at the CIA, who consequently died at the hands of Nikolay's hitman before Michael killed him. That microfilm is supposed to reveal quite a treasure-trove of information. But Thomas' father was killed, in an apparent suicide, before Nikolay could take him out. The money, and microfilm, were never recovered by Nikolay and our guess is that he gave up his search for it thirty years ago."

"Damn Sam, you were listening."

Sam smiled. "You know that's how Bill and I roll. And, in case anyone was wondering," as he pointed at the table, "that's why there's a broken chair on the table. The microfilm was hidden in a secret compartment. Thomas has been carrying around that chair since he was a child."

"So let me get this straight," said Julie as she looked cockeyed at her husband. "Wait…never mind. You're right. This is a lot to take in."

"And if that wasn't enough, I'm afraid the story gets even more tragic," said Thomas. "My mother's car accident was a hit ordered by Kevin, my father's partner at the CIA, because he was a mole as well."

"That's horrible, but I just don't understand," said Julie.

"It was meant as a warning. My father didn't listen. What I do know is that thanks to his heroism, and creative thinking, my grandparent's and I came in to a substantial amount of money. I invested most of it into SANDBOX, as you know."

"I feel like I should be taking notes," said Kim.

"Trust me, you're not the only one," said Laura.

"But that still doesn't explain what Michael wanted to talk to Sam about," continued Kim.

Sam took a breath. "Thomas' father wants to hire SANDBOX to track down Yuri and any Russian sleeper agents. Michael wants justice for the death of his wife and for his country."

"And Kim and I interrupted your answer when we walked in Sam?" Julie asked.

"Listen Julie, I told you before we moved out to Hawaii that I was done. I made a promise to you."

"Sam...I...."

The room became quiet again.

"Listen," said Laura as she stood up, "this is a lot for anyone to take in and there's a significant amount of information we still need to talk about. It's been a very long day. I think that we should all head to bed. Why don't we all meet back here tomorrow for lunch? The kids can play in the pool, we can give you a demonstration and you can ask whatever questions that come to mind."

Bill stood up as well. "Good idea." He motioned to Kim. "Why don't we take off and give everyone time to absorb things."

Sam and Julie followed suit.

D.W. Neuman

5

Saturday October 18, 1997 9:25pm

Laura closed the front door as their friends left. The day had started out with all their kids playing over at Julie's house next door, the wives chatting about their men and their move to Hawaii. The men had visited the Marine base north of where they lived and when they came back the pool party broke up. Then the day changed when Emily summoned Michael and Betsy, Thomas' parents, and they became enveloped in a whirlwind of history. Then, of course, Julie and Kim had walked in on everything. Their foundation of reality, of what is real and what could be real, had drastically changed in the past thirty minutes.

Thomas and Laura walked back to the family room and sat down on the couch together.

"So…one hell of a boring day," Thomas said sarcastically.

"Yup. Not one interesting thing happened."

They leaned back and Laura rested her head on his shoulder.

"Fuuuucck," he said as he let out a deep exhale.

"It'll be okay. We'll be okay. They'll come around."

"I hope so."

"Remember, it took us time to wrap our heads around everything. They'll get over the hurt once they see things with their own eyes and realize how life changing it is. They wouldn't put us in danger."

"I know," he said reluctantly. "It's just that I've known Sam and Bill my entire life. I trust them. Now, I'm not saying I don't trust Julie and Kim, but I'm a little concerned."

"There's nothing we can do about that now but wait and see. Full disclosure comes with a price. There is a bright side to all this."

"Oh?"

"This will bring their relationships closer together. Secrets can be powerful, and stressful. They'll be able to open up and share. That'll help build their communication and trust."

Thomas smiled. "Always the doctor."

She grinned. "You can take the shrink out of the office but you can't turn it off."

"Do you miss it?"

"Do I miss the patients and working them through their problems?"

He nodded.

"Sweetie, the day you walked through my doors and started us down this golden road to Lollipop Land I haven't looked back. It's been one hell of a trip."

"So you're saying I've spoiled you?"

"No. You've ruined me," she kidded. "But in all seriousness, there are days when I miss it. But I wouldn't give up what we have; what we've created together. And it feels like we're just getting started."

Thomas smiled. "I love you."

"I love you too…but tell me something I don't know."

Thomas leaned forward and Laura had to move her head away. He picked up the microfilm that sat on the coffee table next to his dismantled brown chair that contained it for the past thirty years. He held it up and looked closely at it.

"This film is plutonium. It's incredibly powerful and quite frankly I'm afraid of where it will lead us. If we pursue whatever's on this then I don't know if our family will ever be safe again."

Laura sat up. "The future's unknown but we have each other. We have our friends. We just need to be smart about anything we decide to do."

Thomas looked up at the ceiling. "Are you listening to this mom and dad? Of course you are. I know we need to do something about it but I just don't know what that is yet. Maybe tomorrow we'll come up with some answers." He put the film back on the table.

"I keep forgetting that they could be watching," Laura said. "It's a little weird."

Thomas smiled. "Well, they are my parents, why don't we give them something that they don't want to see…"

Laura caught on immediately. "I can't believe you think I'm that kind of woman."

"Oh sweetie, I know exactly what type of woman you can be."

Laura stood up. "First one to bed gets to be on top!" She raced away from the couch towards the stairs.

Thomas laughed and slowly stood up. *It's been a long day but this is going to be one hell of a way to end it.*

* * *

Bill and Kim said goodnight to Sam and Julie as they passed their house and continued on to their own next door. Kim checked in on Sarah and Edward, in their bedrooms, before joining her husband in the kitchen.

"You want a beer?" he asked her. He had one opened in front of him already.

"It feels like I need my own but I'll just share yours." She picked the beer up and drank half of it.

"Damn girl! Yeah, that one's yours." He turned around to the fridge and retrieved another beer.

Kim put it down on the kitchen island. "I guess I needed that."

"You think?" Bill took a more serious tone. "You okay?" He drank from his new bottle.

"I don't know. Everything just seems so farfetched. I did see his parents disappear and that was weird. But the rest of the story…I don't know. I'm still wrapping my mind around it." She drank out of her bottle this time.

"Yeah, it's been pretty extreme. Listening to Mr. Clark's CIA stories was fascinating as hell though."

"Yeah?"

Bill nodded. "Some serious cold war shit went down. The mole in the CIA may still be there."

"I don't even know how to respond to that, you know? It's kind of crazy."

"What part?" he asked.

"I don't know. Everything. What are we supposed to do about it?"

"I don't know yet, but something. Mr. Clark wants to hire SANDBOX to help."

"It sounds more like revenge."

Bill looked at Kim cross-eyed. "If someone took or killed one of our kids, what would you do?"

"I'd bury the fucker," she replied instantly.

"And there you have it," he said taking another swig. "But the implications are larger than that. This is espionage. The well-being of our country could very well be at stake."

"That's a little melodramatic don't you think?"

Bill shrugged his shoulders. "Maybe. I don't know yet. But I will tell you this. If they need my help then I'm going to give it. There's no way I'm going to sit back and do nothing knowing what I know now."

"But aren't there people or groups in the government that can take care of something like this?"

"Probably. But who's going to believe it? And what if they got a whiff of what Emily and Gavin can do…they'd put us all away for life…just lock us all up and throw away the key to get to those kids. And I'm not going to let that happen."

Kim couldn't discredit that.

"Trust me babe, wait till tomorrow and you will see exactly what I mean."

* * *

"Goodnight."

Sam and Julie entered their house after they watched Bill and Kim head over to their own. They closed the door. Sam went to check on Craig while Julie poked her head in on Amanda. They congregated back in the kitchen.

"What's going on Sam? Why have you been lying to me?"

He let out a sigh. *Straight to the point.* "It was in the Clark's best interest not to tell anyone else, including you. The less people that know about what those two kids can do the better. Operational security is paramount. Besides, it's not like you would have believed a word I would have told you anyway."

"Don't give me that crap, I'm your wife!"

"Oh for fucks' sake Jules, since when did this revolve around you? Have I ever told you about the missions that Bill and I have been on? No. It's the same goddamn thing."

"I don't like it. I feel like I'm out of the club."

"Yeah, and now you're in the club. Feel better? We have a secret handshake and everything," he said sarcastically.

"So I don't have a right to be pissed off?" she challenged.

"Not anymore. This isn't about you and it isn't about me. This is about Emily and Gavin. If anyone knows what they can do then their lives are over, period. That's how important this is and that's why I didn't tell you. The responsibility you and Kim stumbled into is more important than us."

"What?"

"Don't take that the wrong way. I love you. I would die for you. But I'd also do anything and everything I can to protect Thomas and his family."

Julie contemplated that for a minute as she cooled down. "Are the stories true? Can they really do what all of you described to us?"

Sam nodded. "I talked to my father."

"I didn't believe it when you said it. Are you serious?"

"Emily touched me and suddenly my father appeared in right front of me. I hugged him. He was tangible."

"I don't...I can't...believe it." She shook her head. "Wow."

"Believe it. It's boggling, and awesome."

She grabbed his hand. "Are you okay with that? Has that been what's been bothering you the last few months?"

He nodded. "That's definitely one of the things that's been on my mind. But at least I can talk to you about it now."

She embraced him. "I didn't know or I would have been there for you."

"I know. I just pushed it in the back of my head and tried not to dwell on it."

"But there's more on your mind. And since I know you I'm going to say it has something to do with being out of harm's way."

Sam broke their embrace and looked at her.

"Are you okay with being out of harms' way?" she asked.

"I made a promise to you about that this morning by the pool."

"Funny how you didn't answer my question though."

Sam shifted uncomfortably.

"So you're not entirely comfortable with the idea of being retired from action, are you?"

Sam took his time before answering. "I thought I was. It's complicated."

"Then let's sit down and talk about it before we go to bed."

D.W. Neuman

6

Sunday October 19, 1997 11:45am

Bill's family was the first one to show up for lunch followed closely by Sam's. The kids were excited, as they had been the previous day, to splash and play in the pool together. When Emily and Gavin didn't join them the kids asked why and were told that they needed to be talked to. The children didn't ask any more questions and immediately jumped in the pool before the same thing happened to them. Laura had prepared hotdogs for everyone and they all quietly served themselves before they settled down in the family room together.

"So," said Laura, "how did everyone sleep?"

Emily and Gavin munched on their food as the adults looked at each other. It'd been a long night for some of them.

"How come everyone is so quiet?" Emily asked between bites.

Kim commented on the small canister on the coffee table. "Is that the microfilm from the story?"

"It is," Thomas replied.

Laura leaned forward. "Do you remember last night when Aunt Julie and Aunt Kim came in while we were talking to grandpa?"

"Uh huh," she replied while nodding her head.

"Well, your aunts are a little scared."

Emily looked over at Julie and Kim who sat next to each other. "Why?"

The two women didn't know how to respond to the six year olds innocent but loaded question.

"There's nothing to be afraid of. Well, most of the time," Emily added and then took another bite of her hotdog.

Laura picked up on her daughter's comment. "What do you mean, most of the time, sweetie?"

"Most of the time they're nice people, but not all the time."

Thomas spoke up. "Em. Sweetie. When have you been talking to these people?"

"When mommy takes us out to the store or something I just touch someone. Then when we get home I go out to the beach, to my private place, and see what happens."

"What do you mean you touch someone?" asked Julie.

"Right, of course, we didn't get in to how it all works last night," said Laura. "The last person Emily touches is the family tree she has access to."

"Oh."

"Back to the beach Em. You're saying that you've been practicing?"

Emily nodded her head.

"For how long?"

"I don't know. Since we moved here. I'm better at it now." She was proud of herself.

The realization hit her parents. "No wonder Em was able to manifest my father for so long yesterday."

"Not to mention your mother at the same time," added Laura.

"You're right. Our little girl has definitely become more powerful."

"But what did you mean when you said that they haven't all been nice?" asked Laura again.

"Just what I said."

"Okay," said her father. "Then why don't you tell us what happened?"

"Oh. Okay. Well, one day we were at the store and I brushed my hand against this other man's hand. When we got home I went out to the beach. When I turned on my power a very scary woman appeared and started yelling at me. I screamed and ran back to my room right away."

"Wait a minute," said Julie.

"What is it?" asked Sam.

"Emily, did that happen a few weeks ago?"

"I think so. It was very scary. I didn't use my powers for a few days after that."

"I remember that happening. I was outside watering the plants and I heard Emily scream. It was bloodcurdling. I rushed to the beach but it was empty. There was no one else out there. I stopped by and asked you, Laura, if Emily was alright."

"That's right, you did," replied Laura. She addressed her daughter. "You didn't say anything to me about this. Why not?"

Emily shrugged. "I dunno. There wasn't anything you could have done to help me. I got scared, that's all. I've seen worse."

"Okay. Hold it," said Kim. "What does she mean by that?"

Out of the blue Gavin spoke up. "Stir ripped the bad man's arm off."

Kim and Julie were shell shocked. "Did I just hear him say what I thought I heard?"

Thomas sighed. "Our kids have been through and seen more than they should have. When I was in the bunker a man named Kirk pointed a gun at me. He was about to kill me when Stir intervened. Stir, via Gavin, saved my life."

Gavin beamed. "Stir's awesome."

"I see, but I don't understand what's going on." She looked at her sister and then back at Laura. "We keep hearing about Stir," said Julie. "When do we get to see him…it?"

"First thing's first so we don't keep jumping all around. Back to you young lady," said Laura. "What else has happened since you started practicing?"

"Does being surprised count?"

"Sure. Why not? What happened?"

Emily continued. "The first time it happened I was surprised, but not since then. When I went to the beach a little girl appeared instead of an adult. She turned out to be really nice and we had a good time digging in the sand. She told me the sun felt really good."

A few seconds ticked by.

"I'm sorry but I'm still trying to wrap my head around this," said Julie.

"Me too I'm afraid," added Kim.

"It took us some time too," said Bill.

Emily became animated. "Mommy, mommy!"

"What is it Em?"

"Do auntie Julie and auntie Kim know what else I can do?"

"There's more?" Julie cut in before Laura could answer. "How can there be more?"

"It's difficult to explain..."

"And even harder to demonstrate I bet."

"Actually no," Laura replied. "This ability is pretty straightforward." She turned to her daughter and then pointed to a blank white wall in the room. "Em, would you please let auntie Julie know that there's a large spider on the wall?"

Julie looked over at the wall and didn't see a spider, just like everyone else. "What are you talking about? I don't see a spider."

Emily scooted over to Julie and placed her hand on her exposed ankle.

Julie's eyes opened wide as she pointed at the wall. She was shaking. "There's.....there's a huge spider on that wall."

"No there isn't sis," said Kim.

"It's right there!"

"Okay Em," said Laura, "why don't you have auntie Julie bark like a dog now please."

"All of this is absolutely ridiculous," said Kim, "My sister would never..."

"Ruff ruff ruff."

Kim's mouth hung open in mid-sentence. She could not believe what her sister was doing.

"That's enough sweetie."

Emily released her grip on Julie and rejoined her mother.

"Julie," Kim said with a concerned voice, "Are you okay?"

She had a perplexed look on her face. "Yeah, I'm fine. But where did the spider go? It was there a second ago?"

"What did you do!?" Kim cried out.

"Take it easy babe, it was just a harmless demonstration," said Bill.

"I'm sorry Julie. Free-will is something we all take for granted," said Thomas. "As you might have guessed, Em has the power to change someone's way of thinking, for lack of better words."

"Are you talking about mind control?"

"Maybe, but we don't know. We haven't tested it thoroughly because we feel it's that powerful. At this point we look at it as manipulating a person's will."

"This...this is all so unbelievable," said Kim. "I just don't know what to say."

"Welcome to our world," said Bill. "You wouldn't have believed us if we told you."

"Could you imagine what the wrong people would do if they had access to her?" said Sam. "Are you beginning to get an idea of why this secret is so important?"

Kim nodded.

"Did I just bark like a dog?"

Emily and Gavin giggled.

Sam rubbed Julie's back. "It was a very cute bark sweetie. It was just a small demonstration. You'll be fine."

"That felt weird Sam."

He nodded. "I can imagine. But you're with family and you're safe."

"Sorry Julie," said Laura. "That won't happen again." She paused for a second. "Maybe we should take this moment to introduce Stir to the both of you."

Julie and Kim nodded slowly.

"Gavin, would you mind bringing Stir out?"

"Okay mommy," and a split second later a little black creature with red eyes appeared next to Gavin. Black smoke seemed to waft around its body as if it wasn't solid. Stir looked around the room and focused on the two that stared back at him. Julie and Kim jumped in their seats.

"Hi Stir," said Emily. Stir thumbed his black tail on the carpet.

"What...what is it?" Kim asked.

"Don't be scared," proclaimed Gavin. "This is Stir. He's my best friend. He won't hurt you unless you're bad."

The two sisters looked at each other and then back at the small creature. *What in the hell have we walked into?*

"Each of you please lower your hand towards the carpet. He'll need to smell you."

"Seriously?" asked Julie.

Thomas smiled. "There's nothing to be afraid of."

"Don't be scared," Gavin reiterated as he petted Stir.

Julie and Kim hesitantly did as they were asked. As soon as Stir moved towards them they changed their minds.

"I...I don't know."

Gavin giggled. "They're scared even though I said not to be. Go ahead Stir. Go say hi."

Stir disappeared out of view, under the coffee table, and reappeared at their feet. He sat and looked up at them. Julie and Kim gazed down at the small black creature. Its eyes were bright red. Wisps of black smoke hovered over its face and body. *Gavin was petting it. Get over your fear.* Julie lowered her hand towards Stir's face. He sniffed it and then looked over at Kim who, having watched her sister come away with her hand intact, did the same. They both began to pet Stir and he started to purr. Everyone watched Julie and Kim's faces change from fear to enjoyment. *He feels weird. It's like he's there and not there at the same time.*

"I can't describe what he feels like," said Julie, "but this is amazing."

"He likes you," said Gavin.

"I like him too," Julie replied.

"Wow, he's pretty amazing," added Kim. "And you can just pop him in and out whenever you want?"

Gavin nodded. "But I like it more when he's with me. I think he does too."

"Did Stir just smile?" asked Julie. "It kind of looks like he did."

"Better a smile than seeing his mouth full of teeth," said Thomas.

"What?"

"Just trust me. I'm just glad he was there."

Stir laid down on Julie and Kim's feet and continued to purr as they scratched him.

Thomas continued. "It looks like he's added you to the family."

"I like him," said Kim.

"Me too."

"You two did better than Bill and I did when we first met him I think," said Sam.

"Yeah, no shit," added Bill. "Oops. Sorry kids."

"Perhaps we should move on to a different demonstration," said Thomas. He turned to Sam. "Did you want to talk to your father again?"

Sam immediately stiffened. "No, not right now. Thank you."

"Right. Sorry. Um, Em, can you bring grandpa out to play?"

"Okay." Emily touched her father's hand and instantly Michael Clark appeared in the family room. Julie and Kim stopped petting Stir as they jumped again. Stir made his way back to Gavin and lay down.

"That's seriously going to take some getting used to," said Julie.

"Hey pop."

"Hi grandpa."

"Hello son." He bent down to Emily and Gavin's level. "Good to see you both again."

"Long time no see," Bill kidded.

"Pop, this is Julie Paige and Kim Nicholson."

Michael walked over to where they were sitting and shook each of their hands. He appeared to be in his late sixties. "Nice to see you again. I apologize for last night. From what we witnessed after we left it appears as if we clearly caught you off guard."

He feels like a real person. "Um, nice to meet you too," they both replied as they shook his hand.

Michael retreated and found a place to sit down. "Laura. Sam. Bill. A pleasure as always."

Thumpthump.

"And yes, I haven't forgotten about you Stir. Hello to you as well."

Thumpthump.

Julie and Kim continued to stare at Thomas' father. *He just appeared out of nowhere. And he looks completely normal.*

"So," said Thomas. "Questions?"

"I don't mean to be rude but can I ask you a question?" said Kim.

"Yes?" replied Michael.

"You're dead, right?"

Julie whispered a little too loudly to her sister. "I can't believe you just asked that."

"Shhh."

Michael smiled. "I don't mind and it's a valid question. I am, for all intent and purposes, dead."

"Then how are you here?" asked Julie.

Sam and Bill leaned forward a little. This was new territory.

"I'm afraid the afterlife, as you know it, is about to take a sharp left turn. This world is just one of many."

"I don't understand," said Kim.

"I don't really, even though I should. My wife is the expert. Emily, would you mind terribly?"

"Okay grandpa." And with that Betsy Clark appeared in the family room next to her husband. Her sudden appearance startled the two sisters.

"Hello dear," said Thomas' mother. "Hello Laura."

"Hi mom."

Laura nodded at Betsy.

"I'm really not used to that at all," said Julie.

"Neither are we yet," Bill added reassuringly.

Michael spoke up again. "Ladies, this is my wife, Betsy Clark." She also appeared to be in her late sixties.

"You were asking about what happens after you die," said Betsy as she took a seat next to Michael and kissed him.

"How? How did you know that?" Julie inquired.

Betsy smiled. "A little while ago Michael said that we clearly caught you off guard last night."

Julie paused. "Yeah, he did, but you weren't around to hear that."

"Don't be too sure dear."

"Then how?"

Kim interjected. "Are you a ghost?"

Michael and Betsy laughed. "It's difficult to explain but I'll try my best." She paused to collect her thoughts before she continued. "There are certain rules that the dead must adhere to."

"Did you just say rules of the dead?" asked Bill.

"Indeed I did. Now, these rules are in place for our protection and yours. The first rule is that we are allowed to witness and observe everything."

"Is that how you know what we said earlier?"

"That's exactly right my dear."

"But I don't understand how that works?" Julie stated.

"We don't know either but, "Michael smiled and started singing, "...we know it when you're sleeping; we know it when you're bad..."

"Dad! Stop pretending to be Santa Clause."

The kids started to laugh.

"Silly grandpa," said Gavin. "You're not Santa Clause."

"I can't get anything by you young man. Thank goodness for that," Michael replied.

"Mrs. Clark?"

Betsy turned her head. "Yes, Bill?"

"Long time listener; first time caller." It was time for all of the adults to smile. "Does that mean you're privy to everything that's happening in the world?"

"Good question. The answer is no. We're only allowed to look in on our relatives."

"Well, there goes that advantage," said Sam.

"But it makes sense Sam," said Michael. "I wouldn't be asking for your help if I already knew the answer to everything, now would I?"

"No sir. It just would have made our job that much easier."

"Indeed."

"Is that the only rule?" asked Laura.

"Oh heaven's no," replied Betsy. "There's more where that came from."

"Okay, so what's another rule of the dead then mom?" asked Thomas.

"We're not allowed to interact with the living."

"Wait a second. Aren't you interacting with us right now?" asked Bill.

"Technically, no. Emily has provided quite the loophole to that rule because she is actually interacting with us instead."

"I can see it now," continued Bill, "all the dead lawyers are rolling over in their graves."

Thomas interjected. "But what about those times you talked to me at the hospital when I was a kid?"

Betsy looked over at Michael and then back at Thomas. "There were consequences for breaking the rules."

"Are you saying you broke the rules with me at the hospital mom?"

She nodded.

Thomas leaned forward. "I didn't know. What happened? What were the consequences?"

"That's not important dear. That's my burden to bear."

"Burden? Mom, what the hell?"

"Hospital?" asked Kim.

"It was the time that our collective buddy Nigel," Bill said sarcastically, "threw Thomas, or Tommy back then, into traffic."

"Oh."

"I'm not going to talk about it Thomas," Betsy stated, "and that's that."

"But mom…"

"No buts Thomas. End of discussion," said his father.

Very interesting. Laura squeezed Thomas' hand as if to indicate 'let it go for now'.

He looked at his wife, understood what she meant, and then turned back to his mother. "You're right. I'm sorry. Please continue. What's the next rule?"

Betsy composed herself before she continued. "The next rule is fairly straightforward. When you die you will grow older, in our world, if you were a good person. You will never grow older if you were a bad person."

"I guess we can assume you two were good people," joked Bill.

"Are you saying we're old?" Michael kidded.

Bill shrugged his shoulders as everyone smiled. "You said it, not me."

"Really Bill," said Sam. "Old people jokes?"

"I can't help it. These rules of the dead are making me nervous. Never grow old if you were a bad person. Did you hear that? What's it mean? What's all of it mean?"

Thomas's face focused as he recalled something.

"You have that look," Laura said.

"Well, it just occurred to me, and you'll forgive me for bringing this up again, but back on Alcatraz, a few months ago, Emily told us that Nigel appeared when she touched his father Harold Clemmings."

Laura frowned. "That bast…that man who stole our children from us."

"Yeah, but that's actually not my point. My point is that Nigel was the same age as when he died. He never grew any older; he just remained the same age."

Betsy nodded. "Exactly. He was a bad person."

"But why?" asked Thomas. "Why all the rules?"

"I just don't have an answer for that."

"Well then....who made up all these rules?"

His mother and father looked at each other before answering. "We can't tell you that either."

"You can't or you won't tell me?"

"It's not for you to know yet sweetie. You're still alive. Stop worrying about the dead. Start worrying about the here and now." She pointed at the microfilm on the table. "That's the elephant in the room." Betsy stood up. "Very nice to have met you Julie. Kim. I'll leave you to it." And with that Betsy vanished.

"Nice to meet you too," replied Kim to an empty chair. *Dammit.*

Thomas looked over at this father. "I haven't seen mom act like that before."

"This is going to come out sounding a little smug, but I'll say it anyway, son. You need to be dead before you come to any conclusions. And, in all honesty, this isn't the time to go into it."

That comment alone stopped Thomas in his tracks. "Fair enough pop, fair enough."

Bill picked up the microfilm and twisted it around in his fingers. "So, what do we do with this?"

Michael answered. "It's time to get it developed. Once you see what's on there I believe the information will speak for itself."

"Well," said Sam, "that film is thirty years old. We can't just go down to the local Photomart to get it developed, not that we'd do that anyway. What we need to do is control the flow of information." Sam got up and paced. "The Marine base might have some old equipment in storage, back from the last war."

"And we can call them up, use our VIP status, and see if they can dig something up," added Bill.

"And if that doesn't pan out?" asked Thomas.

"First things first," said Sam. "First things first."

7

Sunday October 19, 1997 12:30pm

Julie had kept one eye on Sam during the discussion. She saw his excitement rise when they talked about the microfilm and the secrets it would reveal. She shifted her eyes back to Michael Clark and studied him. *How can you be here? How do you exist? Why do I feel like you're going to put my husband in harm's way?* She slowly lifted herself off her seat, met Sam's eyes and headed out to the pool without saying a word.

"Well then," said Laura, "perhaps we should all take a break?"

Bill stood up. "Good idea. Sam and I need to make some calls." He turned to Kim. "It might be a good idea to look in on the kids."

Kim took the hint. "Right." She got up and headed towards the sounds of splashing from the pool.

Sam let out a deep breath. *Fuck.*

"What's the plan Sam?" asked Thomas.

Sam shook his head slightly and looked over at his friend. "I'll make the call."

Michael smiled. "You won't regret it."

"With all due respect sir, you have put me in one hell of a position, and that's me saying it nicely because your grandchildren are in the room. You're interfering with my life and my family." He paused before he continued. "I will get this film developed for you but that's all I will promise you."

"Sam...I..." Michael started in before he was interrupted by his son.

"Pop, just don't." Thomas turned to Sam. "Go. I've got this."

Sam headed off to Thomas' office as Bill shrugged his shoulders and followed.

61

Laura gathered Emily and Gavin and headed into the kitchen as Stir tagged behind.

"Jesus Christ pop."

"What'd I say?"

Thomas scoffed at his father. "You and I both know what you want so please don't play dumb with me."

Michael smiled. "Alright son, fair enough. I want what you want."

"And what's that, vengeance?"

"Justice, plain and simple."

Thomas rolled his eyes. "Justice is mixed in there alright, but it's surrounded by a hard shell of revenge and hatred."

"Get off your high horse Thomas. This isn't a safe world to live in and it never will be. There are monsters out there that continually do harm to others."

"Why don't you just come out and say it. They killed Mom and they tried to kill you. You want to use Sam as your tool, your instrument, without any regard to the consequences."

"Sam can make his own decisions."

"Sam..," Thomas said loudly before he lowered his voice. "Sam has a family to look out for. Sam has made promises to Julie that you're well aware of. But nevertheless you keep pushing."

"It's for the good of this country and it needs to be looked in to. Action MUST be taken."

Thomas pointed a finger at his father's chest. "You're doing it again." He stopped to collect his thoughts and cool down. "You know pop, I thought I knew you pretty well. The fact that we're talking right here, right now, after thirty years continually blows my mind. Hell, anyone would kill for this opportunity. But you know what...maybe I don't know you as well as I think I do. You want to put another man's life, and his family's life, in harm's way to fulfill your own needs. More importantly, he's my family, his wife is my family and his kids are my family." Thomas stood up. "Maybe I'm seeing what the CIA really made you into clearly now.

Michael stood up as well. "You're overreacting."

"You just don't understand."

"What's there to understand?"

"Sam, Bill and their families have been through enough. You don't get to dictate what you want them to do."

"We'll see about that," his father snapped back.

Thomas had had enough as he called out to the kitchen. "Em! Please send grandpa away."

"Right now?" she asked.

"Yes Em, right now."

Em did her thing and Thomas watched his father disappear. Emily walked away.

He spoke out loud to the empty room. "What you don't seem to understand pop is that you have it easy. You're already dead."

* * *

Sam placed the phone back on the receiver on Thomas' desk. "It's all set."

Bill looked at the microfilm in his hand. "This is one hot potato."

"No shit."

"So what do you think's on it?"

Sam reached over and took the canister out of Bill's hand. "More trouble than we can handle."

"You can say that again."

"Yeah." Sam headed for the pool as he pocketed the film. "Time to make nice before we leave."

"Good luck with that brother."

Sam nodded. *This is going to get ugly.*

They walked into the kitchen and ran in to Laura and Thomas. Stir was nowhere to be seen. All of them headed outside.

"Daddy!" Amanda and Craig cried out in unison. They came over for hugs, wrapped in towels and dripping wet.

Sam bent down and scooped them both up in his arms. "How are my two water rats? Are you having fun?"

They both nodded their heads vigorously. "Do you want to swim with us?"

Sam glanced over at Julie and then back at his kids. "Maybe later kiddo. Daddy's got an important errand to run first."

"Poop!" said Amanda from his arms.

The adults smiled as Sam put his kids down. They immediately let their towels drop to the ground, raced towards the pool and jumped in with a big splash.

"Be careful you two," their mother called after them.

"As cute as ever," Laura commented.

"And headstrong, like their father," added Julie.

"Indeed he is," said Bill.

"Thanks Bill," replied Sam. "Jules, Bill and I are going up to MCBH. I talked with Captain Reynolds. He's making arrangements as we speak."

"Whatever," Julie replied. "Do what you want."

"Julie." Kim began to pull her sister towards the house. "Not in front of the kids." Her sister walked away.

The rest of the adults looked around at each other. However, their children remained transfixed as they attempted to splash Emily and Gavin who hadn't joined them in the pool yet.

"Damn it." Sam was clearly embarrassed. "I'm sorry she's acting this way. I'll go talk with her."

Laura put her hand out and stopped Sam. "Let her cool off Sam. She's still coming to terms with everything that's going on around here. Besides, all you're going to do is develop some thirty year old film, right?" She cocked her head and smirked. "Now, how dangerous could that possibly be?"

"The lady's got a point brother," said Bill. "Let's get out of here before world war three starts, shall we?"

"You're not the only one Sam," said Thomas as they walked back inside and gathered at the front door. "Anyway, thanks for taking care of the film development."

"Don't thank me yet." Sam opened the front door and left the house.

Bill remained behind and joked. "Awesome. I'm not sure if I want to stay behind or go with him now. Oh well, hold down the fort while we're gone bro."

"Get out of here."

"Yeah yeah."

Thomas closed the door behind his friend. He turned to Laura. "What the hell are we getting into?"

"Exactly."

* * *

When they got in the car Bill asked Sam a question. "You okay?"

"You're seriously asking me that?"

"Come on brother, Julie's all over your case."

"Just let it be Bill."

Sam started up the car and drove north. The drive to Marine Corps Base Hawaii, or MCBH, took less than ten minutes since it was situated only four miles to the north. Sergeant Lipton was once again manning the gate as they pulled up. He was a big admirer of SANDBOX.

Sam hit the switch and the driver's side window rolled down. "Hello Sergeant."

Sergeant Lipton smiled. "Couldn't get enough of us Marines yesterday, eh sergeants?"

Bill immediately piped up. "We appreciate your advances but the policy is still don't ask don't tell last time I checked." He cracked a grin from the passenger seat.

Lipton played along. "I'll pass that along to my fellow Marines. I know they'll be reaaaal happy to see you again."

Sam felt the conversation had lasted long enough. "Sergeant, did Captain Reynolds call down?"

Sergeant Lipton became serious once again. "Yes sir."

"Don't call me sir, I work for a living." Sam waited a few seconds before he softened his face. "I'm just kidding Sergeant."

Lipton visibly relaxed but remained stoic. "I won't take up any more of your time. Here's the directions to the warehouse where you'll meet up with Gunny Malloy." He handed Sam a sheet of paper. "You'll also need to place this placard on your dash while you're on base, sir." Sam took it and put it on the dashboard. "It's a pleasure to have you both on base again. SANDBOX is very well respected around here."

Sam and Bill both smiled. "Thank you, Sergeant."

Lipton motioned to the other Marine in the booth and the security gate rose out of the way.

Sam handed the paper he'd been given over to Bill as he drove onto the base. "See if you can decipher this."

"Roger that."

A minute later they pulled up in front of a non-descript building and got out.

"Are you sure this is the place?"

Before Bill could reply the door to the building opened and a Lieutenant walked over.

"You must be Mr. Paige and Mr. Nicholson," the younger man said as he extended his hand.

"Call me Sam."

"Bill."

"I'm Lieutenant Dan," he said as they all shook hands. Sam and Bill exchanged smiles. "And yes," as he smiled, "before you say anything the movie Forrest Gump, from three years ago, really made my day."

"I bet," said Bill.

"The word on the street is that you need access to some old equipment. I'll take you inside and hand you off to Gunny Malloy. He's been around since the dinosaurs went extinct. He's excavating what you need presently."

"Thanks Lieutenant," Sam said as they all entered the building.

Canvas tarps covered a wide variety of equipment as Lieutenant Dan led them through the warehouse aisles.

"Gunny! Where are you?"

"Over here 'Leftenant'," a stern voice replied from around the corner.

Gunny Malloy was a no nonsense sonofabitch who'd seen quite a bit of action, in his days, and lived through it. He was a career Marine, grizzled with broad shoulders and white hair that was cut short, as per the regulations. Gunny prided himself that he could still keep up with the younger generation. He got up early, ran his miles and performed PT, physical training, as proudly as he'd done decades prior. All he knew was how to be a Marine, and he still longed to be on the battlefield taking the fight to the enemy, but part of him knew those days were long gone. However, his decades of experience weren't going to waste. MCBH was proud to have a legend to tap for experience available to them, and every Marine gave Gunny the respect that he deserved.

Gunny spoke up as the trio came around the corner towards him. "Are these the two slack-jawed Army pukes the Captain warned me about?"

"I…," Lieutenant Dan stammered.

"You must be the grizzled old man they forged out of the piss and shit of our enemies. You sure they couldn't find anyone older?" Sam countered.

A very faint smile formed on Gunny's face. "I'll take it from here 'Leftenant'."

"Aye, aye, Gunny." He turned to Sam and Bill. "Good luck," he whispered as he left.

Sam extended his right hand. "Sam Paige, sir."

"I know who you both are," was the gruff reply. Sam lowered his hand. "You two paraded around here yesterday like you owned the place. You haven't earned that right. I should kick both your asses' right here, right now."

Bill started to chuckle and the Gunny immediately stepped right up to his face with his fists balled up.

"Something funny asshole?"

"I bet you do one hell of an R. Lee Ermey impersonation, sir," Bill countered.

"Godammit soldier! I will rip off your head and shit down your neck!"

Bill doubled over and died from laughter. Sam couldn't help but crack a smile. Gunny eventually took a step back as Bill composed himself. "Good to see the two of you don't take any shit. I don't help pussies." He looked Sam and Bill over. "Army Rangers, huh?"

"Yes, sir," replied Sam.

"And you two created SANDBOX?"

"That we did."

Gunny scoffed. "Unfortunately, I hear good things about that place and how you treat your people."

Bill spoke up. "Gunny, if you're looking I'm sure we'd be hiring."

"That's not what you came out here for so can that shit and let's get down to business. What'ya need?"

"Fair enough Gunny. We've recently come in to possession of some microfilm that we need developed." Gunny just stared at Sam. "It's from the Cold War era."

"We can't tell you more than that Gunny," said Sam.

He looked right at Sam with hard eyes. "Tell me something."

Sam and Bill exchanged looks and then Bill shrugged.

Sam continued. "This film should give us a solid lead on Russians that have been living in the United States for the past thirty years."

"Well shit," replied the Gunny, "you should have said that in the first place. And here I thought you Rangers were smart." He turned and walked off. "This way," he beckoned. "I found exactly what you're looking for."

* * *

Sunday October 19, 1997 6:45pm

"They're back," said Laura. "They just pulled up."

Throughout the day Julie, Kim, Laura and Thomas had talked while the kids continued to play in and around the pool. The discussion contained a variety of personal topics that Laura helped guide them all through. Thomas and Laura answered whatever questions that Julie and Kim had asked them. During the six hours that Sam and Bill were gone their two wives learned more than maybe even they wanted to know. The past turned into the future and some questions couldn't be answered until the men got back. What would happen next? What about the promises that were made? It turned out to be a long afternoon for the adults but a very fun day for the kids.

Laura opened the front door, let Sam and Bill in and headed to the kitchen. The adults reconvened in the family room while the kids rested on the warm pool concrete. Sam handed a full folder to Thomas as he sat down. Thomas opened it up and flipped through a number of black and white photos.

"Thanks Sam. Thanks Bill."

Sam nodded.

"Anything for you brother," replied Bill. "It was an, um, educational visit. One of these days we'll have to introduce you to Gunny Malloy. He's quite a character."

Laura came back from the kitchen with a handful of bottled beer. "I figure it's been one hell of a day." She opened each beer and handed them out to everyone without any objections and then sat down next to her husband. All of them drank deeply before anyone spoke.

Thomas hefted the file folder up and down. "Pretty heavy."

"Just another reason it took us so long at the base," replied Sam.

"I glanced at some of that info on the way back here brother," Bill said with a little guilt. "Sorry about that."

"Don't worry about it," Thomas replied. "Tonight, whether we like it or not, we're all going to find out the secrets my father has had concealed in my childhood chair for the past thirty years."

"Maybe we should talk to your father first?" Laura asked.

Thomas shook his head. "Not yet. The last thing we need right now is my father trying to talk Sam into something. Let's just see what we have here first."

Laura nodded. However, as the seconds ticked by, Thomas didn't do anything but hold the folder.

"Are you okay?" Kim asked with genuine concern.

Thomas took a few more seconds before responding. "You know, I...uh...well...I thought I wanted to know what my father did for a living. But now that I know I'm not sure that I'm happy about it."

"But from the stories I've heard today he's a hero," said Kim. Julie nodded in agreement.

Laura put her hand on Thomas' leg. "I know, but it's not about that. Not really."

"What is it then?" Julie asked.

Thomas made eye contact with each person. "It's about us. It's about this family that has overcome so many obstacles and grown together over the years. What this folder contains," he said as he tossed it on the coffee table, "could disrupt that dynamic. I'm afraid...I'm afraid that I'll be the one responsible for that disruption and I can't live with that."

Sam and Julie looked at each other. Thomas was clearly talking about them. The family room was quiet for a few long seconds.

Surprisingly Julie was the first to speak. "Thomas. Kim and I learned more about you and Laura this afternoon than I ever thought possible. You've all been heavily involved in some of the worst shit I've heard. And yet here you both are, loving and raising two kids that have extraordinary powers. And behind you are our two husbands who have your back one hundred percent of the time, just as much as you have theirs..., and now ours," she said gesturing at her sister. "We had no idea but we get it now." Kim nodded in agreement. "We really get it. This isn't a normal family, by any stretch of the imagination, but it's a family I'm very proud to be a part of." Julie motioned at Thomas. "So open that damn folder and let's see where the chips fall before I reach over and do it for you."

Everyone was stunned.

"Jules?"

"Yes?" she replied and took her husband's hand.

"What the hell did we miss while we were gone?"

Julie smiled. "Membership to the club. We're all in this together now. No more secrets."

"Deal," Sam replied.

Thomas nodded. "Okay."

"Well shit," said Bill, "let's get to it then."

Thomas opened the folder and spread out the information on the coffee table while the six of them began to pour through it.

A minute later Bill asked the first question. "Who the fuck is Frank Russell?"

8

Sunday October 19, 1997 7:00pm

Frank Russell, age seventy-seven, walked the streets of Washington DC. A cold wind attempted to chill him through his trench coat. He shoved his hands deeper in his pockets and continued on his way.

Damn weather! My arthritis is going to do nothing but act up this winter. I need to get out of this town and go someplace warmer.

Frank made a left at the next corner and casually glanced back to see if anyone was following him. The coast was clear.

Bah. This is a young man's game now.

He entered the first random restaurant he saw and immediately headed towards the back. He was delighted to see a public phone right outside the secluded restrooms. He picked up the receiver and dialed a number from memory. Thirty seconds later the connection was established.

"Yuri," Frank said.

"Please wait," was the reply.

Twenty seconds later a very familiar voice came on the line. "Report."

"And hello to you too, Nikolay." *You old bastard.* Frank heard a grunt from the other end. "The latest mission, as you've seen on television, was very successful. No one has any idea who's responsible or what's coming."

"We've been in this business a long time Yuri and now, while America is distracted in the Middle East, it's the time to strike. They are ripe for the picking, like lambs to the slaughter."

I may have been working with the enemy for the past forty years, but killing Americans like this...somehow it's different. It's

73

not espionage anymore, it's murder, and I've lost my taste for it.
"We've been lucky," countered Frank, "and it's time for me to get out. I've been playing this game for far too long. We're old, you and I. It's time for me to retire."

"No Yuri," came the calm reply. "You will stay and do exactly what I tell you to do, as you have been for the past four decades. You've been extremely valuable to me. Don't think for a second I'd let you live if you tried to walk away."

Goddammit. "Yes, of course, Nikolay. Thank you for reminding me that you own me. However, if anything happens to me, my lawyers are instructed to deliver certain documents to a certain three letter agency."

"Now now Yuri. Your service has not gone unnoticed. Let's see this through and then we'll discuss your future." The line went dead.

Frank hung up the phone and headed back outside to continue his walk.

Fucking Nikolay.

His early espionage days at the CIA, back when he worked for Walt Anderson, the director of Central Intelligence, had been exciting. Stealing information from under the nose of the DCI and relaying it to the Russians always gave him a rush. He felt cleaver and smarter than everyone else. The best part is that no one suspected him, even though he was the DCI's assistant.

Course, I through a few curve balls into the mix.

And Frank had done that very well indeed. Joshua Huntsman had been one of his moles before he had to sacrifice him. Setting Joshua up to be the infamous 'Yuri' had been child's play. Once his hitman Oleg Pavlovskii had finished killing off the rest of Joshua's team, it was easy enough to make the chalk mark to indicate Oleg wanted a meet with Joshua. Of course, knowing that the SOG team was in route at the same time just made it that much sweeter, especially knowing how jumpy Oleg was. After that it was even easier to go to Joshua's house and plant the incriminating documents behind his medicine cabinet. However, the best thing Frank had done had been on a whim as he headed out of Joshua's house. And that was to arrange the refrigerator magnets to spell out YURI. He hadn't planned it but in doing so he really put the extra nail in Joshua's coffin. With Joshua and Oleg both dead, there was no one left to question so Frank's dual identity as Yuri was safe, no thanks to that analyst Michael Clark. But at least the WHITEWASH file was closed.

Then I laid low for four years. But when the invasion of Cuba was on the horizon I had resurface.

With the Bay of Pigs scheduled to take place on April 17, a radio broadcast, on Radio Moscow, said that Cuba was going to be invaded within the next week 'in a plot hatched by the CIA using paid criminals'. That invasion, by the United States, happened four days later.

Then there was Frank's involvement in the assassination of JFK. For both attempts he had access to the President's schedule through the DCI. The first attempt was thwarted but the world definitely heard about the successful attempt in Texas.

And then there was Richard Moore and his continuing crusade to locate a mole within the agency. But Frank didn't know that another investigation had been in progress, by the infamous Michael Clark, led by Richard Moore, until Michael brought it to the attention of the DCI. Michael had discovered that Richard had been stealing weapons, of all things, and had told Walt about his investigation. That was all about the code word, Pinnacle, Michael had discovered. Once the DCI knew, then Frank knew, and he hatched a new plan. Of course, little did anyone know that Kevin King, Michael's partner, had been a sleeper and any new information was immediately passed from Kevin to Frank. It was a nice little package. Richard was framed, much like Joshua had been, but with concrete data that he'd been stealing. However, Frank couldn't help himself but to spell out PINNACLE on Richard's fridge as well. An inside joke that only Frank had laughed at.

Yes, Kevin was going places. I liked that sonofabitch.

But Nikolay didn't see it that way and sent in Vasiliy to kill both Kevin and Michael. The data that Kevin had been acquiring was never recovered, much to Nikolay's dismay, not to mention Frank's. They both would have been compromised immediately. Nikolay ordered a new hit on Michael Clark, but before it could be carried out he had taken his own life. As the days, weeks, and eventual months passed, both Frank and Nikolay relaxed. Business resumed, both in the arms and drug shipments, on Nikolay's side as well as the espionage that Frank loved. He'd learned from his mistakes and became smarter with how he acquired and passed his data. Thirty years later Frank was still alive and had retired from the CIA while he retained his position as Senior Assistant to the Director of Intelligence. Naturally he'd worked for a number of DCI's during his tenure at the CIA.

Frank smiled from the memories that flooded through his head as he walked down the street. He felt empowered from the years that he'd outsmarted the CIA. But his smile faded.

I'm much older now. It's time for this spy to walk away but Nikolay just won't let me.

Frank Russell continued to walk through the cold streets of Washington DC as his mind worked through various solutions to his problem.

9

Sunday October 19, 1997 7:15pm

It'd been twenty minutes since they'd dived into the developed photos Sam and Bill had brought back.

"There is a lot of information here," said Sam. "We've got people, locations, Yuri's identity, money, etc."

"You can say that again," Bill agreed. "My head is spinning." He turned to Thomas. "Maybe it's time to bring in an expert?"

"Yeah, it's a good idea. This is my father's life we're going through. Just watch out for the pitch, okay Sam?"

Sam smiled. "Trust me Thomas, I can handle myself."

Laura took the cue, got up and headed to the open door that lead out to the pool. She called out to her daughter. "Em?"

Emily pulled herself away from whatever conversation the kids were having and came inside. "We'll be having dinner soon," Laura said without receiving any acknowledgement. *Kids.* Emily plopped down next to her father on the couch and Laura took a seat soon after.

"Honey," said her father, "we'd like to talk with grandpa please."

Without saying a word Emily touched her father's bare leg. Michael appeared in the family room. This time Julie and Kim barely flinched at his sudden appearance.

"Thanks Em."

"Welcome. I'm going to go back outside," she said as she got up and made a bee-line for the pool.

"Dinner will be soon," reminded her mother.

"I know."

Michael sat down. "She's getting stronger."

Thomas nodded. "I know. The fact that she doesn't have to be in the same room anymore is quite the change from yesterday when she was with us the entire time you were talking pop." He shrugged. "Something for another time, but for now we need your help."

"I've been watching, and waiting." Michael picked up some of the documents and flipped through them.

"Mr. Clark," said Sam, "what is all this, aside from the obvious?"

"Always with the respect Sam," Michael responded as he shot a hard look at his son, "unlike some other people."

"Then with all due respect sir," as Sam continued, "get to the point. You're not the only person with an axe to grind. And while my time is valuable I'll have you know that my allegiance to your son, and his family, comes before anything else. We've all been through the ringer, as you're well aware of sir. So do me a favor and cut the bullshit you have with Thomas. Let's focus. We got the film developed so do your thing."

The room remained quiet for a few seconds before Michael spoke. "Very well Sam. You're right. We've all lost people during our lives. I lost a wife and an unborn child. My son lost his mother and then me, his father. The fact that the three of you," he said pointing at Thomas, Bill and then Sam, "have supported each other since you were kids is rare enough. I admire your loyalty and respect it Sam. You have created a wonderful and loving family environment. I understand that protecting them while keeping a low profile is your main concern these days, especially now that everyone here is aware of the children's gifts." Michael turned to the documents in his hand and held them up. "This information is important as well. They represent a chance to take the wrongs and make them right."

78

"Pop," said Thomas. "Enough. Can you just take a look at the data and tell us what everything is and why it's important?"

Michael lowered his hand. "Fine." He gathered the rest of the documents and started to go through them. As he did he created different piles on the coffee table. Everyone silently watched him work for five minutes before he spoke up again. "As you can see I've made a preliminary segregation."

Bill interrupted. "Who is Frank Russell?"

Michael grimaced. "Codename Yuri. He's the bastard that ordered my wife killed, amongst other things. He is, or was rather, a high ranking mole in the CIA. He must be in his seventies by now. In any case, as I suspected, he works for Nikolay Dmitriev, the same man I stole the money from. The same money that funded SANDBOX and these lovely homes I might add."

"Pop."

Julie and Kim were transfixed as they observed the interaction. Laura just took it all in.

"The next pile contains names and locations of Russian cells, on American soil, that were in existence thirty years ago. I don't know if the lists that Kevin put together are complete but they are definitely out of date. Still, something that could and should be looked in to regardless."

"You're talking about sleeper agents?" asked Bill.

Michael nodded. "This was the Cold War era. Things were different back then. Russia was the enemy. Attacking your enemy, on his home turf and getting away with it, was part of the game."

"Game?"

"Probably a bad choice of words on my part," said Michael. "Even though the espionage and sabotage was very real it always felt like a game to me partly because I was analyzing so much of the data rather than directly coming into harm's way. I have to admit, to track down leads, correlate data, and find a needle in a haystack did seem like a game."

"It's very different when there's a weapon pointed at you," said Sam.

"Yes, I agree. It became very real for me a few times in my career." He looked over at Thomas. "And even more so when I learned that my son was being bullied. I wanted desperately to protect him at all costs."

"That was a long time ago pop."

Michael shook his head. "Keep telling yourself that but seven years ago you relived all of it and lost your grandparents, my parents, because of one man who was transfixed on you. One man Thomas."

Laura broke in. "I think it's better that we move on before this escalates."

Bill picked up on her tone immediately. "Mr. Clark, what can you tell us about the arms shipments? I came across a few pages that looked like money was diverted away from Nikolay."

Michael paused and refocused his thoughts. "Indeed. That was an enjoyable moment. I stung Nikolay where it always hurts people like him, in the pocketbook. I took the information that Kevin had. I briefly perused what information I could, from the microfilm, and ultimately learned of accounts that Yuri had access to. Surprisingly that information was valid, although it still boggles my mind why Nikolay had shared it. Anyway, I took advantage of that fact and transferred a large amount of money out. As you know, I dispersed some of it to my parents as well as gifting a sizeable chunk to Thomas."

"Wasn't that something like twenty-two million bucks?"

Thomas remembered as he nodded. "It was twenty-two point seven million when I turned eighteen." He turned to his father. "How much did you really take?"

Michael took the time to look around at everyone before he answered. "In total?"

"Yeah."

"Let's see. I gave five million to my parents. I gave twenty-two million to you. The remaining amount of five hundred and fifty three million has been sitting in a Swiss account for thirty years."

"HALF A BILLION DOLLARS!?" Bill practically screamed. "Are you shitting me?"

"Wow…" Kim breathed out in shock.

"Easy there buddy," said Sam.

"Laura," said Michael, "could I trouble you for a calculator?"

Laura got up and returned with one from the kitchen alcove. She handed it to her father-in-law who immediately began to punch numbers into it.

"Well…it's a little bit more than half a billion now. With two percent compounded interest that total is now roughly one billion, give or take a million dollars." That huge sum hung in the air.

Bill whistled.

"Pop. Are you fucking kidding me?"

Michael shook his head. "The numbers never lie."

"No wonder Nikolay wanted you dead so badly," Sam said.

Michael pressed the advantage. "Look Sam, I need your help. I see what you did with the fifteen million that Thomas gave you to start up SANDBOX. Think about what you could do with your company if you were given five hundred million."

"Dammit Pop!"

"I've got this one," said Sam. Everyone stopped and stared at Sam. Julie was the most concerned. "What are you saying Mr. Clark?"

"I want to hire SANDBOX to track down Yuri and Nikolay."

"This is about revenge sir?"

Michael was very careful with how he replied. "It's about justice. It's about stopping decades of leaks. It's about saving lives."

Sam leaned back in his chair while everyone waited for his response. The anticipation could be cut with a knife.

"That's quite an enticing offer sir. It's pretty generous."

Bill couldn't help himself. "Generous? A couple million is generous. When you start talking about half a billion dollars you're talking about real money."

"Bill....please." He addressed Michael again. "As I was saying, your offer is extremely generous."

"Is that a yes Sam?" Michael asked.

"Sir. Thomas is right. We have something good going here. Something we've fought for and continue to protect. On top of that I've made a promise to my wife that I intend to keep." He took Julie's hand as he looked at her. "My answer is no."

"What the fuck brother…"

Julie's eyes watered up and she hugged her husband fiercely. She pulled back as the tears ran down her face. "You weren't lying. You kept your promise."

"Of course. Anything for you and the kids. Our family comes first."

"God how I love you Sam." She wiped her eyes as she turned to Michael. "He'll do it."

"What!?" came the stunned but collective response from around the room.

"Jules…I…"

Julie put a finger over his lips. "I know you've been miserable for the past three months. Maybe miserable is the wrong word. You've been missing something in your life, something that you need and love to do. I don't always like your job but I do love you. Take the job and do what's right. If you don't we'll both know it'll just eat away at you. Take the money Mr. Clark's offering and make SANDBOX even better than what it is today. You can keep your promise to me after this, okay?"

Sam was dumbfounded.

Michael turned to his son. "Thomas. I'm sorry. I'm only human and I'm not perfect. I just want a little justice for your mother and me. But the buck stops with you. Say the word and I'll end this right now."

Thomas chewed on his father's words. There's nothing like being stuck between a rock and hard place. "If Sam and Julie are okay with this then so am I."

Sam looked into his wife's eyes. "What has gotten into you? Are you sure?"

Julie nodded. "I love you Sam. This is what you do. Go with my blessing and do what you need to do. Just promise me one thing."

"Anything sweetie…what is it?"

"Just come back to me, okay?"

"I promise." He pulled her close and hugged her. "I promise."

"Holy shit, this might actually be happening," said Bill.

Michael was pleased and smiled. He waited for a little bit before asking the next question. "What do we need to get this done?"

Bill answered. "Just the little things like planning, money, manpower, equipment and a lot of luck. I'm sure I can come up with a few other things to add to the list," he joked.

Kim stood up. "This might be a good time to get the kids home for dinner."

"Agreed," said Laura. "Everyone go home and get some rest. I have a sense that we're all going to be very busy soon enough."

Michael stood, approached Sam and shook Sam's hand. "Thank you Julie. Thank you Sam."

"Of course Michael," Julie replied. "You're family."

10
Monday October 20, 1997 2:30pm

"From what you've told me about Yuri sir, it might be a good idea to push the timing out."

"Niet." Nikolay paced around his office. "My operation will continue to stay in motion and on schedule."

"Of course sir," said the man on the other end of the line. "Is there anything you wanted me to do about Yuri?"

"He said that if anything happened to him his lawyer would release certain documents. I want you to start looking into where that information could be located." Nikolay stood still and gripped the phone tightly. "Yuri has proven himself to be very resourceful…but he will not get away with threatening me after all these years."

"Very well sir. I'll look into it. Is there anything else?"

"There are seven days until the next incident. I'll talk to you again in six." The line went dead and Nikolay placed the phone back on the cradle. He sat down in his chair, behind his desk, and smiled.

Everything might just come together.

D.W. Neuman

11

Tuesday October 21, 1997 9:45am

In Marin, California, a smartly dressed mid-twenties Caucasian woman with shoulder length black hair opened the front door of SANDBOX. Roberta, the executive admin, had followed the young lady's approach from the parking lot via the CCT, the closed circuit television cameras, from behind her desk. Roberta raised her head as the young woman approached.

"May I help you?"

"Good morning. My name is Rebecca Cross. I have an appointment at ten."

"Yes, of course, Ms. Cross."

"Rebecca, ma'am."

"It's hard to break those habits."

"Ma'am?"

Roberta smiled. "Rebecca, my name's Roberta and we've been expecting you." She closed Rebecca's dossier that lay on her desk, stood and extended her hand. "Welcome to SANDBOX." Rebecca shook the offered hand firmly and let go. "Is there anything I can get you while you wait? Coffee? Tea?"

"No, but thank you just the same, ma'am."

"Very well." She pushed a button on her desk's intercom. "Alex, Rebecca Cross is here."

"I'll be down in ten minutes," came the reply.

"We've got a few minutes before they're ready for you." Roberta gestured towards the plush couches that bracketed the large coffee table adjacent to her desk. "Why don't we make ourselves comfortable and get to know each other." They walked thirty feet and sat down across from each other.

"So Rebecca, why don't you tell me a little about yourself?"

"I'm twenty-seven and enlisted in the army right out of high school at eighteen. I thought about flying helicopters but ended up becoming a combat medic instead. I was deployed and participated in Operation Desert Storm, back in 1991, as well as Operation Desert Strike last year."

Roberta nodded her head as if hearing it for the first time but she was already well versed with Rebecca Cross' entire military career. "And what brings you to our doorstep rather than re-enlisting?"

Rebecca shifted a little in her seat. "May I be direct with you?"

"That's one of the ways we run our business dear."

Rebecca digested what she'd just heard and took it at face value. "I've seen combat and what it does to men, both to their bodies and their minds. During my deployments I've patched up more soldiers than I care to remember."

"Go on."

"What it comes down to is that there are no real winners on the battlefield."

"I see. And why do you think we would hire you?"

Oh God, did I just blow this interview? Crap, I might as well go for it. "There are quite a number of reasons SANDBOX needs me. I'm a seasoned combat medic for one. Two, I know how to handle a weapon. Three, my guess is that SANDBOX has only a few, if any, females on its staff, present company excluded. And four, the Army won't let me, or any other female, on the front lines. I know I'm as good as any man and I'm here to prove it."

Roberta grinned. "Do you really think playing the gender card is the best way to approach this?"

"Ma'am..., Roberta, I'll play whatever card I have to to procure this job. I want...I mean I need to be part of something I actually care about. Your PMC, or private military company, gives me control over my life and the jobs I accept. Being a female, in my opinion, actually gives me an edge over my male counterparts."

"Explain."

"What if SANDBOX gets an offer to protect a HVT, a high value target, but that target is female and requests an all-female protection detail? Not only could I fill that role, since who really expects a female bodyguard, but my skillset and background come in very handy in case something serious does happen to go down."

Roberta changed gears. "Are you married?"

"No."

"Boyfriend?"

"Maybe someday but not currently."

"Drugs?"

"No ma'am."

"Are there any skeletons in your closet that we should be aware of?"

"I…I don't believe so. No." *What do I do? Do I keep answering her?*

They both heard the distinct sound of combat boots coming towards them. Roberta smiled and stood up, as did Rebecca.

"Who do you have for me today Roberta?" said Alex as he walked up to them. He was dressed in a black t-shirt with SANDBOX embroidered on it.

"Alex, this is Rebecca Cross. She'll be starting with us this week."

A stunned look came over Rebecca's face as she looked at Roberta. "I don't understand."

"I'm a pretty good judge of character my dear. Alex runs our Human Resource department."

Rebecca caught herself and then smiled warmly at Roberta. "Tricky. Thank you."

"My pleasure; and you're right you know."

"Right?"

"We do need more women. However, more importantly, we need more forward thinking women like you. It's going to be a long time before the US military allows equality in the armed services. You're smart, level headed and know what you want. SANDBOX is a family and I think you're going to fit in nicely." She turned to Alex. "I'd appreciate it if you wouldn't mind running through all the paperwork with this young lady."

"Of course." He turned to Rebecca. "If you'd come with me please."

Rebecca hesitated.

"Is there something else dear?"

"Am I the first?"

Roberta smiled and nodded. "That you are. Don't let us down."

Rebecca grinned. "Thank you Roberta."

"You're welcome."

Alex led Rebecca Cross towards the stairs that led to the second floor.

Roberta made her way back to her desk and sat down. "See, old habits can be changed." She took Rebecca's dossier, unlocked a file drawer and slipped it back in place.

<u>12</u>

Wednesday October 22, 1997 10:30am

Since Sunday's decision, to help out Michael, they'd all kept busy. Michael, Sam, Bill and Thomas began to work out what they'd need to do as well as the processes to get them done. Laura, on the other hand, fast tracked getting six year old Emily her first passport. Pulling her daughter out of kindergarten hadn't been a big deal. Laura knew she was smarter than most of the other kids in her class.

Julie and Kim continued to support each other now that they had given Sam and Bill the green light to proceed. They knew their men craved the excitement, danger and adrenaline rush that their jobs provided them. For Julie, it had been particularly difficult letting Sam go. She wanted the security of the family life they'd had for the past three months here in Hawaii. She was happy that Sam had turned Michael's offer down flat; that he'd kept his promise to her. Julie knew she could trust Sam to do this one last mission and come home to her. Course, the five hundred million dollar price tag that went with the job was an extremely enticing incentive she couldn't overlook when she'd given Sam the green light.

All in all, Monday and Tuesday had been busy days for everyone involved. And now Thomas, Laura, Emily and Gavin were on the way to the airport to catch a flight.

"Are you sure this is the only way this can be taken care of?" asked Laura.

"I'm afraid so sweetie," replied Thomas. "When my father setup the account he did it from a bank in downtown Orinda. Banks don't mind depositing money. However, removing the money, especially in large amounts, is an entirely different matter.

We don't need to take any unnecessary chances which is why we all decided to do it this way."

"I guess. I'm just worried. Switzerland is on the other side of the world."

"Listen, Emily and I will be fine."

"Yeah mom, I'll be fine."

"And," continued Thomas, "I can't do this on my own. My father has the passcode to access the account. Without Emily at my side none of this moves forward."

The concern on Laura's face didn't change. "You sure you're up for this Em? It's a long flight and it'll be cold there."

"I know," Emily replied. "It's going to be an adventure."

"Good grief. From the mouths of babes," said Laura. "Just promise me that you'll be careful, okay?"

"I will mom, geez."

Thomas chuckled from behind the wheel.

Laura smacked him on the arm. "Don't encourage her," she said with a smile.

Next to his sister, in the backseat, it was Gavin's turn to giggle.

* * *

The five hour flight from Honolulu to San Francisco went without incident. Emily even handled the hour and a half layover with ease. It wasn't until they boarded the plane for Zurich, Switzerland that Emily became a little cranky. Aside from her amazing powers she was still a regular six year old prone to outbursts from time to time. This was her first time flying long distance and it was a little overwhelming. The first class seats helped at least, along with a very friendly staff, and it wasn't long before Thomas' daughter had eaten and passed out in the gigantic airplane seat.

Thomas was nervous on the inside but didn't show it outwardly. He had his own doubts that his mind chewed on. *What if this trip was for naught? What if someone was waiting for them? What if Laura's concerns came true?* He looked over at his daughter in the seat next to him. He put his hand on her leg. *You're an amazing young lady. You're so young and yet you've been through so much already. I just hope I'm doing the right thing for you.* He looked at his watch and calculated the time remaining in his head. *Just another nine, of the nearly twelve hour flight, before we land.* Thomas found his earphones, picked out a movie to watch and pretended that time wasn't dragging by.

* * *

With the eleven hour difference in time between Hawaii and Switzerland, not to mention the roughly nineteen hours of travel they'd taken, both Thomas and Emily's clocks were out of sync. They had left Hawaii at ten-thirty in the morning on Wednesday and arrived in Zurich at four in the afternoon on Thursday. To them it still felt like it was five in the morning Hawaiian time. They were both extremely tired as their town car drove them to their hotel in downtown Zurich. Thomas checked them in, handing over both of their passports before they were quickly ushered up to their room. Their appointment was for the following morning at nine followed by their return flight at two.

* * *

The weather was brisk in Zurich. During the early morning they couldn't sleep so they took that time to summon Michael into existence and run through their scenario. Thomas and Emily had eaten a hearty breakfast in their room before they headed out. At eight forty five a town car drove them from their hotel to the Credit Suisse Bank for their nine o'clock appointment. The three of them arrived on time, got out of the car and walked through the Swiss bank's front doors. The town car parked around the corner and waited for their return. Thomas held on to Emily's hand as they entered with Michael leading the way.

"Guten morgen," said a well-dressed man in a suit.

"Good morning," Michael said in return. "I have an appointment with Mr. Kleiner."

"Ah. Very good. Will you please have a seat while I fetch him? May I offer you something to drink?"

"Perhaps a juice-box for my grand-daughter."

"Of course sir. I'll be back momentarily." The man headed off.

The three travelers sat down on a very comfortable couch with Emily perched on her father's knee.

"They're very polite," Thomas observed.

"And organized. They pride themselves on it," said Michael. "Hopefully this won't take too long but I suspect there'll be some hoops I'll have to jump through to make this happen."

"What? You said this was the easy part."

"Trust me son, it will be. It's just that this account hasn't seen any activity for thirty years. They'll be curious but not overtly so."

"If you say so pop." He turned to his daughter. "How're you doing pumpkin?"

"Thirsty."

As if on cue a man walked over to them with an apple juice-box and presented it to Emily. "Young lady, please accept this with our compliments."

Thomas spoke up. "What do you say Em?"

"Thank you."

The man smiled in return. "You're very welcome." He turned his attention to the eldest Clark. "Sir, I am Mr. Kleiner." He extended his hand and Michael shook it.

"Michael Clark. This is my son, Thomas, and my grand-daughter, Emily."

"Very pleased to meet you." He shook Thomas' hand next and then focused on Michael. "Would you like your family to join us?"

"Yes."

"Excellent sir. Right this way please." Mr. Kleiner headed off with the Clark's in tow to his large office. He closed the door behind them for privacy while they took a seat. "How may I be of assistance to you today Mr. Clark?"

"Mr. Kleiner, I have a rather large account that I need access to today."

"I can certainly help you with that. Before we begin may I inquire as to what you'd like to accomplish?"

"I wish to make the following transfers from this primary account into the ones I have listed on this paper." Michael unfolded a piece of paper but held on to it.

"Of course sir. If you wouldn't mind writing down your numbered account so I can look it up before we can get started." He handed over a small pad and a pen. Michael wrote out the number from memory and handed it back. "Very good sir. I'll just look this up in my computer and we'll go from there." He typed away on his keyboard while Emily walked around the office looking at the various pictures on the wall and sucking on her juice-box straw. "And your passcode Mr. Clark?"

"Dogpatch"

"Thank you. Your account has been verified." He paused for a second. "Oh my."

"Problem?" asked Michael.

"Please excuse me. I don't typically see such a large amount in one account. Are you sure you don't want to discuss this in private sir?"

"They're family."

"Of course. My apologies." Mr. Kleiner's eyes flickered back to the screen. "This account hasn't been accessed for thirty years sir. May I inquire why not?"

Without missing a beat Michael replied, "I've been dead." Then he smiled.

Mr. Kleiner's didn't get it at first but then he chuckled. "A joke. I get it. I'm sorry for inquiring. We're very happy that you've been a loyal customer for this long. May I please see the paper with your instructions now?"

*   *   *

Their flight left on time, just after two in the afternoon. Thomas knew it wasn't going to be easy on his daughter but she was surprisingly in a good mood the entire way home. Their flight landed in Hawaii on Friday morning at eight-thirty.

What they didn't know was that as soon as the Swiss account had been accessed, by Mr. Kleiner, an alert was sent out. That alert had been setup thirty years prior but this was the first time it'd ever become active.

13

Wednesday October 22, 1997 2:35pm

When Laura returned from the airport she puttered around the house for a few hours while trying to ignore the fact that her husband and daughter were on a plane headed out of the country. Julie and Kim had called and asked how things were going. Shortly thereafter they found themselves lounging outside by the pool together. It was eighty-seven degrees with a slight breeze coming in from the ocean. Julie and Kim's kids were at school and would be home shortly while Gavin played on the lawn with Stir.

"So Laura," Kim asked, "how did the airport go this morning?"

Laura knew that they'd been read in on the current plans. There weren't any secrets to keep any longer. "I didn't want to let them go quite honestly."

"I don't blame you for feeling that way," Julie said. "It seems like there are so many unknowns right now. To be honest I don't even know what's really happening."

"Everything is hard to wrap my head around," said Kim.

Julie nodded. "Me too."

"Listen," Laura started, "I'm sorry we didn't tell you. You're my best friends."

Julie turned her head towards Laura. "Kim and I completely understand. Sure, at first I was mad and hurt, but I'm over that now. Realistically, how would you have even broached the topic with us without it sounding completely insane? I mean, look how far we've all come in the past few days. I have an entirely new appreciation for you and your family. Keeping those secrets, not only from us, but from the rest of the world has got to be exhausting."

"It still is," Laura replied. "The good news is that I can talk freely about it now, well, as long as your kids aren't within earshot that is."

"Yeah. A couple of nine and five year olds aren't exactly the best idea for secret keepers," said Kim. She looked over at Gavin from beneath her shades. "I mean, I look over at your son Laura and I still don't believe what I'm seeing. That thing…"

"Stir. His name is Stir."

"Okay….well Stir and Gavin are playing but from the stories we've heard he attacked a man and…"

"Stir saved Thomas' life and protected both Emily and Gavin. I'm extremely grateful."

Kim closed her mouth.

"I just don't care about that. Whatever Stir is and wherever he comes from I'm grateful for him." Laura paused and collected her thoughts. "I don't claim to understand what's going on. I do know that this is the hand we've been dealt. We're not going to have a normal life but I will try my damndest to make it such. I don't know what the future holds but I do know that I need your support to get through it."

"You have it," Julie said immediately. "You have it from both of us. Kim didn't mean anything. It's just that we're four days into digesting this huge data dump, as Sam would put it. It's a lot to take in."

Laura apologized. "Sorry. I'm still a bit edgy."

"I'm sorry too," Kim added. "I can only imagine how tough it's been for you."

Laura smiled. "The funny thing is, it hasn't been tough. Well, not quite yet. Gavin should be in preschool but that's a gamble at best. If Stir makes a sudden appearance then our lives would be

over. We can't take that risk. I might have to homeschool him"
She took a sip of her iced tea. "Emily, I can sense, is going to be a
handful as she grows older."

"She's one smart kid, that's for sure," said Laura.

"I know, and part of that worries me. With her ability to
coerce people just by touching them…, well, that's manageable at
age six. Probably not so much as she hits her teens."

"Rebellious stage?"

"Pretty much. It worries me that our kids won't be able to
have a normal life because of their abilities. Keeping them, and us,
safe is going to be progressively more difficult as they grow
older."

"And let me guess," Julie said, "now that Kim and I know you
have to worry whether we can keep your secret?"

"I…I'm not proud to admit that…but yes."

"I'd say don't worry but I know that won't help. What I know
is that our husbands have been best friends since they were kids.
They've been through things together. They're in their own club.
Well guess what, the three of us have our own club now. Not only
do you have to worry about your family Laura, so do my sister and
I. We're bonded closer than ever now. It's our job to watch out
for all of our families."

"I second that," Kim said as she raised her glass of iced tea.

"To the girl's club then," said Laura.

Laura smiled. "To the girl's club."

"I love you guys."

"Love you too," replied the two sisters in unison.

Their three glasses clinked together in the afternoon sun.

D.W. Neuman

14

Thursday October 23, 1997 10:23am

Sasha knocked on Nikolay's office door.

"Come."

Sasha opened the door and walked in. Nikolay looked up and saw that his butler grasped something in his hand.

"What is it?"

"A telegram just arrived for you."

"Give it here," he said without getting up from his chair.
Sasha walked over and handed it over. "That is all." Sasha exited Nikolay's office and closed the door behind him.

Nikolay ripped open the telegram and began to read.

NIKOLAY DMITRIEV

    SURVEALED ACCOUNT IN ZURICH ACCESSED AFTER THIRTY YEARS –(STOP)– ONE BILLION DOLLARS TRANSFERRED –(STOP)– MICHAEL CLARK ALIVE –(STOP)–

Nikolay reread the telegram twice before laying it down on his desk. *This doesn't make any sense. Michael Clark is dead.* It was verified. He shook his head. *Michael can't be alive but the money he stole from me is real enough.* He picked up the phone and dialed a number.

"I'm moving locations. I'll call you in twenty-four hours. Unless you hear from me the operation moves ahead as planned." Nikolay hung up the phone and stood up. He made his way to the door and opened it. "Sasha."

"Yes sir," was the reply from around the corner as his butler appeared.

"Sasha, we're changing venues. It's time for a warmer climate. We leave in four hours."

"Very well sir."

Nikolay gravitated to the large floor to ceiling windows that overlooked his expansive Florence property.

Oh how I'll miss Italy. The Caribbean sun will certainly warm these old bones of mine as my plan comes to fruition.

15
Friday October 24, 1997 12:30pm

Thomas and Emily's flight arrived on time at eight-thirty and was met with many hugs and kisses. By nine-thirty the tired travelers had arrived back home, courtesy of Laura, and promptly fallen into bed. Three hours later Thomas sleepily wandered into the family room. He was surprised to see so many faces staring back at him.

"What are you all doing here?"

"We heard you got back," said Sam, "and our curiosity got the better of us I'm afraid. How was the trip?"

Thomas sat down on the couch next to Laura and laid his head on her shoulder. "Long." Laura put her hand in his as they shared a lingering kiss.

"Any problems?" asked Bill. "Anything out of the ordinary happen?"

"No. I don't think so. My father handled everything and it seemed to go very smoothly." Thomas sat up and looked around. "How's everyone? Did I miss something?"

Julie spoke up. "You mean other than the fact that Laura missed you terribly?"

"Shush you," replied Laura, but she couldn't conceal her smile.

"You two are making me sick already," Bill joked.

"I think it's sweet," said Kim.

Sam rolled his eyes, grinned and then became more serious. "On to business. The reason we're here is that we need to come up with our plan of attack. Your father took care of the money transfers so we need our next step."

Laura stood up and headed off towards the kid's bedrooms. "I'll see if Emily is up to the task."

"Thanks sweetie."

"How was the flight?" Bill asked filling in the void.

"Thankfully, the first class seats made it more hospitable, but a twelve hour flight, a hour and a half layover, and then an almost five hour flight takes its toll no matter what you do."

"And Emily?" asked Julie.

Thomas smiled. "A few altercations but she's definitely a trooper."

"Laura worried about that. She figured it was a lot for a six year old to take in."

"I know. Sometimes it's hard to imagine that she's only six, especially with what she's experienced in life so far. And now who knows what the plan is…but whatever it is she's clearly involved whether I like it or not. I'd keep her as safe as I could if only I had her power. In any case, whatever the plan is I intend to keep her out of harm's way."

Laura returned carrying Emily and sat back down on the couch next to Thomas.

Sam grabbed one of her big toes through the sock. "Hey there Em. How was Switzerland?"

"Good."

"Did you have fun?"

Emily nodded.

Laura spoke up. "She's sleepy."

Emily looked right at Sam. "You want to talk to grandpa." It was a statement rather than a question.

"Nothing gets by you Em," replied Sam. "And yes, we'd like to talk to your grandfather if that's okay with you."

"Just for a little while sweetie," said her father. "Then you can go back to bed if you want."

"Okay," she said as she yawned. Emily reached over and touched Thomas' face and Michael appeared. Some of the adults jumped a little, clearly not used to this phenomenon yet.

"Hey pop. Long time no see."

"Good to see you too son. You too Em." Michael looked around the room. "Ladies. Sam. Bill." He sat down.

"What's the next step?" asked Sam.

"Well, now that we have positive control over the money we need to take the microfilm data to the CIA."

"And what makes you think they'll listen to us?"

"I don't actually."

"What?" Bill interjected.

"Think about it," said Michael. "Who would? We won't be able to just barge in. We'll need to think out our approach very carefully. Otherwise, for all we know, we'll tip Yuri off."

The phone rang in the kitchen. Laura was still holding Emily so Thomas got up and answered it.

"Hello?" The connection contained a little static.

"Sir, may I speak with a Mr. Michael Clark?"

A puzzled look came over Thomas' face. "This is his son. How may I help you?"

"Very good sir. This is Mr. Kleiner from…"

"Mr. Kleiner. Yes, I remember you."

"Of course sir. I'll come right to the point. I'm sorry to disturb you but as a valued client I felt it was my duty to report this to you."

Everyone had stopped talking and was looking at Thomas.

"I don't understand Mr. Kleiner."

"Mr. Clark, I'm afraid an alert went out when I accessed your family's account."

"An alert? What does that mean?"

Michael stood up.

"We're not entirely sure since it was setup thirty years ago. I'm very embarrassed, as you can imagine, and I felt it was my duty to let you know immediately."

"Thank you Mr. Kleiner."

"Good day Mr. Clark." The phone went dead and Thomas hung it up.

"I caught most of that son. Did he say that some type of signal was sent out because we accessed the account?"

Thomas nodded.

"Problem?" asked Sam.

"I'm afraid so. We might not be acting anonymously anymore and, to top it off, I may have just put your families in danger."

"Danger?" said Julie and Kim at the same time.

"Time for a new plan," said Bill.

"Agreed," said Michael.

"I'm not letting anything happen to us," added Thomas.

Sam stood up. "Everything's going to be okay. However, let's not take any chances. I propose we pack up and head back to the states today. We don't know what to expect but if we stay here then we're clearly at a disadvantage."

"Sam's right," said Bill. "I'm not putting our families at risk."

"I don't want to run," said Julie. "I want to fight."

"Jules, you don't know what you're talking about."

"You're right, I don't. I do know that I'm not prepared for whatever it is, or whoever it is, that's coming for us. At least that's what it sounds like." She looked around and didn't hear any disagreement from anyone. "I like it here. The kids like it here. We don't want to be afraid."

"What are you really saying?" Sam asked.

"I don't know about my sister or Laura…but show me how to fight. Show me how to defend my family Sam."

"I'm in too," said Kim.

106

Bill started to open his mouth in protest. "Kim, you..."

"Shut it mister," as his wife cut him off. "We might not know what we're up against but I can guarantee you that we're invested in this family. And when we say family we mean all of our families. If you think, for one damn second, you're the only one that gives a shit about their well-being...well, you're clearly mistaken."

"I'm in too." Everyone swiveled their head and looked at Laura. "Thomas, we will not sit idly by. Make this happen."

The room quieted down. Thomas looked over at his father, then Bill and finally Sam. "Looks like there's been a significant consolidation of power while I was gone. Sam. Bill. Issues?"

Sam and Bill looked at each other before Sam spoke up. "None." He spoke to the group. "Sounds like you ladies are up for it. This should be interesting. I need to make a couple of phone calls."

The three women smiled. The girl's club was in action.

"Pop."

"Yes son?" Michael replied.

"The CIA portion of this plan will need to be postponed for a bit. We'll be in touch."

Michael nodded. "Don't take too long. Whoever's out there won't wait for you."

D.W. Neuman

16

Saturday October 25, 1997 12:00pm

All twelve members of their families were able to board a red-eye flight to SFO, San Francisco International. Upon arrival they were picked up in three armored Suburban's, driven by SANDBOX personnel, and taken across the Golden Gate Bridge into Marin close to SANDBOX's HQ. The kid's continued to sleep most of the way, as they'd done on the plane, until they reached their destination.

The three vehicles pulled into a driveway and immediately the team members exited, did a once over of the area with their eyes, and then opened up the doors for each of the families. Sam, Bill and Thomas each emerged from their Suburban and then helped their wife and children out. Two of the three SANDBOX personnel, that had driven them to their rental home, headed out to check the perimeter while the third entered the house to clear it for any threats.

It had been hastily rented by Roberta after Sam had called her. It was a five bedroom furnished house that was big enough to hold all three families, although the kids would have to share rooms together. The good news is that it was located only two miles away from SANDBOX itself. The owner had asked for a somewhat ridiculous amount for the weekly rental and had been delighted when it had been immediately accepted. The payment had cleared the bank the very same morning and keys were picked up on the way to the airport.

Sam, Bill and Thomas each adjusted their Glock 17's 9mm handgun's they'd armed themselves with from the Suburban's mobile arsenal, and herded everyone into the house. Their kids immediately took off running around the house to claim bedrooms with Laura, Julie and Kim in toe.

Tony, one of the operators, appeared around the corner and gave the all clear sign to the three men.

"Thanks Tony," said Sam. "Would you mind checking in with the insanity upstairs and see if they need anything?"

Tony grinned as he made his way to the stairs heading up. "You got it." He put his hand to his ear as he started up. He stopped and then nodded to no one in particular. Tony turned back to Sam. "Andy and Matt report the perimeter is all clear."

"Roger that," replied Bill.

"Good to have you back sirs." Tony didn't wait for an answer as he continued his climb, reached the top of the stairs, and headed off after the loud screeching of their children.

"Good to be back," Sam found himself saying.

"Don't let Julie hear you say that brother," said Bill. "She'll tear what's left of your nuts off."

"Hey, fuck you too. I didn't hear you put up much of a fight as you gave up your set to Kim," Sam replied with a smile.

"You see how she abuses me when I say no to her. There was nothing I could do."

Sam and Thomas laughed. It helped to alleviate their current situation.

"The only one left with any balls is our boy Thomas here," Bill continued.

"Yeah, no shit," Sam added. "Laura has had your back ever since we met her back in 1990."

Thomas nodded. "She's pretty damn awesome, that's for sure. But hell, that was some serious shit I put everyone through."

"You didn't put anyone through it," Bill argued. "You were dragged kicking and screaming into it and had the foresight to ask us for our help. There's no way we'd turn our backs on you. Not then and certainly not now."

Sam agreed. "I may have hung up my spurs for my family but we're in this together, like we've always been. Nothing's changed. The good news is that now that Julie and Kim know everything they're clearly onboard. I don't know what the hell we're going to get ourselves into, but I can tell you one thing, I was shocked when my wife asked for training."

"You're not the only one Sam," said Bill. "It's like they're suddenly all on the same page."

"It's weird, right?" asked Thomas rhetorically. "I mean, for months now Julie has been on your case. Then they stumble into my family's secret and now all three of our wives are on the same wavelength."

"I think it's best we stop trying to figure it out and just roll with it." Sam and Thomas nodded. "Besides, we're here to train together. One thing at a time."

"No shit."

"No shit what Sam?" said Julie from the top of the stairs. She started down with Laura and Kim behind her.

"Nothing," Sam replied.

"It didn't sound like nothing," as they reached the landing and joined their husbands. "Something you want to tell us?"

"Thomas?" Laura inquired.

Bill blurted out. "We were just commenting on how you're all synced up on your cycles now or something to that effect."

The three women looked at each other and started to laugh.

"Gross honey," said Kim, "but that's a very succinct way of putting it."

"Yeah, I'm okay with that," said Julie.

"Me too," Laura added.

111

The men just stood there with their mouths slightly open in shock.

"Anyway," continued Laura, "we need to unpack as well as get the kids fed before too long."

Sam recovered. "Roger that." And then his cell phone began to ring. He pulled it out and answered it. "Hello…You've got to be shitting me?...You're the best Roberta…Tomorrow?...Tomorrow it is then…Thank you."

"What's the four-one-one?" asked Bill.

Sam put his phone back in his pocket. "Roberta stocked the shelves for us in anticipation. She told me that we're not allowed to step foot on the property until tomorrow morning."

Bill smiled. "That sounds like our Roberta."

"It's settled then," said Laura. "If you boys wouldn't mind bringing in our luggage then we'll get started on lunch. After that I think we'll all need to get situated and take a nap."

The three wives headed off towards the kitchen leaving the men in their wake.

Bill chuckled as he opened the front door.

"What's so funny?" asked Thomas.

"Oh nothing…other than I was wrong that you still have your balls."

Sam laughed as he headed out the door behind Bill. Thomas grinned at the shit talking. As he walked through the front door the weight of the handgun on his belt left a subtle reminder of just how real everything just happened to be.

* * *

That evening, after dinner, the kids watched television together in the family room in plain view of their parents. The wives swapped recipes, stories and drank wine in the kitchen while the men talked in hushed tones and drank beer on barstools on the other side of the large kitchen counter. They had dismissed Tony, Andy and Matt for the day. The upcoming week, starting that very next morning, would be a somber reminder for everyone just how serious things might get sometime down the road.

Laura, Julie and Kim sauntered over to their side of the kitchen counter and sat down on their barstools facing the men. They'd refilled their wine glasses more than once already. Thomas, Sam and Bill stopped whispering and looked up at them as they joined them. They were all out of earshot from their kids as long as they kept their voices low.

"So just how fucked are we?" Julie asked to start off the conversation.

"Really sweetie?" Sam said as he rubbed his temples.

"I think what my sister means," said Kim, "is what have we stepped in and how bad does it smell?"

The men looked over at Laura as she took a sip of wine. "I explained a few things in more detail."

"Things?" asked Thomas.

She shrugged. "They were both interested so I told them about the night of the assault against Rising Hope Pharmaceuticals."

"And?"

"Well, aside from the fact that you were knocked out with gas…"

"Thanks for the reminder," said Bill.

The ladies giggled. "You're welcome," continued Laura. "But other than that they were very interested to learn that I was armed."

"Okay," said Thomas, "but I'm still missing your point."

"The point, my dear husband, is that we don't know what we're getting into yet."

"Hopefully nothing," said Sam.

"Pfft." It'd been Julie. They all looked at her before she continued. "We're all well past that point. Let's look at what we know." She used her fingers to count off her points. "One; we up and leave, on a moment's notice after receiving a phone call that said someone got tipped off about the Swiss account. Two; armed escorts pick us all up at the airport and bring us here. Three; the three of you are armed. Four; it's getting a little intense and I'm worried even though we all agreed to be here."

Thomas, Sam and Bill glanced at each other and then back at their wives.

Thomas spoke up. "Right now you know what we know. We're merely taking precautions while we track down any threats against our families. I don't believe for an instant that you don't want the same thing."

"I never said…"

Thomas held up his hand and Julie stopped.

"It's okay to be scared. It's okay to be nervous. We don't know what we're all getting into yet. But you know what, we're going to take this opportunity and use it. You're going to train with some of the best and it's going to be fun, scary, hard and exciting all at the same time. The reason you agreed to come is because you want to protect our family. It's not even a question. It is what it is." Thomas paused. "It's true, Laura had a weapon. I had a little training with the one I carried but I've gotten more proficient with it in the past seven years. Do any of us," he said gesturing to the men's side of the partition, "want you to have to use a weapon? The simple answer is no. I don't want to use it, but I'm really glad I know how to defend myself and my family if presented with no other option."

Sam and Bill both nodded their heads in agreement.

"It's better to have a gun and not need it then need a gun and not have it," added Sam.

The women all took a drink from their wine glasses.

"Listen. You're all strong women," said Bill. "You're united like we've never seen before. We don't know what to expect so we're being overly cautious for the time being. Learning how to shoot is just another toolset that you'll have access to."

Laura nodded. "You'll both like it. I do."

Thomas picked up where he left off. "This week you're going to learn some new things. We'll have the kids looked after…"

"By bodyguards," stated Julie. It wasn't a question.

"Um…well, technically, yes."

Julie shook her head. "How much fun is that going to be for them? A few armed men, not to mention that they're strangers, hanging around our kids while we're gone. They're not nannies. Are they trained for dealing with children and their needs?"

"She's got a point," added Laura. "Maybe I should stay behind?"

"Crap," admitted Sam, "you got me there. Is there anything else that we've missed?"

"Females," said Kim.

"Females?" Bill repeated.

Kim nodded. "We can't have just a bunch of armed swinging dicks looking after our kids. We need a nanny and activities for them to do. Do you think our kids are going to love being holed up in this house for a week? They won't hesitate to let us know exactly how upset they'll be."

Julie raised her glass to salute her sister. Laura smiled along as Sam's plan began to unravel before his eyes.

"It's okay sweetie," said Julie. "We know how much you tried. Nothing like getting bested by your own children." Wine glasses 'tinked' together on that comment.

Sam and Bill could plan missions into hostile territories all day long, but they'd definitely run up against the wall on planning this one out on short notice.

"Fine," replied Sam between clenched teeth, "I'll make some calls."

Bill chuckled. "If it weren't for those meddling kids."

* * *

Early the next morning, during breakfast, Sam's cell phone rang.

"Hello?...right." He placed it back in his pocket as he approached the front door. He opened it and Roberta walked in followed by a woman with black hair. They both followed Sam back to the kitchen area.

"Everyone. I'd like to introduce you to Roberta." A variety of hi's and hello's came from the room. "And Roberta brought…"

"Rebecca Cross," said the twenty-seven year old woman with the black hair, "but you can call me Becca." She drifted over to the children immediately and didn't wait for a reply from any of the adults. "Hi," she said cheerily to the six children. "I'm Becca. What're your names?"

"Amanda," said Sam and Julie's youngest.

"I love your black hair Amanda. It's just like mine."

"Thank you," replied the five-year-old.

"I'm Sarah," said the girl sitting next to her.

Becca knelt down next to the other five-year-old. "Well hello there Sarah. Aren't you a doll?" Bill and Kim's youngest giggled.

"And who might you be?" she asked as she moved around the table.

"I'm Emily. Are you going to be our new friend?"

Becca glanced over towards the adults who were watching. They gently nodded their heads almost in unison together without even realizing it. She looked back at Emily. "Do you want me to be your new friend?"

Emily nodded and grabbed Rebecca's hand. Thinking her daughter was about to bring someone into existence Laura stopped herself from removing Emily's hand off of Rebecca when nothing happened.

"You wanna see our room?" Emily asked as she, Amanda and Sarah got up from the table with the full intent of dragging Rebecca upstairs.

"You betcha. But I haven't met everyone else."

"Don't worry about them," said Sarah as she pulled on Becca, "they're just boys."

Rebecca smiled. "Well, nice to meet you boys, but apparently I'm heading upstairs now." And with that the three young girls took their new friend out of the kitchen, up the stairs and to their room they were all staying in.

Edward and Craig, both nine-years-old, rolled their eyes at their sister's antics. "Whatever." They were too cool.

"She's funny," said Gavin as he continued to eat cereal.

The adults moved to the kitchen.

"I think the girls just found their new BFF," said Laura.

"BFF?" asked Bill.

"Best Friends Forever," Kim answered.

"Oh."

"Boys." Julie shook her head and smiled. "Ladies, shall we go see how things are going upstairs?"

Julie, Kim and Laura took their leave and headed up after their youngsters.

"Well. That went better than expected," said Roberta who was very pleased with herself.

"Who is she" asked Sam. "How long has she been an employee?"

"Her name's Rebecca Cross. Officially this will be her fifth day."

"Her fifth day Roberta!"

Roberta stood right up to Sam. "Don't take that tone with me. I vetted her myself. She's a Combat Medic and has seen action. She's qualified."

"I see." Sam calmed down.

"Did I forget to mention that she's the only other female, other than myself, that works at SANDBOX? You should be thankful she hasn't been deployed and was available, along with me."

Sam back off. "You're right Roberta. I'm sorry." Bill and Thomas smiled.

"Damn right you're sorry," continued Roberta without missing a beat. "You know this is going to cost you."

It was Sam's turn to smile. "Roberta, I can't pay you what you're worth."

"And why's that?"

"Because you're priceless," Sam said in his most convincing voice.

Roberta smiled back at Sam. "You old softy."

"Don't I know it. Thank you."

"You're welcome." She then gently slapped his face. "But you know you still owe me big time for this."

Thomas and Bill couldn't help but laugh.

* * *

A few minutes later a sharp double-knock sounded on the front door. Thomas was the closest and cautiously opened it. Tony O'Neill, Andy Carter and Matt Jackson, the same operators from the previous day, had arrived. Thomas welcomed them in and closed the door behind them. Before anything could be said a chaotic stampede erupted on the staircase above. Their daughters raced down the stairwell while their wives and Rebecca casually followed after them. They gathered at the now crowded front entrance.

Roberta took charge. "Rebecca. I'd like to introduce Tony, Andy and Matt. They'll be working with you. Gentlemen, this is Rebecca Cross, our newest addition to the SANDBOX family."

Respectful handshakes and nods were exchanged.

Roberta then turned to Sam and Bill. "What's the game plan?"

Laura spoke up instead. "The adults need to get going. Roberta, thank for allowing us to invade your life like this."

Roberta smiled. "My pleasure dear. It's been some time since my own children grew up and moved out. I'm sure we'll all have a splendid time together."

Emily pulled on her mother's pant leg. "Can Becca stay and play with us?"

Laura picked her daughter up. "Absolutely. In fact, these three men are going to look after you for the day as well."

"So no bad guys can get us?"

Roberta tilted her head a little. Laura nodded. "Yep. We want you all to be safe. You're going to have a good time." She put Emily down.

"Let us know if there's anything we can do," said Julie.

Roberta smiled. "Everything will be just fine. I think we might visit the Exploratorium today." She bent down to Emily's level. "I hear they have this wall that captures your shadows."

"Cooool."

Everyone smiled. Even the two nine-year old boys thought it sounded intriguing.

"Okay. Scoot," Roberta ordered. "You have my mobile number and we have yours."

"Thanks Roberta," said Bill.

"Yes. Thank you," Sam added.

Roberta smiled. "That Christmas bonus is coming up, isn't it?"

Sam put his hands up in mock defense. "Deal." He put his hands down and whispered to his three male operators. "Keep them safe."

"Roger that sir."

* * *

All six adults found seats in one of the three Suburban vehicles that were parked in their rental driveway and headed out towards SANDBOX. The remaining two vehicles would be used to transport the six children, four operators and Roberta to wherever they needed to go. Julie looked back as they drove away and Sam caught her doing it in the rearview mirror.

"They'll be fine honey."

"I know. That doesn't stop me from worrying though."

There were a few seconds of silence before Kim spoke up. "What are we going to be doing?"

"I'll field this one," said Bill. "The goal for this week is to inundate you with small arms, hand-to-hand combat and defensive driving."

"Why not throw us out of a plane while you're at it?" his wife joked.

"We actually considered some tandem jumps for you....but since it's pretty cold out, and it doesn't really fit the curriculum, we decided to skip it this time."

"Gee. Thanks," said Julie sarcastically.

"You'll do great honey," said Sam. "The best part about this is that we won't be the ones training you."

"Why's that the best part Sam?" his wife insisted.

Sam chuckled. "It's really for our personal safety. There's a better chance you'll listen to someone else other than Bill and I. In all seriousness though, you'll need to focus this week."

"So what are you and Bill going to do while the four of us are in training?" Julie asked.

"Refreshing our own skills," Bill answered. "Don't worry, we'll be around, we just won't be hovering."

"Thank God for small favors," said Kim.

Everyone had a good laugh as SANDBOX came into view.

* * *

The group had been led to an underground shooting range. Currently they were in a side training room.

"Hello everyone. My name is Mack Morgan and I will be one of your instructors this week." Mack was an imposing six-foot-two, brown hair, muscle toned man in his early thirties. He had an air of self-confidence and assertiveness that just seemed to flow from his mere presence. He had a gentle face which also made him easy on the eyes, at least from all three of the wives' perspective.

Introductions were made all around and then everyone took a seat while Mack continued. Sam and Bill positioned themselves in the back off the room.

"Who here has fired a weapon before?"

Thomas and Laura raised their hands. Julie and Kim squirmed in their seats a little.

"Good to know. My goal is to bring you up to speed, as quickly as possible, with the proper method of safely carrying, loading, unloading, discharging and the cleaning of a variety of small arms. We'll practice with the Glock 17 nine-millimeter, the Heckler and Koch MP5, as well as the AR-15 that fires the 5.56 millimeter NATO round." Mack stopped and looked over his students. "If I ever yell at any one of you please don't take it personally. I'll be yelling because you're violating safety and putting either you or someone else in immediate danger. Deal?"

Thomas, Laura, Julie and Kim looked around at each other and nodded in agreement.

"Perfect. Are there any questions so far?"

"When do we get to shoot?" Julie asked.

Mack, along with Sam and Bill in the back row of the room, smiled.

"First things first." Mack turned around and picked up four Glock 17's from the large training table that also held the MP5's and AR-15's he'd talked about. The Glocks were locked open and none of them contained a magazine, effectively making them inert and completely safe. He handed them out. Thomas and Laura left there's on the table in front of them while Julie and Kim inspected theirs and got used to the feel of the handgun.

"Safety is my number one concern and it needs to be yours as well. Here are a few simple rules to follow so you don't find me yelling at you. One; never point your weapon at anything you're not willing to shoot. Two; while we're on the shooting range keep your weapon pointed downrange at all times. Three; always assume your weapon is loaded and treat it as such. Questions?"

There were none.

"I'm going to walk you through handling your Glock 17; how to load and unload it safely. Once I'm satisfied we'll move on to tactical reloads and…"

"Tactical reloads?" asked Kim.

"Yes ma'am. There are two different types of reloads. The standard is when you've expended all your ammunition and your slide locks open. The empty magazine is ejected, a new mag is inserted, and the slide is charged to make the weapon hot again. Tactical reloading, on the other hand, is similar but different. In a tactical reload there is still ammunition left in your magazine. With the tactical reload you're ejecting your mag and replacing it with a new one while your weapon is hot the entire time."

"Can you give me an example of why I'd use one type rather than the other?"

"Excellent question. Real world situation. You've just assaulted a location and have fired a large number of rounds from your weapon. Maybe you remember how many rounds you've discharged or maybe you've lost count."

"We're supposed to count and remember our shots?"

Mack smiled. "Not right away, but it helps. Anyway, instead of waiting for your slide to lock open, and out of ammunition, the proper course of action is to perform a tactical reload so your weapon is full."

"Thanks," said Julie. "I think I understand."

"I'll have you practice extensively on the handguns until I'm satisfied."

"Are you saying we'll be experts?" asked Kim.

Mack chuckled. "No disrespect, but no. That can take years. What you will see, and I guarantee this, is a huge improvement from when you first start sending lead downrange to when I'm done with you. You might not hit the bulls-eye every time but you will definitely be hitting your target where it counts."

Mack glanced back at Sam and Bill who gave him the thumbs up.

"I'll also get you familiar with the HK MP5 and AR-15 platforms but my primary focus will be on your use of the Glock 17 for now. Questions?"

"I'm excited," said Julie. "Show me what to do."

Sam and Bill chuckled and got up. They came forward and kissed their wives.

"Have a good time." Sam turned to Mack. "Don't go easy on them."

"No, sir," he said with a smile.

17
Sunday October 26, 1997

Fidel Castro had been very pleased to take Nikolay Dmitriev's
phone call the day before. He was even more pleased when
Nikolay told him he'd be relocating to Cuba. It had been a number
of years since he'd talked to his old Russian friend but, more to the
point, he missed the transactions that put Nikolay's hard currency
in his pocket. Castro had assured Nikolay that he'd have the full
cooperation of the military and the government upon his arrival.
Nikolay ended the call telling Castro that a sizeable money transfer
was underway. Castro hung-up the phone, smiled and lit a cigar.
Of course there'd be money; that's how friends conduct business.

* * *

One hundred miles southwest of Havana, Cuba, is a small
town called Pasa de Marin. Nikolay's entourage had arrived
without incident and proceeded to his villa on the outskirts of
town. His advance team, along with a contingent of military
soldiers, had prepped for his arrival and the location was locked
down tight. Nikolay's team consisted mostly of ex-KGB and ex-
Spetsnaz Special Forces personnel and were escorted by a well
armed military convoy all the way to his new home. This
procession would have raised a number of questions in the States,
but in Cuba the inhabitants had learned not to see or hear anything
lest they face harsh consequences.

As Nikolay stepped out of his vehicle the door was closed
behind him. Sasha, his butler, stood by his side as he'd done so for
years. The villa itself was ten years old and rested at the top of a
large hill that just had magnificent and panoramic views of the

Caribbean Sea. Directly east was the Gulf of Batabano. Nikolay had chosen this location for his retirement, its natural beauty, and of course, for the security it provided. When it came to security there was only one road in and out for starters. The trees and jungle that surrounded his property were extremely dense which meant that any attack would have to be made on foot. Furthermore, the beach that bracketed his property was three-thousand feet away at the base of the hill.

His men armed themselves with traditional Kalashnikovs, the AK-47 assault rifle, the advance group provided. Orders were barked out and several groups of two men each headed out to the four guard towers around the property. Four stayed with Nikolay and Sasha while they took their time inspecting the grounds before they headed inside.

"Status," Nikolay ordered as he entered his villa.

"Phone lines are working," replied the ex-KGB officer. "The satellite uplink has been established. Encryption protocols have been tested and are secure."

"Very well." With a wave of his hand he dismissed the man.

Nikolay had been here once before right after he'd had it built. *That was ten years ago when I was sixty-seven and in good health.* He grunted. All of his plans changed when the great Soviet Union toppled in 1991. He lost his power and was cast out in the blink of an eye. The people had spoken and Democracy had taken over. *Pfft. What did they know? Damn ingrates.*

"Blyadischas!" he spat out. *Whores!*

Nikolay had breathed only war his entire life. From fighting on the streets of Russia; to taking over his father's roll in the Politburo; to fighting the Americans and their allies during World War Two; to running assists and covert missions during the Cold War; Nikolay had experienced it all. He'd also grown old and bitter over the years but he didn't mind. Everyone who didn't take what they wanted was weak in his eyes. He'd taken obscene amounts of money from his own government selling weapons to foreign countries. Nikolay smiled for a brief second before his frown returned due to a distant memory.

Michael Clark, that goddamn bloodhound. You continued to hinder and disrupt my plans as you attempted to track down Yuri, my mole deep within the CIA. You stole from me and got away with it. You killed Vasiliy. How is it that thirty years have gone by and yet you're accessing my money just now? I should have killed your son and your parents the same week you shot yourself.

Nikolay continued to wander around the interior of his villa, familiarizing himself with it as Sasha trailed behind him.

Democracy, bah! The Americans will continue to pay...in blood.

He turned on his heels and headed towards his office. His butler hurried to catch up as Nikolay opened the door and let himself in.

"Is there anything you need sir?" Sasha asked behind him.

"I'm hungry. And bring me some vodka. I have things to attend to."

"Right away sir." Sasha closed the office door behind him on his way out.

Nikolay walked over and sat down behind his desk.

This isn't Italy but it'll do. At least Cuba is still Communist.

He picked up his phone and dialed.

* * *

It'd been a week since Frank Russell had spoken to Nikolay and motivated himself to leave the country by any means necessary. He needed to cover his tracks while he looked over his shoulder. Frank knew that it was difficult to stay off the grid and yet need it at the same time. He figured he had maybe a week before he could establish the necessary plans to get out of the United States for good. He'd worked for Nikolay for forty years and knew that this day would eventually arrive; the day where his usefulness came to an end and he'd become a liability. Nikolay only cared about Nikolay, it'd always been obvious. Frank knew he'd been coerced into his role as a Russian spy back in the day but the reality, as he well knew, was that he enjoyed the adrenaline rush. The act of getting away with such grandiose acts of espionage, all under the nose of the DCI, the Director of Central Intelligence, had always brought a smile to his face.

But those events were all part of history now. Frank knew that if he was caught he'd never see the light of day again. At his age there might be a chance to negotiate a deal if he gave up his handler and Nikolay knew that. And, after hearing Nikolay's tone on the phone, he knew he had to act.

Even after retirement Frank lived in Washington D.C. He had come to two conclusions in the weeks that followed. One was that he missed the action. The second was that his subconscious had begun to plague him. His dreams were sometimes filled with anxiety; flashbacks of how he'd potentially hurt people over the decades. He didn't particularly enjoy them and had begun to drink heavily to numb himself. Frank's level of self-preservation never diminished but his tradecraft, over the years, combined with his intoxication certainly hindered his effectiveness.

A man watched Frank from across the street from a doorway. He'd followed Yuri for the past two hours and had to give the old spy credit when he changed trains, doubled back on his path and stopped to check behind him from time to time. However, it was apparent that Yuri was no longer the same man he used to be. From the man's perspective Yuri looked weak, haggard and scared as he entered one of the many Law offices that dotted the D.C. area.

* * *

Alexei Vorobyrov's satellite phone chirped. He removed it from one of his jacket pockets, established the connection and waited for the encryption protocols to sync. Fifteen seconds later the line was secure.

"Yes?"

"Report," said Nikolay on the other end.

"I'm looking at him right now. He just entered a lawyer's office."

"Track his movements for the next few days in case he has more than one place he's keeping his secrets."

"Yes. Of course sir."

"Good. Now, what's the current status on tomorrow's mission?"

"Nothing's changed. Situation normal."

"Excellent. I'm moved to the final location. Call me if anything changes." The line went dead.

Alexei put the phone back in his jacket pocket and moved out of the doorway. He took up another position that would prevent Yuri from eyeballing him as he exited the building.

Alexei was his real name and he'd been raised as an orphan by the state until he was adopted five he'd been adopted by a Russian couple at age five. That couple worked for Nikolay and were paid handsomely to give up their new child. Alexei was taken and placed in a very special program, along with many other young boys and girls. That program, along with its top secret location, was geared to westernize those children. They were taught and expected to speak only English. They watched the Brady Bunch,

Sesame Street, Three Stooges and many other American television shows. They participated in celebrating holidays such as Halloween, Thanksgiving and Christmas. But they were also taught how to fight, the use of small arms, espionage and so on. Their training lasted for years before they would immigrate to America and begin to live their lives there. The goal of the project, naturally, was a long term infiltration of the United States as Russian sleepers.

And it worked.

Alexei was thirty-one, five-eleven with short black hair. He was not built as a wrestler, due to his average size, but he was very strong and wiry. He'd arrived in the US when he was eighteen with false papers. He attended college and began his new life as an American Citizen. But he never forgot who the real enemy was, where he'd come from or what his mission was.

Nikolay had activated him two years prior and since then Alexei had been handling special circumstances for Nikolay ever since. Not once had Alexei wavered in his convictions and his loyalty was never questioned.

Alexei sat down on the stairs at the end of the street that permitted him an unobstructed view of the lawyer's office Yuri had entered. He took out his satellite phone and dialed a number. He waited the same amount of time for the secure connection to be made.

"Update."

"We're good on this end. Tomorrow is going to be a late Fourth of July."

"Disappear."

"It's like we were never here sir."

Alexei grinned as he ended the call. He wondered how the citizens of the United States would react after tomorrow's demonstration.

* * *

Monday October 27, 1997 6:15pm

At 6:14pm Gladys Knight waited patiently amidst the large crowd of people that gathered for their commute home. She stood in Union Station Washington DC, a major train and rail hub. Gladys looked down at her watch as she heard the Metro train approach. All around her the mass of people jockeyed for positions as they came and left work.

The underground Metro train arrived, opened its doors, and more people spilled out onto the platform, just as the clock changed to 6:15.

Two bombs simultaneously exploded in the middle of the platform. They sent out hundreds of metal objects into the thick crowd.

Later it was determined that the two initial blasts killed seventy-nine people. The other eighty-seven casualties were primarily from people trampled during the ensuing mass panic. An additional two hundred plus were never named because they recovered from their injuries, even though some of them would never walk or hold a utensil properly again.

The heart of the nation, Washington D.C., had been openly and blatantly attacked by an unknown enemy. The nation cried out, as a whole, for blood.

D.W. Neuman

18
Friday October 31, 1997 2:35pm

"Cease fire! Cease fire! Actions open and emptied."

Thomas, Laura, Julie and Kim immediately stopped shooting. They ejected their magazines, cleared their handguns and placed them on the mats in front of them. As each finished they stepped back, removed their ear protection and turned to face their instructor.

Mack couldn't help but to smile at his four students. It'd been a long week, full of bruises, sore muscles and calloused hands. But they'd all stuck it out and their progress was very evident. And, as promised, Sam and Bill had been doing their own variety of training away from the group because there's nothing like comparing yourself to experts and instantly realizing your own skill level isn't up to par. Mack believed that had definitely helped the four adults and hadn't discouraged them.

Aside from spending quite a bit of time in one of SANDBOX's shooting houses they had also spent time in the dojo. Mack had brought them up to speed on a few moves, mostly quick attacks and escape tactics. Eyes, nose, throat, groan and knee jabs; weight pivoting; biting and scratching. Mack only covered the basics because in a fight there isn't time to do much of anything else. Leave the long and choreographed fights to the movies. Nevertheless, he had them practice those moves for hours until their muscle memory became fluid and automatic. Mack told them, more often than not, that indecision and hesitation would get them killed.

"Great job. I'm really quite impressed with everyone's commitment this week."

"Forget about that; who's the best?" teased Kim.

Mack smiled, as did the rest.

"We're about to find out," Mack replied.

Puzzled looks crossed their faces but before they could ask another question Mack motioned for them to follow him. He led the way out of the shoot house to a new building. Sam and Bill opened the door and came outside as they approached.

"What'ya bring us Mack?" Bill asked. "And hi honey." He winked at Kim.

"I'll let you two be the judge. I've molded them as best as I could in the time provided. Course, the fact that they actually listened to me and took directions is a big plus. You both could learn that from them," he joked.

Sam and Bill laughed. "Tell us something we don't know." Sam turned to his wife. "How's it going sweetie?"

"What else do you have for me that I can master?"

"Oooo," said Bill. "Them's fighting words brother."

Sam took it all in stride. "We'll see in a minute. Thomas. Laura. How're you two doing?"

"Sore," replied Laura, "but it's been a very educational week. I think I've got this shooting thing down." She grinned.

"Heh. Thomas?"

"Better and better. Thanks for this Sam."

"You don't get to thank me. We get to thank you. Anyway, I'm glad you've all learned a few things this week."

"You do what you have to do when your family's in danger," said Julie.

"What?" asked Mack.

"Nothing," she replied.

"As I was saying," continued Sam, "welcome to your graduation test."

"There's more?" asked Kim.

"Just one more thing honey and you'll love it," said Bill.

Shadows of the Past

"Welcome to the Kill House. In this building are a number of rooms. Some rooms contain bad guys. Some rooms contain hostages. And as you might imagine, some rooms contain both. Your test will be to clear this building."

The four graduates nodded in anticipation. They'd seen each other improve during the week but shooting at targets on a range, although beneficial, was not terribly realistic. Secretly they'd each wanted to try their skills out in a real-world environment. But that didn't mean they weren't nervous.

"It's okay to be nervous, or even scared," said Mack. "Just remember your training. You know what to do because you've been doing it extremely well for me all week. In this test no one will be shooting back at you. However, innocent hostages are also at risk, from you. Get your sight picture, check the background and know what you're shooting at before sending anything downrange."

Sam nodded at Mack and then said. "Any questions before one of you begins?"

When no one replied Laura piped up. "Let's get it done."

"Roger that Laura. Who's first then?"

Kim stepped forward.

"That's my girl," said Bill. "Follow me." Bill and Kim opened the Kill House door and walked inside.

Everyone else sat down at one of the exterior picnic benches.

"So Mack, they've been keeping everything tight lipped this week. I've been trying to get them to open up about their training, back at the house at night, but no one's talking."

Mack smiled. "That'd be my fault sir. The less you knew the less you could interfere with the way I trained."

Julie, Laura and Thomas laughed.

Sam rolled with the punch. "Oh. It's like that is it? There goes your bonus."

"I think I can survive without the extra five dollars sir." Mack grinned.

"Nice Mack. But on a serious note, how'd my family perform?"

"You've got a family of shooters now, that's for sure."

"That good?"

Mack paused. "Just about."

"What does that mean?"

Julie interjected on Mack's behalf. "Let's just say that my sister struggles a little."

It was Sam's turn to laugh. "More ammo for me to use against Bill. I love it."

They heard the muffled gunfire start up in the Kill House. Pop Pop. Pop. Kim's test had begun.

* * *

The door closed behind Bill and Kim. He led her over to a table that contained a Glock 17 and three seventeen-round magazines.

"Go ahead and gear up," Bill instructed," but don't touch the weapon yet."

Kim secured the holster around her waist and inserted two magazines in the quick draw holders on her left hip. She then donned her ear and eye protection.

"There are four rooms containing an unknown number of bad guys and hostages. Your mission, should you choose to accept it, will be to single handedly save them while eliminating the opposition."

"Cute honey."

Bill smiled. "Anyway, long story short, the bad guys are in white while the good guys are in black. Do me a favor and don't shoot the hostages."

"No promises," she kidded.

"Great," he groaned. "Go ahead and make ready."

Kim picked up the Glock, slammed the last magazine home and chambered a round. The weapon was now hot. She held it in both hands at a downward angle in front of her. She was ready.

Bill held up a digital stopwatch. "As soon as you breach that door," he said as he pointed to the only door on the opposite side of the room, "the time starts. I'll be right behind you. The time stops when you yell clear."

Kim nodded and moved to the far door. She held the weapon in her right hand, nodded at her husband, and then turned the door handle with her left.

The door swung open and across the other side of the new room stood two white bad guys behind a couch. A hostage blocked half of the terrorist on the right.

As Kim's weapon came up she added her left hand to stabilize and fired off two quick rounds towards the right target.

Pop Pop.

She shifted towards the left and fired another round.

Pop.

With both targets down she advanced to the next door. *Fourteen. I have fourteen rounds left.* No need to reload. She breached it and continued with her test.

With Bill trailing behind he saw that all three of her rounds struck the targets. The first shot had taken a chunk out of the hostage's leg while the second shot embedded itself in the bad guy's neck. Her third shot, on the left target, had entered high in the chest.

Bill wondered about a few things in his head as he silently followed behind Kim. *Why didn't she shoot both targets twice? Did she mean to shoot the hostage? Did she literally follow Keanu Reeves advice from the movie Speed?*

In the next room Bill watched as Kim emptied her magazine, all remaining fourteen rounds, into three targets before the Glock's slide locked open. Bill quickly counted nine hits, from leg shots to head shots. Bill grumbled to himself but kept quiet. She thumbed the mag release and grabbed a replacement from her hip, inserted it and released the slide lock.

Two rooms later Kim yelled, "CLEAR!" Bill stopped the clock.

"Safe your weapon."

She did so and then placed it in her holster.

"Great job sweetie."

"Yeah right. Don't think I don't know that tone."

Bill sighed. "What can I say, you know me."

"Which is exactly the reason why you didn't train us. You and I wouldn't have lasted two hours without yelling at each other."

"I know, I know. Can I ask you one question before we head out?"

She took a hard look at him. "What?"

"Any reason you unloaded your entire magazine in the second room rather than putting two rounds into each of the three bad guys?"

"I had fourteen rounds left. I didn't want to have them sitting there, unused on the floor, if I'd done a tactical reload."

Bill looked at her cross-eyed.

"I didn't want to waste them," she insisted.

He began to laugh. "I love you, you know that, right?"

A puzzled look crept over her face. "Yeah…"

"That's it. Just I love you." He led her back to the front room while Mack came in to set everything up for the next person's run.

An hour later the results were in. Laura had performed the best hitting every target in the least amount of time. Julie barely beat out Thomas but they also hit every target. Kim had only, but thankfully, injured a total of two hostages while eliminating the opposing force in her own way.

Hugs and handshakes went out to Mack Morgan. Bill quietly thanked the stars that they wouldn't be testing his wife's defensive driving skills. He already knew that she could beat him up pretty well so there was no need to worry about the hand-to-hand skills she might have picked up.

The group headed back to their rental7 house. They were tired but elated. It had been a long week, but it had also been very educational. A new level of appreciation was acknowledged, especially from Julie and Kim, of what their husbands actually did for a living, not to mention the dangers they put themselves in because of it.

Their kids had been kept busy during the week and tonight was no exception. It was Halloween and their parents had promised to take them around their old neighborhood for trick'or'treating that evening. As they pulled up to the house they hoped that Roberta and Rebecca had been able to take care of any and all costume requests that had been made of them. They couldn't wait to see what their kids were going to be dressed up as.

As they turned off the car, and stepped out, Sam acknowledged Tony O'Neill watching the house from the trees. Tony nodded in return and used his radio. Sam paused before he closed the car door. *We have protection but nothing's even begun yet.*

The group spilled out of the Suburban and headed towards the front door which opened for them.

Craig and Edward had decided on Spiderman and Batman costumes. Gavin finally settled on a ghost but complained out loud that he wanted to have Stir with him. The kids asked what a Stir was but Laura covered by saying that's what Gavin called monsters. Thomas gently pulled Gavin aside and reminded him that Stir needed to remain a secret and that no one would understand. Gavin told his father that he missed Stir a lot this week. Thomas told him that he could see him tomorrow when they were home in Hawaii. That brought a smile to Gavin's face and suddenly he was back to normal and ready to head out to collect candy.

The girls were another issue altogether. Two wanted to be Princesses and a minor argument has ensued. Rebecca sat them down and told them that families shouldn't fight but instead that they should support each other. Amanda told Sarah that she could be a Princess and Sarah's face lit up. Instead, Amanda decided to go as a Ballerina which was the next best thing to being a Princess. Emily, on the other hand, surprised everyone by wanting to be a Secret Agent. As it turned out she just wanted to dress like Rebecca.

After a week or intense training at SANDBOX a night out with their children was just what the doctor ordered. There were plenty of costumed kids out and about in their old neighborhood. The roads had been temporarily closed and everyone was relaxed and enjoying themselves, especially the six kids with their ever-growing candy bags. They filtered out the fact that Tony, Andy, and Matt always remained in close proximity. No one was in any danger. Naturally the three girls wanted Rebecca to go with them as they rang each doorbell and insisted that their parents stay on the sidewalk while they did so. The two older boys took Gavin with them and waited for their sisters to get out of the way before they could take their share. All in all it was a very relaxing evening.

* * *

Aside from the initial sugar rush it didn't take long for the six youngsters to pass out. It'd been a long week for them as well with various trips around the Bay Area that kept their attention and wore them out at the same time. Everyone was ready for the plane ride back home in the morning. The adults sat around drinking and talking after they'd put their kids to bed. The television was on in the background.

"It's been one hell of a week," Julie stated.

"You can say that again sis. Can you imagine how long it would have felt if they," she thumbed towards Sam and Bill, "had been the ones training us."

"Oh no shit," replied Julie. "We might have been filing for divorce," she kidded.

"Hey now," said Sam.

Everyone chuckled.

"Just remind me," said Bill, "not to be a hostage if Kim has to save me."

Kim punched him in the shoulder. "My hostages lived you sonofabitch."

Laura raised her glass. "To Kim and her injured hostages."

"To Kim," and glasses clinked around the room.

"You all suck," she said but couldn't hide her smile.

"Don't you worry," said Julie. "We now know that Laura knows what she's doing. Good job for kicking ass this week."

"Thanks."

"Yeah, you really rocked it babygirl," Thomas added.

"Oh, I know," she kidded.

Everyone had a nice laugh.

"Back to business I'm afraid," said Sam.

They had all been thinking it but now that Sam had said it out loud they knew it was time to talk about it.

"Quite frankly I still don't know what to expect when we head back home tomorrow. I don't know if we should feel more secure now that everyone can handle a weapon...or...if I should still worry for our safety."

"Let's get home," said Thomas, "and talk with my father. We'll get his perspective and go from there."

"Yeah, there's no way we're going to wake up Emily tonight," Laura added.

"Sounds like a plan then," said Bill.

"The girls have been talking nonstop about Rebecca," said Kim. "They're upset that they have to say goodbye to her."

"I have an idea," Laura offered. "Why don't we take her back to Hawaii? We still need some type of protection, and she'll blend in easily."

"I love the idea," added Julie. "Sam?"

"Not a bad idea. I'll talk with her. It appears she's grown pretty fond of the kids too. And your reasoning is sound Laura. Good thinking."

"Thanks. Like Julie said earlier, when our families are being threatened you do what you have to do." Everyone nodded. "And this might not be the right moment to mention it but we do need to protect ourselves. I'll come right out and say it. There's a billion dollars on the table now. That's not going away and we're an extremely rich target. I'll go out on a limb and say that money is not an option when it comes to making sure our families are safe."

"That's not even a question," said Thomas. "Our job will be to make sure that's exactly what our families are when we get home, safe. We don't know the road we have to go down yet but we don't have a choice either. The ball's already in motion."

"Well said brother," said Bill as he raised his glass.

"Here here," added Sam.

"What's this?" Kim picked up the remote control and turned up the volume. On the television the camera panned around a graphic scene as a reporter spoke.

"It's been four days ago since the explosion at Washington DC's Metro transportation hub during the evening commute. The body count has currently capped at one hundred and sixty-six while over two hundred others were injured during the attack. The federal task force, put together after the Sun Valley Mall bombing a month ago, has yet to disclose any leads. Whether that bombing, the bombing at the Las Vegas Convention Center, and now Washington DC's, are connected in any way has yet to be determined or even talked about. Government officials are tightlipped but my sources tell me that no one has taken responsibility for any of the three attacks. Reporting live from Washington DC I'm Vicky...."

Kim muted the television.

D.W. Neuman

19

Saturday November 1, 1997 1:30pm

The flight home was uneventful. Getting the kids up and packed in time had been the real struggle. The children settled down once the flight lifted off from SFO because they knew they'd be back to the warm weather, the beach and their pools soon enough.

Roberta had seen them off personally. The wives couldn't thank her enough for all her help during the past week. Sam eventually pulled her off to the side while the rest waited in the check-in line.

"Please tell me that Rebecca hasn't been scheduled for any job yet?"

"I'm afraid she has Sam."

"What!? How? What location?"

Roberta smiled. "She's been assigned to a protection detail in Hawaii."

Sam visibly relaxed. "You had me going."

"The kids loved her and she enjoyed looking after them. It's none of my business, other than the fact that you pay the bills, but continued protection seemed like the right course of action."

"Nice call."

"Are you sure that you want only her out there?"

Sam looked around and then met her eyes again. "It's too early to tell. I'll let you know if additional bodies are necessary."

"I'll make the arrangements just in case," she said. "Rebecca will be on a later flight."

"What would I do without you?"

"You don't want to know." She smiled and walked off as Sam rejoined the large group that was headed back home.

* * *

In the early evening the three weary families walked through their respective front doors in Hawaii. It'd been one hell of a busy and exhausting week. As much as they wanted to relax and unwind they agreed to meet for dinner. That gave each family a few hours of downtime before they gathered at the Clark's house.

* * *

After dinner the adults remained at the main dining room table while the kids hung out in the family room. The doorbell rang shortly after eight. Thomas and Sam got up from the table and headed towards the door. They both adjusted their weapons on their hip before Thomas opened the door. Rebecca Cross stood on the doorstep.

Thomas extended his hand. "Rebecca. So very nice to see you again. Won't you please come in."

She shook his hand and entered with her luggage behind her. "Thank you sir."

Thomas smiled. "Please, call me Thomas."

She turned to Sam. "Reporting for duty sir."

"BECCA!" Emily ran towards her new big sister and grabbed her hand before Sam could say anything else. Amanda and Sarah followed behind trying to act cool but obviously very excited.

Sam smiled and stepped back to give the girls room to crowd their big sister. Rebecca gave Sam the 'sorry' eyes, leaned down and picked up Emily.

"Oof. I think you grew a foot since I saw you yesterday."

Emily giggled. "You're silly."

"And how was your trip home girls?" she asked giving the other two girls some attention.

"Good."

"Okay."

"Well, that's better than bad." She put Emily down. "I'll visit more with you in a bit. Right now I need to talk with your parents. Okay?"

The three girls scampered back to the family room without any argument.

"Sorry about that sir," she said to Sam.

"Looks like I'll need to take some lessons from you Rebecca. Please join the rest of us and we'll bring you up to speed."

Rebecca left her luggage at the front door. The women each gave her a hug and plenty of compliments on how the kids loved her. She shook Bill's hand and then sat down.

"Can I get you something to drink Rebecca?"

Laura took the opportunity to refill everyone's drinks.

"Iced-tea will be fine ma'am."

Laura smiled. "We don't go on ceremony around here Rebecca, not to mention we need to keep a low profile. You need to use first names with us, okay?."

Rebecca nodded and handed her the glass of iced-tea. They all stared at her.

Thomas spoke up. "I'd like to take this opportunity to thank you."

"Thank me?" she responded.

"We know you just started with SANDBOX and we've monopolized your time already. You didn't join the company to babysit."

"Actually sir, I mean Thomas, it's a refreshing change of pace. As a Combat Medic I'm subjected to experiencing some pretty ugly things. That being said I'm no dummy. I realize that my gender led to your obvious choice, especially since Roberta and I are the only females available. Some men can work with children but they don't always have the patience."

"Whatever you're paying her you should double it right now," Kim stated with a smile.

"Thanks a lot honey," Bill said.

Everyone laughed and relaxed a bit.

"So yes Rebecca," said Julie, "thank you."

"You're welcome…Julie."

Sam had remained quiet until this point. "Rebecca, your mission hasn't changed. You're still tasked with protecting this family."

"May I ask from who si…Sam?"

Sam looked around the table and then back at Rebecca. "We're currently still figuring that out. However, in the meantime your primary responsibility is to safeguard our residences. We live next door to each other but will most likely be spending our waking hours together in one location."

Rebecca nodded. "I'm currently unarmed."

"I'll take care of that," said Bill. He took off his sidearm, along with his extra magazines, and slid them across the table to her. "I'll show you the armory later."

Rebecca took the holster and clipped it to her belt, along with the extra ammunition. It was then that she noticed all of the adults carried side-arms. *Interesting.*

Sam continued. "For the time being you can bunk at my house in our guest bedroom. As Laura mentioned it's all about fitting in. Since you'll be in Hawaii for a while you might need a new wardrobe. We'll take care of that tomorrow. I'll also get you a cellphone. Do you have any questions?"

It had been a little hectic getting used to her new job. The hours had been long but the three men she'd worked with, from

SANDBOX, had been very professional and answered many of her questions the previous week. Now she was on her own and it seemed daunting.

"My initial assessment is that there aren't enough personnel here to do the job correctly. No disrespect intended of course. It's just my gut feeling that as soon as you figure out what you're working on you might take off on me."

Sam nodded. "You're absolutely right. Roberta had made arrangements, if they're necessary, for additional personnel to be stationed here. If that happens they'd be under your direct supervision. In the meantime, we need to keep a relative low profile until we know exactly what type of threat we're dealing with. It's not an ideal situation Rebecca, but all of us trust you. More importantly our kids love you. However, let me be clear, you're not under any obligation to accept this job."

Rebecca didn't hesitate. "I'm in. It'd be an honor. I won't let you down. With that being said I'll need schedules; get used to the property and get situated."

"Down to business. I like it," said Bill.

"Honey, why don't you and Kim take the kids back home, show Rebecca her room and the lay of the land. We need to stay here and figure out our next course of action."

Julie got the clue. She and Kim got up from the table. "Come on kids. Who wants to show Rebecca the guest room?"

* * *

Emily was disappointed that Rebecca left but Laura assured her that she'd spend time with her in the morning. Thomas put his son to bed, but not before Stir made an appearance. Stir snuggled right up to Gavin and a soft purr emanated from his small black form. His red eyes blinked a few times and then closed. Gavin fell asleep with a smile on his face.

Back in the family room Sam, Bill, Laura and Emily waited for Thomas to rejoin them. Emily knew what they wanted and touched her father's hand as he sat down. Suddenly Michael Clark appeared next to them.

"How's my little granddaughter?"

Emily giggled. "Gooood." She began to play with a doll to occupy the time.

"Hello Sam. Bill."

Sam and Bill nodded with respect.

"Always a pleasure Laura."

"Hello Michael," she said.

"Hey pop," said Thomas, "it's been awhile. We were busy last week."

Michael smiled. "Don't I know it. Your mother and I watched you train. Looks like Laura happens to know what she's doing."

"Dammit pop."

Sam and Bill laughed. "We tried to have our skills rub off on him. At least he knows which end of his weapon to point downrange."

"Ha ha Bill. Very funny. But you know what?"

"What's that brother?" asked Bill.

"At least I know not to shoot the hostages." Thomas grinned.

"He's got a point there," Sam chuckled.

Bill rolled his eyes. "You're never going to let me forget about that, are you?"

Thomas shook his head.

"Well, what can I say? Kim loves to pull the trigger. Annnnnyway…back to business."

"Bill's right," said Sam. "As much as I'd like to reminisce we actually need to figure out what the hell we're doing."

"A week ago," Michael stated, "you received a phone call that some alert went out when we accessed the money in Switzerland. I haven't seen any reaction as a result from that, correct?"

"That's correct, as far as we know. But that doesn't give me any comfort. I don't like standing around and waiting for something to happen. We need to be proactive."

"Sam's right," said Bill. "With the training under our belt we need to get back on track. We can give credence to the alert or not. Either way we still need someone to look at the microfilm."

"I believe I have an idea about that," said Michael. "It's been thirty years, and I don't know who to trust, but we need to make a trip to the CIA."

They all looked around the room at each other.

"The CIA?" asked Bill. "How's that going to work? I doubt we can just waltz right in."

"I have an idea about that too."

Laura caught on right away. "You mean that Emily will need to be there, don't you?"

Michael nodded. "It's unavoidable."

"I don't like it."

"I understand. From my point of view I know that a great blow has been dealt against this country. It started while I was working for the CIA and I'm sure has continued since I died thirty years ago." Michael leaned forward. "Nikolay Dmietriev is probably still out there. Aside from him Yuri has to be dealt with as well. We can't do that from Hawaii. We have little choice but to go to the CIA and present the evidence."

Thomas squeezed Laura's hand. "I don't like it either, but my father has a point. If we do nothing then justice will never have a chance to be served. Emily will be safe with us, I promise."

Sam spoke up. "If there's nothing else then it sounds like we have a preliminary plan. I'll book us four tickets to Washington DC."

"It's Saturday," said Laura. "Put off the trip until Tuesday, or Monday night at the latest. We're all exhausted and need to rest up. I don't want Em getting sick."

"It's going to be okay," Michael assured her.

"There's no way you can know that. Michael, please don't make promises you can't keep." She picked Emily up off the floor and headed down the hallway. "Time for bed sweetie."

20

Saturday November 1, 1997 10:20pm

Thomas climbed into bed and joined Laura. She hadn't been her usual self since the conversation a few hours before. He turned off the light and snuggled in close to her.

"Penny for your thoughts," he said.

"I'm just worried, that's all."

"About Emily?"

"About everything. There are so many unknowns."

"For all I know we'll have the meeting with the CIA, hand off the information and be done with it."

"Then why does our daughter have to go? You know the only reason she needs to be there is so your father can appear."

"Having him available is a huge resource. There's going to be questions. We need to be able to consult him. I can't carry off a meeting without knowing how to act and what to say."

Laura chewed on this for a bit. "I suppose."

"It doesn't mean I like taking her to DC. The attack on the Metro station is pretty horrific as it is."

"And yet you still want to take her there."

"I don't want to honey. But what other choice do we have? My father is a cornucopia of information. We need his expertise."

Laura pouted a bit but finally turned over to face her husband. "You'll keep her safe."

"You know I will."

"And you'll keep yourself safe?"

"I'm not out there on the front lines. Besides, Sam and Bill will be with us. You know those two can handle just about anything."

"Fine. But it still doesn't mean I can't worry."

Thomas kissed her forehead. "I'd be very surprised if you didn't."

They were silent for a few seconds before Laura spoke up again. "You know, maybe I should use that magical phrase on you…"

"Hey now, don't even kid around about that. You were supposed to disable that during my hypnotic regression sessions."

"Did I? I can't quite remember."

'Well then, I'd better give you a reason not to use it…"

* * *

Rebecca made her rounds around the perimeter of the houses. Nothing seemed out of the ordinary. The gentle ocean breeze danced through her hair. *A person could get used to this.* She walked off the beach, past the pool and into the house. With everything locked up tight she armed the alarm and headed to the guest room to turn in.

Upstairs in the master bedroom Sam and Julie climbed into bed and continued their conversation they'd started in the bathroom.

"So you, Bill, Thomas and Emily are headed to Washington DC in two days. What's the plan?"

"Basically it'll be an informational handoff. Maybe it'll end there. We don't know."

"So when you hand off this information we'll be safe?"

Sam shrugged. "I don't know anything more than you do. I need to know if there is a threat against us for starters. If there is one then we'll figure out what to do from there. What I will do, and you know this, is to protect our family at all costs."

Julie sighed. "I know. I'm just worried."

"It'll be okay Jules. Rebecca is here looking after everyone. You're all armed now, which is strange enough as it is."

"I know, right?"

"But you kicked ass in the Kill House. I'm really proud of you. I know for certain that if push comes to shove you'll definitely be shoving."

Julie laughed. "I have to admit, it was fun."

"You're a natural."

"Stop trying to distract me. I know what you're doing Sam."

He smiled. "Guilty."

"Just promise me that you'll be careful."

"You got it sweetheart."

"Promise me"

"I promise."

* * *

"What am I supposed to tell the kids?" Kim asked.

"I've been gone on jobs before. Hopefully this one will be over before it starts."

"You can't know that for sure."

"No, you're right. I don't know that for sure. What I do know is that if we don't do anything then the bad guys will continue to win. That doesn't sit well with me. And, currently my gut tells me that we're potential targets. I have an obligation to change that. We're not going to want to walk around with guns for the rest of our lives, looking over our shoulders, right?"

Kim thought about that for a second. "No, of course not. Just promise me one thing."

"Anything."

"Promise me you'll be careful."

"I promise."

Kim smiled. "Good. Because if you didn't promise I'd have to kill you." She jabbed him in the ribs.

"Hey!" Kim giggled as he smiled. "You know that you hit like a girl, right sweetie?"

"Oh, it's like that, is it?" And with that she jumped on top of her husband.

21

Monday November 2, 1997 8:30pm

Nikolay basked in the afterglow as his plan came together. He had watched, with great intensity, the various CNN reports that covered the Washington DC attack over the past week. They tried to make sense of the destruction but none of their conclusions mattered.

Let them squirm and rot.

He spat at the television. The phlegm found its mark and slowly slid down the screen.

It'd been a week since he'd moved to Cuba. Time seemed to stand still in this part of the world. The food was spicier than he remembered but his system was slowly getting used to it. And, he had to admit, the weather soothed his tired bones.

At least I won't have to deal with my doctor distracting me anymore. Nikolay chuckled. *Like I gave a shit what he thought anyway. I have more pressing matters to attend to.*

He turned away from the picturesque view his balcony provided and headed back inside his office. His compound's security was extremely tight with two men roaming the interior, manning the main road and the guard towers. Nikolay felt very secure. *Not that I have anything to fear. The Americans, even if they eventually figured out I was the one behind the bombings, can't reach me here.* He smiled and sat down at his desk.

He picked up his phone, dialed a number from memory and waited. A female voice, distinctly American, answered after the encryption synced.

"Your call is unexpected."

"But necessary. Report." His tone was dismissive.

"Final preparations are being made."

"Issues?"

"None. Sunday the eighth is right on schedule."

"Good. Get it done and disappear," he said and hung up.

Nikolay smiled a little too much as he leaned back in his office chair. He was clearly enjoying himself.

I alone am making war on my enemy and succeeding. I alone will be responsible for the destabilization of the United States, something even the great Soviet Union was unable to do during her glorious reign.

He began to violently cough. He covered his mouth with his handkerchief to stifle it. When he pulled the cloth back it was dotted with blood. He threw it in the trash bin with anger and disgust. This wasn't the first time it'd happened and he didn't plan on letting it slow him down.

I have work to do.

The various cells Nikolay had in place throughout America were staggering. He had had the foresight, the tenacity and the money to invade the US long before the Cold War ended. He knew that a direct or nuclear attack would fail. He had dismissed those courses of action decades ago. His ideology and ego led to the idea of his specific brand of sleepers.

My children.

Nikolay played the game to win and had never stopped playing. The long game was the correct way to win and he knew that given the proper amount of time he could position his pawns, rooks, knights and bishops exactly where he wanted them. When he was ready he would then use them to strike.

And that time was now. Some of his children had been in the US for a significant amount of time. Learning; adapting; employed in government jobs; and waiting. They were more than happy to hear from their 'father' and what he demanded of them.

Nikolay broadened his smile. *It's my time now. I will prevail where my forefather's failed. I will take back what was taken from me, my dignity and respect. The United States will continue to pay, and they will pay in full, with their blood.*

His smile faded and was soon replaced with a scowl. *Taken from me. I can't forget about Michael Clark and my money.* He made a note on a piece of paper in front of him. *I'll get to you in good time. Durak huesos. Stupid cocksucker.*

D.W. Neuman

22

Tuesday November 3, 1997 10:00am

For the third time, in as many weeks, Thomas and Emily were on a plane yet again. His daughter slept next to him in first class while Sam and Bill were in seats directly behind them. Their flight had left Monday night. With the six hour time difference between Hawaii and Washington DC, combined with the long flight time, the jet lag would be significant.

Thomas' mind drifted. *A billion dollars. That's a lot of money.*

Thomas has never particularly seen the need, or had the urge, to spend his money in such a way as to invite attention. Sure, he'd always lived in relative comfort, but never gone out of his way to advertise that he had money. Although, during the plane trips he'd recently taken he'd made sure they'd sat in first class and would never regret that decision. *Some things just make life easier.*

He hadn't given a lot of thought to the new influx of money his father brought to the table. *I don't even know if it's mine.* All Thomas knew was that his father had a serious grudge, and rightfully so, and had promised half-a-billion dollars to Sam and Bill in exchange for their help. *Five hundred million dollars.* It was an obscene amount of money that was difficult to comprehend. The money he'd received on his eighteenth birthday had blown his mind and was nearly impossible to wrap his mind around. But the money his father had left him all those years ago was just a drop in the bucket compared to the billion dollars they'd just unearthed. *Crazy.*

Thomas looked over at his daughter and smiled. The butterfly effect had hit his family square in the face and never looked back at the damage in its wake. The laundry list had grown almost exponentially since his own childhood. First his mother had been taken away from him, then his father. Both their deaths were part of two different conspiracies; his mother due to his father's work and his father's due to Nigel's fucked up family. Then, years later, he'd become the center of a bizarre plot of revenge. Injected with psychotropic and mind altering drugs, which caused him to think he'd killed people. Those events directly led to Thomas meeting Laura. They married, had two children who, due to the nature of Thomas' altered DNA, developed abilities that came straight out of a science fiction novel. Those powers allowed his children to become the target of yet another conspiracy. But because of those powers Thomas was able to learn of his father's history with the CIA first hand. And now here they were, on a plane to Washington D.C., with thirty year old evidence of a mole, with an enemy potentially after them. Of course, they were a billion dollars richer.

Thomas rubbed his temples as he squeezed his eyes shut. *Fucking insane is what it is. But the funny thing is that I wouldn't change any of it.* Thomas glanced back and got a nod from each of his friends before he turned back around. Sam and Bill had been there for him since they were kids and they'd stayed loyal their entire life. You couldn't ask for better lifelong friends than that. And then there was his wife Laura. *She's downright amazing.* Thomas found himself smiling without even realizing it. *I might still be living in the mountains if it wasn't for her. God I'm lucky.*

He looked over at Emily who was cuddled up against him. She had wanted the window seat but had promptly fallen asleep as soon as the plane had taken off. After a quick lay-over in Los Angeles she'd repeated the same process. *I don't know how you do it Em. I don't know if what you have is a gift or a curse but here we are. You're so young. I'm sorry I did this to you.* A silent tear broke free and trailed down Thomas' cheek and he wiped it away. *I just want you to have a normal life. After all the horrible things you experienced in that bunker I was hoping Hawaii would be a fresh start. Now look where we are. You shouldn't have to do this but what choice do we really have? I hope you can forgive me when you're older, both you and your brother.*

The plane hit a mild patch of turbulence that jolted Thomas around but didn't disturb his daughter. *Everything will be fine, it's just another adventure. This time there won't be anyone to take you hostage.* He paused. *Nice Thomas. Just relax for fuck's sake.*

* * *

The plane landed at Dulles International at ten in the morning. A large town car was waiting for them outside baggage pickup, after they'd retrieved their locked weapon's case. Soon they were headed to their hotel. All of them needed to freshen up and get something in their bellies. After that final preparations would be reviewed and finalized. There was no going back, not with their families in the crosshairs.

They checked-in to two large but adjoining rooms in one of the upscale hotels in the downtown area with plans to meet up thirty minutes later. The eighth floor views allowed them to see a number of the historical locations that D.C. had to offer. Thomas turned away from the window and headed towards the bathroom. Emily stood still transfixed by the view. He stopped, picked up the phone and hit the room service button. Thomas ordered a variety of breakfast items including omelets, cereal, bagels, fruit and orange juice to be delivered about the same time they'd all be gathering.

"Em, I'm going to take a quick shower. Don't open the door or leave the room please."

"Kay."

The adjoining doors between their rooms were open. Thomas poked his head in to Sam and Bill's.

"I'm going to jump in the shower real quick. I have some food coming up for us."

Sam jerked his thumb towards his own bathroom. "Bill already beat you to the punch on our side. I'll make sure Em's okay."

"Thanks."

* * *

Breakfast arrived and was devoured by all four of the travelers. No one had particularly spoken while they'd eaten.

"So what's the plan?" asked Bill as he wiped his chin.

"Right now it feels like we're winging it," said Sam. "We should talk to your father Thomas. We need some solid direction. I highly doubt we can just walk into the CIA."

"Yeah," replied Thomas, "I had the same thought." He turned to Emily. "Sweetie?"

She briefly touched her father's exposed wrist and Michael appeared. She went back to drinking her chocolate milk.

"Gentlemen. I've been waiting."

"Take it easy pop. You're not the only one who's nervous."

Michael walked over to the windows and gazed out over the city. "My apologies. God this city has changed in thirty years." He looked around some more and then joined them back at the table. "You're right, I am nervous. I don't know why, I'm already dead. There's nothing that anyone can do to me."

"Seriously, pop."

"I just love the reassuring speech Mr. Clark," said Bill.

"Sorry that I'm not being terribly positive at the moment. It's just that I'm nervous sending my son and grand-daughter into the CIA with the microfilm. It might not be the best idea right now."

"Any particular reason sir?" asked Sam.

"You know as well as I do that they could still be compromised. I can't have you talking to just anyone."

"What do you think about asking for a meeting with Victor Bannon?" Thomas suggested.

"Who's he son?"

"He's the current DCI."

Bill scoffed. "How do you plan to manage that? He's not going to take a meeting with anyone raving about a CIA conspiracy."

"Indeed," Michael replied. "I do have an idea about that though."

* * *

Tuesday November 3, 1997 2:15pm

They'd rented two cars, split up after leaving the hotel, and they kept in contact through their cell phones. Thomas and Emily headed across the Potomac River and drove north up the George Washington Memorial Parkway towards the Central Intelligence Agency. Sam and Bill were going to pass the time by taking in the various sights. Doing that was better than just waiting around in their hotel rooms.

As Thomas got closer he swallowed hard. He knew he was nervous but he didn't know how nervous he was until that exact moment. The microfilm in his pocket felt like a boulder. The briefcase, sitting in the back seat contained the developed documents. *Maybe those documents won't save our families.* His palms were clammy and his throat was parched.

Emily sat in the front passenger seat. She was enjoying their trip and knew she played an important role. Although only six she considered herself pretty grown-up and responsible. *I'm more responsible than Gavin, but he's only a baby so I can't really blame him.* She looked over at her father and immediately sensed how nervous he was. She wanted to help, so she did.

"Daddy?"

"What's up pumpkin?" he replied with somewhat shaky voice.

She reached over, stretched out and touched his hand on the steering wheel. "There's nothing to be scared about."

And just like that Thomas' fear and nervousness dissipated. His entire demeanor instantly shifted and he relaxed.

"Much better, thank you Em. I don't want you to make a habit of just doing that without asking me in the future, okay?"

"Kay." She grinned because she knew she had done the right thing and helped her father. It'd been some time since she'd been able to utilize that particular ability she possessed. Her parents knew how powerful her 'suggestive ability' was and had told her not to use it unless asked. Emily had nodded her head and done what they'd asked of her. She'd seen a hint of fear in their eyes and didn't like it. However, what they hadn't said was not to use her power to summon dead people, so she had practiced that ability without their knowledge on her own.

Thomas took the exit and rolled up to the massive gates that led to the CIA buildings. Guards were prevalent as he came to a stop and rolled down his window. He wondered how many men with weapons pointed at him he didn't see.

"Identification." The voice was respectful but forceful.

Thomas remained calm and collected. He handed over his Hawaii driver's license. "Thomas Clark. I have a meeting with Victor Bannon."

The guard's eyes quickly jumped back to Thomas when he mentioned the DCI's name and then slid back to the card he held. A second guard walked around the rental car with a mirror that extended underneath. He was looking for explosives.

"You're on the list sir. Please proceed up and to your right to visitor parking. Enter through the main entrance. Someone will be waiting for you." He handed Thomas' id back.

"Thanks." Thomas drove through the gate. The extremely large building loomed as Thomas pulled into the parking lot.

"That's a big building."

"You can say that again."

"Grand-pa used to work in there?"

Thomas nodded. "That he did."

"And he caught bad guys?"

"You don't miss much, do you kiddo?"

Emily smiled as they walked towards the front entrance. The buildings before them were absolutely massive. The front doors opened automatically and Thomas saw two things right away. The first was the large CIA crest that was built into the marble floor. The second were the stars on the wall that represented the numerous intelligence officers that had fallen in the line of duty. Thomas drifted over to the wall and looked at it while he held his daughter's hand. The stars were organized by year. He scanned for 1967, the year his father was killed, but it wasn't listed.

"Mr. Clark?"

Thomas turned around. A woman in her sixties stood there. "Yes?"

"Hello. I'm Patricia Reed, Mr. Bannon's executive admin. He asked me to come down here and escort you."

"Hi Patricia. Nice to meet you."

Patricia smiled. She looked at the little girl with Thomas. "And you must be Emily."

"Hi," said Emily.

She focused back on Thomas. "Would you please put these badges on," she said as she handed them to Thomas, "and then follow me. Please don't remove them."

Thomas clipped his on first and then the other to his daughter's jacket. He didn't ask how she knew what his daughter's name was. Patricia waited for him to finish and then walked towards a guard booth that bracketed one of the electronic entrances.

Emily looked around as they followed Mrs. Reed. She saw vendors selling food. They all wore dark glasses.

"Daddy?"

"Yes sweetie."

"Why are they wearing sunglasses inside?"

Thomas didn't know but Patricia spoke up before he could say anything. "They're blind Emily."

"Oh. You mean they can't see?"

"That's right."

"Oh, I see." Then Emily giggled at her own joke.

Mrs. Reed flashed her badge to the guards and told them that the two visitors were with her. After the briefcase went through the x-ray, and all three passed the metal detector, they were on their way up the private elevator that led directly to the executive floor. The doors opened and she walked them down the hall to her desk. Two massive doors were closed beside it. She sat down.

"Nice place you have here." A little bit of his nervousness had returned.

"Mr. Clark. I've been instructed to inform you that you have ten minutes of Mr. Bannon's time and that you should be lucky to have that." She picked up the phone and hit a button. "Mr. Clark is here sir. Very well." She hung up and pressed a hidden button. One of the doors popped open and she returned to her work.

Thomas took his cue and opened the door the rest of the way. His daughter walked in and he closed the door behind them. The DCI's office was large and Victor Bannon stood behind his imposing desk.

"Won't you please come in Mr. Clark."

Thomas put the DCI in his mid-sixties. He had some gray around his temples and a slight pudginess to his stomach. To Thomas he looked like any other person on the street except for his impeccable suit and the obvious way he carried himself.

Thomas shook the man's hand. "Nice to meet you sir." The DCI's eyes didn't miss a thing as he examined Thomas. "This is my daughter Emily."

"Hello there." He extended his hand and gently shook hers. "Please, have a seat," as he gestured to the couches further in the room rather than to the chairs opposite his desk. They all sat down. Emily's feet dangled off the side.

"You're lucky to have caught me in town Mr. Clark. I keep myself pretty busy around here as you might imagine."

Thomas didn't miss a beat. "I appreciate you carving out some time from your schedule sir. I believe I have something here that you'll want to see."

Victor held up his hand. "Before we get into whatever it is you think is important, I must admit that I'm intrigued."

"Intrigued, sir?"

"You're damn right I'm intrigued. Excuse my language Emily."

"I've heard worse."

The DCI was not prepared for the six year olds retort and had to collect himself before he continued. "You might imagine that it's not often I get the President of the United States asking me to take a meeting with a civilian on a moment's notice."

"No," a mostly relaxed Thomas replied, "I suppose not."

"But I didn't argue so here we are. However, I'm still interested. What possible pull do you have with President Clinton that would allow this meeting to occur between us?"

"I just needed two words sir." He looked closely at the DCI's eyes. "But you already know what they are. In fact, I'd bet you already know who I am."

Bannon smiled. "Tell me anyway."

"WHITEWASH and DOGPATCH."

"Indeed. Those two codenames are highly classified and have been buried for decades. Out of nowhere you call the White House switchboard, request a meeting with me and drop those two names. You must know they traced the number you called from but you gave them a call back number anyway."

"It took them twenty-two minutes."

"Oh, I know. I was part of the decision making process. My concern was why you have knowledge of top secret and classified coding's. Quite frankly Mr. Clark if it weren't for your father's reputation I would have sent a grab team to your hotel instead of letting you waltz in here on your own."

Thomas wasn't fazed. "Did you know my father Mr. Bannon?"

The DCI weighed his response. "I knew of him but we traveled in different circles. I've been working for the CIA for most of my life, come to think of it." He hesitated. "I'm sorry for your loss. You were very young."

Thomas nodded. "It was a long time ago."

"Again, I must apologize. I've been perusing your father's file to bring myself up to speed. Your phone call caught me off guard as well as the President's. But down to business. Why are you here? Are you looking for some type of closure? How did you know about those classified codenames? And what did you hope to gain by bringing your daughter with you?"

"Mr. Bannon, I understand you have a lot of questions and concerns. I'll do my best to answer them."

"Very well. Go on."

"Sir, I recently learned of my father's work from a reliable source."

"Source? What source?"

"That's not important at the moment. What is important is why I'm here. The fact that I was able to procure a meeting with you clearly shows your level of curiosity; which I will now fulfill. My father earned JFK's respect as well as Walt Anderson's, the DCI of the time. DOGPATCH was the codename assigned to my father, in secret, by JFK. It was given to him for two distinct reasons. The first was for WHITEWASH. WHITEWASH was a very hush hush operation, run by Richard Moore, my father's boss, to ferret out a mole in the agency. The other was that my father discovered a plot to assassinate JFK and then foiled it."

"You're very well informed," the DCI said matter-of-factly. "That level of detail could be construed as treasonous. My gut tells me you know a lot about what your father did for us and, quite frankly, I'm uncomfortable with that fact. Bringing your daughter was a mistake. She won't protect you from walking out of this building." The DCI began to stand up.

Fuck. He just went from good cop to bad cop and I haven't even begun to tell him why I'm here. Thomas tried to remain calm. "Sir, I understand your concern. I should have gotten to the point of why I'm here sooner. If you feel the need to detain my daughter and I afterwards then so be it."

The DCI froze and then sat back down. "Alright. Our country owes that much to your father so I'll extend that courtesy to you. Proceed."

"Thank you, sir." Thomas opened the briefcase and pull out the documents he'd brought with him. He also removed the empty microfilm canister and placed it on the table. "Mr. Bannon, I regret to inform you that WHITEWASH should never have been closed."

"I'll play along Mr. Clark. Richard Moore was the mole. Your father was the one who discovered it."

Thomas shook his head. "Richard's only crime was stealing munitions for profit. He wasn't Yuri or a mole."

"Yuri was an old wives tale made up to keep young agents like me wary in our early days with the agency. Just because they slapped that name on Richard doesn't mean there was ever a real Yuri working as a mole."

"I'm afraid not sir. The real Yuri worked tirelessly behind the scene. He planted evidence and framed other agents, including Richard, and got away with it. My father had a gut feeling. However, before he could pursue those instincts, and the data he'd collected, he was killed."

"Your father's file says he killed himself."

Thomas sighed. "That's a long story and not relevant to what I'm talking about."

"I see," the DCI replied not quite believing what Thomas had just said. He pointed to the documents that Thomas had placed on the table. "Would those happen to be the data your father collected by chance?"

Thomas nodded. "Yes, sir. The majority of this raw information was retrieved from Kevin King, an agent of Yuri, who had been collating it."

The DCI got up, walked to his desk, retrieved a file and returned. "Kevin King. Ah yes. The man who worked with your father. Hell, it says here they were even roommates at Yale." He looked up at Thomas. "You're saying he was a mole, just like Richard?"

"Kevin worked for Yuri. Yuri worked for Nikolay Dmitriev. Richard was not involved."

"Now that's a name I haven't heard for a long time. Nikolay used to be a member of the Central Committee, the youngest member admitted at twenty-nine after his father was assassinated." Bannon stopped and stared at Thomas. "And you're saying Yuri worked for this Russian?"

"Yes, sir."

"And if Kevin King worked for Yuri then you're saying that Yuri was the top mole, so to speak?"

Is he messing with me? "Yes, sir."

"So, from all of this, you're here to tell me who Yuri really is?" It came off as a bit too flippant.

"You don't believe me?"

"I'll tell you what I do believe son." The DCI stood up. "I believe you're here in some misguided attempt to follow in your father's footsteps. I don't know how you know the level of detail you've been telling me. Maybe it has something to do with your career as a writer or maybe your father left you a journal."

"Sir, I..."

"Enough Mr. Clark. Right now I have too many unanswered questions and not enough answers. That will change. You are a walking liability. This ends now." He walked to his desk and pressed a button. "I need security in here right away."

Emily had mostly ignored the entire discussion between her father and the man they had come to see. When his tone changed to anger she looked up and took hold of her father's hand.

The DCI released the button and turned around to look at Thomas. Someone else was in his office now. *What the hell?* A man in his sixties stood there in a suit. Mr. Clark and his daughter still sat on the couch.

"What the fuck? Who the hell are you? How did you get in here?"

"Mr. Bannon, my name is Michael Clark. I'm Thomas' father. I'm Dogpatch."

Joke or not this man posed a real threat. Victor moved behind his desk. "I don't know who you are but security will be coming through that door any second."

Michael continued. "Sir, that's hardly relevant at the moment. You wouldn't believe me if I told you anyway. You're standing exactly where Walt Anderson stood thirty years ago. When you open your top right hand drawer you will remove a loaded handgun." Bannon twitched as Michael continued. "Your position means something. It has integrity, just like you do. There is, or has been, a high level mole in this agency. I'm here to tell you exactly who that person has been."

The double doors to the DCI's office burst open and two security men rushed in with extended HK MP5 PDW's. They immediately covered the three strangers in the room.

"DON'T MOVE! HANDS ON YOUR HEAD. NOW!"

Michael didn't budge and didn't raise his arms. Emily retreated into her father's lap.

"This isn't necessary Mr. Bannon. My family and I are no threat to you."

"HANDS!"

"Stand down."

"Sir?" Both security guards waited for another order from their boss.

"I said stand down."

The guards lowered their weapons.

The DCI pointed at Michael. "Pat him down."

One of the security men advanced. "Please raise your arms sir." Michael complied while the guard searched him. "Clean sir." He moved back.

"Very well. One of you bring me a DFSU. The other waits outside."

"Right away, sir." Both guards left and closed the door behind them.

Victor Bannon raised a finger and pointed directly at Michael. "Stay right where you are. You're absolutely right about my weapon. If you are who you claim to be then I'll know very shortly. I don't know what game you're playing and I don't like it. How the hell did you get in here?"

The door opened and the DFSU was brought in and placed on the DCI's desk. The guard waited for additional instructions.

"That'll be all. Please wait outside."

"Yes, sir." The man retreated and closed the door.

Bannon picked up the piece of equipment and turned it on. The DFSU was short for Digital Fingerprint Scanner Unit. He walked over to Michael. "Place your right hand on the scanner." Michael complied. The unit ran its scan and then beeped. Bannon retreated back to his desk and waited. Another beep sounded fifteen seconds later. The DCI looked shocked at the results.

He shook his head. "You have got to be shitting me. You really are Michael Clark."

"Yes, sir."

The DCI recovered. "It would appear that the report of your death was greatly exaggerated." The DCI came around his desk and approached Michael. He extended his hand. "Victor Bannon. A pleasure to meet a hero. I guess I should take this opportunity to welcome you back to the agency. You certainly scared the crap out of me. How'd you do that?"

Thomas and Emily continued to watch from where they sat on the couch. His father was running the show now.

Michael sidestepped the question. "Mr. Bannon, please let me walk you through the information we brought you. I wouldn't have come out of hiding, after thirty years, if it wasn't that important."

Thomas suppressed his grin.

Victor gave Michael a hard stare and received the same in return. He got up and pressed the same button on his desk. "Patricia, clear my schedule."

* * *

Victor hadn't interrupted once as Michael went through the documents. He added his own insights about Joshua Huntsman, the original spy set-up to look like Yuri; Kevin King, his long-time friend who killed Betsy, Michael's wife; and Richard Moore, the man who lost his entire family, began to steal from the US Government and was ultimately framed as Yuri.

"You're telling me that Frank Russell was Yuri?"

"Yes," replied Michael. "You used the past tense. Is he dead?"

"Retired a few years back. He would have been one of my executive assistants."

"Where'd he retire to?"

"I don't think he left the city." The DCI sat down. "My God this is unbelievable. The ramifications are enormous."

"No sir, more like frightening. He was an employee of the Central Intelligence Agency for thirty plus years."

176

"I need to send a team to arrest him immediately." The DCI headed for his desk.

"Before you do that may I make a suggestion?"

Bannon paused and turned around. "What is it?" He'd come to like Michael Clark in the short time he knew him.

"I don't know how to phase this so I'll just come out and say it. You don't know who else is involved. Frank wouldn't have retired without leaving others in play. Nikolay wouldn't have allowed that. I'm sorry to say that you don't know who to trust now."

Shit. He's right. "That doesn't leave me with very many options Michael."

"Actually sir, I'd like to give you a very viable option."

"I'm all ears."

"Have you heard of a PMC, private military company, called SANDBOX?"

"I've heard a few good things about them. What's that got to do with this?"

"My son Thomas co-owns that company. His two childhood friends, Sam Paige and Bill Nicholson, who founded it, are here in town. They are currently waiting for our phone call."

"What are you saying?"

"I propose we go after Yuri utilizing outside support. This effectively compartmentalizes who has knowledge about this operation."

The DCI thought about that. "You really think the agency still has a leak?"

"It's my assumption that it still does sir. Quite frankly, can you take the chance that it doesn't given the current level of evidence I just presented?"

"I don't like it. There are already a number of people that know your son was meeting me and pulled your file."

"True. But what none of them know is what we talked about, not to mention that I came out of hiding. I'm supposed to be dead. It's better we keep it that way, for the time being, while Yuri is pursued and then interrogated. Having him slip through my fingers was bad enough; I don't want it to happen again. If this information leaked out the embarrassment for the agency would reach epic proportions."

"Goddammit Michael. Who do you think you are? You can't just come in here and bark orders at me."

"We're well past that stage sir. Just because you don't like the current situation doesn't mean it's going to resolve itself on its own. We must act. Give me Frank Russell's address so we can do just that. The evidence is irrefutable!"

Thomas watched his father work his magic. He knew how close to the razor's edge he walked.

The DCI relented. "Fine. I'm going to give you the benefit of the doubt. Send your men."

"Thank you," replied Michael.

"Don't thank me yet. You'll stay here while this goes down." The DCI walked over to his desk and pressed the button. "Patricia. Two things. I need refreshments for four."

"For four, sir?"

"Yes, you heard me, for four. Secondly, the men outside my door are dismissed." He let the button go, picked up his phone and dialed an extension. "Bannon here. I need a tactical unit prepped and ready to move on the following address." He relayed Frank's home address. "Additional information to follow."

Michael inwardly groaned. *There goes our window of opportunity.*

Thomas pulled out his cell phone and made the call that Sam and Bill had been waiting for.

Monitors and television screens lined the large room. Technicians and security personnel watched live and pre-recorded video feeds from hundreds of cameras that covered CIA Headquarters. Two techs were tasked with the post-mortem of the DCI's security request earlier that afternoon. Both of the security guards that had responded watched the replay, along with the two techs, of their dynamic entrance into the DCI's office.

"Textbook entry," one of the techs said offhandedly.

One of the guards turned and glared at the man.

"You said there were two men and a little girl in his office?" the other tech asked.

"That's correct."

He hit a button and the video played backwards until a single man and the little girl appeared from the elevator. They followed Mrs. Reed down the hallway to her desk and then they all watched as she let them in the DCI's office.

"I'm not seeing a second man enter Mr. Bannon's office whatsoever."

"He was there, no doubt about it. I patted him down myself."

Video, from a number of various angles popped up on new screens. "Here they are," the tech said pointing to one screen, "coming in from the parking lot. On this other screen they pass security and we can follow them right to the executive elevator. I can't begin to tell you where your mystery man came from."

D.W. Neuman

<u>23</u>

Tuesday November 3, 1997 5:25pm

Sam hung up his phone. He pulled out a map of Washington D.C. and located the street. "Let's do this."

* * *

Frank Russell opened the garage door to his house when his phone started to ring. He walked the short distance to where it hung on the wall and picked it up.

"Hello?"

There was a computerized voice on the other end of the line. "Firestorm. Firestorm. Firestorm." The line went dead in his hand.

Yuri dropped the phone, went to his gas stove and turned on the four burners. They lit up and he blew out the flames. The raw gas continued to pump into his house. He set the egg timer, connected with wires attached to the electrical outlet, for two minutes and headed out to the garage. The wires would touch in two minutes and create a spark. Out of a beat up bin, behind some old wood against his back garage wall, Frank pulled out his 'Go' bag. It contained various passports, currency, a change of clothes, a weapon along with other necessities. He opened the driver's side door of his BMW and tossed it inside.

He'd made up a list of codes years ago as part of a plan. The specific code Firestorm indicated he needed to leave immediately while destroying any evidence left behind. Frank had a number of contacts that could have called to warn him. The computerized voice he'd heard was clever.

Shit. Documents.

181

He took a few seconds to weigh the pros and cons and then jumped in his car, opened the garage door and hurriedly left his house behind.

* * *

Bill turned right. They had finally made it to the street Thomas had provided them. Sam looked out the right window and eyeballed an address as Bill continued to drive.

"It'll be on this side of the street. I'm guessing about two blocks down."

"Roger that."

Sam put on an earpiece and clipped the wire to his collar. The other end he inserted into his phone. He pressed the speed dial and Thomas picked up on the first ring.

"You're on speaker Sam. I've got Victor Bannon, the DCI and my father here listening."

"Your father is there? Nevermind. We're two blocks from the target's house."

"Mr. Paige, this is Victor Bannon. I have a tactical team a few minutes behind."

"Dammit Thomas, I thought we were going to keep this compartmentalized?"

"I made the same argument Sam," said Michael.

"Great. Mr. Clark, so good to know that you're alive and well. Anyway, we're a block away now. I'll keep this line open as we..."

"Holy shit, there's a car leaving the property," Bill interrupted. "I'm goin..."

KA-BOOM!

The front side of Frank's house exploded with tremendous force. A huge fireball shot out of the front windows.

Bill swerved and sideswiped one of the many parked cars along the left side of the street.

"Fuck!"

"What happened Sam?"

"Go Bill! Get after him," they heard Sam say. "Frank Russell's house just blew up. We're in pursuit. Send a fire-engine and secure the scene with your tac unit."

* * *

Frank raced out of his garage and took a right. A few seconds later his house exploded behind him. In his rearview mirror he saw a Jeep Explorer veer and sideswipe a parked car. Instead of stopping the Explorer gained speed and closed the distance behind him.

"Fuck! That was fast!" Frank's heart raced. Years of espionage had kept him used to the adrenaline rush. He loved the rush. Sometimes he'd had close calls and had always skated away free. He looked in the rearview mirror again. *Fuck!* This time it was different. Now they were after him and closer to catching him than ever before. *Not like this. Not like this.*

Frank turned a corner and headed against rush hour traffic back downtown. He accelerated and tried to increase the distance between his pursuers, whoever they were.

* * *

"Stay on him!"

"I see him."

"He just took a right. Dammit, the street name was covered by a tree. It looks like he's heading back downtown."

No one was more surprised about Frank's house exploding than Alexei. He sat in a car down the street and watched Yuri arrive home not two minutes earlier. He'd spent the past week trailing Yuri to various locations around Washington and made notes along the way. Alexei was sure that Yuri only had three lawyers that held documents. Nikolay had instructed him to only watch Yuri and not take any direct action as of yet.

When Yuri's garage door re-opened Alexei turned the key of his car. What he hadn't expected was the house blowing up seconds later and spewing a huge fireball out into the street and into the air. Alexei had literally jumped behind the wheel of his Ford Taurus.

A Ford Explorer, nearly caught in the blast, had sideswiped a parked car. Instead of stopping the vehicle accelerated. Alexei saw too animated men in the jeep as it passed by him. Alexei pulled a one-eighty and chased after the two men.

* * *

"You're not going to believe this," said Bill.

"What?"

"I think we have company."

Sam turned in his seat and looked behind them. Sure enough a Ford Taurus was hot on their trail. *Who the fuck is that?*

"It appears Frank has backup," Sam said to the hands-free device.

The DCI responded. "What do you mean he has backup?"

"We're being pursued by a Ford Taurus. We're still following Yuri towards downtown." Sam covered the speaker. "This complicates things a little," he said to Bill.

"Just a tad brother."

Sam pulled out his Glock 17 and chambered a round.

* * *

Almost there!

Yuri knew Washington D.C. like the back of his hand. He'd managed to miss all traffic heading back into the city while maintaining enough speed to stay ahead of the car after him. He blew through stop signs and barely avoided other cars in his way, but he had no other choice but to attempt to disappear into the city he'd sold out decades before.

With his adrenaline pumping he flew south down 24th St NW and screeched to a stop next to the George Washington University. As fast as his old body would let him he grabbed his bag from the front seat, got out and started to jog east towards the Foggy Bottom Metro Station. Behind him he heard his pursuers squeal to a stop as well. Yuri ducked behind a tree, opened his back and removed a Skorpion vz 61, a small Czechoslovak full-auto submachine gun. He inserted a twenty round magazine, pocketed two additional magazines in his coat pocket and slung his bag over his shoulders. He chambered a round and peaked out from behind the tree.

* * *

"He just stopped. He's getting out!" yelled Sam.

"I see him."

They both watched as the man they were after headed into the plaza carrying a bag.

"We've still got trouble behind us."

Sam relayed their update. "Yuri has exited his vehicle at 24th and I St heading east. No visible weapon. We've got company."

Bill hit the brakes and slid the Explorer's back-end one-hundred-eighty degrees so the hood faced the oncoming threat. He opened his driver door, pulled out his weapon and used his open door for cover. Sam, gun in hand, popped open his door and ran after Yuri.

*   *   *

Alexei knew he'd been made shortly after the pursuit began but he didn't care. He knew he'd have to prevent Yuri from being captured, even if it meant shooting him. It went against his current orders to identify the lawyers that Yuri was using, policing up any documents, and eliminating him. But there was nothing Alexei could do about that now. He had little choice but to react to the situation.

In the distance he saw the BMW grind to a halt and Yuri flee on foot. The Explorer in front of him did something completely unexpected and pulled a one-eighty. Moments later two doors opened. One man sprang from the vehicle, with a gun, and headed after Yuri. The other remained behind his door and aimed his weapon at Alexei.

Well this just got interesting.

Alexei skidded his car ninety degrees to the left, forty feet from the Explorer, and came to a full stop. He popped his seatbelt, quickly extracted a Beretta FS situated in a holster on his hip, and began to rapidly fire towards the Explorer from inside his own vehicle. His passenger window exploded outward from the initial barrage.

*   *   *

Yuri just peaked out as the muffled sounds of gunfire began. *I'm not being shot at.* He saw an armed man enter the plaza and head in his direction. Yuri determined the car that the man had exited was the one taking fire, and he wasn't going to let that stroke of luck go to waste. He pointed his Skorpion at the man and depressed the trigger.

BrrrrrAapppp!

* * *

Bill aimed down his sites at the approaching Taurus. Forty feet away it slid to a stop. His eyes locked onto the eyes of the unknown man with black hair as a gun came up. Bill ducked down as fifteen rounds began to hit the Explorer and the door he used for protection.

* * *

Sam heard the gunfire behind him and then saw movement from behind a tree fifty feet ahead.

GUN!

Sam dived behind one of the plaza benches, which gave him very little cover as the cement, and the benches around him, were peppered with bullets. People had already begun to run from the shooting and a crowd of students began to scream as the long automatic burst of gunfire filled the air.

* * *

Thomas, Victor and Michael listened to the audible handgun sounds.

POP POP POP.

They heard an umph as Sam hit the ground and then the long BrrrApppppp from an automatic weapon. People's screams were clearly heard through the speakerphone.

* * *

Yuri watched the man dive for cover as he quickly emptied his twenty round magazine. People screamed and ran away. He broke from cover behind the tree, swung his bag around and dumped the Skorpion back inside. He joined the panicked crowd and headed for the subway entrance, lost in a sea of students.

* * *

Bill endured a second volley of fifteen bullets that hit the Explorer moments after the first fifteen had finished. He was pinned down without Sam's help.

Fucking hell!

* * *

Sam ran through his mental checklist and immediately determined that he wasn't hit. He popped his head up but Yuri was gone.

Fuck!

More shots rang out from behind him. He got up, turned around, ran north to the building's wall and moved with purpose back the way he'd run.

Fifty feet later Sam arrived at the corner of the building. He immediately saw that the Explorer was taking fire and was full of bullet holes. He moved his Glock from his right hand to his left, leaned out from behind cover and engaged the Taurus.

* * *

Alexei rapidly emptied his first magazine. He'd briefly looked into the man's eyes, seen a warrior stare back at him, and didn't hesitate to open fire. Fifteen rounds later his Beretta locked open. In a blur he thumbed the magazine release, inserted a fresh one and thumbed the slide lock. He continued his barrage.

Rounds suddenly penetrated his windshield from a new direction. One whistled right by his head and embedded itself in the headrest. Alexei ducked, yanked the wheel to the left, punched the accelerator and sped off the way he'd come. His back window shattered before he'd driven out of range.

A mile down the road he dialed a number on his satellite phone.

"We've got a problem."

* * *

"Sam! Sam, what's going on!? Are you alright!?" yelled Thomas. The gunfire had abruptly stopped.

"I'm fine. Checking on Bill." A moment later they heard Bill yell, "I'm going to fucking kill that guy!"

"Bill's fine. We're in a shitting situation here. Yuri got away in the confusion, our transportation is shot to shit and I can hear siren's in the distance. I don't believe any civilians were injured so we have at least that going for us."

"Mr. Paige," said the DCI, "remain where you are. I'm making a phone call to the DC Chief of Police. You won't be detained. What the hell went down out there?"

"Yuri had help sir. We would have had him otherwise."

"I understand. Once you're cleared I want you both to head back to his house. The tactical team is there now waiting on the fire department to put out the flames."

"Roger that sir." The DCI ended the call and immediately dialed a new number and talked with the Chief of Police. After that quick call he rejoined Thomas and Michael.

"I'm not particularly thrilled, as you can imagine, on how this day has turned out. So far we've got an explosion, a car chase and a firefight in a populated area with nothing to show for it."

"That's not true sir," Michael said. "We actually know more than we did before."

"Oh? How's that?"

"I knew Frank Russell was Yuri. Now you do too. We also know he has at least one accomplice. Our course of action would be to immediately start peeling Frank's life apart. There are phone records and we have his house."

"Or what's left of it."

"I'd like to head out there and see it for myself," Michael insisted.

"Fine. I'll walk you out of this building myself," said the DCI.

* * *

"Roger that sir." Sam pulled his earpiece out when the call terminated.

"I didn't even get a motherfucking shot off!"

"Take it easy Bill. You're not hit I take it?"

"Just my pride."

Sam chuckled. "At least that's the only thing. However, we have a bigger problem. In about thirty seconds the police are going to show up. The DCI assured me that we'd be spoken for but I'm not counting on it. Dump you weapon in the front seat so we don't spook any of these blue shirts."

* * *

The DCI escorted the three of them out to their car in the parking lot.

"You know you've caused quite a shit storm."

"Actually sir," replied Michael, "the shit storm was always there. We're just trying to contain it."

Victor Bannon smiled. "I like your style Michael. I don't know where you've been hiding for the past thirty years and I know you're not going to tell me. What I do know is that you have a knack for this type of thing. I have some damage control to attend to. I'll make sure you have clearance at Frank's house by the time you get there. What do you need from me?"

"I need a small team that has been handpicked and reports directly to you."

"Team? What type of team?"

"A couple of techs that can help us go through anything left at Franks' house for starters; evidence bagger and taggers. We'll also need an analyst, aside from me of course."

"Anything else?"

"We shouldn't meet at your office anymore. We'll need a location to run this operation."

"Done. I'll make it happen."

"Thank you, sir."

"On a side note, I must insist that I meet Mr. Paige and Mr. Nicholson."

"I'll pass that along."

"I'll call you later with a location we can meet at tomorrow morning. I'll expect a full report."

* * *

Michael, Thomas and Emily arrived at Yuri's house just as Sam and Bill had exited their taxi. The tactical unit had the perimeter locked down and a fire engine was still on the scene.

The unit leader watched with interest as four men and a little girl approached the property.

"This is a restricted area," the unit leader said forcefully. A short barreled CAR-15 was slung across his chest within easy reach.

Michael stepped up. "You've been instructed by the DCI to grant us full access to this location."

"Your name?"

"Michael Clark."

"Yes, sir. Your tech team is in route."

"Time?"

"Five minutes, sir."

"Very well. We'll start without them."

The unit leader spoke into his throat mike. "Let them through, they've been cleared."

The group walked past him as Thomas held Emily's hand.

Sam and Bill gave nods of respect as they passed. The unit leader spoke up. "I know you."

Sam stopped and gave the man a hard look. "No, you don't."

The man got the picture right away. "No, of course not."

24

Wednesday November 4, 1997 10:30am

Rebecca continued her patrol, and then headed inside the house which left Laura, Julie and Kim lounging by the pool. Four kids played and splashed around after being taken out of school for an indefinite amount of time. Gavin was in the family room playing on his own. A fresh pitcher of iced tea sat on a tray; the condensation dripped down the sides of the glass container. Birds fluttered just outside and their chirps added to the ambiance that was Hawaii.

"I haven't heard from Sam," said Julie. "Other than a call saying that they landed safety."

"You worry too much sis."

"Kim, how am I not supposed to worry? Just because you're not dealing with it…"

Laura interjected. "Seriously? Take it easy on each other."

The two sisters glared at each other but kept their mouths shut.

Laura looked at them. "What's going on?"

Julie finally spoke up. "I know I gave Sam my blessing but now I'm not so sure. What if something happens?"

Laura nodded. "Well, you're not the only one who has a reason to be worried."

"What do you mean? Oh right, Emily."

"You two worry too much," said Kim. "We just have to trust that they know what they're doing. They're not going to keep us in the dark, especially not now."

"Why do you say that?" asked her sister.

"Our husbands just had to worry about each other and how their jobs affected us. Now our children, hell, our entire families are part of the equation. To be blunt, they're not going to fuck around."

Kim's logic was sound and they quieted down for twenty seconds. The only constant sounds were of the ocean, their kids making a ruckus in the pool and a few birds.

Julie broke the silence. "Speaking of our kids, mine have started to ask a few questions."

"Mine too," Kim added.

"What kinds of questions?" Laura asked.

"Like where Daddy and Uncle Bill are."

"And why we have a nanny around." Kim looked around to make sure Rebecca wasn't in the area. "But truth be told, I'm kind of glad Bill isn't around. I might just catch him staring at her."

Julie and Laura laughed at Kim.

"What?"

"Sis, Bill wouldn't be caught dead looking at another woman. You two are just too stupid for each other."

Laura chuckled. "I have to agree. You have nothing to worry about."

"You think? I don't know. I think my boobs are starting to sag. What do you think sis? Are they?"

"We're twins. If you think your boobs are sagging then that means I'd have to admit mine are too, and that's never going to happen."

"Oh please," said Laura, "you're both thirty-seven and look fantastic. I hit forty-two a few months ago. If anyone should be complaining it's me."

Julie and Kim looked at each other and then over at Laura. "Shut up!"

"Yeah, shut up," said Kim. "If anyone has a smoking body it's you Laura."

Laura smiled. "Really? You think so? Thanks."

"Don't give us that 'really' shit," added Kim. "You don't even have to work on yourself. Your natural beauty makes us sick."

Julie agreed. "Sick to our stomachs."

"And you have great tits."

Everyone started laughing.

"You both suck," Laura said as she tried to catch her breath.

"I'm sorry to intrude." The three women, with smiles on their faces, looked up at Rebecca. "May I join you?"

Laura responded. "Of course. Please."

"Hi Becca," said Sarah from the pool.

"Why don't you come in and swim with us?" Amanda asked.

"Hey you guys. Maybe later." Rebecca sat down on an empty lounger. She was appropriately dressed for the weather now in khaki shorts, a white t-shirt, sandals and sunglasses. The only thing that stood out was the handgun strapped to her waist.

"How's everything going? Is there anything you need?" asked Laura. She poured a new glass of iced tea for Rebecca and handed it over.

"Thank you." She took a sip and put it down. "I'm actually not sure how to answer your question."

"Why's that?"

"I've only been working for SANDBOX for a few weeks now."

"Let me guess. Culture shock," said Julie.

Rebecca nodded. "I think that's it exactly. This job is completely different than what I was expecting."

"Different bad or different good?"

"I'm not sure how much you know about me actually."

The three wives looked around at each other and then back at Rebecca. "Sam told me you were a Combat Medic and served in '91 and '96," said Julie matter-of-factly.

"That's correct."

"I don't want to sound insensitive," said Kim, "but that must have been difficult."

"Sure, at times, but not because of the job. Fixing soldiers up after they've been wounded was the easy part. It was difficult because I was a woman in a man's war."

Laura probed. "Okay, we're all ears."

"I had to prove myself each and every day. Over time it became exhausting. I just wanted to do my job and be respected for my work. But not all men are created equally, as they say. There were times I narrowly avoided being raped and I'd heard plenty of stories, from others, who weren't as lucky." Rebecca paused. "So I lost faith in the system that was supposedly there to protect me. But I still wanted to do my job, to complete my mission."

"I had no idea it was like that. I'm sorry," said Julie.

"It's not your fault. Anyway, I just wanted to say thank you. You and your husbands have been nothing but professional and treated me with respect. They want this job done right and that's what I'm going to do."

"From what we've seen," said Kim, "you deserve it."

"It's the three of us that should be thanking you," added Laura. "The kids, well, at least the girls all love you. You take care of business and have been keeping us safe. I imagine the only thing you're having a tough time with is our location."

Rebecca smiled. "Laura, you're right. I absolutely hate this place."

Julie, Kim and Laura smiled as well. "We do too," said Kim.

"Tell me about it. This place is pure torture," said Julie.

Rebecca laughed as she drank more of her iced tea. "Time to walk the perimeter," she said as she stood up.

"Thanks Rebecca," said Laura.

"You're welcome," she replied and headed off towards the beach.

"Okay, she's a keeper," Kim admitted.

"Yeah, she's alright," her sister said.

"Okay. I'm sorry but I have to say this," continued Kim, " but she's got great tits. Did you see them? Don't tell me you two weren't looking? I couldn't help myself. I'm definitely glad Bill's not here."

"Sis!"

"Too funny!"

They all had a good laugh and went back to soaking up the morning sun.

* * *

In the family room Gavin worked on his coloring book while Stir watched with interest. He'd been cautious about summoning Stir with the other kids around but he knew they'd never drag themselves out of the pool. With Emily gone he didn't really have anyone to play with or talk to. He liked the other kids; it was just that sometimes he wanted to be by himself. Stir loved Gavin's company and he tracked his young master's crayon movement with his red eyes.

Gavin stopped and looked right at his pet. "I love you Stir."

Stir's tail thumped against the carpet. He inched closer, on his belly, and gave Gavin some tongue kisses.

"Heh heh. That tickles. Quit it." That only egged Stir to elevate his assault.

A loud thump against the window made them jump. Gavin and Stir looked over at the window but he didn't see anything. He dropped his crayon, walked over to the edge and looked down at the ground through the glass. In the bushes, on the ground, there was a bird. It just lay there.

"Stay here Stir," he said as he rushed outside.

The bird hadn't moved the few seconds it had taken Gavin to open the sliding glass door, take a right and walk behind the bushes. He crouched down and picked up the unconscious animal, cupping it in his hands as he did.

"Gavin. What are you up to honey?"

"There's a bird. He hurt himself."

"Don't touch it." He heard his mother walk towards him.

Gavin couldn't help but stare at the bird. "Please be okay."

"Gavin Clark. I told you not to touch it." Laura appeared over his shoulder.

He looked up at his mother. "But he's hurt."

"Put him down right now. I'll take a look at it once we go inside and thoroughly watch your hands."

"But…"

The bird's eyes blinked a few times and his black eyes stared at Gavin. Suddenly it shot out of his hands, beat its wings and took off into the air.

"See, it's just fine. Let's go, time to wash your hands."

Gavin stood up and followed his mother into the bathroom. She helped him scrub his hands.

"Birds and wild animals have germs sweetie, that's all. I'm not mad at you."

"Are you sure he'll be okay?" His eyes pleaded with hers.

"The window just stunned him is all." She turned off the water and dried his hands with a towel. "Now, do you want a popsicle?"

Gavin nodded his head.

"Okay then. I forgot where the kitchen was. Can you help me?"

He smiled. "You're silly. It's this way." He headed off and she followed behind.

In the kitchen he waited in front of the refrigerator.

"What color?"

"Purple."

"Purple it is," as she opened the freezer door. She found what she was looking for and took off the wrapper for him. "Here you go."

"Meow....meow."

"Did you hear that mom?"

Laura paused and listened as she held the popsicle in her hand.

"Mew...mew....meow."

Gavin forgot all about the cold treat and raced towards the front door.

"Gavin!"

He turned the knob and pulled. The door swung back and he darted outside.

"Gavin. Come back here!"

In the bushes, beneath the front windows, was a cat. Gavin got on his knees.

"What'ya up to champ?" said Rebecca out of nowhere.

He looked up. "There's a kitty."

"Meow."

Laura came out the front door, saw that Rebecca had Gavin under control and relaxed.

"Here kitty kitty."

"Meow." The bushes shook a little as the cat made its way towards Gavin's voice.

"Gavin," said his mother, "be careful."

"Here kitty kitty."

A large cat emerged and walked straight up to Gavin. It was a long haired tabby, orange and had a white chest. Some of its fur was matted. It rubbed against Gavin and began to purr.

Gavin petted the cat. "Ickers."

"What was that sweetie?"

"Mom, it has ickers."

Laura walked closer and held out her hand to the cat. The cat carefully smelled her hand and then rubbed his head against it. She looked closer at the cat's matted fur. Sure enough it had stickers in it.

"You're right. It has stickers."

Gavin continued to pet the cat and received a nice loud purr in return. "Can we help him?"

Laura looked up at Rebecca whose only response was to smile and shrug. *Good luck saying no now.*

"Let me see if he…"

"His name's Stickers."

If it's not one animal it's another. "Fine. Let me see if Stickers has a collar." Naturally the cat did not.

"Can he come inside? Please mom?"

"O…okay sweetie."

Gavin produced the biggest smile as he proudly picked up Stickers and carried him through the doorway.

Laura turned to Rebecca and smiled. "And here you thought your job was tough."

<u>25</u>

Wednesday November 4, 1997 11:00am

Thomas parked outside a warehouse along the waterfront and took a long look at it. The place looked abandoned. Weeds grew out of cracks in the pavement and the building was in severe need of a new coat of paint.

"You sure this is the place brother?" Bill asked.

"It's the address he gave me."

Sam, Bill, Thomas and Emily got out of the rental and closed the doors behind them.

"Time for the family picture." Thomas took Emily's hand in his own and then smiled at his daughter. She smiled back as Michael appeared next to all of them.

"Morning pop."

"Good morning son. Sam. Bill. And how's my little angel this morning?" He tickled his granddaughter.

"Teeheehee. Quit it," she teased.

"Let's get this show on the road," said Sam. "I'm not taking any chances. Give us a second."

Sam and Bill drew their weapons, advanced to the building's entrance and carefully opened the door. It creaked loudly as it swung inward. They nodded to each other and entered. The interior of the warehouse was dark, dirty and there were puddles of water everywhere from the leaky ceiling. In the far distant corner a large portion of the warehouse wall began to roll open. Sam and Bill positioned themselves behind some steel support beams and pointed their weapons at the potential threat.

A voice called out from the new opening. "You two must be Sam Paige and Bill Nicholson. I assure you that you're in the right location. If you'd be so kind as to lower your weapons and invite the Clark's inside so we can get started."

Sam and Bill nodded at each other and holstered their side arms. Bill jogged to the outside door and beckoned them inside.

"Looks like you're up Mr. C. This cloak and dagger stuff is your ball of wax." Bill pointed towards the hidden wall that had rolled open at the back of the warehouse.

Michael smiled and led the way as they crossed the large but empty warehouse. As the group approached, two men stepped out of the shadows. One of them was Victor Bannon. The other was the unit leader that they'd talked to the night before. His CAR-15 was in his hands but he held it at a neutral angle.

Everyone exchanged handshakes while Michael made the introductions.

"Mr. Bannon, this is Sam Paige and Bill Nicholson."

"Very nice to finally meet you both. I've heard a lot about you."

"The pleasure's all mine, sir," Sam replied.

"Yes, thanks for the get out of jail free card yesterday," said Bill. "Our rental pretty much shot to shit."

The DCI smiled. "The least I could do given the circumstances. That incident was filed away as a drive-by shooting with no fatalities."

Curtis, the tactical unit leader, spoke up. "I knew I knew you," he said to Sam. "I believe I have some buddies that work for you Mr. Paige. You need anything just let me know."

Sam nodded to Curtis, one operator to another.

"And I see it's bring your daughter to work day again," said the DCI in passing. "Shall we get started?" He led the group further in the private area and the hidden door rolled closed behind them.

Directly across from the entrance was a small room. Bill poked his head in and determined it was used for interrogation. Curtis led the way down a corridor lined with surveillance cameras. At the end of the hallway they saw a thick metal door with a security panel embedded in it. Curtis punched in a code and the door opened inward. The group entered the new area and looked around.

The CIA, and other TLA (three letter acronym) groups, are notorious for a variety of offsite, and sometimes off the book locations. All over the world there are safe and resupply houses to detention and surveillance facilities. This particular location was a black ops surveillance and operations site. High tech equipment, communications, computers and work stations filled a portion of the sixty-by-sixty work space. Large monitors adorned the walls whose main purpose was to relay information from various sources around the world from satellite images to cell phone tracking. The large space maintained a certain hum. A large table was in the middle of the room while a comfortable looking couch adorned the back wall. An offshoot room contained a refrigerator, stove, and bunk beds along with a full bathroom.

"Nice place you have here Director," said Bill. "It's been awhile since I've been in a TOC." He saw a puzzled looked come over Thomas' face. "Sorry. Tactical Operations Center. It's where missions are handled from."

"Indeed," replied the DCI. He waved his arm around. "Welcome to Operation Briar-Patch. This is your new home away from home."

In chairs facing the onslaught of information sat two men. Both were white and in their late twenties. They got up, came over and introductions were made.

"For the sake of security you can call them Calvin and Hobbes. Apparently they came up with the names on their own. They're your technical support as well as your liaison to me. Curtis is your security. This entire operation, as you might have guessed, is off the books."

The DCI walked over to the table where they all took a seat.

"You're saying we can trust everyone in this room?" Michael asked.

"They have all been fully vetted and read-in on the current situation. Suffice it to say that a leak about a mole in the Agency, going back to the Cold War, would have serious ramifications. I cannot turn over any portion of this investigation to the FBI nor can I legally run a CIA sanctioned operation on United States soil. Any way I look at this problem is a nightmare."

"There's egg on the entire country's face, sir," Michael stated.

"Maybe, but we're dealing with it on my watch so it's my responsibility. I can't trust the normal chain of command because I don't know who or what's been compromised. That's where you come in." He turned to Sam and Bill. "This operation will require plausible deniability. To that end I recommend we use SANDBOX personnel."

"We're on the same page, sir," said Sam.

"Good." The DCI moved on to Michael. "You will have full access to the Company's resources through Calvin and Hobbes. You'll track down and capture Yuri, aka Frank Russell. I want the network dug up and exposed." He paused. "On a side note, and nothing personal, but why are your son and granddaughter here Michael?"

"They're an essential part of this process and will be working with me. Having another set of eyes is never a bad thing."

The DCI's eyes narrowed. He knew Michael had just sidestepped his entire question. "Very well."

Michael continued. "What additional resources will be at our disposal?"

Hobbes spoke. "We have the ability to task a satellite if necessary. We also have a pipeline into the NSA, the National Security Agency."

"How'd you manage that?"

"I called in a favor. They are unaware of our actual operation and that's all you need to know," added the DCI.

Sam spoke up. "How's this all going to work, logistically speaking?"

"Mr. Paige," replied Calvin, "you and Mr. Nicholson will remain in the field. We have a separate location for your team, a safe house. Information will be relayed to you via these encrypted satellite phones." Hobbes opened a container and handed out the phones.

"Why satellite phones? Why not cell phones?" asked Thomas.

"A few reasons," Calvin replied. "For one they've already been setup and tested. Two, who's to say this operation won't spill out of the US. You don't want to find yourself someplace with a phone and zero cell coverage."

Thomas nodded. He looked back at his father and watched how animated he was. *Right back where he left off.* Thomas knew it wasn't going to be easy. Not on him, not on his daughter and certainly not on Laura. *What the hell did I get us all into?*

The DCI stood up. "If there's nothing else you need from me I still have a day job to get back to." He looked at Calvin and Hobbes. "Keep me informed."

"Of course, sir."

"I'll need one additional person to fill out the team," said Michael.

"Fine. Authorized. Anyone else?"

Thomas stood. "May I speak with you for a moment, sir?"

Michael cocked his head slightly at his son before he turned back to the table and spoke up. "To start with I want to go through what was found at Frank's house."

The DCI and Thomas walked over to the steel door, away from the group.

"What's on your mind?"

"I don't know how else to say this so I'll just say it. My father is ill."

"I don't understand. He seems fine to me."

"The specifics are hardly important other than to say that its terminal."

Victor's face turned concerned. "Cancer?"

"Something like that. Anyway, my point wasn't to worry you. He's clearly enjoying being back in the game."

The DCI nodded. "Once a spy always a spy. Your father's file clearly represents the dedication he puts into his work. That reminds me, where the hell has he been for the past thirty years?"

"If he wants you to know he'll tell you."

He sized Thomas up. "Fair enough. If you have any medical needs just let me know."

"Fair enough. Also, I wanted to make a request."

"Fire away."

Thomas whispered into the DCI's ear, shook his hand and watched him depart. He then headed back to the table.

"How're you doing Em?"

"A little thirsty."

"Sorry to intrude," said Hobbes, "but there's some juice boxes in the frig."

"Thanks," said Thomas. He went to retrieve one as the conversation continued.

"As I was saying," said Calvin, "we found some items that hadn't been destroyed."

"Good," replied Michael. "However, we're going to take a trip there. I need to go through it myself. I can do that this afternoon while the laundry list is being worked on."

"Laundry list?" asked Calvin.

"We need groceries. We need toys for Emily. Sam and Bill need to organize their team and setup at their new location. Also, the extra analyst I need has to be acquired. I'll provide you his name. So yes, there's plenty of foundational work to be done."

Calvin and Hobbes looked at each other and then back at Michael. "You're in charge so whatever you want. On a side note, and not to sound too sappy sir, but you're a legend from the Cold War days and we're honored to be working with you."

Michael stopped. To him it felt like he'd picked up right where he'd stopped working. But that reality was thirty years in the past. *Christ. A legend. The Cold War. Time has really marched on without me.*

"Listen closely. Yuri is still out there," Michael replied. "He knows we're coming for him. We have nothing else on our plate but finding him."

"Yes sir," said Calvin.

"Absolutely," added Hobbes.

Bill nudged Sam. "Let's go make the call."

"Well do it enroot to the new location," replied Sam. "We're going to need some wheels."

"I can help you with that," said Curtis. "We've got some stashed in the back. I'll also get you keys and the safe house address."

Michael stood up. "After that's done Curtis I'll need you to take us over to Frank's house."

"Who's we?"

"Thomas, Emily and I."

Curtis gave him a strange look.

"Problem?" Michael asked.

Curtis paused before replying. "No, of course not."

Michael turned away, wrote down a name on a piece of paper and handed it to Hobbes. "Here's the name of the analyst I need."

26

Wednesday November 4, 1997 11:05am

The recoil, from Frank's Skorpion, was something he wasn't prepared for. The majority of the twenty rounds he'd shot high as he wrestled with the weapon's kick. The good news was that his pursuer, whoever he was, had been forced to eat dirt. Combine that with the large crowd of screaming students and Frank had instantly created a recipe that allowed him to escape to the subway.

Frank Russell had been sought after before, but never to this extreme. His seventy-seven year old body wasn't as nimble anymore and his body constantly reminded him of that fact once he'd hit the subway. His breathing was labored and his bones ached. But he still didn't know who was after him. He had only seen two people in the car behind him, not to mention his savor. *I have a strange suspicion who that man might happen to be.* It was just another indication that he needed to get to his safe house and off the street.

Frank took the subway two stops, exited, dumped his cell phone and boarded the next bus that pulled up. He rode it five stops, got off and waited a few minutes for a new one that headed north. Three hours later, after circumventing the city more than once, Frank knew he hadn't been tailed. He took his last bus ride and exited three blocks from his safe house. Not one of his tell-tale signs, on the outside of the house, had been disturbed. He extracted the key from a secret stash in the garden and let himself in.

It'd been a few weeks since Frank had spent any time at his safe house. Junk mail littered the entrance doorway all under a false name; the same false name that was on his rental lease. Frank scooted the collection aside with his foot, let his bag hit the floor and headed to the kitchen. He didn't store fresh food in the house because it would spoil. Instead he kept food that had a longer shelf life like crackers, chips, nuts and cookies. In his freezer he stocked a decent amount of frozen dinners, lasagna, chicken strips and whatever else he'd purchased from Costco. Soda, bottled water and beer filled the fridge while his Scotch whisky sat on the cabinet shelf waiting for him.

Frank quickly opened a bottle of water, drank half of it and then opened up a box of cookies. He had surprised the hell out of himself how fast he'd reacted back at his house.

Hit the stove, timer, go bag and got the fuck out.

Without going back he'd never know how much evidence he'd been able to destroy.

I can't go back. I can never go back. It's time to lay low.

The evening news had briefly covered his house fire, the downtown shooting and then moved on to more important topics. There was no correlation that either was connected.

Nor should there be.

At five minutes past midnight Frank, having changed clothes, exited his safe house. He walked the four blocks to a gas station and checked for any surveillance. Frank was certain he was alone by the time he reached the station. The payphone was one of many on his mental checklist. He picked up the receiver and dialed a local number. An answering machine picked up after the fourth ring and Frank quickly left a message.

"Anita, this is your father. It's time to come home. I expect to see you in the morning for breakfast."

Frank didn't want to make the call. However, the simple fact was that he'd torched his house. He was burned; and that meant this city was locked down. Any attempt to leave by train, ship or air would be complicated.

* * *

"We were wondering if you'd give us a call." Alexei had been waiting for Frank at the rendezvous indicated in the coded voice message. The park made it easy to watch anyone coming and going. Frank sat down on the bench next to Alexei.

"Hello Alexei. Fancy meeting you here. I assume you're the one I have to thank for interfering yesterday? I've seen you around this past week, more than once. You're good, I'll give you that, but I've been playing this game longer than you have."

Alexei shrugged.

"So what now? Are you going to kill me?"

"Another time perhaps. Right now we both know there are more pressing issues to deal with. Tell me what happened."

"I want to talk to Nikolay."

Alexei shook his head. "That time has passed. You have fallen out of favor."

"I don't give a shit. You might hold my life in your hands but he knows I can say the same thing about him."

"He doesn't care."

"Bullshit. If he didn't then you wouldn't have shown up this morning. The game is still afoot and we're all playing it whether we like it or not."

Alexei didn't react. He didn't deny what Yuri had said either.

"Get Nikolay on the phone or I walk."

Alexei just sat there.

"Sure, you can let me go to take my chances. Who's to say I make it out of the city, or even the country before I get picked up and make a deal for immunity. Or, maybe you just kill me now. You do that and you know the information I have socked away exposes him sooner than later."

Alexei still didn't budge.

"Well, it's a shame really. We both know you're smarter than this. His plans will be ruined. Say goodbye to him for me, will you." Frank stood up and started to walk away.

"Wait."

Frank stopped, turned around and sat back down.

Alexei pulled out a satellite phone and waited for the secure connection. "He's here and wants to talk to you." He handed the phone over to Frank.

"You play a dangerous game Yuri," said the voice on the other end.

"It's a game we've both been playing for a long time. Did you really expect that I'd roll over without a fight Nikolay?"

"Alexei was there to look after your well-being my old friend."

Frank laughed. "We both know he's been following me for a week to find out what law offices I've stashed the information you're so afraid of. Maybe I didn't visit all of them Nikolay, you think of that?"

Silence.

"My safety should concern you. If certain parties don't hear from me, on a specific schedule, then it's all over Nikolay."

"Very well. I believe you. You have my word, Alexei won't kill you."

"Not very comforting but I'll take that for now."

"Great. Moving on. Tell me what happened?"

"I received a code from someone I've been handling within the agency. The code told me that I was completely burned. I blew up my house but was not prepared for an immediate car chase by two strangers."

"Who are they?"

"I don't know yet."

"Get your man to look into the situation for you. If you're not safe then I need to know about it immediately. My operation is paramount."

"I'll use some back channels and see what I can find out."

"You do that. In the meantime you and Alexei are going to be best friends."

"Lucky me." Frank handed the phone back to Alexei who listened to what Nikolay had to say.

"I understand." Alexei put the phone back in his jacket and looked at Frank. "Looks like you just gained a roommate."

D.W. Neuman

27

Thursday November 5, 1997 12:35pm

Thomas had been driving south on I-95 for the past two hours. He traveled through Richmond, Virginia and taken an exit twenty-five miles later. He pulled into the Petersburg Correctional Complex visitor's parking and turned off the engine. Emily sat in the front while Curtis rode in the back seat.

"I thought your father would be taking care of this?"

"My father has his way of doing things. He asked me to come and make the offer. It's his show."

Curtis nodded. "Yeah, he's definitely a force to be reckoned with."

Thomas nodded. "I'm beginning to come to that conclusion myself."

Thomas opened the door and all three of them got out.

"I'll watch your daughter sir."

Thomas shook his head. "No. She doesn't leave my side. We'll be back when it's done."

"Bye," said Emily as they walked away.

Curtis watched Thomas take his daughter's hand and head off to the facilities entrance. He leaned against the vehicle.

There's definitely something odd about that family, that's for sure.

* * *

One of the guards at the entrance checked Thomas' name off his list and escorted the two of them inside. Ten minutes later they were shown into the Warden's office.

"Have a seat."

"Thank you."

The Warden looked over the request he held in his hand. "This is highly unusual Mr. Clark."

"That may be but the paperwork speaks for itself."

Emily swung her legs back and forth as she sat in her chair. Thomas couldn't help but notice that the Warden kept glancing in her direction.

"I'll come right to the point. This is my federal prison and I don't like being dictated to even if it's a direct call from the Director of the CIA."

Thomas leaned forward. "I don't blame you. These are unusual times. I'm not here to upset your apple cart. With that being said, I don't want to make this day any worse for you with a simple phone call. I'd rather be out of your hair sooner rather than later, wouldn't you agree?" He leaned back.

The Warden had a tough time reading the man who sat across from him. *And to bring his little girl with him; who does that?* With one last glance at the child he picked up his phone and dialed an extension. "Set it up. No surveillance. Yes, you heard me. Get it done." He hung up the phone as he stood. "You're right Mr. Clark. I'd like to get you and your daughter out of my hair as soon as possible."

* * *

A different guard led them down a series of hallways and checkpoints until one specific door was opened for them. It was a conference room that contained a large table and several comfortable chairs.

"Can I get you anything?"

"Juice please," replied Emily.

"Apple for her, if you have it."

"And you?"

"I'm good, thanks," said Thomas.

"It'll just be a few minutes." The guard closed the door behind him as he left.

"How're you doing pumpkin?"

"Okay. I'm starting to get used to it."

"Used to what?"

"That we won't be going home soon."

Shit she's growing up too fast. "I'm sorry Em. I'm going to try my hardest to get us there. You understand that as soon as we help grandpa out, and get the bad guys, then things can go back to normal, right?"

Emily nodded her head.

"You're doing a great job sweetheart. I'm really proud of you."

"What about you daddy?"

"What do you mean?"

She cocked her head to the side. "Are you okay?"

From the mouths of babes. But he had to think about his daughter's question. Things had dramatically altered. His life, here and now, was drastically different than it was seven years prior. Instead of getting out of bed to write children's books he woke up to his wife and children now. Laura's professional life, her career as a therapist, had all but been left behind. Their children were thankfully angels, but they still possessed powers that they were just coming to understand. Powers that everyone were still getting used to. *So many damn things have changed.*

Thomas smiled at this daughter. "I'm getting there."

Emily smiled back. "Me too." She paused before she continued. "Do I do what we talked about earlier?"

"Absolutely."

"He might get sad."

"I know. It's a chance we'll have to take."

"Okay daddy."

The conference room they were in was just that, a regular conference room. Thomas couldn't locate anything out of the ordinary that appeared to contain an audio or video device. Other than the guards who waited in the hallway the conversation they were about to have was going to be private.

The door opened inward and two guards came in. The first brought in the refreshments while the second led an elderly man to one of the empty chairs. The man's hair was white and he had piercing dark eyes. He tried to hide his confusion but he clearly didn't know why he was in this room, especially not with a man and a little girl.

"Please remove his handcuffs," said Thomas. The guard complied.

"Thanks for the juice," said Emily.

"You're welcome." *What the fuck is the kid doing here?*

"Please close the door behind you." The two guards turned and walked out the door. They knew enough not to ask any questions.

The prisoner wore a traditional orange jumpsuit. It might have fit him years ago but it hung loose off his body. Neither one of them said a word as they sized each other up. Thirty seconds ticked by before the man spoke.

"What's with the kid?"

"This is my daughter Emily."

He turned his gaze on the little girl. "How old are you Emily?"

"Six."

"This place must be scary for you?"

Emily shrugged. "I've seen worse."

The prisoner didn't know what to make of that. "I see. Do you know why your father brought you here today?"

Thomas watched the interaction with interest.

"My daddy needs your help."

"Oh, is that right." He turned to Thomas. "Who the hell are you?"

"Your name is Richard Moore. You worked with my father, Michael Clark, quite a long time ago." Thomas let the words hang in the air. Richard's eyes widened as his jaw clenched. Thomas could see his mind working as he put things together.

"Michael...Clark. That's a name I haven't heard in a very, very long time. And you say you're his son?"

"Yes sir."

"You're telling me that you're his boy Tommy?"

Thomas nodded.

"Well I'll be damn. You've really grown up. You look a lot like him." Richard's face turned compassionate. "I'm sorry about your parents. I attended their wedding. Betsy really brought a smile to your father's face. I was sorry to hear about his passing as well. He was a good man."

"Thank you, sir."

Richard looked around the room again. "You have me at a disadvantage..."

"Thomas."

"Thomas. Of course. Listen. I've been incarcerated for over thirty years. I'm seventy-seven years old. Are you looking for some type of closure or something?"

"No. I'm actually here about Yuri."

Richard's fists balled up and his lip curled. "I don't know how you know that name Thomas, but judging from the fact that we're even talking is proof enough that you must know something. My own agency threw me in a dark hole when they concluded I was

219

Yuri. I was tortured and interrogated for years. Hell, I even led the team that was after that sonofabitch and the CIA had the gall to think it was me!" He slammed his fist down on the table and Emily jumped. Richard's eyes softened immediately. "I'm sorry Emily. I didn't mean to startle you."

"The day's still early," she replied.

Richard smiled. "I can see your father in her too. She's smart, just like he was. You know Thomas...it was your father that figured out that I was stealing from the government."

Thomas cut in. "But it was Yuri that set you up to look like the mole."

"I know. Your father thought the same thing. He was one hell of a bloodhound. When I heard that...well...he'd taken his own life I couldn't believe it."

"It wasn't true. He was killed. Murdered."

Richard sat up straight. "What? What happened?"

"That's a story for another time. Right now I have a question to ask you."

"Alright. It's your dime. Fire away. I have plenty of time."

"We need your help to take down Yuri. You were part of the original investigation. Will you help us?"

Richard wagged a finger. "Yuri's got to be long gone by now."

"And if he isn't?"

"Then I want to nail that bastard to the wall for what he put me through, not to mention the damage he did to this country." He briefly paused. "Wait. You said we. Who's we?"

Thomas made a signal under the table to his daughter.

"He's referring to me," said a new voice from behind Richard.

Richard jumped in his seat and turned around. He blinked his eyes a few times. *No, it can't be. It's impossible. But he's older, just like me. I don't understand. What the hell is this?*

"Hello Richard," said Michael as he took a few steps forward and extended his hand. "It's been a few years."

Richard was dumbstruck but reached out, shook the man's hand and held onto it. "How...? Michael...is that really you?" He finally let go.

Michael took a seat next to his son and granddaughter. "It's really me."

"But I...I don't understand. I thought you were dead?"

"Who's saying I'm not?"

Richard scoffed. "What the hell does that mean? You're sitting right here. So unless this is some sick joke I..."

"Go easy my friend. This isn't a joke," said Michael. "I'm actually here for a few reasons. The first is that I need your help taking down Yuri."

"You take it easy. I've just seen a ghost. But what about Yuri? He hasn't been captured after all these years?"

"The situation is more complicated than that. Listen to me. I know who Yuri is."

"What!? When?"

"I've had that information for thirty years."

Richard was exasperated. "What the fuck Michael? Nothing that you're telling me adds up, you know that? You're talking in circles. There's no way you'd sit on information that vital for thirty years. That's not how I remember you."

"No Richard, you're right, I wouldn't have. Not unless I wasn't given a choice about the matter."

"A choice? So why are you here now? What can I possible offer from my prison cell to make you come out of hiding after all these years?"

"Just a few things like vindication, justice and revenge. Do any of those work for you?"

Richard looked his old protégé in the eyes. "Come on, what are you really saying?"

"I'm saying that you've paid your debt. You're a free man."

"Oh bullshit. You can't come in here, bring up the past, and toss hope in my face like that."

Thomas spoke up. "My father is actually serious. Your imminent release is real. However, it comes with one condition."

A skeptical look passed over Richard's face. "Okay, I'll humor you. What's the condition?"

"That you come and work with me," said Michael. "We have Yuri on the run and there's isn't much time."

"And let's say we do catch him. Then what? Am I looking at a trip straight back to prison or what?"

"No. You'd be a free man. If the government doesn't set you up then I'll personally finance your new life."

"Pfft. Even if I were to believe you why would I want to help the same government who refused to believe me? I begged them to relook at the evidence during my interrogations. Do you hear me? I begged them. They just turned a blind eye. They closed the file and screwed themselves over for the past thirty years. It's not my problem. Hell, they made sure it wasn't my problem by keeping me behind these damn bars. I'm old Michael, I'm tired and I'm angry."

"It's alright. I understand you're bitter. Quite frankly I didn't think you'd be an easy sell."

"What the hell does that mean?"

"You said it yourself. You're angry at the Agency for not listening to you."

"And now I'm angry at you Michael. Where the hell have you been for the past thirty years? You said you've known who Yuri was and yet you've done nothing, including setting the record straight with me. I've been locked away and forgotten about until today. And yet you have the gall to ask me for my help? Give me a break. I'd rather stay in here."

Michael nodded. "I understand."

"You couldn't possibly understand."

"I do my old friend, and so will you. I'll ask you again. Help me get Yuri."

"I don't think so."

Michael sighed. "Time is short so you'll forgive my tactics." He stood up. "I was there, in your house, when they found the evidence. The magnets on your refrigerator spelled out PINNACLE."

"We already had this conversation thirty years ago. You damn well know that wasn't me."

"Oh, I know. My point is that I found myself staring at a few of your pictures on the wall. One was taken at Yosemite National Park. The picture was of you, your wife and your daughter. Do you remember? The falls were in the background. The other was professionally taken at a studio years before. The three of you looked like a very happy family."

"Don't you dare you sonofabitch."

"What I didn't know until right then was that your wife Katie and daughter Olivia were killed in a massive pile up."

"Stop..."

"The fog was so thick that morning. You probably knew you shouldn't be on the road but you drove anyway. You couldn't have been more than thirty-five years old when it happened. I'm guessing your Olivia was probably only nine at the time."

"How dare you bring them up. What kind of a sick bastard are you?"

"Like I said before, we don't have a lot of time. You're going to help me. I know you want to but you've turned into a stubborn old man. I don't blame you but it's preventing us from moving forward." He turned to Emily. "It's time sweetie."

Emily got off her chair. All eyes were on her as she walked around to where Richard sat.

Richard didn't know what to make of the situation. Nothing made any sense. Emily came around the table towards him. *What the hell is she doing?* The little girl looked up at him and then gently reached out, briefly touched his hand and stepped back. A woman materialized out of thin air in front of him. He jumped for the second time.

Thomas had expected his father to disappear as the woman appeared. Michael had been expecting the same thing but he remained exactly where he stood.

Michael slowly sat down as Emily made her way back to her chair.

"Hi daddy" the woman said.

Richard's mouth hung open. His heart pounded in his chest.

"Daddy. I'm Olivia, your daughter." She reached out to her father but he recoiled.

"Don't…don't touch me."

"It's okay. Mom and I have been looking after you since we died."

"This isn't happening. I must be hallucinating."

"Daddy please. It's me, Olivia. I've missed you so much."

"No….this is impossible. My daughter's dead."

"You need to stop blaming yourself for what happened. It was an accident."

Richard stood up and pointed at Michael. "I don't know what this is but I want it to stop right now."

Olivia continued. "It's okay. There's no need to be afraid."

He whipped around. "I don't know who you think you are but this isn't funny anymore."

"Do you remember that time when you gave me that teddy bear for my fifth birthday? I was supposed to be asleep but I snuck out of my room and overheard you talking to mom. You told her that I was your…"

"…world," he said. Tears brimmed.

"I loved that bear. When I'd hug it I would imagine it was you who was hugging me back."

Richard looked at her with new eyes. "Olive?"

She nodded. "It's me daddy. It's really me." She opened her arms and he embraced her.

"Oh my God," he said with tears coming down his face. "It is you. How is this possible?"

"I missed you. Mom and I both have," she said crying along with her father.

Michael looked over at Emily, as was Thomas.

Thomas whispered, "I thought it was only the last person you touched."

"I didn't know I could do that until just now."

Her father smiled. "That's pretty cool Em." *Wow. Her powers are getting stronger and stronger.*

Emily was very pleased with herself as well. She returned the smile.

Michael stood back up.

Olivia pulled broke the embrace. "I have to go now."

Richard wiped away some tears. "No, wait. I don't understand. Don't go."

"There will be time later."

"No please. Don't go."

"Bye daddy. I love you." And with that she disappeared.

"I love you too," he replied to the empty space where his daughter had just stood.

"Are you okay?" asked Michael.

"I…I don't know." Richard quietly sat back down.

"She's nice," Emily stated. "Not everyone is like that."

Michael took the opportunity to take his own seat.

"What was that? What just happened?"

"That's a very long story," Michael replied. "What you need to understand, right now, is that I've just put my family at risk. This is how much I trust you Richard."

He took it in. "You're saying that my daughter, who passed away, was just in this room."

"I am."

"You're also telling me that you weren't lying to me. You're really…"

"…dead?"

Richard nodded.

"I really am."

"Holy shit. How is this possible?"

Michael looked over at his granddaughter. "Emily has some amazing powers but this isn't the time or the place to go into any details. Like I said, I have just put my family at risk with this demonstration. I can't take it back or make you forget what you just experienced."

"My Olive…I held her in my arms."

Michael nodded. "That can happen again Richard. I'm sure your wife Katie would like to visit you as well."

"Michael, you have my full attention. What do you need from me?"

"I want you to know that you're not the only one who's suffered at the hands of Yuri. I need your help to put him away."

"As long as I get to see my family again you have my word. Besides, that bastard has had it coming for far too long. I've always wanted to finish what we started."

Michael smiled. "You're going to be in for a wild ride." He turned to Thomas. "Son, he's all yours."

"Bye grandpa."

"I'll see you later Em." And with that Michael disappeared.

"Holy hell," exclaimed Richard.

"Mr. Moore?"

Richard slowly met Thomas' gaze.

"We're going to walk out of here now. I'm sure I don't have to remind you that the wellbeing of my daughter now rests in your hands."

"I understand completely." He smiled. "To tell you the truth I'm feeling quite invigorated. I don't know how any of what just happened is possible but it doesn't matter. I got to hold my little girl again." He stood up and headed for the door. "I'm ready to go get that sonofabitch."

D.W. Neuman

28

Thursday November 5, 1997 7:30pm

"Hi sweetheart."

Laura smiled from her home in Hawaii. "It's really good to hear your voice. I miss you both so much. How are you?"

"I'm a little tired. We've been going gangbusters since we got here. I can tell you with certainty that our daughter's one hell of a trooper."

"I already knew that."

"Cute honey. So, ah, what are you wearing?"

Laura laughed. "You can imagine me in one of my bikinis right now....laying out by the pool....perspiration trailing down my neck, down past my cleavage..."

Thomas smiled. "Ooo yeah. That does paint one hell of a vivid picture. That'll last me for a while. Thanks babe."

"Anything for you. Where's Emily?"

"She's right here. She wants to talk to you."

"You asked that in front of our daughter? Have you no morals?"

"Not when it comes to you babe. Hold on a sec."

Laura heard the phone change hands. "Hi mommy. I miss you."

"I miss you too my little angel. Are you doing okay out there?"

"Uh huh. I've met a lot of new people. Most of them are nice. Grandpa works a lot though."

"I bet. Are you getting enough sleep? Daddy's taking care of you, right?"

"I'm fine. What about Gavin?"

"What do you mean sweetie?"

"How's he doing?"

"Funny you should ask. He was wondering the same thing about you. Just yesterday he found a cat outside and twisted my arm to make it part of our family."

"A cat? Neat! I can't wait to come home and see it." Thomas gave his daughter a weird look.

"Oh how I miss you. Love you. Put your father back on please."

"Love you too." She handed the phone off.

"What was that about a cat?" Thomas asked.

"Your son heard it meowing out front and got it to come to him. It's actually the sweetest cat. I had to brush its coat out because it was full of stickers."

"What's its name?"

"Stickers."

"No, I heard that part. What's the cat's name?"

Laura chuckled. "Your son named it Stickers."

Thomas got it. "Stickers the cat…gotcha. I've got to ask. How's Stir and Stickers getting along?"

"It's too early to tell."

"I see. And don't think for a second I didn't hear you call him 'my son' instead of 'our son'."

Laura giggled. "What? You heard that? Guess you'll just have to come out here and spank me."

Thomas smiled. "Not like I've haven't thought about it. On a serious note though, how's everything? Any issues?"

"So far so good. I don't think Rebecca's getting enough sleep though. She takes her job seriously and needs a break. I'm sure Julie will mention it to Sam but would you mind talking to him about it just in case?"

"Good idea. I'll bring it up when we head to dinner in a bit." He paused and she picked up on his hesitation.

"Honey, you okay out there?"

"I don't know. No worse for wear. Can I just say that it's weird seeing my father back in his element? He definitely has a knack for this line of work. I just feel like I'm along for the ride."

"From my point of view you have the most important job of all."

"What's that?"

"Looking after and protecting your daughter."

"She's our daughter."

"You're damn right she is. Watch out for her and watch out for yourself. Get it all sorted out so we can raise our children in peace, okay?"

"That sounds like a plan sweetheart. I love you."

"I love you too. Be safe."

"Always. I'll talk to you later. Bye."

* * *

Sam drove while Bill continued his conversation with his wife. They were on the way to meet up with Thomas and Emily for dinner.

"Kim, we've only been here for two days," said Bill over the phone.

"And yet you've been involved in a shootout already."

"What?"

"I've been following the news in Washington. That shootout had both of your name's written all over it so don't pretend otherwise."

Shit she's good. "Everything's fine." *Go for the joke.* "I didn't even get shot this time."

"I'll be the one that shoots you when it comes down to it," she teased. "Just be careful out there."

231

"You know me…Mr. Careful."

Kim heard Sam snicker in the background as Bill told him to shut the fuck up. "Tell Sam that Julie's right here and would like to speak with him."

Bill passed the phone to Sam. "Here you go brother. Your turn."

Sam rolled his eyes. "Hello? Jules?"

* * *

The four of them sat down to eat together, at a corner booth, at Denny's.

"Hey Em. How was your day?" Sam asked after their drinks.

"We met Olivia today. She was nice."

Sam looked over at Thomas.

"Richard was somewhat uncooperative at the beginning. Em re-introduced his daughter that he'd lost over thirty years ago."

"So he knows."

Thomas nodded. "My father trusts him and he's properly motivated."

"Sounds like playing with fire if you ask me, but there's nothing we can do about it now. You okay with it?"

Thomas shrugged. "Time will tell. He's at the TOC now. Curtis, Calvin and Hobbes are bringing him up to speed."

Bill spoke up. "Thirty plus years in the pen. That has to really mess with your head."

"What about you guys?"

"We've got six operators on standby to jump out here on a moment's notice," said Bill.

"Any reason not to bring them out right now?"

"You've got a point Thomas," stated Sam. "Things could go sideways at any moment for all we know."

"I'll make the call after dinner. What'ya think…want them here tomorrow or Monday?"

"Shoot for Monday. Unless we catch a huge break tomorrow I think we'll just be sitting on our asses."

Emily giggled.

"Speaking of more people," Thomas started to say before Sam interjected.

"Let me guess, our wives are suggesting more support be sent out."

"It makes sense. Rebecca is only one person. There's quite a bit of property and family members to look after."

"It's already been taken care of. As soon as I got off the phone earlier I called Roberta."

Bill chuckled. "He couldn't get off the phone with Julie fast enough."

"Oh that's rich coming from the guy who shoved the phone into my face, right Mr. Caution?"

"Mr. Caution?" asked Thomas.

Bill smiled. "It's a long story. Suffice it to say I'm glad to be out here with you guys regardless of the circumstance. We're going to take care of business and get things back to normal."

"Easier said than done but I love your enthusiasm," said Sam. He raised his glass. "To our success, wherever it may lead us."

D.W. Neuman

29

Friday November 6, 1997 10:30am

Rebecca Cross had expected their arrival and opened the front door for her fellow SANDBOX operators. On the doorstep stood Tony, Andy and Matt, the same men she'd worked with in Marin the week before.

"Come on in," she said after they'd greeted each other. They put their bags down and Rebecca led them out back to the pool. The kids seemed to live in the water while the ladies lounged around the pool.

Laura heard the sliding glass door open, slowly reached under her towel and gripped her Glock that was hidden from view.

Rebecca walked up with the three men. "Julie, Kim, Laura. You remember Tony, Andy and Matt."

"Hello again," said Laura as she removed her hand from underneath her towel.

Polite re-introductions were made before Rebecca spoke up again. "I just wanted to let you all know that they had arrived. I'll get them situated."

"Thank you," replied Laura.

* * *

Rebecca led them back inside the Clark's.

"Listen, I'm here to protect this family just like you are but I know I'm new to all this. Sam put me in charge but I think that was a bad call. I thought we worked really well together in Marin and I'm letting you know that I'll take my queues from you. The bottom line is that our job is to successfully protect this family."

Tony, Andy and Matt grinned as they stared back at her.

235

"What?" she asked.

Andy spoke up. "Sam was absolutely right when he put you in charge."

"Why's that?"

"The three of us are just a bunch of knuckle draggers," said Tony.

"Thank God you're here to run interference for us," Matt added.

"Run interference? What?"

"Andy wants banana. Ooo Ooo Ahh Ahh." The three men chuckled while Rebecca's face contorted for a second. She joined in shortly thereafter.

"You got me," she said.

They all smiled. "We're just fucking with you," said Tony. "We think you did a great job last week."

"Thanks."

"Our pleasure," said Matt. "Don't worry about being in charge. We all have each other's backs. What's there to worry about? It's not like we're guarding the boss's family or anything…"

"Yeah, no shit. No added pressure or anything," said Tony.

"Well, we could be stuck in some other dark corner of the world."

Rebecca smiled. "You're not going to get any complaints about Hawaii from me." She picked up two of their heavy bags. "Now, if you're done razzing the new chick then follow me. Otherwise you can all sit and spin."

"Lead on o'fearless and apparently strong leader," Tony joked.

Everyone smiled as Rebecca walked away carrying the two large bags.

"Yeah," Matt added, "this job is just going to suck so much. Please, give me my sunscreen already."

Thirty minutes later the three new operators began their patrol of the beach estate. Before that they'd dropped off their gear and were issued side-arms and radios after Rebecca introduced them to the armory that had been secretly built into each of the three houses. AR-15's and HK MP5's were also available but had not been drawn since they would be difficult to conceal as they walked around the property. There was no need to alarm the neighbors.

They had discussed a few egress plans on how to escape the property with the families. The Suburban's were the primary mode of escape. The Marine base was a few miles away and was the ultimate go to location, especially since Sam had told them he'd made an agreement with the Gunny who worked there. They also considered, if push came to shove, that the beach ran both north and south. Escaping along it was also an option.

Rebecca's job changed from walking the property to watching the families. While Tony, Matt and Andy kept the perimeter clear of threats she now had the time to integrate herself back in with the wives and children.

She let a quick smile dance across her face as she took up her spot alongside the pool. *How horrible.* She pulled out her walkie and pressed the transmit button.

"This is Juliette. Thirty minute check-in. Primary secure."

"This is Delta. Clear," said Tony, "nothing to report."

"Foxtrot here," said Andy. "Clear as well."

"This is hotel," said Matt. "All clear and my sunscreen is working."

"Roger that," she said. "Keep your heads on a swivel out there boys while I sip on my iced tea by the pool."

"Kiss my ass," Andy said as he chuckled.

"Yeah, mine too," Matt added.

D.W. Neuman

30
Saturday November 7, 1997 9:15am

"Play it again," instructed Michael.

"Sure thing," Calvin replied. He tapped a couple of buttons and the video they'd just viewed started over. Michael, Richard and Thomas watched as Frank Russell entered the metro station during the chaos he'd created. They clearly saw him enter through the turnstile and then another camera caught him boarding a train.

"It took time," said Hobbes, "but I finally found him again."

"Where?" asked Richard.

"Two stops later he exits and heads topside."

"Cameras?"

"Way ahead of you. I've got a feed from a bank cam that shows him boarding a bus. But that's all I could find."

"Shit," said Michael.

"We'll keep looking."

Richard stretched and headed back over to the large conference table. It was filled with items from Frank's house that hadn't been destroyed in the explosion and ensuing fire. Michael and Thomas joined him while Emily continued to play off to the side, clearly content to be by herself.

* * *

Two days prior Sam and Bill had taken a walkthrough of Yuri's house and packed up whatever they'd found. Yesterday Thomas, Emily, Michael and Richard made the same trip, the day after his release, to look for anything that may have been overlooked. The two old spies took their time sifting through the remains of what had once been a very lovely home. The two of

239

them plied their old tradecraft in an attempt to locate any type of camouflaged or concealed cache.

"What's it like?" Richard asked.

"What's what like?" Michael countered.

"Being dead...I guess. What's it like?"

Michael shrugged. "It's not unlike being alive quite frankly."

"I don't understand."

"You're not supposed to Richard. You're still kicking."

He grabbed Michael's upper arm. "Then how is it that you're here now? You feel real. I want to know how I was able to hug my daughter I buried decades ago." Richard released his grip.

Michael stopped what he was doing, turned and faced him.

"I know it's all new to you. Trust me I know. Having the opportunity to talk with my son again; to meet my grandchildren; there are no words. When I'm not here, in your world, I just live in another."

"You mean Heaven?"

Michael shook his head. "Heaven and Hell are overly simplified concepts that barely scratches the surface when it comes to describing what the human race knows of the afterlife."

Richard's eyes widened with curiosity. "Tell me."

"I can't."

"You can't? Or do you mean you won't?"

"You don't understand Richard. There are rules. And there are the consequences for breaking them."

"You're talking in riddles Michael. I need to know where my wife and daughter have gone to."

"Ask them yourself and see if you receive a different answer. There are things you and this world are just not ready for."

Richard tried a different tact. "Are you breaking the rules being here right now?"

Michael just stared at his old friend and mentor.

"Well?"

"Do me a favor and don't ask a question that clearly has nothing to do with you."

"I see. So what you just admitted is that even your son doesn't know."

"You don't know what you're talking about."

"Maybe not. However, I do know that I'm actually talking to a dead person. I'm not blind Michael. It's obvious that the two techs, Curtis and the DCI don't know who you really are. Why's that?"

Michael poked his finger hard in Richard's chest. "You're right, they don't. The less anyone knows about this the better. Emily is a very sweet child. Without her you would have never seen your daughter again." He dropped his hand. "The fact of the matter is that I have a vendetta against Yuri and Nikolay. They took everything from me. I will not have my son, and his family, turned into targets."

Michael's demeanor hadn't deterred Richard's interest. "Always the spy; talking in circles and riddles. The fact of the matter, as you so succinctly put it a second ago, may indeed be about your vendetta. I can actually swallow that part of your story. What you haven't told me is why your family would become a target. As far as Nikolay's concerned his worries were over when you died."

Michael didn't say anything as Richard studied his face.

"Tell me why they're suddenly a target?" Richard insisted.

Silence. "You're a sonofabitch, you know that?" Michael finally said.

"What is it? Talk to me."

Michael sighed. "Fine. You'll love this. I stole over half a billion dollars from Nikolay."

Richard smiled. "Oh my…a half a billion. I can't help but taste the irony. I steal from the good guys and get put away. You steal from the bad guys and get away with it. So my assumption is that Nikolay somehow found out about this?"

Michael nodded.

"No wonder he's pissed at you."

"Tell me something I don't know."

Richard chuckled. "I knew when I recruited you that you were something special, but damn Michael, you really outdid yourself. What cajones!"

"Keep it down will you."

Richard lowered his voice. "So what'd you do with all that money? Take it to the grave with you?" He smiled.

"Funny but you're pretty close to the truth. I gifted some to my parents. I also made sure Thomas got a nice chunk when he turned eighteen."

Richard whistled. "That must have caused him to question what his old man did for a living."

"You have no idea how right you are."

"And the rest of it?"

"A Swiss bank account."

"With compounded interest?"

"Of course."

"So let me get this straight. After thirty years…half a billion dollars is roughly what these days?"

"Just over a billion."

Richard whistled. "Wow. So you weren't kidding."

"Weren't kidding about what?"

"You weren't kidding that you'd finance me yourself if the government didn't."

"No, I wasn't. And now you know the truth. Happy?"

Richard grinned. "A little to tell you the truth. I thought the high and mighty Michael Clark was a man of integrity; a man of honor. To think you had a greedy side to you kind of blows me away."

"I took Nikolay's money to hurt him."

"Oh, I'm sure you did. The fact that you used the money the way you wanted to, rather than giving it to the government, had nothing to do with it."

"What do you know?" he said testily.

"I'll tell you what I know Michael. I know that you were one hell of an agent thirty years ago. I know that you followed the rules, tracked down your leads and that you put me away. I know your wife was killed on orders from Yuri and or Nikolay. I now know you took his money and didn't give it up. And I know that your family has been living in peace for the past thirty years until you somehow came back from the dead, due to some anomaly in your granddaughter's DNA." He paused. "What I don't know, or the part you haven't told me yet, is why you think they're suddenly in danger?"

"Fine. Have it your way. My son took Emily to the bank in Switzerland. She popped me into existence and I moved the money. When they got back home we received a phone call that an alert had been put on my account."

"You're telling me that Nikolay was already onto you before you died? That he knew you took his money, found it but could never access it?"

"Yes."

"So he essentially had your account bugged for the past thirty years?"

"That's my assumption."

Richard thought for a second. "But why? If you were dead then why do that?"

"I was close to exposing him. He was after the microfilm I took from Kevin that exposed Yuri and his sleepers. The money was the least of his worries at the time. Losing his power, his people and his network into the CIA was paramount concern. He must have tracked my deposit, put the alarm on it just in case, and then came after me. Course, by then I was dead and he never located the microfilm. With you in jail Richard, and the trail cold, he was never exposed. He must have chalked up the financial loss and moved on."

"I can see why you're concerned. I have to agree that your family is definitely in the crosshairs. The worst part of that story is that you know you put them in danger."

"No shit. Now help me look for something; anything."

Michael went back to searching for a hidden compartment as he stepped into Frank's bathroom. Richard checked the attached master bedroom. The back part of the house had not fully burned due to the reaction time of the firefighters.

"So Michael…when do you think I can talk to my daughter again?"

"When there's time; after we catch this bastard."

"You know, all of this is just so weird."

"What is?"

"You told me that you and Betsy watched Thomas grow up."

"That we did."

"So my wife and daughter have been watching over me?"

"In a sense. They could if they wanted to. But I can't really talk about that. I can say that by your daughter's reaction the other day my gut tells me that she really missed you."

"Thanks." Richard continued to search the bedroom. "I've got another strange question."

"You haven't stopped asking a slew of them today already. Go ahead. What's your question?"

"Hey, go easy on me. I'm talking to a dead guy, remember? And speaking to such, were you ever a ghost?"

"That's not as strange as I was expecting."

"And?"

"Yes and no. It's just not that black and white."

"So I don't understand. Why so much gray area?"

"There are specific rules and guidelines to our world."

"Okay," Richard replied.

"My wife broke the rules."

"And...?"

"And she paid the consequences."

"What..."

Michael interrupted Richard. "And don't think for a second that I'm going to go into that with you."

"You and your goddamn secrets."

"This isn't the time or the place."

"Well, then when is a good time?"

"When you're dead," Michael replied as he felt around the medicine cabinet. He popped a small nodule and it released from the wall. He pulled the cabinet out. "Bingo. Found something. Once a spy, always a spy."

* * *

Back at the TOC conference table Richard and Michael poured through the evidence that had been collected.

"This feels just like old times," said Richard. "Lucky you found the stash behind his medicine cabinet."

Michael grinned. "You wish it was luck."

"Credit will have to go to your teacher then."

"That old fool? He couldn't have taught me my spy craft. He was busy stealing munitions."

"Ouch."

Thomas smiled at the two old men needled each other. *All my life I wondered what my father did for a living and now I'm knee deep in it.*

"Penny for your thoughts son."

Thomas returned his gaze to the task at hand.

"Nothing."

Michael continued to read through documents found at Yuri's house. Water damage had literally turned a large portion of the paper in the house into mush. The documents and papers that had survived were now segregated in ten boxes of miscellaneous bills, tax returns, receipts and what not. The only other actionable intelligence that was recovered was from the secret cache Michael had discovered behind the medicine cabinet.

Michael carefully looked through the few documents he'd recovered.

"Well well well. You might be interested in this."

Richard looked up as Michael handed a couple photos to him. "Damn it," replied Richard as he looked at both of them.

"What are they pictures of?" Thomas asked.

"My old house actually. Yuri had a picture of the exterior and another one of my fridge."

"Why?"

"To me they look like trophies. The one of my fridge shows the word PINNACLE spelled out on it. He must have snapped these when he set me up. Damn. I can't wait to get my hands on him." Richard handed the photos back to Michael. "Thanks for the trip down memory lane."

"My pleasure."

"Asshole."

"Were you two always like this?"

Michael and Richard looked at each other. "Actually no," Richard replied. "I used to work your father pretty hard when he started out. I think it's just that we're older now and don't give a shit. It's an old person perspective"

"I concur," said Michael. "After all these years I'm just now catching up on giving him shit." His face contorted. "Wait a second. Hold the horses."

"Got something?"

"Maybe. Seeing that it was tucked away I have to assume it's important."

"What is it?" inquired Richard.

"It's a recent newspaper clipping about a theft at some construction yard in Sacramento, California."

"What was stolen?" Thomas asked.

"A good deal of explosives."

"May I see it?"

Michael handed it over to his son. Thomas read through the article and then looked at the date. *September 18. Something tugged on Thomas' mind.*

"Hey Hobbes."

"Yo."

"What date was that Sun Valley Mall bombing?"

"Give me a sec." They heard furious typing. "That was on the twenty seventh of September."

"Okay. Thanks."

"No problem."

"What're you thinking Thomas?" his father asked.

Thomas shrugged. "I don't know. They could be related. I don't have enough data to corroborate anything yet."

Richard smiled. "The apple doesn't fall far from the tree, now does it Michael."

Michael smiled as well. "Like my son said, it's too early to tell."

31

Sunday November 8, 1997 10:45am

"So you're the infamous Sam and Bill duo I've heard so much about," Richard said as he shook their hands.

"And you're the infamous Richard Moore," replied Bill. "You were a highlight during Michael's CIA career. How's freedom treating you?"

Richard cocked his head to the side as he tried to read Bill's inclination. "The world's changed quite a bit since the last time I experienced it. Thirty years is a long time."

"I bet."

Sam and Bill had joined the rest of the team at the warehouse after breakfast. They were antsy for any information that would generate a lead. They, naturally, had heard about Richard's release but hadn't met him face to face until now. As for the others, Calvin and Hobbes always seemed to be glued to their computers while Curtis maintained the security of the facility.

Thomas, Michael, Richard, Sam and Bill gathered around the conference table while Emily kept to herself in her play area. Thomas worried about his daughter but nothing really seemed to faze or distract her. Maintaining her grandfather's presence didn't even register on her face anymore. She'd come a long way with developing her abilities in the last few months.

"You mind bringing us up to speed?" Sam asked.

"You got it," replied Michael. "Have a seat." Everyone took a seat around the table as Michael continued. "Yesterday we were able to gleam a few leads from the evidence collected at Yuri's residence. The first things we looked into were his phone records. Calls through his cell and house phones are being scrutinized and cross referenced as we speak. Secondly, he had information squirreled away about a heist of explosives. That information included a news clipping as well as the particulars on how to use them."

"By particulars do you mean the actual plans? Schematics?" asked Sam.

"I'm afraid so."

Bill shook his head. "Fuck. That's never a good thing."

Sam continued. "Has anything come out of that information?"

"Yes, as a matter of fact. The materials used to construct the two devices, used in the Sun Valley Mall bombing on September twenty seventh, match the list of materials to a tee. They also correlate how those bombs were prepared, placed and executed. Residues along with parts of the devices were recovered at the scene. Thomas was the first to see the connection."

"So what you're telling us is that Yuri is responsible? He's behind that bombing?"

Richard chimed in. "It appears he's involved in some capacity Sam. Whether he's the mastermind behind it all is too early to determine."

"That sonofabitch," said Bill. "Killing and injuring innocent civilians with bombs is just insane. How crazy is he? What's he plan on gaining from it?"

"Your guess is as good as ours. No group has taken responsibility for that horrific event."

Calvin and Hobbes had been listening in from their workstations. They took that moment to join the group.

Bill didn't like it. "It's not as if Yuri isn't bad guy number one already…but now you add this on top of it all….damn it. We've got to get him."

"The bad news doesn't stop there we're afraid," said Calvin.

Hobbes took up the reins. "We took a look at the evidence from the other two bombings that happened in Las Vegas and right here in Washington D.C. The recovered elements, from both sites, are an exact match."

"That's an FBI case. How were you able to 'look at the evidence'?" asked Sam.

Calvin and Hobbes both slightly grinned when they glanced at each other.

"Never mind. I don't want to know."

"As I was saying, the same MO, the method of operation, was used in all three bombings. Video surveillance, reviewed from all three locations, clearly indicates that the actual waste containers, that housed the bombs, were replaced."

"By whom?"

Calvin took over. "It would appear from the recordings that the people involved were actually janitorial and maintenance staff. Or they could have just been wearing the proper uniforms."

"And no one's going to look twice at a maintenance worker replacing a garbage bin," Bill acknowledged. "Fuckers."

"As you can imagine, there's a large task force already running that investigation," said Michael as he regained control of the meeting. "Our job is to find Yuri. Moving our focus back to his phone usage." He looked over at the two techs. "What've you got for me?"

They nodded. "We've set up a program to dissect his phone usage over the past ten years. Of course that information is based on the phone numbers we know he actually owned," Calvin explained.

"He's a trained spy so we don't expect to get any solid results," Hobbes said. "However, our biggest lead might just be the last person that called him. The phone company records indicate it came in minutes before he burned his house down."

"That sounds promising," said Richard.

"Yes and no," Hobbes warned. "The call originated from a phone within Langley."

"From inside the CIA building?" Bill asked in disbelief.

"That's the good news. The bad news is that whoever made the call knew what they were doing. That particular phone is located in a common but populated area of the third floor. Video feeds, of the area, clearly show that the phone wasn't in use at the time the records indicated it was."

"How is that possible?" asked Michael. "You just said that's the phone that was used."

"We have a theory on that. Do you want the long or short version?"

Michael gave Hobbes a blank stare.

"Fine. The phone was cloned."

"Cloned?"

"That's correct. A better way to explain it might be to say that your house has two phones; maybe one in the kitchen and one in the bedroom. They both ring on an incoming call. If you answer the phone in the kitchen someone can still pick up the extension in the bedroom and naturally hear what's being talked about in the kitchen."

"The CIA doesn't set up their phones blindly like that," Michael countered.

"No, of course not. However, the people that set up the phones themselves would have the access, the ability and the opportunity to make this happen."

"What people?"

Calvin answered. "People like us actually. IT."

"IT?"

"Sorry. It stands for Information Technology." He received a few of blank stares. He sighed. "Nerds. People who work with computers and technology. You know, it's the group that has access to everything."

"What do you mean by access to everything?" Richard probed.

It's like talking to my parents, they just don't get it. "Back in your days you kept everything in a file folder that was then stored in a file cabinet, right?"

Richard nodded. "Go on."

"Okay, well, with the use of computers that process hasn't changed except that a lot of that information is now stored digitally on computer hard drives. Those computers are called servers. Access to those servers is controlled, in part, by IT."

"But you said the phone was cloned? What am I missing?"

Calvin sighed. "It's two different things but handled by the same group. Our theory is that someone in IT temporarily cloned the phone, used it, and then covered their tracks. Furthermore, the individual absolutely knew that the call would be recorded."

Michael leaned forward. "Are you saying that you have that recording?"

Calvin smiled. "Indeed we do."

Hobbes walked back over to his computer console and tapped a few keys. On one of the larger screens an audio file began to play.

"Firestorm. Firestorm. Firestorm."

"It sounds like the computer voice from WarGames," Bill observed. "You know...shall we play a game? The movie with Matthew Broderick."

"Nice reference and you're absolutely right," said Calvin.

"Great work," said Michael. "Now, where's this lead us?"

"We're looking into it. There are a lot of factors involved. Who was on duty; their location based on the time of day; who had access; etc."

"Get it done. This is your new priority," Michael ordered. "And just in case you didn't like me already you still need to work on tracking Yuri down."

"Is there any indication that he's skipped town?" Sam asked.

"Unlikely," said Michael. "My bet is that he's holed up somewhere in the city. Maybe a safe house we don't know about."

"Why wouldn't he just leave the country?" Thomas asked.

"It's just a hunch. But based on the phone call, he was warned as soon as the DCI ordered the tactical unit. I don't think he had enough time to plan his escape. If he did he wouldn't have left any evidence behind. At this point he knows he's blown. He has to think that his face is on every agency watch list. Getting out of town, let alone the country without help, would be difficult. He's not going to risk getting caught now, not after all these years. No, my guess is that he's biding his time to plan his next move."

Richard nodded. "I agree. He's still in town." He turned back to Calvin and Hobbes. "Tell me you two nerds have something hidden up your sleeves?"

"Ahh…maybe," Hobbes replied hesitantly. "Give us a second."

The group watched the two techs stepped back and began an animated discussion. It lasted a full minute before Michael interrupted.

"Gentlemen. Time is of the essence. What's the hold up?"

Calvin and Hobbes stopped and rejoined the group.

"Problem that I can help with?

"No sir," replied Hobbes. "Calvin and I have been working on a facial recognition algorithm together."

"And?"

"It's not exactly ready for testing."

"Yes, it totally is," Calvin argued.

Michael looked back and forth between the two. "Are you wasting our time? Is this a viable option or not?"

Hobbes stared at Calvin but finally relented. "Fine. I'll load the program up." He walked back to his station.

Michael focused on Calvin. "What's the problem?"

"The issue is too technical to go into. Suffice it to say that our program is not one hundred percent reliable."

"How reliable is it?"

Calvin winced. "About eighty percent."

"Will it do the job?"

"That's why I didn't want to use it," said Hobbes. "I haven't perfected the software."

Michael didn't bat an eye. "You'll live. What's the coverage?"

"The NSA is tapped into just about every security system that's out there. The main one is going to be the Department of Transportation. We'll piggyback on their access."

"Excellent. Good work."

"Fuck me," said Bill. "Is there anything the two of you can't do?"

Calvin smiled and walked back to his station.

"At least it sounds like we've got a solid lead," said Richard. "From the sound of the IT group's scope an individual, with that kind of broad access, is frightening."

Sam spoke up. "I can think of only one other position that had just as much access, if not more than IT."

They all looked over at Sam.

"Who would that be?"

"Janitors. I would endeavor to think that no one thinks twice about some geek coming to fix a computer. That holds true for the same person who empties out your trashcan. They see and have access to everything. It comes with the job."

"I can't argue that point, especially with how we've heard how those explosive devices were delivered to each location," said Michael. "Let's take a breather before we dive back in to see if we've missed anything."

Everyone stood up and stretched. A large beep emanated from one of the computers.

"What was that?" asked Bill.

The group walked over.

"Oh shit," whispered Calvin.

"Oh shit what?" Sam asked.

"I set up a program to alert me to specific key words. I then incorporated that program into a variety of sources to…"

Bill interrupted. "Not in geek speak. Try English."

"Oh, right, sorry. An alert just came in over the news wire. There's been an explosion at an Indoor Water Park. Lots of casualties."

"Goddammit. Where?"

"Wisconsin."

32

Sunday November 9, 1997 11:00am

"Happy Birthday to you. Happy Birthday to you. Happpppyyy Birrtthhhday tooo Booobbbyyy....Happpyyy Birttthdaaay tooooo yoooouuu."

A few of the other kids kept singing. "And many more on channel four. And Scooby Doo on channel two. And Frankenstein on channel nine. And..."

Bobby's mother cut them off. "Make a wish and blow out your candles honey."

Bobby Banes was celebrating his ninth birthday in style thanks to the new Great Wolf Lodge indoor water park that had been completed earlier in the year. Located in Wisconsin Dells, WI, the indoor water park was the first of its kind.

Bobby's obesity ran in his family. He was a chubby third grader who was just trying to find his place in life and in the schoolyard. He had a few friends and they all kept to themselves for the most part. Being bullied and made fun of was something they all endured but it still hurt. He'd told his parents about it in tears the year before and only been told a simple rhyme in return.

"Sticks and stones may break your bones but words can never hurt you."

Bobby comprehended the meaning of the phrase and it hadn't changed anything. The first time he'd recited the line to one of the sixth graders, who'd cornered him the following week, he'd paid for it with bruises. He'd covered up those bruises and never complained to his parents again. Grownups just didn't care or understand.

Living in Wisconsin Dell, Bobby and his friends were well aware that the water park was under construction. Each of them

257

couldn't wait for the grand opening. Their anticipation, as the date drew closer, took on a life of its own. And with Bobby's birthday rapidly approaching he finally made his pitch to his parents. And here they were, on his birthday, about to have the best day ever.

His three friends watched him blow out the nine candles and cock his head to the side. The sounds of kids yelling, screaming and enjoying the water rides distracted even the birthday boy. His friends turned their heads as well as Bobby's mother began to cut his cake.

"Mom. I wanna go on the rides now."

"There's more than enough time for that honey. It's time for you and your friends to eat some cake."

"And then can we go in the water?"

"You can't go swimming for thirty minutes after you eat. Everybody knows that."

Bobby was dejected. "No! It's my birthday and I want to go have fun. You can have my cake." He began to get out of his seat.

"Don't sass me young man. You'll do as I say."

Bobby's butt returned to his seat while his face turned red. "Mooomm. You're embarrassing me."

Bobby's father was a larger man, just like his wife, and he finally spoke up. "Marge, he's not a baby anymore. Bobby, you and your friends go and have fun."

The four kids scattered off towards the large structure called Fort Mackenzie at a speed that wouldn't get them hollered at by one of the life guards.

"Hank!"

"Don't Hank me woman. You baby him too much and look how he's turned out because of it. And who cares if he doesn't want to eat cake. It's his birthday. Get over it."

Marge pouted and began to eat her own slice.

Shadows of the Past

Bobby and his friends, on the other hand, were ecstatic. To have waited nearly a full year; the fun just inches from their fingertips, and then be told to wait had been agonizing. When Bobby's father told them to go play not one of them waited around for a final verdict. They had already paid their dues and now it was time to collect.

Fort Mackenzie, in the water before them, towered a full four stories high. They were wide eyed as they took it all in. There were cargo nets, rope bridges and a multitude of water slides that exited the top story of the fort. Who knows where they would end up or adventures they'd encounter.

"Let's go!" Bobby bellowed. "Attack that fort!"

He and his three friends scampered up the huge structure floor by floor. At each level there were water stations to spray each other and dump water on the kids below them. They were having the best time of their lives. They co-existed with happiness. The four of them finally made it to the top level and prepared to take one of the loopy slides down to the bottom.

The two bombs detonated simultaneously in the water park's food court.

The force of the explosions tossed people into the air as if they weighed absolutely nothing.

Ball bearings ripped through everything they came in contact with. Tables; chairs; strollers; children; adults, structures. Everything was perforated.

The once full and organized food court had been transformed. Bodies and body parts were strewn all over. Some hung haphazardly from the indoor palm trees and large imported ferns.

The wounded moaned and began to drag themselves around the ground as best they could, clearly confused.

Children screamed and cried. Some of them weren't able to do either.

Splashes of blood decorated everything.

In the birthday area Bobby's parent's, Hank and Marge, had been killed instantly. They had sat only twenty feet from one of the two waste receptacles that had detonated.

Bobby and his friends, however, survived without a scratch. They, just like many of the other children playing around the fort, began to cry when the water feeding the slides took on a reddish hue.

33

Sunday November 9, 1997 5:15pm

"I've got a visual," Bill spoke into his radio that was situated in his left cuff. He began to casually tail the man down the street.

"Roger that," replied Sam from the van that was a few blocks away. Bill heard Sam in his earpiece.

Thomas, Richard and Michael were back at the TOC and monitored the situation with Calvin and Hobbes. Their suspect, Jonathan Lane, age thirty seven held a senior IT role at the CIA and had just left the movie theater. He'd seen Starship Troopers, which had opened the previous Friday, to great reviews.

Thank God you're alone. It'll make this that much easier.

Bill continued to trail Jonathan towards the midtown college bar area.

An early movie, a few drinks and maybe you'll get lucky. Is that what you're hoping for? Sorry, but that's just not going to happen you fucking traitor.

A few minutes later Jonathan crossed the street, made a bee-line for McGill's Pub and stepped inside.

"Suspect has entered McGill's Pub," Bill said casually as he pretended to brush his hair with his left hand. "I'm heading in."

"On my way," Sam said. "I'll let you know when I'm in the back alley."

Bill entered thirty seconds later and walked up to the bar. The place was full of students that were either old enough or had procured a fake id in order to drink.

"Can I get you something?" he was asked loudly.

Bill turned his attention away from the crowd and towards the female voice. The bartender wore jeans, a thin white t-shirt and a black bra. She was pretty and couldn't have been more than twenty-five. He caught himself not making eye contact right away and brought his gaze up.

"Beer. Whatever you have on tap."

"Coming right up cutie."

Fucking hell. To be young again.

He placed a five dollar bill on the counter and let his eyes wander around the room as he waited for his drink. He caught sight of his target at the far end of the counter checking out the single women.

Nothing wrong with having a thing for younger woman pal, it's just going to be the last time you'll see one.

Bill saw a couple of waitresses come out the rear hallway carrying food for people.

"Here you go." The bartender placed his beer down and picked up his money. "I'll be right back with your change."

"Keep it." *We both know you dress like that to get better tips anyway.*

She smiled and then walked away to serve someone else. Bill refocused on his prey and observed Jonathan as he headed towards the restroom.

Did you have a large drink at the movie? Tough luck for you but it saves me some time.

Bill picked up his beer in his left hand, took a sip and then kept the bottle close to his mouth. "I hope you're going to be here soon, he just went to the head. Thirty seconds."

"Almost there. It'll be close," Sam said in his ear.

Bill took another sip, put his beer down and headed towards the restrooms.

Twenty three.

He casually pushed by a few rowdy patrons.

Twenty.

The bathrooms came into view.

262

Seventeen.

He paused in the hallway like he was waiting for his turn to use the men's room.

Fifteen.

The kitchen door opened and a young waitress brushed by him with a tray full of appetizers.

Thirteen.

The woman's restroom door opened and two college women exited. One of them looked Bill up and down and smiled as she sauntered back to the bar. He chuckled to himself. *Still got it.*

Nine.

The men's door opened and his target emerged.

Eight.

As Jonathan began to turn Bill grabbed his left wrist.

Seven.

"What the…"

Bill sucker punched him in the solar plexus and Jonathan doubled over.

Six.

He grabbed Jonathan by the back of the neck and pushed him through the kitchen door.

Five.

"Hey! You can't be in here."

Four.

Bill ignored the cook and focused on the exit ten feet away.

Three.

"Excuse me!"

They were through the kitchen and at the exit.

Two.

The door opened and the two men emerged in the back alley. A black van was thirty feet away and drove towards them.

One.

Sam pulled up. Bill cranked open the side door, pushed Jonathan inside and climbed in afterward. Sam accelerated as Bill rolled the van door shut. He then turned around and secured Jonathan's wrists.

"Who are you? You can't do this!" he screamed.

Bill gave him a hard stare. "It's already done." He gut punched him a second time and proceeded to put a black bag over his head.

"We've got him," Sam said over the com-link.

* * *

"Run us through it again," said Richard.

"No problem," replied Hobbes. "We used a program to correlate the different variables that were available."

Calvin jumped in. "We used things like duty schedules; access logs; computer activity; etc."

"Exactly. The time window of the phone call was limited, which actually helped the process. Anyway, there were four IT personnel that fit the various variables."

"And you narrowed it down to our suspect, Jonathan Lane, because of internal video surveillance?"

Hobbes nodded. "As you may or may not know every nook and cranny of the CIA has video coverage."

"It didn't take us long to match up the timing of the phone call with Jonathan's activities," Calvin added.

"But why make such an obvious error? He must have known this could be tracked or, at the very least, he'd had a better way to cover his tracks," Richard inquired.

The two techs nodded. "We thought of that as well and came up with two possible solutions."

"Two?"

"The first," said Calvin, "is that he didn't have any time to prepare. When the DCI made the call to activate the tactical unit the order was logged in the computer system. Our assumption is that Jonathan had a program in place to alert him if Yuri's address came up."

"And the second?" asked Michael.

"The second hits a little bit closer to home. It's not uncommon for members of the IT community to view themselves as superior to others. His ego could have played a role in thinking he wouldn't get caught; that he was smarter than everyone else."

"Calvin and I actually believe that our two ideas actually overlap each other," Hobbes concluded.

Michael and Richard shared a smile.

"Soooo, can you relate when it comes to this IT ego hypothesis?"

Calvin and Hobbes looked over at each other. "We have no idea what you're talking about."

Everyone chuckled. "Fair enough. Thank you for locating our man. Is the location prepped?"

Calvin nodded. "Everything's set. We've got audio and video. The observation window is ready to go."

"Good," said Michael. "We're going to take the first crack at him."

"But sir, the Director is sending a professional team to interrogate him."

"Yes, I'm well aware. But time is of the essence. The faster we get any information out of him now the faster we can locate Yuri. I know you don't have a problem with that."

* * *

Sam pulled the van through the open door, parked and turned off the engine as the outer door rolled closed behind them. Once it was secured Sam got out, walked around the front and yanked open the sliding van door. Bill man-handled Jonathan, who had remained hooded and quiet, into the empty warehouse.

Sam led the way towards the hidden back wall. It silently slid open and Curtis stood there.

"He's all yours," said Bill.

Curtis took Jonathan by the arm and led him to the interrogation room. Sam and Bill watched through the one way glass as Curtis sat him down in the steel chair and restrained his hands to the steel bolt in the table. He left the black bag on over his head. He left the room and headed back to the TOC. As Curtis entered, Thomas, Emily, Michael and Richard walked out and joined Sam and Bill. They all took a long look at their prize.

"Nice job," Michael said.

Bill shrugged. "My pleasure."

"With that being said we don't have a lot of time. The DCI has an interrogation team on its way."

"And that's not business as usual?" Bill asked.

"He," as Michael jerked his thumb towards Jonathan, "might not break right away. We have a tool, so to speak, at our disposal that will allow us immediate results."

Everyone but Richard casually glanced down at Emily.

Richard didn't understand. "I'm missing something."

"What do you need from us?" Sam asked.

"That room is naturally wired for audio and video. We're going to need those disabled. And please take Richard with you."

"Michael," Richard said, "what are you talking about? You're not making any sense."

"We're on it," said Bill as he gripped Richard's arm.

"Let go of me."

Thomas spoke up. "Richard, there are some things you don't need to know about and this is one of them."

"Bullshit."

Thomas continued. "We don't have time. My family doesn't have time. If you don't leave I'm afraid I can't allow you to see your wife and daughter ever again."

Richard's nostrils flared.

Michael added. "You don't have to like it my old friend, you just need to do it."

"Very well." Sam, Bill and Richard returned to the TOC and the door closed behind them.

"Well played son."

"I wasn't kidding."

"Oh, I got that."

* * *

The secure door closed behind the three of them when they entered the TOC. Sam and Bill walked up to Calvin and Hobbes. One of the large overhead screens displayed the live feed of Jonathan Lane in the room next door.

Sam bent down and whispered into Hobbes' ear. "Disable the audio and video feeds."

"What? Why?" Hobbes replied.

"You sure you want to get into a heated discussion with me? Turn them off now." Sam straightened up.

Hobbes swallowed hard. *What the fuck?* He started typing. Five seconds later the overhead blinked off.

"Hobbes, what just happened?" Calvin exclaimed.

"I'm...um...running diagnostics on the equipment. It'll be completed in five minutes."

"Shit man. You shouldn't have done that. We have our orders."

Curtis didn't like the exchange. "Problem?"

"Nothing. We're fine. My colleague here just pulled a boneheaded move for some reason."

"Sorry," replied Hobbes. "I just wanted to make sure everything worked before the team showed up."

"Forget it man."

Hobbes fingers worked his keyboard as Sam walked away. An instant chat window silently popped up on one of Calvin's monitors.

Sam just threatened me to turn off the surveillance.

Calvin read it and responded. *What the hell? Why? I knew you wouldn't do something that stupid.*

Hobbes typed. *No idea. It's bullshit. I've already activated the silent mode.*

Good.

*   *   *

Michael waited until the red light on the video cameras turned off.

"We're on." He opened the door to the interrogation room.

"Who's there!? Where am I!? Do you know who I work for!?" Jonathan yelled from beneath the dark hood over his head. He'd found his voice again.

"We don't have much time Mr. Lane."

Jonathan stiffened.

Thomas watched as Emily approached. She stood ready.

Michael continued. "I'm going to set the stage for you Mr. Lane. After that you're going to tell me absolutely everything."

"What's this about? Leave me alone. I'm nobody."

Shadows of the Past

"You warned Frank Russell, also known as Yuri, to an impending attack. The message you sent used a prerecorded message that contained the word Firestorm."

"You have the wrong person!"

Michael continued to ignore Jonathan's outbursts. "Now for my question. Who do you work for?"

Emily touched Jonathan's bare arm with her hand. He immediately stiffened.

"Who do you work for?" the little girl asked.

"I work for Frank Russell."

"Are you a spy?" Emily repeated her grandfather's question.

"Yes."

"What is your name?"

"My name is Jonathan Lane. I was born Stefan Nikolaev."

"How long have you been a spy?"

"Ever since I can remember. We were all raised to become spies."

Thomas pointed at his wristwatch and his father nodded.

"Who raised you?"

"Nikolay Dmietriev. He saved us from the orphanages. He's our father."

"Where is Frank Russell?"

"I don't know."

"Do you have a way of contacting him?"

"Yes."

"Are there other spies working within Langley?"

"Yes."

Bill opened the door to the room. "The team just arrived. Thirty seconds."

Michael didn't ask a question this time. Instead he had Emily make a request for him.

"You will cooperate fully." Emily did her magic.

"I will cooperate fully."

Emily stepped back and rejoined her father just as the four man interrogation team the DCI had sent arrived. Two members moved to remove Jonathan.

The team leader spoke directly to Michael. "I'm not going to ask you what happened in here. As far as I'm concerned you never got a chance to talk to this man. With that being said I have my orders. We're taking this man to another location. I was told to inform you that we'll be cleaning up our own mess. He said you'd know what that meant. Any leads will be shared with you immediately, of course." He tried not to look at Emily on his way out.

Michael nodded as they led Jonathan away.

Sam and Richard rejoined the trio. They watched the team depart.

"What the fuck was that all about?" Richard asked. "Why'd you strong arm me?"

"My apologies," Michael replied. "Don't take it personally. It was for our protection. Now, do you want to continue busting my chops or are you more interested in what we learned from him?"

Richard was stunned. "Wait. You're kidding. He talked to you?"

"He did indeed. He confirmed he's a spy; that he worked for Frank; that he was raised by Nikolay; that there are other spies in the agency; that there's a way for him to contact Frank; and that he'd fully cooperate with any other questions asked of him."

"Bullshit. No he didn't. You're pulling 7my leg."

Michael just stared back at his old boss.

"No, I can tell, you're not kidding. How did yo....never mind, I don't think you're going to tell me." He collected his thoughts. "It sounds like we'll soon have some solid leads on how to get our hands on Frank."

"Why don't we head back inside and figure out our next moves then," said Sam.

They left the interrogation room behind, opened the secure door and entered the TOC. Calvin and Hobbes looked over their shoulders and gave each other a 'what the fuck' look as the group sat down around the conference table.

"Sam, where are we at with additional personnel?" Michael asked. "This shit's going to hit the fan sooner than later."

"They'll be here tomorrow afternoon. I've got six more joining Bill and me."

"Good."

Before Michael could continue Calvin and Hobbes joined them.

"Sorry to interrupt. We thought you'd want to hear this."

"What's up?" asked Bill.

"We just intercepted the preliminary report on the water park bombing from earlier today."

"Let me guess. It's the same MO?" Michael asked.

Hobbes nodded. "Yeah, it looks that way."

D.W. Neuman

34

Monday November 10, 1997 12:35pm

Nikolay had tuned into CNN the day before and hadn't changed the channel since then. He'd muted the volume and sat transfixed watching image after image of the carnage he had orchestrated. The news station had covered little else than the waterpark horror from the previous day. The vodka he'd drunk only added to the jubilance he felt for having struck yet another blow to the Americans. To say the least, Nikolay was very pleased with himself. He raised his glass into the air.

"Thank you father. Without your assassination I would have never taken a seat on the Central Committee. I would never have had the opportunity to grow my power, my loyal followers, and my money over the years. I would never have been able to infiltrate the United States, the CIA and others with my children. And without those children I would never had been able to execute such bold chess moves against the nation that took Mother Russia away from me."

In one gulp Nikolay finished off what remained in his glass. The television, once again, panned over the numerous and various sized body bags as they were removed. One camera zoomed in on a female paramedic who had just fallen to her knees. She was crying uncontrollably.

Nikolay only smiled at her pain.

D.W. Neuman

35

Monday November 10, 1997 1:30pm

Sam and Bill met the six SANDBOX operators after they landed at Dulles. Strong handshakes were exchanged along with the normal amount of banter. After the team collected their gear they all drove them to the safe house. Once they settled in Sam pulled them all together for a team meeting.

"I'm going to talk for a bit. After that I'll take any questions that you might have." Sam paused for a second. "Okay then. The reason Bill and I chose you six is because, as a unit, you fit together like a jigsaw puzzle. Each one of you will take on a different role based on the needs of the mission. We may need sniper support; three of you have it. We may need all six assaulting; and you all fit that bill.

Second. Based on current intelligence we may have a target as early as this evening. What that means is immediately following this chit chat I want your gear prepped and ready to go. That means hitting the armory, loading magazines, prepping vests, etc. When the word comes down the pipe we're ready to move out, period.

Also, depending on the level of intel that's gathered there is a possibility that we'll be conducting missions outside our country's borders. That's pure speculation at this point but be prepared for that eventuality nonetheless. Questions?"

"What's the mission?"

"On the wall behind me you'll see a current picture of our target. His name is Frank Russell. He's also known as Yuri. He's seventy seven years old. We've been tasked with apprehending this HVT, high value target, here in Washington D.C. Frank is a known CIA mole that works for a man called Nikolay Dmietriev."

"A Russian?"

"Yes. Nikolay's an ex-Soviet Central Committee member who apparently has a hard-on for the US."

"Is there any particular reason why this isn't being handled internally?"

"Good question. The unfortunate reality is that our government has been penetrated by an unknown number of foreign agents. The Director of Central Intelligence doesn't know who to trust. SANDBOX is a neutral solution to this very volatile situation. Our operation is black and off the books. With that being said it gives the DCI, as you can imagine, plausible deniability. The seriousness of this national security breach is far reaching and we're only one part of the solution to correct this problem that our country now faces. If you don't want in let me know right now."

Not a single operator opened his mouth.

"Excellent. Get ready to take down the bad guys. Gear up."

As the men headed off to prepare, Bill smiled at Sam. "Nice speech. It almost brought a tear to my eye."

Sam smiled back. "Yeah. Fuck you too."

"So what'ya think? The shit is about to hit the fan, eh?"

"We'll find out soon enough."

36

Monday November 10, 1997 4:30pm

Babysitting Frank Russell, at his safe house, had become stagnant and boring. Alexei Vorobyrov had been an elite member of the Spetsnaz, the Russian Special Forces, before going to work for Nikolay. He was a trained killer and over the past ten years his skills had been put to a much better use. Sitting around a house looking after an old man was not what he wanted to do no matter how well he was being paid.

Alexei's satellite phone chirped. He answered it and waited for the encryption to sync.

"Yes?"

"Can you talk?" Nikolay asked.

Alexei looked around the living room before he answered. "Go ahead."

"I've been told that Jonathan didn't show up for work today. He also hasn't checked in through regular channels."

Alexei kept listening. He knew that Nikolay wasn't finished with his thought.

"Someone's after Yuri and now another agent has gone missing. I don't believe in coincidences."

"What do you want me to do?"

"At this point the final part of my plan cannot be stopped. The fact that Yuri's lawyers hold documents that will expose me now works in my favor. Through them the United States will learn that I am the one responsible for striking fear into their hearts. That I am the one responsible for the deaths of their fellow countrymen. That I am the one to fear."

"Your orders, sir?"

"Yuri's usefulness has come to an end. Do what you do best."
The line went dead.

Alexei smiled as he put his phone away. *Finally.*

He pulled out his Beretta and extracted a silencer from a hidden coat pocket. He began to screw it on the end of his weapon.

"Yuri?"

* * *

"Go ahead."

Frank had been sleeping in his bedroom when he heard the phone chirp, not that he'd been sleeping very well this past week. And the fact that Alexei watched over him didn't help his nerves. Relaxing wasn't an option.

Frank put on his shoes and snuck out of his bedroom. The living room was right down the hallway but he headed to the kitchen instead.

"What do you want me to do?"

Frank cringed when he reached the kitchen and heard Alexei ask that question. Frank knew Alexei had to be talking with Nikolay.

This was going to end badly.

He quietly opened a kitchen cabinet, took out the container of flour and dumped it all out on the counter.

No knives or my Skorpian. Alexei saw to that.

"Your orders, sir?"

Shit! I'm running out of time!

Frank slid open the utensil drawer and placed his hand around the rolling pin.

"Yuri?"

On the opposite side of the kitchen was the living room. Frank heard the sound of a silencer being screwed on.

He grabbed a huge handful of flour with his right hand and held the roller in his left. He tried hard to control his breathing as he hugged the kitchen wall.

"Yuri?"

"In the kitchen," Frank replied casually.

Frank poised as he saw the silencer appear around the corner.

As hard as he could Frank slammed the rolling pin down on top of the weapon.

Pop!

The weapon discharged into the floor. Frank brought his left hand up and threw the flour into Alexei's face.

* * *

"In the kitchen."

Alexei crept towards the kitchen with his weapon extended.

Out of nowhere came a blur of movement that hit his weapon.

Pop!

The weapon discharged into the floor.

What the…

Fine powder struck his face. It covered and filled his eyes.

…FUCK!

* * *

Frank's toss had been perfect. The majority of the flour had hit Alexei square in his eyes.

Without pausing he stepped in and swung the rolling pin.

It connected.

* * *

Alexei stumbled backward from the first blow and instinctively brought his weapon up.

CRACK!

His world went black.

* * *

Frank was exhausted from his efforts. He knelt over Alexei and relieved him of the Beretta. Then he went through his pockets. He took Alexei's cash, identification and satellite phone. Frank looked at the Beretta and then at the unconscious man who had just tried to kill him.

"Nikolay is not going to be pleased when you have to report that you lost me."

Frank unscrewed the silencer, pocketed everything he collected and walked out the front door of his safe house. He needed a place to stay and knew exactly what part of the city to head to.

On his way a variety of city-owned video cameras recorded his movements.

37

Tuesday November 11, 1997 8:45am

"We're connected and secure," said Calvin. "Sir, can you hear us?"

"I can hear you just fine," replied Victor Bannon, the DCI. "Who's there this morning?"

Michael spoke up. "Sir, Richard, Thomas, Sam and I are on the line."

"Very good. The interrogation of Jonathan Lane was unlike any other I've seen or been involved in. He was absolutely forthcoming. It was the damndest thing."

Michael and Thomas shared a slight smile.

"Yes, sir," said Michael. "Did he provide any actionable intel?"

"Nothing that's going to require boots on the ground yet. However, he did provide us with the location where he stashed a satellite phone he used to communicate with Nikolay Dmitriev. We'll be sending that unit over shortly. Other than admitting his involvement he doesn't know where Frank is nor does he claim to have talked with him since placing the phone call."

"We understand sir. Hopefully that phone will give us a solid lead."

"Sam," said the DCI, "what's the status of your team?"

"We're ready to go at a moment's notice sir. Curtis has provided us with small arms, the tactical gear and vehicles. However, I want to bring up a larger concern."

"Which is?"

"Two things. One. What if the intelligence leads us outside the United States? Two. If we are sent overseas then what support will we have at our disposal?"

"Sam. I can guarantee you'll receive any equipment you deem necessary. I will also guarantee a ride to wherever you go and back again. However, you and your team will be on your own, if and when an overseas mission occurs. That's the nature of this game and I know you understand."

"Yes, sir. I hear you loud and clear."

"I knew you would. Calvin, are you still there?"

"I am sir."

"What's the current status on your side of the house?"

"Our program continues to run through video feeds. There are an incredible amount of cameras in this city, sir. So far we haven't received any hits."

"Very well," replied the DCI. "Meeting adjourned. Calvin, take me off speakerphone."

* * *

Sam got up from the table as the conference call ended.

"Unless you need me for something I'm going to head back to the safe house."

"Thanks Sam. Say hi to Bill for me," said Thomas.

"Will do brother, will do." Sam walked over to Emily. "Hey cutie, how're you doing?" He gave her a hug.

"I'm good. I miss home though."

"You know what?"

"What?"

"Me too."

"You do?"

"You betcha. It's tough to be away from home and family for so long."

"Yeah," she replied.

Sam noticed she was a little sad. "I miss my family. I know your mom and your brother miss you."

She just looked at him.

"Anyway, I wish I was half as brave as you are Em. We couldn't have done this without you."

She perked up.

"I've got to go now. Take care of your dad for me."

She giggled. "You're silly."

Sam smiled. "That's what they tell me. See you later cutie."

* * *

Calvin punched a button and the speakerphone disconnected. He punched another one to add Hobbes.

"Sir, it's just the three of us now."

"What's the status of the job I gave you?"

Hobbes spearheaded the answer. "Sir, we looked into your request. There is no record of power, water or phone bills. We looked for tax records and checked out the flight manifest. Zilch. For all intents and purposes Michael Clark has been off the grid since his reported death thirty years ago."

It was Calvin's turn. "We took a look through the CIA surveillance feeds. From what we've seen he never entered that building. We have no idea how he got into your office."

The DCI was silent on the other end.

"Sir?"

"Thank you."

"There's one other thing sir," said Calvin.

"What is it?"

"Mr. Paige requested…"

"He demanded," Hobbes interrupted.

"…fine…demanded that the interrogation room's audio and video feed be disengaged prior to the other team's arrival."

"That's highly unusual."

"Right. Well sir, Hobbes recorded what happened in that room anyway."

"How's that possible?"

Hobbes jumped in. "It's a combination of programs I've inserted into the…"

The DCI cut him off. "Nevermind. Send it to me."

"Yes sir," replied Calvin.

*   *   *

Thomas walked over to his daughter as Sam left.

"Did you want to call home sweetie?"

Emily nodded.

"We'll do that later today. With the time change mommy and your brother are still sleeping right now."

"I hope they're okay."

Thomas smiled. "They're fine. They've got some good guys looking after them."

"So the bad guys don't get them?"

"That's right."

"They'll be fine then."

"Oh hell yes!" Suddenly Calvin screamed from his desk.

Everyone scurried over and crowded around.

"You got something?" Richard asked.

"You're damn right I do! The facial recognition program hit pay dirt." He clicked a few buttons and the image transferred to the overhead screen. They watched the video as Frank Russell walked down the evening street and off screen.

"This is from last night?"

284

"Yup. But now that we know where this video camera is located, as well as the time, our search area has been exponentially reduced."

"What about tasking a satellite?"

"Good call actually. In the meantime Hobbes and I will backtrack all the available cameras in the area we just saw Frank."

"How long?" asked Michael.

"Depends on a number of factors actually."

"Fine. Best guess."

Calvin and Hobbes looked over at each other.

"Anywhere from two to eight hours."

"Get that satellite in play then," said Michael. "We need to narrow down where he's hiding right now."

"I'll give Sam a call," Thomas added.

D.W. Neuman

38
Tuesday November 11, 1997 9:00am

Rebecca Cross sat back in her lounge chair next to Laura, Julie and Kim. The pool was filled with splashing and laughter, as it had been most days since she began her protection duty.

The weird thing is that I haven't caught a whiff of danger. I don't know who or what we're protecting them from but I can't deny that Hawaii and my pay are phenomenal.

"Do you know anything Rebecca?"

Rebecca heard her voice and looked over at Julie. "I'm sorry, were you talking to me?"

Laura and Kim laughed. "Yup, you're fitting in just fine."

"We were wondering out loud whether or not you knew what our men were up to. Do you?" Julie asked.

Rebecca straightened up in her chair. *Did I just doze off?* "I'm afraid not. I haven't talked with Mr. Paige since he hired me." She paused. "My apologies. I think the sun got to me for a second." Rebecca got up. "I'm going to go check the perimeter."

Laura smiled. "We've got a radio if we need you."

They watched as Rebecca headed towards the beach.

Julie turned to Laura. "So what do you think Laura, are we in danger? I don't believe anything's changed around here."

"No, you're right. I haven't felt the slightest hint of danger. But you know how our men are."

"You mean overprotective?" said Kim.

"That's the one."

"Don't get me wrong," added Julie, "our week of training had its moments, but I don't know anymore."

"Something on your mind?" Laura asked.

"Here we go again," Kim added.

287

D.W. Neuman

Julie ignored her sister's comment. "What was I thinking letting Sam go off to save the world?"

Kim rolled her eyes. "Any chance you want to be a bit more dramatic. Come on sis. We've been down this road more times than I can remember. I miss my husband too, but I don't sit here and whine about it like you do."

Julie opened her mouth to say something, shut it and just glared at her sister.

"I know how you feel, okay," Kim said offering an olive branch. "We love our men. Waiting around, not knowing what's going on and hoping that they're okay can be torture. However, let's be realistic. They're going to do what they're going to do and we knew that when we married them. And don't delude yourself, you weren't going to let Sam go and do a damn thing until you heard about the payout. Then you crumbled. We all saw it."

"No I didn't," Julie said unconvincingly.

Laura had stayed out of way until now. "It's okay Julie. I probably would have done the same thing. Five hundred million dollars is an unfathomable amount of money. The risk to reward perspective was considerably skewed. I don't know anyone who could have said no to that proposal."

"That has nothing to do with needing Sam to come home safe to me."

Laura continued. "I agree. I'd give up absolutely everything I owned to make sure Thomas, Emily and Gavin were safe."

"Sorry," said Julie. "For whatever reason I tend to forget we all have something at risk right now. I don't mean to come off like some spoiled bitch who wants everything her way."

"Too late." Kim smiled as she said it.

They all had a good laugh while the tension evaporated.

SCREEEEECHHH!!

All three of them jumped in their chairs.

"That sounded really close," said Kim.

"Right out front actually. I'm going to go take a look." Laura got up and headed inside.

* * *

Stickers continually wound around Gavin's legs and purred loudly. Stir watched the new cat with great interest, as he had for the past week. At first Stir didn't know what to make of the feline. He'd approached Stickers to sniff him and had been rebuffed with a paw to his nose. But even that hadn't deterred his curiosity and, while Stir was active in this realm, his attention was focused on figuring out what Stickers was all about.

"Meow." Stickers bumped his head against Gavin's hand.

Gavin scratched him under his chin with his right hand as he petted Stir with his left. Stir took the opportunity to inch closer to Stickers yet remain outside of paw range. Stir's little black nose constantly sniffed the air.

"Purrr."

"Okay, you two play nice. I'm going to go get a popsicle." Gavin got up, walked out of his room and down the hall towards the kitchen. Stickers followed Gavin and Stir followed Stickers.

As Gavin entered the kitchen he looked out the window and saw his mother, along with everyone else, out by the pool. He'd been told to keep Stir a secret from the other kids as well as the people protecting them.

"Even Becca?" he'd asked his mother.

"Even Becca honey."

He'd nodded his head in compliance.

Back in the kitchen he opened the lower freezer compartment and removed a green popsicle. He unwrapped and began to lick it. Stickers had stayed by his side the entire time while Stir kept up his observation of the cat from a few feet away. Stir quietly inched forward and sniffed Sticker's tail end. He backed off before Stickers noticed what he was up to.

Stickers wandered off towards the front door and began to paw at it. Gavin walked over to the door and opened it. He knew he wasn't supposed to go outside unless an adult was with him but he just wanted to see what Stickers wanted. The orange tabby suddenly bolted through the open door to the front yard. Stir, unable to contain himself, raced after his new friend.

"Stickers!"

The cat, with Stir hot on his tail, ran across the street.

SCREEEEECHHH!!

The neighbor's car had little time to react and immediately applied her breaks. She helplessly felt her front bumper hit the animal.

Thump!

Gavin had seen it all unfold before his eyes.

"Stir! Nooooooooo!"

Gavin dropped his popsicle. It broke in two when it hit the walkway.

He ran towards the dark and unmoving form that lay in front of the car. Tears ran down his face as he scooped Stir into his arms.

"Pleasebeokay. Pleasebeokay." He petted and stroked Stir's wispy body.

Laura appeared in the doorway.

"Gavin!" She hurried over to him as the elderly neighbor got out of her car. "What happened? Are you okay?" Laura didn't see any blood on her son.

"I'm so sorry," the neighbor said. "I didn't see them until it was too late."

Gavin stood up with Stir in his arms and ran back inside the house. Stickers appeared out of nowhere and ran back inside with him.

"Gavin?" She watched her son leave as she turned back to the neighbor. "What happened?"

"I think I hit one of your cats. I'm terribly sorry. I hope it's okay."

"I have to go." Laura turned and hurried back inside, closing the front door behind her. "Gavin?" She found him in his room holding onto Stir tightly.

He son's face was covered in tears. He looked up at his mother when she appeared in his doorway.

"Stir got hurt."

She sat down next to him. "Is he going to be alright?" Laura saw Stir begin to move.

"Stir!" His tail began to thump and he licked Gavin's face. Gavin hugged him. "I was so worried."

He put him down and Stir began to act as if nothing had happened. Stickers sauntered up to Stir and they sniffed noses much to his delight. Stickers started to give Stir a tongue bath.

Gavin wiped the remaining tears off his face.

"Why were you outside? You know the rules. You scared me to death."

He nodded. "I know. I'm sorry. Stickers wanted out. I just opened it a little and they both ran out. I saw Stir get hit by that ladies car. He didn't move."

Laura pulled her son to her. "It's okay sweetie. I'm just really glad that nothing happened to you. I guess we now know that nothing bad can happen to Stir, right?"

Gavin nodded. They both looked over as Stickers and Stir took turns licking each other. They'd become best friends.

The phone rang in the kitchen.

"Are you going to be okay?"

"Uh huh," replied Gavin.

"Okay, well why don't you stay here and make sure Stir's okay while I go answer the phone." Laura stood up and headed towards the kitchen. She picked it up on the fourth ring.

"Hello?"

"Hey babe."

Laura smiled. "Hey honey. It's good to hear your voice."

"Yours too," said Thomas.

"How's DC?"

"We're closing in actually. I don't want to go into details over the phone, but things are coming to a head."

"That's great."

"I had to wait until later to call you. I know how you like to sleep in."

"It's just not the same without you. You know that."

"Tease."

Laura smiled. "How's Em holding up?"

"Why don't you ask her yourself." He handed the phone off.

"Mommy?"

"Hi sweetheart. How's my little girl?"

"Good. I miss you."

"I miss you too. Are they taking good care of you?"

"I'm stronger now."

"Stronger?"

"Daddy says I can't talk about it on the phone."

"I see. I love you Em. Be good. Can I talk to Daddy again please?"

"I love you too."

"Hey again," said Thomas.

"What does she mean by stronger?"

"How can I put this…..let's just say that my father and another individual were available at the same time."

"Seriously? Wow."

"That's pretty much how I experienced it too."

"And aside from that, how's everything else?"

"We've been staying pretty busy actually. Richard and my father have kept at it. Sam and Bill are ready to rock and roll. All in all it hasn't been that bad. A little stressful but I think Em's been handling it better than I have actually."

Laura chuckled. "She's a little trooper. Just make sure to stay safe."

"We will. Speaking of safe; how's the home front?"

"Not a peep of hostility. We were just talking about that. Still, it feels weird to be looked after."

"They're there for a reason."

"I know. Oh yeah, before I forget, Stir just got hit by a car."

"What? That couldn't have hurt him, right?"

"That was my assumption too. I guess it stunned him because when I got to Gavin's room he was coming around and started acting like it didn't faze him."

"So Gavin's okay?"

"He was frightened, that's for sure, but no harm done."

"Whew."

"I miss you."

"I miss you too babe."

"Love you."

Thomas smiled on his end of the phone. "I love you more."

Laura chuckled. "You wish you did. I've got that end locked up and you know it."

"You never fight fair."

"Just wait till you get home."

"Oooo. You're one hell of a tease, you know that?"

"Tell me something I don't know."

Thomas sighed. "I miss you sweetie."

"I miss you too. Get home safe."

"We will."

39

Tuesday November 11, 1997 3:00pm

"All teams report in," Sam ordered.

"Alpha One and Two are covering the front and are in position."

"Bravo One and Two have the rear entrance covered."

"Charlie One has eyes on the south side of the building."

"Charlie Two reporting west side covered."

* * *

Thomas had just gotten off the phone with Laura when Calvin and Hobbes tracked down Frank's location at one of the hourly rate motels. They narrowed down his movement through the city's CCTV, or closed circuit television system. Sam was called and his team of eight immediately deployed to the location.

The motel's cliental primarily consisted of street walkers and their johns. The DCI was able to get the local police to cordon off the area while Sam and his team moved in to do the actual assault.

* * *

As he drove Alexei looked down at the device he held in his lap. The signal from the tracking device he'd placed in one of Yuri's heels was getting stronger. Next to him sat Brutus and Sergio was in the back seat. Alexei had brought the extra muscle with him just in case. Play time with Yuri had come to an end as they fingered their AK-47's they held in their laps. If necessary they'd be able to bring the weapons up and start shooting instantly.

Alexei turned the corner and immediately pulled over to the curb. He saw that the police had the area locked down. He scanned the area.

Two snipers, one on each building that overlooks the motel. That's where the signal is emanating from. From his vantage point he saw four armed men moving up the side of the motel. *They'll probably have additional men in the back, but not as many.* He pulled out his satellite phone and made the connection.

"Tell me you have him."

"Not at this moment. However, it looks like members of the police are about to take him."

"Explain."

"We're at a motel. The roads are blocked off by police. They have snipers and a group of four men moving on a motel room as we speak."

"Yuri must die."

"Of that I have no doubt."

"Don't call me again until you've handled it." The line went dead.

Alexei put the phone away and began to observe the unfolding situation.

* * *

Something's not right.

The headboard, from the adjoining room, hadn't resumed its banging in more than an hour. Frank knew what this motel was used for, and had even used it on occasion back in the days. But the pretty twenty-five year old blond named Summer, that rented the adjacent room, was always entertaining clients.

Something's not right.

Frank rolled off the bed, fully clothed, and peaked out the closed drapes. For a full fifteen seconds he scanned and waited.

No traffic.

He caught a slight movement on the roof of the building from across the street.

Oh shit!

Frank left the window and entered the bathroom. He took a quick look through the window panes. Two men had it covered.

Dammit!

He moved back to the bedroom, pulled out the Beretta he'd taken from Alexei and chambered a round.

* * *

Sam and Bill took the right side of the motel and moved as a team towards Frank's room. Alpha group mirrored their movement from the left.

"Bravo has movement from the rear window. We're made."

"Roger that," Sam said into his throat microphone. "All teams prepare to engage."

Sam and Bill quickly moved up to the right side of room six while both alpha members stacked up on the left side with their MP5's. Charlie, using sniper rifles, covered everyone from different angles across the street.

Sam pounded on door six.

"Frank. We know you're in there and you know we have this place surrounded. It's over. I'd rather not have to come in there by force. What'ya say Frank?"

"I have a gun."

Sam shook his head and spoke into his mike. "Hold." He then raised his voice so Frank could hear. "It doesn't have to go down this way. It's over. Let me take you in."

Two rounds punched through the door.

"Hold! Hold! Hold!"

"Don't come in here! I'd rather shoot myself."

Sam gripped his weapon tighter. "You don't want to do that. You're more valuable to us alive."

"Go fuck yourself."

Bill spoke up. "Listen dipshit, you're obviously smart because you've lasted this long. But my guess is that your usefulness came to an end with Nikolay a long time ago. If you want to go out this way then there's nothing we can do about it. But if you want to make him pay then you have the power to do just that. Give it up and rat him out. Sure, you'll go to prison but think about how far your cooperation will go. You can do that or you can just splatter your brains across the room. Your call."

"What the fuck was that?" Sam whispered to Bill.

"Just appealing to his sense of survival. It's not like he's going anywhere."

The lock on room six clicked and the door swung open. Sam, Bill and the two alpha members readied their weapons. Frank Russell, the deep cover Russian mole, stood before them with his hands raised above his head. The Beretta lay on the bed, well out of reach.

"Clear it," Sam commanded. He spoke into his mike. "Securing suspect now."

Alpha One and Two entered room six, bypassed Frank and quickly made sure no one else was in the motel room. Sam and Bill kept their weapons trained on Frank.

"Clear!"

"Secure him."

Alpha slung his weapon and secured Frank's wrists in front. He then patted Frank down and emptied his pockets onto the bed.

"He's clean."

Meanwhile Alpha Two picked up the Beretta, ejected the magazine and cleared the remaining live round in the chamber.

"Weapon secure."

Sam and Bill lowered their weapons and took a long look at the man they'd been hunting.

"Nice speech. Good work," said Sam.

"Every once in a while I get it right brother."

Frank stood there, with his wrists secured, in a daze. "I can't believe this is how it's going to end."

"Maybe it's the end for you," said Bill, "but somehow I think your capture is only the beginning."

* * *

Alexei looked through his binoculars. He watched as Yuri was led out of the motel room and into one of the two black Suburban vehicles. He also observed the two snipers stow their equipment and come down off the roof positions. Two more members appeared from behind the motel and joined up with the main assault force.

Eight men.

* * *

Bill peeled off and began to talk with the police unit commander while Sam addressed the rest of the team.

"Great job everyone," said Sam. "Excellent work. Now, Alpha team will ride with Bill, myself and the prisoner. Bravo and Charlie, go ahead and head back to the safe house in the second Suburban. We'll debrief later."

Bill walked over. "We're all set. The police will secure the scene so the DCI can send over a unit to search the motel room."

"Sounds good. Let's mount up and head back to the TOC."

Alpha team flanked Frank in the backseat. Bill drove and Sam rode shotgun. The two Suburban's pulled out of the motel's parking lot and headed away from the scene.

* * *

Alexei pulled away from the curb and began to follow the two black Suburban's from a distance. Fifteen minutes later the second vehicle peeled off and headed in a new direction. Alexei knew that Yuri was in the primary vehicle and didn't alter course. He smiled.

Only four men now.

* * *

Bill turned right and entered the warehouse district. Just then he heard another car's engine gun. He checked the rear view and saw it bearing down on them.

"We've got company!"

Bill swerved to avoid being t-boned and the advancing car ended up on his driver's side.

Automatic weapons fire erupted from the right side of the pursuer's vehicle that left holes in the vehicle's armor. Windows cracked as the heavy 7.62 rounds peppered their left side.

"It's him!" yelled Frank. "He's going to kill me!"

"Fucking hell!" Bill's window had taken a number of direct hits and was splintered. Its integrity had been compromised.

Bill slammed on the breaks and swung the Suburban to the right. It came to a stop in the middle of the street.

The pursuing vehicle shot by and it screeched to a halt forty feet away. Three men jumped out, all with AK-47's and unloaded rounds in their direction.

"Move!" Sam yelled. "Out and take cover!" he said while keeping his head low.

Bill crawled over the center console and followed suit as Alpha team forcefully pushed Frank out onto the street. They huddled behind the large tires.

The Suburban's left side was thoroughly pummeled by incoming rounds. The AK-47's automatic fire hadn't let up.

"Suppressing fire!"

Alpha One switched his MP5 from his right to his left hand, extended it from behind the rear of the Suburban and depressed his trigger. 9mm rounds soared towards the sound of the AK-47's as he fired blind to force their attackers back.

Sam, who had exited first, brought his weapon up over the hood and blind fired as well.

The AK-47 fire ceased for a few seconds as their attackers were forced to take cover behind their own car.

Bill keyed his mike. "We're under attack! We need backup!" He gave them their position.

"Roger that. We're five minutes out."

"The sooner the better," Bill replied.

"On our way. Don't have too much fun without us."

Sam pulled his MP5 down and reloaded the thirty round magazine. He looked to his left and saw that Alpha Two had a secure grip on their prisoner. The last thing they needed was for Frank to panic, run and get gunned down.

The enemy fire started up again, but more sporadically. Sparks sprayed up a few feet from the Suburban as the steel AK rounds ricocheted off the street.

"How's your ammo?" Sam asked.

"You know what they say…you can never have enough," replied Bill.

Sam fired off another burst over the hood while Alpha One did the same at the rear.

* * *

The warehouse district was relatively light on traffic. Alexei punched the accelerator just as the black Suburban turned right but the man driving it must have seen him coming and swerved. Their windows had been rolled down so both Brutus and Sergio, as they passed by, unloaded their AK-47's from ten feet away. The Suburban's windows cracked and its armor turned into Swiss cheese as sixty rounds found new homes.

The Suburban slammed on its brakes and Alexei followed suit coming to a halt forty feet away.

Brutus and Sergio inserted new magazines. All three of them popped open their car doors, got out and unloaded their weapons as they walked forward.

"Suppressing fire!"

They saw an MP5 appear from the rear of the Suburban and another one appeared from over the hood.

They stopped their advance and ran the five feet to cover as both of the MP5's opened up. Some of the 9mm rounds struck the street while others hit their car. All three made it to the other side of their car without being shot.

Alexei, Brutus and Sergio reloaded their weapons and spread out behind their car for cover. They popped up and started to shoot again. 7.62 bullets hit both the street and the Suburban as they kept the pressure up.

More shots from the enemy's MP5's peppered their car.

* * *

"This shit isn't going to get any better," said Bill. As Sam finished firing Bill shouldered his MP5 and stood up from his crouched position.

Three men.

He quickly sighted in on one man on the far right whose upper body was exposed above the car hood.

Bill depressed his trigger.

* * *

The sudden movement caught Alexei's attention.

He traversed his weapon to the left.

In his peripheral vision he saw Sergio's head snapp back as a round entered through his eye.

Alexei fired his AK-47 and saw the man tumble backwards.

He ducked down and looked over at Sergio's unmoving body.

Now we're outgunned.

"Brutus. Grab Sergio's body while I cover. We're out of here."

Alexei sprayed the Suburban to keep the enemy's heads down as Brutus loaded Sergio's body into the car.

* * *

Bill watched the man's head snap back right before he was hit by a runaway train.

Bill tumbled back as the round hit him squarely in the upper chest and he hit the ground hard.

"Bill!" Sam pulled his unresponsive friend to him.

A solid stream of gunfire drilled the Suburban and forced Alpha One to disengage.

Sam saw the 7.62 entry in Bill's upper chest.

The shooting stopped. A second later the car peeled out. Alpha One watched it take the next left and disappear from view. Hundreds of shell casings littered the road where the car had been. A pool of blood remained as well.

"Bill Godammit!" Sam checked his friend's neck for a pulse and couldn't locate one. He hurriedly checked the other side and finally felt something. Sam unzipped the front of Bill's tactical vest and the 7.62 round now stuck into his ballistic vest. The bullet had compacted upon impact and would have caused massive damage, if not death, if he hadn't been wearing protection.

Bill's eyes fluttered and then opened with a pained expression on his face.

"Fucking hell that hurts."

"Can you sit up?"

"Get this thing off me, will ya?" He started tugging on his vest before Sam helped him slowly remove it. After it was off Bill pulled up his shirt. "Oh shit yeah. That's a massive bruise already."

"You're one lucky sonofabitch, you know that."

Bill pulled the compacted 7.62 round, that had embedded itself in his vest, out and looked at it. "Not today motherfucker."

"You going to be okay brother?" asked Sam.

"Peachy." He coughed and then winced. "I don't think we should tell the girls about this. Kim might actually kill me."

Sam smiled. "Glad you're not dead. Ballsy move. Course, not the brightest move, but ballsy nevertheless. Looks like you nailed one of them."

Bill just stood there with a blank look on his face. "I got shot."

"Yeah, no shit. We just covered that."

"No." He shook his head. "What I meant is, the guy who shot me….he's the same sonofabitch who gunned at me the other day while you were off playing with this jerk." Bill motioned towards Frank.

Alpha Two had pulled Frank up off the ground but kept a hand on his shoulder.

Sam spoke at Frank. "Looks like they want you dead pretty badly." Frank didn't reply.

"Inbound on your position," said the voice in everyone's ear. The second Suburban turned the corner and pulled up. Bravo and Charlie teams spilled out.

"You guys okay?"

Bill coughed and winced again. "You missed all the fun."

"What do you need us to do?"

Sam replied. "Secure the scene. For all I know they'll come back. We still have a mission to complete. We're taking our HVT back to the TOC."

Sam reached into the shot up Suburban and removed the evidence bag from the motel.

"Let's go."

* * *

Sam drove the last mile to the Tactical Operations Center and pulled in. Curtis met them as they disembarked.

"Heard everything over the wire as it happened. Glad to see you guys are okay."

"Thanks. So are we."

"The DCI has been made aware of the situation, both the attack and Frank's capture. He's on his way here now. I'll go pick up the rest of your team and bring them back here for now."

"Appreciate it Curtis."

Sam took positive control over Frank and walked him towards the private facility. The hidden door opened. Richard, Thomas, Michael and Emily stood there as Sam and his team approached.

Michael stepped right up to Frank. He took his time as he looked over the man known as Yuri; the man he'd chased after so many years ago; one of the men responsible for his wife's death. Michael's fists balled up.

Frank Russell stared back at the man in front of him. *Who is he? Why does he look so familiar?* He continued to study the face. *No. It can't be.*

"But...you're dead."

Richard stepped forward and joined Michael. "How about me Frank? Remember me?"

How is this possible? The shock on Frank's face was clearly visible. "How...?"

Michael spoke up. "After all these years...we finally got you Yuri. And now you're going to tell us everything."

* * *

The DCI arrived twenty minutes later. By that time a few things had already occurred. The first was that Sam had been able to hand off the satellite phone they recovered and Calvin assured Sam that he'd start breaking it down right away. The second, and certainly the most rewarding, was that Frank actually did tell them a few things. And that was all without any help from Emily.

When Victor Bannon arrived he watched as Frank Russell was loaded into the back of his vehicle. Eight men had arrived with the DCI, in three cars, to secure the prisoner and take him away.

"Great job." The DCI shook everyone's hand. "I'll keep you in the loop on what we discover from Frank. It's going to be a long time before we're done with him."

"Calvin's working on cracking the satellite phone we covered," said Sam.

"Excellent. With any luck that will get us one step closer to ending all of this. Anyway, great work out there today. Take a break tonight and enjoy yourselves. You've earned it."

The DCI and his security crew mounted up and departed. Everyone headed back inside the TOC as Sam pulled Thomas aside.

"It got pretty hairy out there today. I'm not sure I can stomach you and Emily in harm's way."

"Where's this coming from Sam?"

Sam looked around. "You didn't hear this from me but Bill took a round in the chest today."

"What?"

"His vest stopped it but he's sore and has one hell of a bruise. You and Emily need to get to safety. These guys came at us. Who knows what's going to happen next."

"While I appreciate the concern Sam, we're not going anywhere. There's still work to do. You know this thing isn't over yet. There have been four bombings that Nikolay has orchestrated."

"My point exactly. I can't look out for you and Em at the same time everything else is happening."

Thomas stood his ground. "It's not your call to make. Without Emily my father can't be here to do his work. Just think, the sooner we track down Nikolay the sooner we can put this all behind us."

Bill walked over when he noticed the heated discussion. "Hey guys. What's going on?"

"Sam's trying to send me and my daughter home. He says it's too dangerous. What do you think?"

Bill looked at Thomas, over at Sam and then back at Thomas. "You're needed here. I may not like the fact that Emily is in danger but I know you can handle yourself. It's also your call." He turned back to Sam. "Worry about the shit you can do something about. You knew Thomas wasn't going anywhere. Besides, the last time I checked his father was running the show. Let's just be smarter and pull Charlie team back here to look after everyone. Deal?"

Sam's face softened when he realized he'd overstepped. "Sorry about that Thomas."

"Don't worry about it. I totally get it, especially after Bill got shot today."

"Goddammit," said Bill. "You told him? I can't believe you ratted me out like that." Bill said as he winked at Thomas.

"Does it hurt?"

"Fuck yeah. It really hurts. Nothing's broken but I don't recommend the experience."

"I'm really glad you're okay brother," Thomas replied. "I don't know how many times it'll be until your luck runs out."

"Are you kidding? Sam's my lucky charm."

"Great," said Sam. "Bill, any chance you could call and up the man count in Hawaii before your lucky charm gut punches your ass?"

"Good idea. I'll take care of it." He walked off to make a few phone calls.

"So we're good?" Sam asked.

Thomas smiled. "We're brothers. Of course we're good."

* * *

Tuesday November 11, 1997 6:00pm

Alexei entered the bus terminal and proceeded to the locker area. He located one, unlocked and removed a bag. Around the corner he sat down on a bench and extracted a backup satellite phone. He checked the battery status, liked what he saw and made the call. Ten seconds later the secure line was made.

"Report."

"He's still alive and in custody. I attacked them in route but had to withdraw."

"Goddammit Alexei. I told you not to call me until this matter was taken care of."

"I'm afraid it's out of my hands now sir."

Nikolay sighed heavily. "So you're saying that as of right now you have no idea how much they might know?"

"They could very well know everything."

"This does not bode well." Nikolay paused. "No matter. I will not make any changes to my plans at this point. Anything else?"

"Yes sir. I identified the men who scooped up Yuri."

"How's that help me?"

"Actually sir, I think you'll find it to your liking. The two men, Sam Paige and Bill Nicholson, run a Private Military Company called SANDBOX based out of Marin, California."

"A PMC. Interesting. Go on."

"As it turns out they're good friends with Thomas Clark."

"Thomas....the son of Michael Clark?"

"The very same sir."

"You were right to bring this to my attention. They've made this personal. I should have sent you to kill them after they moved my money." Nikolay chuckled. "But payback's a bitch, even thirty years later. This is what I want you to do. Get someone to find out where they live and tap their phone lines...discretely. I need to know more about Thomas Clark, his friends and his family. They'll soon learn they should have never fucked with me."

"Right away sir."

40

Tuesday November 11, 1997 8:30pm

Laura, Julie and Kim worked on the late evening meal together as they often had the past week. Rebecca watched over them all. Julie's kids, Amanda and Craig watched television with Kim's kids, Sarah and Edward in the family room. Gavin, on the other hand, had spent most of the day in his bedroom ever since Stir had been struck by a car that same morning. He'd fallen asleep an hour before with Stir and Stickers curled up next to him.

"Why hello Gavin," said Betsy, his grandmother.

"Hi grandma." He reached out and she took his hand. She smiled. "It's good to see you."

"You too."

"I just don't understand. What are you doing here?"

Gavin's face contorted and then he screamed.

Stickers jumped off the bed in fright.

Rebecca reacted immediately and raced down the hallway, weapon drawn. Laura and the group followed.

Gavin woke up with a start to find Stir licking his face.

Rebecca and Laura entered his room.

Rebecca didn't know what she saw. She raised her weapon but Laura immediately stepped in her way.

"Don't. It's not a threat."

"It's…it's attacking him." Rebecca's sidearm was still up.

"No, he's not." Laura turned and went to her son. Stir jumped out of the way as she picked Gavin up. She stroked his hair.

"It's okay sweetie. More nightmares?"

"I don't know. I saw grandma."

"What is that thing?" Craig pointed at Stir from the doorway as the other kids crowded around to get a view. Stir stood on

311

Gavin's bed and looked back at everyone with his red eyes and wispy black body.

Oh shit. "It's just a cat," Laura said.

Rebecca holstered her weapon and took everything in.

"Nuh uh," Craig insisted.

Laura pleaded with her eyes at Julie and Kim.

"Come on kids," said Kim as she pulled them out of Gavin's bedroom. "Back to the family room. Gavin was just having a nightmare."

"No. Gavin, tell us. What is it?"

Laura didn't know what to do. *We are so fucked. I knew this would happen, I just knew it.* She whispered to her son. "Go ahead. You can tell them now."

Gavin turned his head towards his bedroom door where the kids had congregated. "His name is Stir. He's my imaginary friend." Laura put her son down. Gavin walked over to Stir and picked him up. Stickers came out of nowhere and started to wind around his legs as Gavin walked towards the door to show them.

Julie and Kim were apprehensive because they had heard all the stories. The kids, on the other hand, showed absolutely no fear and immediately crowded around Gavin.

"Wow, he's neat."

"Where'd you get him?"

"Does he bite?"

"Can I touch him?"

The adults watched as Gavin sat down on his carpet with Stir in his lap. The kids took his queue and did the same. Stir became excited and apprehensive at the same time.

Gavin petted him. "It's okay," he told Stir. "They're my friends." Stir's tale thumped against Gavin's leg as he relaxed.

"Can I touch him?" asked Craig.

"Yeah, me too," said the others.

Gavin nodded. "One at a time. Be gentle."

Stir hopped off Gavin's lap and walked around to each of the four children. They were eager and did their best to contain their curiosity. One by one they each petted Stir as he came around, but only after he sniffed them.

"He's soft."

"He's soooo cute."

"His red eyes are awesome."

"You're so lucky."

"Okay kids, everyone back to the family room. Dinner's going to be ready soon," said Kim.

Gavin and Stir led the way and the other kids followed right after him. Stickers trailed behind the group leaving Rebecca and Laura alone in Gavin's room.

"My apologies for over reacting."

"Actually Rebecca, I couldn't have asked for a better response." Laura paused as she studied Rebecca's face. "But I can tell its not really what you wanted to hear. You want to know what that was all about."

Laura sat down on her son's bed. "I can't get into the specifics mind you. What I can tell you is that Stir is my son's imaginary friend."

"Come on."

Laura looked at her square in the eyes. "I'm not bullshitting you nor do I care what you think. You're here to protect our families. Telling you anything at this point is a courtesy I'm extending you." Laura stood up. "Listen. My son is special and that's all you need to know."

"I didn't mean any offense Mrs. Clark. I'm very fond of your family and I'm just trying to do my job. Surprises like this shouldn't be happening. I won't ask any more questions." Rebecca turned to leave but Laura placed her hand on her arm.

"Sorry. You're a good person and I know you're just doing your job. The reality of the situation is that we've been down this road before."

"I don't understand. What road?"

"The road where we've kept our secret but someone finds out about it and our family is suddenly at risk."

"Mrs. Clark..."

"Laura."

"...Laura. From Julie and Kim's reactions I can tell that they already knew, which by default means that Sam and Bill must be in the know. With those conclusions I can easily ascertain that the circle of trust is limited to your three families. I don't know what to believe or to think at this point. My job is to protect you and that's exactly what I'm going to do. If, at some point down the road, I need to be in the know then so be it. Until then I'll do my best not to overthink what just happened in here."

"Thank you Rebecca."

She nodded and left the room.

Laura lay back on Gavin's bed and brought her hands up to her head. *Oh boy.*

* * *

Julie picked up the phone on the second ring. She had just tucked the kids into their beds. They were still excited about meeting Stir.

"Hello?"

"Hey Jules," said Sam.

"How are you Sam? You sound tired?" She looked at the clock. It read 9:30pm. "What are you doing up so late? Isn't it two thirty in the morning or something out there? Is everything okay?"

Sam chuckled. "Slow down sweetie. Everything's fine." Sam took a second. "We got him."

"You got that Frank Ru..."

Sam cut her off. "No names over the phone....but yeah, we got him."

Julie was ecstatic. "So, it's all over then? You're coming home?"

Sam shook his head before he responded. "Not quite yet I'm afraid."

Her demeanor sunk. "What do you mean? I don't understand."

"There's more to the puzzle Jules. We're trying to go after the head of the snake."

"But you promised."

"You're right. I did promise. I promised to see this thing to the end. The bottom line is that we're not going to be safe until I do just that."

Julie pouted. "I just want you to be safe and in my arms Sam. Is that too much to ask?"

"I want that too babe, more than you know." He hesitated.

"What is it?"

"I'm sending more men out to look after all of you. They'll be there in the morning."

"Are we in danger? Wait, are you in danger?"

"Hopefully not, which is exactly why we're taking precautions. I know it hasn't been ideal but I need to know you're being looked after."

"I miss you Sammy Bear."

"Miss you too. I love you. Hugs and kisses to the kids."

"I love you too."

"Bye babe."

* * *

The phone rang at the Nicholson residence. Kim picked up the phone on the third ring.

"Bill?"

"Hey there lover," he replied. "Miss you."

Kim smiled. "Miss you too. How's DC? Everything okay?"

"Why? What'd you hear? I'm fine."

Kim was instantly on guard. "Spill it mister. What happened?"

"So you didn't hear anything?"

"No. Now tell me what happened right now."

Oh dammit. "Well…um…I guess I should tell you before you hear it from anyone else."

"Tell me what? Spill it," she insisted.

"I'm obviously fine honey, cause we're talking and everything."

"Biillllll, if you don't tell me I'm going to strangle you."

"There might have been an incident today where I…uh…got shot."

"YOU GOT SHOT!"

"Now calm down sweetie, just calm down."

"Bill Nicholson, I swear to God, you're going to give me a heart attack. And when I do you KNOW I'm going to haunt your ass."

"You're not making this any easier….I mean…the idea of you haunting me is…well…hot."

Kim was not expecting that. Her train of thought evaporated and she found herself laughing. "Okay, I was not prepared for that. You're okay though, right?"

"Just a bruise. I'm fine."

"Good. At least I'll have another place on your body to apply pressure. I can't wait to make you scream."

"Gee sweetie, you really know how to get to my heart."

"You know I love you."

Bill smiled. "You've made that abundantly clear. I love you too. Now, on a side note, I have a few things to pass along. I just want you to listen."

"Okay."

"The first part of our mission is complete....we got him. However, we're not done yet. Expect more men tomorrow."

"Are we in some kind of danger?"

"That's the point of sending more men out to you...that way you won't be in danger," he answered. *Whew, dodged that one.*

"Be careful out there. The kids and I really miss you."

"I miss you all too. I'll be home soon enough. I've got to go. Bye sweetie."

"Bye."

* * *

A similar phone call was currently in progress between Thomas and Laura.

"So you got him...that's awesome. And how's our daughter holding up?"

"Emily's a rock star. Nothing seems to faze her."

"Good."

"Anything new on your end of the world?" he asked.

"Today's been a full day actually."

"Do tell. I'm all ears."

"Well, it started with Stir being hit by a car."

"He's still okay, right?"

"Yeah, like nothing happened. Weird. Anyway, this evening Gavin dozed off and had some kind of nightmare, while everyone was over. Long story short, the other kids all met Stir."

Thomas winced. "Oh shit."

"Yeah, you can pretty much say that a few million times. But there's more."

"More?"

"Rebecca also had the pleasure of nearly shooting Stir when she saw him licking our son's face."

"This just keeps getting better and better. Fallout?"

"She's a professional. But she's seen things she can't un-see."

"Well, we're going to have to deal with all that later. Once we take care of business over here in D.C. we can try and get things back to normal. And unfortunately, that's going to get worse for you starting tomorrow."

"Why? What do you mean?" she asked.

"They're sending more people out to look after all of you."

"What aren't you telling me?"

"I swear it's purely precautionary. There was a firefight today and Bill took a round in the chest."

"What!? Why didn't you tell me that sooner? Is he okay?"

"He's fine. Sorry, I would have mentioned it earlier if it was a big deal."

"It is a big deal. Are you saying because of that incident that we're in danger?"

"There's nothing definitive to answer yes to that….but I'm not saying no to more people looking out for your well-being either. This isn't over yet and until it is we're all potentially at risk."

Laura sighed. "Be careful out there…please."

"Unless I happen to get a paper cut we're going to be just fine. Seriously, you should see some of the toys we have. Video cameras, satellite coverage and access to a ton of information. My father's in heaven, so to speak."

Laura chuckled. "Nice one."

"Yeah, I thought so. Anyway, we're fine. Just do me a favor and watch your back out there. I only wish I was with you right now."

"I wish you were here too. I really miss you."

"You have no idea how much I miss you too. Anyway sweetie, it's late and who knows what tomorrow will bring. I'll call you when I can. I love you."

"I love you too. Bye."

"Bye babe."

D.W. Neuman

41

Wednesday November 12, 1997 7:00am

Rebecca was outside when the taxi pulled up. The sliding van door opened and three men, dressed in casual clothes, exited. They retrieved their gear as she paid off the driver. The taxi drove away. The men followed her inside.

"Welcome to Hawaii. My name is Rebecca Cross, team leader."

"Jeff Russell."

"Adrian Shelton."

"Joseph Pickens."

"Nice to meet you all," she said. "Currently there are four of us on site. With your arrival that number jumps to seven. Now, I don't know if you're aware of the current situation so I'm going to review it with you right now. We're in charge of protecting three families. On site there are five children and three adults, all female. On a typical day they'll congregate here, at this property, which makes our job easier. The pool area can be accessed from either the beach or through where we're standing. Any questions?"

"Who are we protecting them from?"

"I've been told that this is merely a precautionary move, but let's be honest, the bar doesn't get raised this high for no reason. Keep your eyes open and your heads on a swivel. Anything else?"

"What about the lay of the land?"

"We're going to walk the entire property as soon as you've pulled small arms and radios. The handle I answer to is Juliette. My additional three operators are Tony, Andy and Matt. They answer to Delta, Foxtrot and Hotel. We'll have a meet and greet once you're familiar with the area. As for each of you...Jeff, you're Oscar; Adrian, you're Whiskey; and Joseph, you're Yankee. Let me show you the house armory so we can draw your weapons."

* * *

An hour later, and introductions to the rest of the team out of the way, Rebecca stopped by Gavin's room and peaked in. Sure enough, Stir and Stickers lay next to him on his bed.

What the hell is it?

"Still trying to figure out what Stir is all about?"

Rebecca was startled.

"Sorry Rebecca. I didn't mean to sneak up on you."

"I was so engrossed I didn't hear you come down the stairs. But you're right, I'm intrigued. I've never seen anything like him."

"No one has. Would you like some coffee?" Laura asked.

"Sure."

Laura headed down the hallway and Rebecca followed.

"Have a seat."

Rebecca adjusted the weapon on her hip and sat down on a bar stool. "Three additional team members arrived this morning."

"That makes seven," Laura said as she prepared the coffee. "Should we be worried?"

She shook her head. "Not that I'm aware of."

"So why the extra protection?"

Rebecca smiled. "You're no dummy Laura, that's for sure. The fact that more operators are on site tends to indicate that something might happen. However, my team hasn't experienced threats whatsoever."

"Any threat…yet…you mean."

"If there's anything I've learned in life it's that anything's possible, but that's why we're here."

"This type of protection duty must be very different than your Combat Medic role."

"It is. It's almost a night and day difference." Laura handed her a cup of coffee. "Thank you."

"You're welcome."

"Do you enjoy this type of work more?"

Rebecca smiled. "I'm not sure I'm the right person to ask that question to. I just joined SANDBOX. Your family is my first assignment."

"So you don't enjoy it?"

"Oh, I didn't say that. Being responsible for other human lives isn't new to me. The distinctive difference is that now my job is to prevent harm from coming to you rather than saving your life after you've been injured."

"And you're okay with that change?"

"I'm loving it actually. Okay, that came out wrong."

Laura chuckled. "I get what you mean."

"I like the fact that I can concentrate on protecting everyone from danger rather than trying to save someone from bleeding out. What do you think?"

"What I think doesn't matter. It sounds to me like you enjoy helping people and just found your calling in the military."

"Yes, that's a good word for it. A calling. I can't explain it."

"You don't have to. I see the exact same thing in Sam and Bill. They're motivated just like you. Hell, you should probably talk to Julie and Kim about it."

"Why?"

"Maybe sharing your perspective on why you do what you do could be enlightening, especially from a woman's point of view. Just a thought."

"Hmm. Maybe. Anyway, I've got rounds to make. Thank you for the coffee."

"Anytime Rebecca. I've got to get ready for another day by the pool with everyone tromping through my house."

Rebecca chuckled. "The sacrifices we all make."

Laura smiled. "Tell me about it."

42

Wednesday November 12, 1997 12:00pm

The room that housed Frank Russell was small, made up of four walls with a table affixed to one of them. There were no windows. Multiple surveillance cameras covered every angle of the holding cell. Frank had finally managed to fall asleep, after a very long night, when the door to his cell abruptly opened.

He opened his eyes and rolled off his bed. "And who might you be?"

"My name is hardly your concern," said the man as he closed the door behind him. "However, to keep things civil, you may call me Mr. Black. Are you hungry Frank?"

Frank nodded.

"Very well."

The door opened and Mr. Black was handed a plastic tray that contained a carton of milk, a red apple, a ham sandwich and a cookie. As the door closed he turned around and placed it on the table. Frank sat down opposite Mr. Black as the tray was pushed towards him.

"Is there anything else you need?"

Why are they being so polite to me?

He picked up the ham sandwich and took a bite. It was actually quite delicious.

"Frank, your debriefing…"

"Don't you mean my interrogation?"

Mr. Black smiled. "We both know what we're talking about. I've been brought in to facilitate this process. I'm going to be straight forward with you and my hope is that you'll return the same courtesy."

Frank didn't respond as he ate.

D.W. Neuman

"I'll get to the point. The CIA has a considerable amount of egg on its face because of you. In time you will tell me your entire story. You will leave nothing out. I've been instructed to tell you that the more you cooperate the easier your future will be."

"You mean something like taking strolls on a sandy beach?"

"Funny you should say that because you're not that far off. We have detention facilities all over the world and not all of them have walls. On one such island you'd have the ability to walk wherever you wanted; and due to its remote location the vast ocean would effectively be considered your jail cell. Of course, you could always swim to freedom."

"Not at my age."

"Probably not. Moving on. Refusing to answer my questions, or misleading me, will earn you two things. The first punishment will be a windowless room where you will never have the option to feel the warm sun on your face ever again. The second is my displeasure. So far the two of us are having a very pleasant and civil conversation. I would recommend that you keep it this way. The tone of this conversation, and ultimately your future, rests entirely in your hands Frank. Also I've been told that if your role, as a Russian mole, were to become public you would find yourself stripped of any benefits whatsoever."

Frank finished his sandwich and moved on to his cookie.

"So Frank, are we on the same page?"

"If I cooperate with you, and share my knowledge, you're telling me I can live out my golden years in relative comfort? Do I have your word Mr. Black?"

"Yes, in fact, you do have my word on it."

Frank studied his face and believed him.

*   *   *

Two and a half hours later Mr. Black concluded his initial talk with Frank and left the cell. The surveillance cameras had recorded everything that had been said.

Frank knew there was little point but to cooperate especially since his loyalty to Nikolay had been shattered the moment Alexei attempted to kill him.

Payback's a bitch.

Frank informed Mr. Black about the information packets he'd put together, what lawyers had them and how to retrieve them before they were distributed. He told them about Nikolay Dmitriev and how they'd stayed in touch over the years using covert drops and other spy trade tools. And Frank told them about a cell, located in D.C., that he had worked with as well, along with their location.

As Mr. Black left the cell Frank's thoughts drifted off.

I've had a long run at this but I'm tired.

He lay back down on his bed and closed his eyes.

I just want to feel the sand between my toes again before I die.

* * *

Mr. Black stepped into another room.

"First impressions?" asked the DCI.

"He's motivated. He knows he'll never be free, but Nikolay's also burned him. He'll cooperate."

"Motivated out of revenge, eh? That seems to be a common denominator these days."

"Sir?"

"Nothing. Keep me informed of your progress. I have some phone calls to make."

"Yes sir. I'll give him a couple hours before the next session."

43

Wednesday November 12, 1997 3:00pm

"Here's what we know about the location." Sam laid out the residential blueprints in front of his men. Alpha, Bravo and Charlie teams gathered around the table while Bill hovered next to Sam. "Unfortunately we have zero time to prep for this incursion."

"What are we up against?"

"The intel supplied says that this location is utilized by a cell. That cell is apparently responsible for the Metro Station bombing."

"That's pretty specific information."

Sam smiled. "No shit. Motivation does wonders." He turned serious and pointed to the plans. "As you can see the target is a detached, two story unit with three bedrooms and a basement. There are three entrances; the front door, the garage and a door from the backyard."

"Number of opposition?"

"That's unknown. We also don't know what we'll find inside. Regardless, we're still going in. Unless anyone has any objections this is how I want the breach to go."

Sam began to go over his plan. Fifteen minutes later the eight men geared up and headed out.

* * *

The two Suburban's quickly came to a stop as they pulled up in front of the house. Each team member was dressed in black wearing body armor and tactical vests. Non-lethal flash bang grenades hung at the ready. Each of them carried an HK MP5SD 9mm submachine gun. The integrated suppressor on their weapons would significantly reduce the sound of any gunfire.

Glock 17's hung low off each man's right leg as their backup weapon.

Doors popped open and the eight men spilled out. Alpha team flanked left and headed for the garage door. Bravo team flanked right and moved towards the back of the house. Charlie team took positions behind each Suburban's hood and covered the front while Sam and Bill made their way to the front of the house.

Sam and Bill stacked up at the front door. Two large windows were to their right. Bill poked his head over and looked inside.

"Looks quiet. No movement."

Sam nodded.

"Alpha team in position."

"Bravo team in position."

"Eagles One and Two are ready," Sam said into his throat mike. "Zero movement out front."

"Negative movement from the garage."

"Negative movement from the back."

"Check your doors for booby traps and report back." Sam covered Bill while he began to inspect the front door for traps.

"I can't tell from out here," said Bill. "But I have an idea."

Bill checked the front room for movement again. Not seeing any he moved in front of the window before Sam could stop him. Bill tried to look at the inside of the front door but he didn't have a good angle. As he moved back he caught a glimpse of something in the mirror that hung on the wall opposite the front door entrance.

"Fuck."

"What've you got?" Sam asked.

"Well, I'd say we're at the right house. There's a M67 fragmentation grenade attached to the front door."

Sam immediately spoke into his mike. "Hold hold hold. Front door is wired."

"Alpha holding."

"Bravo holding."

"I've got an idea," said Bill, "but it isn't pretty," as he pointed at the front windows, Sam understood right away.

"Command, you copy?"

"We're here Eagle One," Calvin replied.

"Anything on satellite?"

"Negative." Calvin zoomed in and adjusted the overhead picture. "No movement other than your team."

"Roger that. Alpha. Bravo. Collapse to the front door. I'm not taking any chances. We're entering together."

Twenty seconds later six team members were outside the front door as Charlie continued to cover them from behind the vehicles.

Sam nodded to Bill who then turned, brought up his MP5SD and shot out the closest window with a three-round burst.

Cough Cough Cough. The silenced rounds did their job and the window fell apart.

CRASH!

Bill butted a large section of glass that hadn't fallen out of its frame and quickly stepped through the new opening. He kept his weapon up and at the ready.

Nothing. No movement.

Sam, along with Alpha and Bravo, filled the living room behind Bill.

Bill pointed to his eyes and then pointed at the front door. Then Bill, with his left hand, mimicked scissors. Alpha One moved to the front door to disarm the booby trap while Alpha Two covered the hallway that led to the back of the house.

Bravo One and Two carefully moved right and traversed through the dining room and into the kitchen.

Sam and Bill bypassed the front door and began to clear towards the garage.

Alpha Two lowered his weapon as Eagle One and Two passed his location. He then pointed his MP5SD at the second floor stairs to cover his teammate.

Alpha One slung his weapon and pulled a pair of wire clippers from his front vest. He knelt down and inspected the grenade.

Open the door and it pops the pin. Hold the grenade's spoon and cut this wire.

He made the cut and the booby trap became instantly inert. He pocketed the M67 grenade and brought his weapon up to cover the stairs as well.

Bravo team quickly swept through the kitchen and then stopped at the hallway junction. To their right was the garage and in front of them was the door to the basement. They kept their weapons trained on the basement door.

Sam and Bill cleared a small room used for storage on their left before they continued down the hall to the garage. Bravo was on their right, in the kitchen, and they passed by. The two of them stacked up on the garage door. Sam nodded and Bill opened it. It swung inward as Sam made entry.

Nothing.

The garage door that led outside, the same one Alpha was initially going to breach, had another crude but deadly trap attached to it. Bill examined the mechanism and quickly disabled it. The two of them left the garage and headed back towards the kitchen.

"Hold while we clear upstairs."

Eagle team moved to Alpha.

"First floor is secure. Move up to the second."

Alpha nodded and ascended the stairs. Their weapons were up and ready. Sam and Bill waited two seconds and then followed behind.

Nothing. No movement.

At the top of the stairs were three bedrooms, exactly like the blueprints they'd memorized. Alpha team turned left towards the master bedroom as Eagle team headed straight.

Alpha swept into the master bedroom together.

Nothing. No one.

Sam and Bill hit the first bedroom on the right. The door was open but the room was empty.

Together they moved to the hallway bathroom and quickly cleared it.

The last bedroom door was closed. Bill tried the handle but it was locked.

Sam grimaced. *Here we go.* He made the signal for forced entry.

Bill obliged and kicked in the door with his boot.

The grenade's pin was pulled out by the wire. The spoon flew off the grenade, armed the detonator and went sailing across the room from the force of Bill's kick.

They both heard the familiar *twing* sound of a grenade.

"GRENADE!"

The grenade bounced off a wall and skittered across the floor.

Alpha Team, who had just emerged from the master bedroom, hit the carpet.

Sam and Bill ran past the bathroom and dove towards the stairs just as the grenade exploded.

BOOOOM!

The bedroom's doorway and part of the hallway were obliterated. The interior of the bedroom took the majority of the damage as shrapnel embedded itself in the walls and furniture. Where the grenade had detonated a new entrance to the garage had been created in the floor below.

Pieces of wood, plaster, wall and carpet flew over Sam and Bill's heads. Dust filled the hallway.

D.W. Neuman

Back at Command Thomas yelled into the microphone. "Sam! Bill! Are you guys okay!?"

Sam and Bill coughed a few times. Alpha team appeared around the corner.

"Well that was fun," said Bill. "I'm volunteering you to kick in the next one."

"There's been an explosion. Eagle's One and Two are down but appear okay."

"Confirming the explosion," said Calvin. "We saw a blast come through the bedroom wall."

"Really Calvin?" Bill said testily. "It's not like we experienced it first hand or anything."

Sam and Bill accepted Alpha's help as they picked themselves up from the carpeted hallway.

"Forget about us. Go clear that room," Sam commanded. Alpha team went and did just that. "Command. We're fine. No injuries. Bravo, Eagle One and Two are heading downstairs to you."

"Roger that."

Sam and Bill went down a flight, turned right and rejoined Bravo at the basement doorway.

"You guys okay?"

Bill nodded. "Just another day of earning my paycheck. After you ladies."

Bravo One slowly eased the basement door open. It creaked as it opened. Stairs led down into the unknown darkness.

"Bang it," said Sam.

While Alpha One covered the stairs with his weapon, Alpha Two pulled a flash bang from his vest, pulled the pin and underhanded it down the steps. The four of them turned their heads, closed their eyes and covered their ears.

BOOM!

The pitch black basement illuminated with an intense flash while, at the same time, an incredibly deafening sound filled the room.

Bravo team rushed down the stairs followed by Sam and Bill.

At the bottom of the steps Bravo team hugged left while Eagle team went right. The basement encompassed the entire underside of the house.

Work benches filled the area. Various supplies were stored in wall racks.

Wires.

Ball bearings.

Cement.

Each of them had their weapons up as they moved forward to clear the area.

"Basement's clear," said Sam.

"Alpha's clear on the second floor as well."

"Roger that," Sam replied. "Calvin, send your crew in. Zero tangos on site. All teams; don't touch anything. Who knows what else is booby trapped." Sam moved over to one of the work tables and took a look at some of the papers. He decided to pick one up.

"Something interesting?" asked Bill.

"You tell me." He handed it over. "Looks like some sort of schematic."

Bill scanned it and nodded. "I'd have to agree." He picked up another. "Well shit."

"What've got?"

"Oh nothing major. Just a cutaway sketch of a trash bin…along with how to build it out as one huge improvised explosive device."

* * *

Thursday November 13, 1997 9:00am

The next morning Sam and Bill met back at the TOC while the rest of their assault team rested at the safe house.

"Nice job," said Michael.

"Ahh. You mean aside from the booby trap I tripped," Bill replied.

Sam smiled. "Thanks." He turned to Bill. "Besides, we all know a little explosion can't hurt you. You took a bullet the other day and you're still walking around. So far no one's collected the pool money on you yet."

"Very funny."

Richard spoke up. "You'll be happy to hear that your risk was worth the reward."

"Okay," said Bill. "I'm all ears."

Hobbes pushed a few buttons and some images appeared on the large overhead screens.

"Whoever used that house used it to make bombs. Combing through the evidence our unit confirmed that whoever made the DC Metro bombs made them there."

A variety of pictures taken of the basement showed various materials used for bomb making. A new picture filled the screen. It was of a torn and tattered badge. The symbol on the top matched the Department of Transportation's logo. The ID picture, on the front of the badge, was missing.

"This badge, discovered in the same second floor bedroom room that the grenade went off in, was recovered. It, in itself, doesn't prove that there's any connection....but..."

A new set of documents appeared on the overhead.

"We cross referenced DC Metro employees that have gone missing since the bombing. The initial thought was that those employees died in the explosion and haven't been identified yet. However, it would appear that one of the employees actually owns the house you hit yesterday."

"You're shitting me," said Bill.

"Two others, that are missing as well, have the exact same home address listed on their employee paperwork."

"You're telling me that they didn't even attempt to cover up their identities?"

"What it means," said Michael, "is that Nikolay has always been playing the long game. He's willing to go to all this trouble; setting up a cell; establishing jobs and history, maybe even for years; building bombs; and more. He's playing the long game. He must have a number of other cells throughout the United States that are responsible for the other bombings.

"I have to agree with Michael," said Richard. "I'm afraid we're not going to see an end to any of this for quite some time. It's bigger than we thought."

Sam interjected. "So let's go after the head of the snake. Let's go after Nikolay directly. Take out the leadership."

"Exactly," replied Michael. "Calvin."

Calvin took his turn. "The satellite phone you recovered from Yuri, for lack of a better description, was encrypted. The NSA was able to hack the unit and look at the call log. The actual number Yuri called is no longer active, but from that phone we now know two things."

"Which are?" asked Bill.

Michael answered. "We know the satellite that's receiving the calls."

"And how does that help us?"

"The calls were traced to Cuba. We've asked The NSA to actively track all calls from that particular satellite for us. Once those calls are intercepted it's only a matter of time until we have a solid fix on his location."

"Cuba?" said Bill as he looked over at Sam.

"Is the DCI in the loop about this?" Sam asked.

Calvin nodded.

"Good. He made me some travel guarantees. Looks like we'll be finally taking the fight to where it belongs."

44

Thursday November 13, 1997 1:30pm

"Mom, I want to go out on the beach."

"You know you're not allowed out there by yourself sweetie," Laura said to her son. "The water is dangerous."

Gavin didn't budge. "I don't want to go in the water; I just want to play in the sand. And Stickers will be with me so I'm not alone." He thought his explanation was well thought out.

Laura smiled. *Oh to be young and innocent again.* "Well, if Stickers is going to be with you then how can I say no? Just stay back from the water's edge please."

He excitedly skipped down to the beach gate and opened it. Stickers followed right behind Gavin as he planted both his feet in the soft warm sand. Gavin made his way out towards the water but stopped well short of it. Stickers took his time walking on the sand before he joined Gavin.

Laura watched her son plop himself down and began to digg in the sand. She turned to Rebecca.

"Would you mind…"

"Already on it." Rebecca spoke into her radio. "This is Juliette. Anyone on the beach?"

"Whiskey is on the beach. From my vantage point it appears as if an epic sandcastle is under construction."

Laura and Rebecca smiled. "Roger that Whiskey. Do me a favor and make the beach your new home for the time being."

"You sure? It's horrible out here."

"I'm sure you'll manage. Juliette out."

"Thanks," said Laura.

"No problem."

339

* * *

Out on the beach Gavin used his hands to dig his moat. He piled up the unearthed sand in the middle.

I'm going to need some wet sand.

He got up and walked ten feet to where the ocean waves crested high up on the beach. He scooped up as much damp sand as he could and made his way back to his creation. In the distance he never noticed the man lean against a palm tree and watch over him. Stickers looked on in earnest at Gavin's progress while he occasionally scratched himself.

* * *

The cordless phone next to Laura rang. She picked it up on the second ring.

"Hello?"

"Hey Laura, it's Nick Raynes, Thomas' publishing agent."

"What? Who is this?" Laura paused for a second. "Just messing with you Nick. You think I forgot what your voice sounded like?"

"Well...I..."

Laura grinned. "How are Susan and little Lisa?"

"I keep forgetting that you and Thomas live on sarcasm. Susan and Lisa are doing great, thanks for asking."

"Did your daughter enjoy Disneyland?"

"Thomas told you about that?"

"We're married Nick. Would you like me to chat with Susan and tell her how much you enjoyed the 'It's a Small World" ride?"

Nick laughed. "Oh for the love of God, please don't. I almost about lost what little sanity I had left. All I heard from my daughter was 'again daddy, again'. I can't go on that ride ever again."

Laura smiled. "Sounds miserable. Maybe you should take them out of Los Angeles for a few days and visit Hawaii. I know we'd love to see you."

"You know, we might actually have to take you up on that at some point. It sounds delightful. Certainly much better than the lovely smog that lingers here in LA. And, speaking of adventures, I'm taking tomorrow off to take the family to the zoo."

"Well, you'll definitely have fun. And just think, there aren't any rides for your eight year old to drag you on."

"Tell me about it, thank God. Anyway, I didn't mean to talk your ear off. Is Thomas available? I haven't spoken to him in three weeks and wanted to touch base, see what he's up to. You know...the usual agent gibber jabber."

"I'd love to help Nick but he's away on business."

"Business? Don't tell me he's looking for another agent?"

"How'd you know that?"

"Wait....what?"

"Gotcha again Nick."

"Damn. You got me. You're quick with the wit Laura, I'll give you that."

"You know he's not going to go through anyone but you. Tell you what though. I'll let him know that you called when he checks in. Anything you'd like to relay?"

"Nah. Nothing specific other than my normal badgering on whether he's writing anything new."

"Got it. Normal badgering."

"Thanks Laura. Hey, I forgot to ask how the kids are doing."

"They couldn't be better, thanks for asking."

BLAM! BLAM!

All four women shot out of their chairs.

"I've got to go Nick." Laura thumbed the end button, dropped the phone and grabbed her Glock 17 from underneath her towel. She raced after Rebecca towards the beach where the gunshots came from, and where her son was playing.

* * *

Stickers was bored and began to paw at one of the towers Gavin had created.

"Stickeerrrrrsss....cut it out."

The tabby's constant pawing undermined that tower. It toppled sideways and fell into the empty moat.

"Awww." Gavin moved to repair the damage while Stickers moved out of his reach and started pawing at something else.

"Come on Stickers. Quit it."

The cat looked at his master. "Meow."

Gavin sighed. "I'd play with you but I want to finish this."

"Meow."

"You're not being reasonable Stickers."

"Meow." He began to paw at another tower.

"Stickers!"

The cat looked straight at Gavin again. "Meow."

"Fine. You win." Gavin looked around the beach and didn't see anyone. A split second later Stir appeared next to him, his black tail wagged while his red eyes focused on his new feline friend.

"Happy now Stickers?"

In response Stickers leapt off Gavin's island creation and tackled Stir where he stood in the sand. The second tower he'd pawed at toppled over as he'd sprung.

"Awww man."

342

Stir watched Stickers fly through the air at him. They tussled in the warm sand and pretended to nip and bite each other as they played. Suddenly Stickers took off like a shot up the beach. Stir loved to chase his friend and took off after him with Gavin far behind.

* * *

Whiskey scanned the north side of the private beach. As he traversed his head south to check on Gavin again he saw some kind of animal as it chased down the family cat.

What the hell?

He pulled his sidearm, took aim and fired.

BLAM! BLAM!

* * *

Gavin's head snapped up at the sound of gunfire. He watched Stir tumble a few times and come to a rest on his side. He didn't move. Gavin was up and running towards Stir on his short legs without even thinking.

"STIR!"

* * *

BLAM! BLAM!

Rebecca bolted out of her chair and yelled at Julie and Kim. "Keep your kids here!" She drew her weapon and ran towards the beach.

She saw Gavin get up and run. *Thank God he's okay.*

"STIR!"

343

Rebecca bee-lined to intercept Gavin, but then she saw Whiskey approach the small black animal, known as Stir, that lay motionless in the sand. *Oh fuck me.*

"Stand down!"

"GET AWAY!" screamed Gavin.

Whiskey still had his weapon out. "That wild animal was after the cat."

"I've got this Whiskey. Secure the area."

Whiskey gave Rebecca a weird look but finally moved away.

* * *

"Mew." The sound that emanated out of Stickers was pitiful.

Stickers circled Stir's body and headed butted his friend. He didn't get a response.

"Mew."

* * *

Laura caught up with Gavin just as he reached Stir. Her son was hysterical.

"GET AWAY!"

"I've got this Whiskey. Secure the area."

* * *

"STIR!"

Gavin ran as fast as he could across the soft sand. He reached Stir's body just as Rebecca did. A man, with a gun, approached.

"GET AWAY!"

"I've got this Whiskey. Secure the area."

Gavin scooped up Stir from the sand and cradled him in his arms. Tears flowed down his face. Stickers kept up his sad mewing.

A single bullet hole had penetrated Stir's side but there wasn't any visible bleeding. Stir's normal wispy black body had subsided somewhat and his red eyes were closed.

"You'regoingtobeokayyou'regoingtobeokayyou'regoingtobeo kay."

Gavin pulled him to his chest.

Rebecca stood off to the side, finally holstered her weapon and pulled out her radio. "This is Juliette. Stand down. We're secure."

Laura put her hand on her son's shoulder.

"Please don't leave me Stir. You're my best friend in the whole world. You can't die, you just can't," he pleaded.

"Gavin….it's okay sweetie."

"It's not okay! It'll never be okay!"

"Mew."

He rocked back and forth on his knees with Stir in his arms. "Please be okay Stir. Please be okay."

Nothing. Then something. Stir's red eyes opened and slowly his tail began to move.

"Stir?"

"Mew?"

While they watched the bullet hole slowly closed up on its own.

"Oh my God," Laura breathed out.

Stir began to struggle in Gavin's arms.

"Stir!"

Gavin put his friend and guardian down in the sand. Stickers immediately began to lick Stir's face and head.

"You're okay! You came back to me!"

Stir jumped up and began to give Gavin his own tongue bath. Gavin giggled with absolute joy.

Laura's legs finally collapsed and she abruptly sat down on the beach.

Holy shit, I think I'm reaching my breaking point.

* * *

Alexei listened to the taped conversation one more time and then called Nikolay.

"Report."

"Thomas Clark's wife, Laura, just had a conversation with a close friend in Los Angeles. Their family is taking a trip to the zoo tomorrow."

Nikolay smiled from his Cuban compound. "It's a start. I want you to take care of this personally. Let's see how much they like their lives fucked with."

"Very good sir. I'll be in touch."

45
Friday November 14, 1997 9:45am

Calvin answered the incoming phone through his headset.

"Good morning Director."

"Is everything prepared?"

"Yes sir."

"Very well."

Calvin turned in his chair and called out. "Mr. Clark?"

"What?" replied Thomas.

"Yes?" replied Michael at the same time.

"Oh, right…sorry. The Director's on the line for Michael. You can take it over there," Calvin said. He pointed to an open computer.

"Thank you." Michael made his way to the computer, sat down and donned the headset. "Director?"

"Good morning Michael. I thought you and I should have a conversation."

"Sure. What about?"

"You actually."

"Me sir?" *What the hell is this?*

"Start it up."

"Yes sir," Calvin said as he punched a few keys.

"Why is Calvin looped into our conversation?"

"Don't worry about that Michael," replied the DCI. "You should be seeing images on the screen in front of you now."

The computer screen came to life in front of Michael.

"It's live sir," stated Calvin.

"I'm seeing it on my end as well," the DCI said. He changed gears. "Now, Michael. What you're looking at are from various camera angles here at Langley."

"Okay." Michael watched a number of camera feeds in different squares on his screen.

"You'll notice the time stamp on each of them is from ten days ago, the fourth. If you recall that was the same day your son and granddaughter came to visit me."

Oh crap.

"That's also the same day you bypassed heavy security and appeared in my office. Now, as you're well aware, the CIA takes security breaches very seriously. As you can see, the video you're watching follows your family's movements from the time they parked, entered the building and arrived at my office."

Michael could do nothing but watch as the videos tracked Thomas and Emily's movement.

"The fact that you were able to completely circumvent the building's security has been a conundrum for me. But let's put that aside for the moment. You have been out of the game, or off the grid, for thirty years now. Where have you been? What have you been up to? How have you managed to stay hidden? These are all questions that have bothered me since your reappearance. I needed to know more so I had Calvin and Hobbes tear your life apart."

Michael looked over at Calvin who didn't return his gaze.

The DCI continued. "I started off small with your visit to Washington D.C. Your name wasn't found on any flight manifests. Sure, there's a chance that you traveled under another name."

A new video popped up that tracked Thomas and Emily's movements at Dulles International.

"And yet you didn't arrive with your family. That doesn't mean much but it's interesting nevertheless. Moving on."

The screen displayed a video of Richard being led into a conference room.

Oh shit.

"Sir, you assured my son that that room was clean of surveillance."

"That's a moot issue at this point, don't you think."

The video continued to play.

"This is my favorite part," said the DCI.

On the screen Michael suddenly appeared out of thin air and Richard jumped as it happened.

Michael shifted uncomfortably in his seat. "Where did this come from? Who has seen it?"

"Why don't you let me worry about that Michael."

Goddammit.

The video continued to play.

"And then there's this part."

On the screen a woman appeared. Richard was shocked but his attitude eventually changed.

"Enough," said Michael.

"Just one more. Bear with me."

The screen changed once again. What played were two angles of the interrogation room. They clearly showed Michael, Thomas and Emily in the room with Jonathan Lane, Yuri's protégé and IT Specialist. The audio kicked in.

"Who's there!? Where am I!? Do you know who I work for!?" Jonathan yelled from beneath the dark hood over his head. He'd found his voice again.

"We don't have much time Mr. Lane."

Jonathan stiffened.

Thomas watched as Emily approached. She stood ready.

Michael continued. "I'm going to set the stage for you Mr. Lane. After that you're going to tell me absolutely everything."

"What's this about? Leave me alone. I'm nobody."

"You warned Frank Russell, also known as Yuri, to an impending attack. The message you sent used a prerecorded message that contained the word Firestorm."

"You have the wrong person!"

Michael continued to ignore Jonathan's outbursts. "Now for my question. Who do you work for?"

Emily touched Jonathan's bare arm with her hand. He immediately stiffened.

"Who do you work for?" the little girl asked.

"I work for Frank Russell."

"Are you a spy?" Emily repeated her grandfather's question.

"Yes."

"What is your name?"

"My name is Jonathan Lane. I was born Stefan Nikolaev."

"How long have you been a spy?"

"Ever since I can remember. We were all raised to become spies."

Thomas pointed at his wristwatch and his father nodded.

"Who raised you?"

"Nikolay Dmietriev. He saved us from the orphanages. He's our father."

"Where is Frank Russell?"

"I don't know."

"Do you have a way of contacting him?"

"Yes."

"Are there other spies working within Langley?"

"Yes."

Bill opened the door to the room. "The team just arrived. Thirty seconds."

Michael didn't ask a question this time. Instead he had Emily make a request for him.

"You will cooperate fully." Emily did her magic.

"I will cooperate fully."

Emily stepped back and rejoined her father just as the four man interrogation team the DCI had sent arrived. Two members moved to remove Jonathan.

The screen turned off.

Michael glared at Calvin. "That camera feed was turned off for a reason. Do you have any idea what you've done?"

"My job."

"Focus Michael," said the DCI over the headset. "No need to get hotheaded."

Michael gritted his teeth. "You don't know what you're getting yourself involved with. Leave it alone."

It was as if the DCI hadn't heard him. "You know, the common denominator seems to be your granddaughter Emily."

"You leave her the fuck alone."

"So this is what's going to happen Michael. You're going to fill me in on exactly what I just watched."

"Like hell."

"Are you sure that's what your answer is? We're allies, you and I. We're on the same side. From where I'm sitting all I can see is enormous potential."

I royally screwed up. Why was I so stupid? How did I not see this coming?

Michael took a deep breath. "Sir, you need to back off, permanently delete what you just showed me and pretend you never saw any of it...ever."

"I see. I assume that's for my own protection?"

"No. For my family's."

"I don't think so. I will leave you with this gem though. Michael, if you tell anyone about our conversation I will rip your granddaughter away from you so quickly it'll leave your head spinning. On top of that, you, your family are now prohibited from leaving the TOC. Consider yourself my guests."

"You...you can't do that!"

"The order had already been given. Curtis will not hesitate to use lethal force. I'm sure you understand."

"Goddammit!"

"Now," continued the DCI, "I'd suggest getting back to work. Nikolay is still out there and he's our primary concern."

Michael seethed but remained silent.

"Can I take your silence as a yes?"

Fuck.

"Yes. I won't say anything. Don't hurt my granddaughter."

"Excellent. I'll leave you to it then." The line went dead.

Oh my God. What have I done?

Michael took off the headset and gently laid it down. He got up from his chair and slowly walked back to the table.

"Everything okay pop?" asked Thomas.

Michael forced a smile. "Yep. Everything's fine."

At that moment a new message popped up on Hobbes' screen. He read it and then joined the group.

"An alert just came in. Another phone call was made to Nikolay that bounced through the same satellite that's orbiting Cuba."

"Did it give us a solid location?"

"Yes and no. They were able to track that the call originated right here in D.C."

"Do they have an address?" asked Richard.

"Yes, which actually doesn't seem to make much sense actually."

"Why's that?"

"The call originated from a landline rather than from a satellite phone."

"Maybe whoever called Nikolay got sloppy," said Thomas. "What about the destination? Did they pinpoint Nikolay's location?"

Hobbes shook his head. "The transmission was quick but it does point to the west side of Cuba."

"At least we're closing in."

Michael finally spoke up. "Get Sam on the phone so they can pay that address a visit."

* * *

Victor Bannon, the DCI, terminated the conference call with Michael Clark.

I wonder what all of it means. Can Michael turn invisible? Is that how it works? But how'd that female suddenly appear in the conference room? I don't understand. And what about the child? There's something special about her that's for sure. It really appeared as if she bent Jonathan Lane's will.

He began to jot down notes on his legal pad. He consolidated what he knew and his theories. He didn't stop until he had six full pages. The DCI ripped them off his pad and stapled them together. On the top of the first page he wrote a title. Psychological Operations. Below that he made a shortened version. PsyOps.

D.W. Neuman

46
Friday November 14, 1997 10:15am

"We're so close to catching Nikolay that I can practically taste it," said Richard.

Thomas, Michael and Richard sat at the large table in the Tactical Operations Center. Emily put down some toys she was playing with and wandered over as Curtis lingered by the secure doorway that led out to the warehouse.

"Daddy?"

Thomas pulled her up to sit on his lap. "What's up cutie?"

"I don't feel good. I want to go home."

"Are you feeling okay?" He felt his daughter's forehead. "You're a little warm. Maybe I should have a doctor take a look at you."

"I'll go with you," said Richard. "I haven't seen much of the outside and we could definitely use a break."

"What'ya say pop? Care to stretch your legs?"

Michael knew what his son meant. He couldn't exactly remain here if Emily traveled out of her range. "Sounds like a plan. Let's go have my granddaughter checked out."

Michael and Richard got up from their chairs. Thomas hefted Emily up and she put her arms around her father's neck. All four of them walked towards the secured door towards Curtis.

"Hey Curtis, my daughter's not feeling well. We're going to go see a doctor."

"I'm afraid not."

Puzzled looks crossed everyone's face but Michael's.

"What do you mean? I don't understand," said Thomas.

"Stand aside," Michael ordered.

355

Curtis, in one smooth motion, chambered a round and brought his rifle up. That action caused the group to step back.

"My apologies but I have my orders."

"Orders from whom? The Director?"

Curtis didn't reply.

Thomas stepped forward with Emily in his arms. "My daughter is sick goddammit, get out of our way!"

Curtis aimed his weapon. "Step back sir. Do it!"

Thomas had little choice but to move away.

"No one is leaving this facility. If you attempt to come near this door, myself, or the two technicians, I will not hesitate to shoot. Now go sit down. I'll have some medicine delivered."

There was nothing they could do. They didn't have any weapons and were effectively trapped. With little choice they moved back to the table and sat down. Thomas held onto Emily as she rested her head on his shoulder.

"What the hell is going on?"

"Whatever it is this can't bode well for us," said Richard.

Michael spoke up. "Listen. I just had a conference call with the DCI. He knows."

"What?" said Thomas. "What do you mean he knows? Knows what?"

"He had me watch a few surveillance feeds." Michael described what happened during the meeting.

"That sonofabitch."

"I don't think he has a full picture of what's going on but he's certainly on the right track. He wants Emily." Michael looked around the enclosed TOC. "And from the looks of it he currently has his wish."

"And the two techs?" asked Richard.

"They've been working for him the entire time, peeling apart our lives like bloodhounds."

"We have to get in contact with Sam and Bill. They'll get us out of here."

"They're not going to let us near a phone, let alone let us talk to them," said Michael. He paused before he continued. "I can't believe I didn't see this coming."

"You're not the only one pop; you're not the only one." Thomas held Emily close and began to stroke her hair.

Think Thomas think.

D.W. Neuman

<u>47</u>

Friday November 14, 1997 11:00am

Sam and Bill, along with Alpha, Bravo and Charlie teams screeched to a halt in the parking lot outside the supplied address. As the eight men piled out of the two Suburban's they took a look at their objective. The two story building, located just outside the city limits, had plywood over the windows and entrance. The establishment had been a bar but right now it definitely looked abandoned.

"You sure this is the right place?" Bill asked.

"No shit. This doesn't feel right," replied Sam. He turned to the team. "Okay, I don't know what we're about to walk into here but we have a job to do. Since this place used to be a bar we're all going in the front, nice and slow. No more surprises. Questions? No? Alright then, let's do this."

Everyone put their game face on and quickly rechecked their gear. Once satisfied, they moved in two columns, four men deep, with weapons up towards the front entrance. As they moved each of them covered a different attack zone. At the bar's front door Sam made the crowbar signal towards the plywood and Bravo Two shouldered his weapon and extracted an all-in-one tool. Sam gave the signal and he applied pressure. The board popped off, fell face down onto the walkway and revealed the glass door behind it.

"Careful."

Bill took a quick peek through the glass door and pulled his head back. "I don't see anything attached to the door. No movement either."

"Roger that. Check to see if it's unlocked."

Bill gently pushed on the door handle and it swung inward a couple of inches. He looked over at Sam. "Dynamic entry?"

Sam shook his head. "No. No flash bangs. We go as planned."

The team readied itself. Two seconds later Bill pushed open the door and led the charge. The other seven team members followed right on his heels.

Alpha and Bravo team peeled left.

Sam and Bill moved straight in towards the bar counter.

Charlie team flanked right to cover.

Each team member, with their weapons up, hunted for threats as they cleared their assigned areas. All eight men easily swept through the entire first floor, clearing out the bar, kitchen, bathroom and storage areas within twenty seconds.

"I've got nothing."

"Ditto. No contacts."

"Moving upstairs."

Bill led the way slowly up the stairs, from the main area, and watched for movement, booby traps or any other threat. He crested the landing and discovered it was another large space that, at one time, must have contained a number of tables.

"There's nowhere to hide up here," he called down the stairs. "It's just a big loft."

"Roger that. Come on down and let's figure out our next course of action."

Bill, and the other team members, retraced their steps back to the main bar area. They had lowered their weapons but kept them ready.

Sam motioned Bill over to him. "Thoughts?"

"I don't know. Someone might have been here but I'm just not seeing any evidence of it."

"It doesn't add up."

Rinnnnnng.

The sound of a phone ringing from behind the bar caught everyone off guard. Weapons instantly came up.

Rinnnnnng.

Bill sidestepped to the end of the bar, where it was open. Everyone else stood their ground, ready.

Rinnnnnng.

Bill inched his way behind the bar until he saw the phone. It was tucked under the counter at the very end.

Rinnnnnng.

He made his way towards the phone and scanned everything with his eyes. Nothing seemed out of place.

Rinnnnnng.

He squatted down and took a look at the device. The phone sat on an empty shelf with a single phone cord that extended out of the wall.

Rinnnnnng.

Bill gently placed both hands on either side of the phone and gently picked it up.

Rinnnnnng.

He pulled it out from underneath the counter and placed it on the bar top.

Rinnnnnng.

Bill shrugged. Sam strode over and picked it up.

"Who is this?" he demanded.

"It's about time you answered Mr. Paige."

Sam's face contorted. "Who is this?"

"Don't be naïve. While I know you're not the brains behind this operation, we both do know that you're just the muscle, now don't we?"

"Hello Nikolay."

Bill and the other team member's jaws dropped.

"Hello Sam."

Bill motioned to the other team members to check the front and back entrances for any new threats.

"So what do I owe the pleasure?"

"You're part of the crusade to take me down. I admit, watching my handiwork unfold on CNN has been absolutely delightful."

Sam's hand turned white when he gripped the phone tighter.

Nikolay continued. "But the reason I called was to tell you that you're too late."

"Too late for what?"

"You're too late to stop the game of course."

"Have we been playing a game Nikolay?"

"No. Certainly not between you and me Sam. Apparently you're too stupid to realize what I'm saying so I'll just go ahead and tell you. You're just a pawn. My chess game will come to its inevitable conclusion long after you've been removed from the playing field. Goodbye Mr. Paige."

Sam let go of the phone and yelled.

"MOOOOOVVVVEEEEE!!"

It felt as if his legs weren't fast enough.

Bill turned towards Sam, away from the front door, when Sam yelled.

Brave One and Two also began to turn their heads.

The phone hit the counter and toppled off behind the bar.

Bravo Two finished swiveling his head.

Bill completed his turn just as Sam plowed into him.

The momentum carried Bill, Sam and Bravo Two through the covered front window just as the bar exploded.

* * *

"Report in!" Sam yelled into his throat mike.

"Alpha and Charlie team...no injuries."

"Come to the front!"

"Fucking shit!" yelled Bill. "Get off me!"

"Talk to me."

"I'd be a lot better if you got your heavy ass off of me."

Sam rolled off the two men and landed on the glass littered concrete. Bravo Two didn't move and Sam checked on him. He didn't find any bleeding and his pulse was strong.

Good. He's just knocked out.

He stood up and looked around for Bravo One. Sam now saw his crumbled form a second later. Bravo One was laying face up halfway out of the bar's entrance. Sam rushed over.

Bravo One's body seemed to float in a pool of his blood. The number of injuries he'd sustained from the glass was absolutely staggering. It was as if his body had absorbed every bit of the front door as he was propelled though it. Blood continued to ooze out from beneath him. His face, surprisingly, only contained a couple of scratches. Sam immediately knew there was nothing he could do.

Sam knelt down and took Bravo One's left hand in his own. Before Sam could say anything it gripped him.

Bravo One's eyes popped open and focused on Sam.

"You're going to be okay," said Sam as he tried to reassure him.

"Bull...shit. You were...always...a...bad liar," Bravo One said as his life force pooled out of him. His eyes changed. "Tell....tell..my wife that I lov..."

Sam watched as his team member died. His vacant eyes remained open and focused on Sam's.

Goddammit. God fucking dammit.

He gently placed the man's hand back on the ground and carefully closed the soldier's open eyes.

"Shit," said Bill behind him. "Motherfucker."

Damn you Nikolay. Damn you.

48

Friday November 14, 1997 1:00pm

Charles and Alice Brown walked around the Los Angeles Zoo for their very first time. They were a young couple, in their mid-thirties, and were longtime residents of LA but, for whatever reason, had never once visited the zoo. As they walked through the various enclosures they held each other's hands. They smiled as they enjoyed the variety of wonders the zoo offered.

Throngs of children, led by a few teachers, wound their way towards the monkey enclosure. They all gawked and pointed as the animals jumped from tree to tree while using the variety of ropes to effortlessly maneuver around their cage. Charles and Alice stood farther back and smiled. After a few minutes the teachers herded the children towards the next enclosure.

"Why don't we go that way," said Charles and pointed to the opposite direction the stampeding group had departed.

"Good idea," Alice replied. "I'd hate to be one of those teachers right now."

"You and me both."

The couple giggled and moved up the path towards the tigers. When they arrived they read the information plaque and then gazed out over the ten foot drop in front of them. Alice pointed at one of the tigers that was relaxing under a tree in the back. Two others wrestled with each other, playfully swiping at each other's rear ends while they tussled.

"Oh daddy daddy! Do you see them!? They're playing!" exclaimed a little girl a few feet to their left.

Charles and Alice looked over at the excited girl and watched her point at the felines.

"I see them honey," replied her father.

"They're soooo cute."

Her mother and father both smiled at their daughter's energy level.

Alice walked over with Charles in tow.

"Excuse me."

The two adults turned their heads.

"Yes?"

"I'm sorry to intrude. I just wanted to say that your daughter is just adorable."

"Why thank you," replied the girl's mother.

"Don't mind my wife," said Charles. "We've been trying for a child of our own."

The woman laughed. "Oh I don't mind. Little Lisa is our own little slice of heaven."

Charles extended his right hand. "I didn't mean to be rude. My name is Sebastian Rogers. This is my wife Cynthia."

The man took his hand. "Nick Raynes. My wife Susan and our daughter Lisa. Nice to meet you."

"Nice to meet you as well."

"Now they're playing tug of war! I want a tiger." Lisa pulled on her father's pant leg. "Daddy, listen to me."

"Sorry." Nick bent down. "Sweetie, I don't think the zoo will let us take one home with us. Besides, where would it stay?"

Lisa didn't miss a beat. "It can stay in my room."

"I thought that's where the unicorn was going to live."

"They can be friends."

"I see!" Nick said as he stifled a smile. "Tell you what; why don't you watch them play for a bit while we have a talk with these nice people?"

"Okay." Lisa went back to watching the tigers run around after each other.

Nick stood up. "So where were we?"

Charles pointed over Nick's shoulder. "Do you know that man? He seems to be waving at you."

Nick and Susan both turned to where Charles had pointed.

Charles took that opportunity to chop the back of Nick's neck and it sent Nick to his knees.

"Oof."

At the same instant Alice grabbed Lisa.

"Stop it!" yelled Lisa.

"Wha.." Susan was stunned. She did the only thing that came natural to her. She screamed.

Other zoo patrons stood mesmerized as the commotion unfolded around them.

Charles then kicked Nick in his side, heard a rib crack and turned on Susan.

Susan's scream was cut short when Charles backhanded her. She stumbled backwards, dazed.

Alice lifted Lisa up and tossed her over the low fence into the empty concrete moat that surrounded the enclosure.

Lisa vertically traveled ten feet to the concrete below. There was a sickening crack. She didn't move.

Susan had recovered enough and witnessed her daughter being thrown over the railing.

"LIIISSSAAA!"

People couldn't believe what they'd just witnessed and finally a couple of them ran over.

Charles and Alice fled from the scene.

"THERE'S A CHILD IN THE TIGER PEN!"

* * *

In the closest bathroom the two of them removed their wigs, turned their reversible jackets inside out and took separate paths towards the zoo exits.

Alexei sat in his car, in the parking lot, and watched as the Russian sleeper agents individually exited the zoo's entrance. Charles combed back his hair as he walked.

There's the signal. Success.

Alexei started up the car and slowly pulled out of the zoo parking lot.

49
Friday November 14, 1997 1:17pm

Rinnngg.

The kitchen phone rang and Laura picked it up.

"Thomas?" All she heard was crying on the other end.

"Hello?"

Sniffles. "Laura? Is that you? I just hit redial on Nick's phone. Please tell me it's you Laura."

"Yes, it is. Who is this?"

The woman was hysterical. "Oh my God! Laura! I don't know what to do! Lisa was thrown into the tiger cage! We were attacked!"

Laura's mind raced. "Wait? Susan? Is that you?"

More crying. "Idon'tknowwhattodo." She was mumbling incoherently. "Idon'tknowwhattodo."

Laura took charge. "Susan. Listen to me. What happened? Are you alright?"

"I can't...I just can't..." Susan pulled the phone away from her face. "GET MY LITTLE GIRL OUT OF THERE!"

Laura heard Susan screaming her head off followed by the sound of the phone as it hit the pavement.

What the hell is going on? "Hello? Susan? Hello?"

"SAVE HER GODDAMMIT!"..."Ma'am...please calm down. We're doing everything we can."

"Hello? Hello?"

A new voice came on the line. "Hello?"

"Who is this? Where's Susan?" Laura demanded.

"I'm sorry ma'am. There's been an incident. Are you family?"

"Excuse me?"

"I asked if you were family ma'am."

"Yes. Now tell me what's happening. Who are you?"

"I'm just a zoo ranger. This woman's…"

"Her name is Susan Raynes."

"I see. Well, her daughter was just thrown into the tiger pen."

"What!? Did you just say thrown?"

"That's what everyone here is talking about."

"Is Lisa okay? Did they get her out?"

"That's happening as we speak ma'am. The tigers came over and sniffed her but left her alone. The handlers were able to lure them away. The park medics are working on her now. She's still unconscious but appears to have a broken leg."

"Oh my God."

"I need to go."

"No. Wait." Laura held the phone to her ear but all she heard was a dial tone.

* * *

"Is it done?" Nikolay asked.

"Before I left the zoo I watched them do it myself. The Raynes family was attacked and the little girl was thrown into the tiger's pen."

"Excellent. Will she live?"

"I do not have that information."

"No matter. That should send a clear message that fucking with me is a bad idea. Now, where are you with the next stage?"

"It's doable, of course, but I don't like the timing or the location."

"Just get it done Alexei.

"You know me. I'll take care of it."

"I know you will." Nikolay smiled on the other end. "And be glad that you're going to be well clear of D.C. tomorrow. I've waited years for this day to happen but even now I find it's difficult to wait even one more."

"Your patience and planning, as always, will be rewarded," said Alexei.

"As will your dedication to me." The line went dead.

* * *

Alexei, and five other men, boarded a Los Angeles flight bound for Hawaii.

D.W. Neuman

50
Friday November 14, 1997 4:00pm

Rinngg.

"Hello?"

"Hey Jules."

"It's really good to hear your voice Sam. I miss you."

"I miss you too. I love you."

Julie smiled. "I like that. Say it again."

"I love you."

"I love you too Sam." She got serious. "How're you doing?"

"I'm good. I'm surprised you picked up the phone. I expected you to be over at Laura's."

"We would be but there was an incident yesterday."

"What do you mean there was an incident?"

"One of your men mistook Stir for a wild animal and shot him."

"What? Really? Shit. Is Stir okay?"

"As far as anyone can tell. Gavin was beside himself of course. But Stir woke up, or whatever he does, and was fine. Laura needed some time for them to just chill out so we're all back at our own places for the time being."

"Interesting. Do you know if Thomas has heard about this?"

Julie shrugged. "I don't know. I don't think so. She didn't mention that Thomas called. She definitely would have because Nick Raynes family was attacked at the zoo earlier today."

"Wait. What?"

"Apparently their daughter was tossed in the tiger's pen or something. Laura gave me a quick rundown. She doesn't have a number to contact Thomas. She's stressing out."

"I hear you. I'll check in with him, see what's going on and have him give Laura a call."

"Perfect. Thank you. How's everything going out there?"

"That's one of the reasons I called. Did you catch the news last night?"

"Of course. Kim and I watch it every night. Why? Were you involved in that building explosion?"

"Yes, I'm afraid so."

Julie shifted uncomfortably. "Sam, you sound funny. I know you can't talk about things but please tell me that you're okay."

"Bill and I are fine."

"But…"

"Jules, most of us got out in time. I lost David Thompson. He died right in front of me."

"I'm so sorry Sam."

There was a long pause. "Me too."

"What can I do?"

"I don't think there's anything you can do. We're getting close to nailing this sonofabitch. My goal is to make sure our families will be safe."

"Me too. The kids and I just want you home again."

"That's the plan sweetie, that's the plan. Speaking of the kids, how're they holding up?"

"As strange as it is to admit they're getting used to the men guarding us. I don't know if that's a good or bad thing. Aside from that it's still Hawaii. We have the sun, pool, beach and the ocean. They're keeping busy. It's you I worry about."

"I'll be home soon enough and we'll take our own vacation, just the two of us."

Julie smiled. "That sounds delightful. You know I'm going to hold you to that."

Sam chuckled. "You wouldn't be you if you didn't. I love you Jules. I'll talk to you later. Bye."

"Bye Sam. Be careful."

D.W. Neuman

51
Friday November 14, 1997 5:00pm

The computer beeped. Calvin pushed his screen to the large overhead.

"Looks like the NSA caught another transmission to Nikolay and used it to pinpoint its location. We might have a target. Accessing the satellite for imaging." He began to type. "Inputting coordinates." More typing. "That should do it."

A new image appeared on the large overhead screen. Richard and Michael walked over. Thomas continued to cradle Emily in his arms. Despite the medicine she'd ingested her fever hadn't broken.

"Not too close," Curtis warned.

"Relax, we know," said Michael.

They both watched as the island of Cuba magically appeared. The satellite zoomed in, sector by sector, at the coordinates requested on the southeast portion of the island. The clarity was uncanny.

"That's downright scary," said Richard.

"Are you kidding," said Hobbes. "It's great for looking at the nude beaches all over the world."

They just stared at him.

"Well...I mean...if one was to do that."

The image on the screen froze and hovered at five hundred feet above the ground.

"Well look at what we have here," said Calvin.

The sprawling compound, from a bird's eye view, contained two major structures, walls and four towers. It rested on top of small hill that overlooked the ocean to both the east and the south.

"Nice vacation rental," Hobbes joked.

"No shit," replied Calvin. "Let's see what else is going on."

Calvin zoomed in closer as everyone watched. The image settled at two hundred feet above the ground.

"Are those people moving?" asked Richard.

Hobbes nodded. He typed a few keys. "The computer estimates twelve targets."

"But those are the visible targets, right?" asked Michael.

"Correct. We should assume there could be more inside both structures."

"Zooming in for a closer look."

The image changed once again and stopped twenty feet above two men. They were talking to each other and both carried AK-47's.

"That's definitely not a vacation rental," commented Hobbes.

Calvin spoke up. "Those guys look pretty serious. Combine that with what appears to be guard towers, along with the number of men we've seen, I have to assume that the secondary building is the guard's barracks. I think we found Nikolay's base of operations."

"I'd have to concur," said Michael.

"Good. I'll get the DCI on the horn."

* * *

"What's your confidence level?" The DCI spoke from his Langley office.

"Extremely high. Ninety percent sir," replied Calvin. "We've got a guarded and very secluded compound sitting on top a defensible hilltop. There are only twelve guards that we've seen so we can comfortably double that number to twenty four. The NSA tracked the satellite phone signal to this exact location. The only thing we haven't been able to confirm is that Nikolay

Dmitriev is actually onsite. That's why it's only a ninety percent recommendation."

"I see. Michael. Richard. What about you two?"

"Go to hell."

"Temper temper Michael. You can't tell me that after thirty long years you're not the least bit interested in taking Nikolay down?"

Silence.

"Regardless of what you might think of me I do have this country's best intentions in mind."

"You mean by holding us prisoner against our will? Go ahead and feed me another line of your bullshit."

"You need to focus on the task at hand. Everything else will work itself out in time. Get Mr. Paige on the line and make sure your end is muted."

"Yes sir." Hobbes dialed up a new number and muted his side.

"Yes?" said Sam as he joined the conversation.

"Mr. Paige. This is the DCI."

"What can I do for you sir?"

"We have a hard target for you. It appears we've located Nikolay. I need your team to deploy right away."

"Cuba sir?"

"That's right."

"You have a way in and a way out for us?"

"Get your team to Andrews Air Force Base asap. There's a C-130 Hercules that's been prepped and is waiting for your arrival. Your gear will be onboard. Are you and your team up for a night drop?"

"You'd better believe it sir."

"Excellent. On the way you'll have time to go over the satellite images and form a plan of attack. I can't emphasize the necessity of bringing Nikolay back alive."

"I understand sir."

"Good. Any questions?"

"Just a request. I need to talk to Thomas."

Calvin unmuted his headset. "I can give him a message for you Mr. Paige. Emily's sick and he's at the doctor's with her."

Sam paused before he responded. "I see. Would you tell him to call home? His wife needs to speak with him."

"I'll do that."

52

Friday November 14, 1997 11:45pm

The C-130 was waiting for the seven operators when they arrived at Andrews AFB. Sam, Bill and the other five SANDBOX members boarded the plane, it was immediately cleared, and taxied down the runway. It took off and headed south towards Cuba that was 1200 miles away.

The huge Hercules briefly landed at MacDill AFB in southern Florida, on the coast of the Gulf of Mexico before taking off again. Soon after that the C-130 took up a SSW course, in a commercial flight path, and squawked as passenger airliner. To any radar installation tracking the plane it would appear as if it was on a direct course to Cancun, Mexico. The C-130 would pass within fifty miles of Cuba's northwest coast.

The DCI hadn't shortchanged their equipment load out whatsoever so Sam and his team had all the bells and whistles at their disposal to gear up with. Each operator dressed in a full black outfit that would double as a wet suit. On top of that suit they wore tactical vests outfitted with smoke, flash, fragmentation grenades and a knife. Radios fit in their backs and were wired to their throat mikes. Suppressed 9mm pistols protruded from thigh holsters along with additional magazines for it on their right leg. The left leg carrier held additional MP5 thirty rounds magazines. Night vision goggles, or NVG's, hung around their necks along with their suppressed MP5SD 9mm sub machine guns.

* * *

Before they geared up they had all taken a look at the packet of satellite photos that had been left for them.

"What'ya think?" said Sam over the roar of the engines.

"Nikolay's compound in Pasa de Marin is an interesting place," replied Bill. "We have to successfully get there first. I hope the prevailing winds are on our side or it's going to be a long swim."

Sam nodded along with some of the other team members. "I was thinking the same thing. I'll have our pilot verve off course ten miles or so. That should give us more room to work with. Anything else?"

"Attempting to land on the compound is too risky. Too many things can go wrong and we'd lose the element of surprise. I think a water entry followed by an assault from the beach is our best course of action. There are just too many trees around his property to land any closer, or any safer."

"Agreed." Sam pointed to a stretch of water just south of the compound. "This is our point of ingress. Set your global positioning to the following coordinates." Each man looked at the large watch-like device on his left wrist and punched in the numbers Sam gave them.

"Now, as for the enemy, our understanding is that they're most likely ex-Spetsnaz and KGB. We're grossly out-numbered but we have a job to do. Our target is Nikolay Dmitriev. He's seventy-seven and should be located in this building." Sam pointed at the larger of the two structures provided by a satellite photo. "As a reminder, he's our primary target and needs to be taken alive. Now, prior to that we'll have to neutralize the four guard towers, the barracks and any resistance inside the main house. We're seven men going up against an estimated twenty-four. The only thing we'll have on our side is the element of surprise, the dark, speed and violence of action."

"And a little luck," Bill added.

* * *

All seven team member's headsets crackled. "Sorry about that," said Calvin. "I had to synchronize the encryption."

"Is there something you wanted to add Calvin?" Sam asked. "We're a little busy getting ready."

"Trust me. You'll want me in your ear when the time comes."

"And why's that?" asked Bill.

"Because when it comes to killing the enemy we're going to cheat."

* * *

Each of the seven SANDBOX operators had donned a parachute, enclosed helmet and a respirator system. Flippers were tapped to their legs. Watches were synchronized and every man double checked his gear to make sure it was secured. If something fell off after exiting the plane they'd be shit out of luck. This team knew they were on their own once they jumped.

Forty miles off the coast of Cuba the C-130's rear door lowered five and a half miles above the earth.

"Final comm check," Sam ordered.

"Eagle Two," said Bill.

"Alpha One."

"Alpha Two."

"Bravo One."

"Charlie One."

"Charlie Two."

"Eagle One," said Sam, "I read everyone five by five."

The red light above the loading door began to blink.

"Stay tight, in formation and keep your eyes on your GPS. The last thing you want is to be left out here all by yourself."

The seven men huddled together with an arm on another man's shoulder. The red light stopped and changed to solid green.

"Let's do this thing!" Sam yelled.

As a group they jumped out the back of the C-130 and into the pitch black night. The roar of the plane quickly faded as they plummeted towards the ocean below. Each member immediately fanned out in their own direction. They had only been out of the plane for five seconds when Sam yelled the command.

"PULL!"

Each man released his primary chute and then looked up to make sure it extended properly.

"Eagle Two, good chute."

"Alpha One, good chute."

"Alpha Two, good chute."

"Bravo One, good chute."

"Charlie One, good chute."

"Charlie Two, good chute."

So far so good. Thank God for the little things.

"Roger that. Check GPS and follow me in. We've got some significant hang time ahead of us gentlemen. Stay vigilant."

Five miles up seven black parachutes glided through the night, invisible and deadly. With each passing minute they drifted closer and closer to Cuba. Each man kept checking his GPS and updated the direction his steerable parachute was pointed. Winds buffeted the group around and pushed them off their target more times than they could remember. Minor course corrections were constantly made as they drifted towards the distant lights of like birds. During their initial fifty minute descent each man checked to make sure his gear hadn't dislodged. Every few minutes they all checked in to verify they were on course. In the dark they just couldn't see each other.

They passed over Guadiana Bay and then over the town of Manuel Lazo towards their Caribbean Sea water landing. Two members had lost more altitude than the others and their feet came dangerously close to touching the tops of the jungle before the land pitched down to the sea. The ocean wind gave them enough lift to bank left and parallel the beach a mere five hundred feet off the southern coastline.

"One minute," said Sam.

Each man ripped his flippers off his leg, put them on and then immediately concentrated on the upcoming water landing.

"Thirty seconds."

Heading east seven parachutes descended out of the night sky one after another. Each man held his respirator to his mouth as he splashed down to make sure it didn't jar loose. As soon as each man hit the water he immediately hit the parachute release, kicked twenty feet in the direction he'd hit and surfaced clear of the floating entanglement. The sea was relatively calm. The red lights that emanated from each man's helmet allowed them to quickly gather together in the water. They'd all made it.

Sam pointed towards the beach five hundred feet away. The group submerged and swam together into shore just underneath the surface. Just as they neared the shore they collectively stopped. Bill continued forward and rode a small wave right onto the deserted beach. He knelt in the sand and let his respirator fall from his mouth. He put on his night vision goggles as he detached his MP5 from his chest rig where it had remained secure. He scanned the beach. It was empty. The only sounds were the waves constantly lapping up against the shore.

"Clear," said Bill.

He kept watch as the remaining six members made their way to him. Then, as a team, they moved to the tree line where they discarded their flippers, helmets and respirators.

"I've got you on satellite," said Calvin. "Nice clean insertion."

"Fantastic," replied Sam. "Use the comm for something actually useful and tell me how far away we are."

"Right. Sorry. You're about three thousand feet south of the compound's outer wall. You'll need to make your way north up the mountain side."

"Roger that. Radio silence from everyone from this point on until otherwise ordered. Let's go."

The seven member team silently moved out and began their trek up the mountain.

* * *

Nikolay couldn't sleep nor did he want to. His end game would come to its fruition in a matter of hours. His years of planning and waiting were coming to a head. He was excited.

He spoke out loud in his office. "They will pay. I will watch them burn and I won't be able to stop laughing."

He giggled as he fingered his favorite Russian Makarov pistol that lay on the desk in front of him. He'd owned it for decades.

"Yes, the world will finally know the power and foresight I possess. They'll realize that no one is safe, especially the Americans."

He picked up his satellite phone, dialed and waited for the encryption handshake.

"This is my final acknowledgement. Report."

"Everything's set on our end sir."

"I'm glad to hear that." He paused. "Steve, the most American name I know of. You were one of the best students I ever had. I could tell, even at a young age, that you were a true believer. You wanted to hurt America just as much as I did. I could see it in your eyes. Now, you have been given the opportunity to do just that. Do not squander it. I will not accept failure."

"No sir. The switch-out is scheduled for early in the morning. There has been no indication that our plans are in danger."

Nikolay smiled. "Very good. Continue on and God bless."

"It's been an honor working for you sir."

"I know it has." He thumbed the end button and put the phone down.

I can't wait to see how the world reacts when America's President steps aboard his helicopter, Marine One, in the morning for the very last time.

* * *

Making their way up the mountain had taken longer than they'd planned. The first two thousand feet they'd bee-lined straight up the mountain without worrying too much about their noise level. However, the last thousand feet they'd they made sure they took their time, stepping over anything noisy that might give them away as they remained hidden. The good news was that this was a night mission. Surprise is everything.

Sam stopped his team three hundred feet from the southern wall. Two guard towers, one on each corner, were visible. Bill pulled out his binoculars, zoomed in and whispered.

"Two men in each tower. Looks like they're bored. They're smoking. Too bad for them."

Sam nodded and whispered into his mike. "Calvin, what have you got for us?"

"I've been watching the compound feed since you exited the C-130. Confirming two men in each of the four towers. There are also two roaming the grounds, individually, and two more at the front gate. That's twelve up and active that I can verify."

"Roger that. Right now we'll assume the rest are sleeping in the barracks or in the main house."

Calvin responded. "I saw a guard change earlier. Two of them headed inside the main house while the rest went to the barracks."

"Fine. That's doable. Splitting the team and heading out to our pre-assigned waypoints."

"I've got you on satellite. I'll guide you in just like a video game."

"Did that fucker just say that this is a video game?" Bill said without transmitting.

"Fuck Calvin. Get your head in the game brother."

Sam gave the signal to move out and the team split in two. Sam and Bill, along with Alpha One and Two, quietly made their way towards the east side of the wall. Bravo One, Charlie One and Charlie Two began to creep to the west side of the wall.

Calvin, and everyone else back at the TOC, watched the events unfold in real time through the overhead satellite feed. Calvin had switched the view to infrared thermal long ago. The compound, up on the screen, appeared in black and white. Any heat source was brightly illuminated. They observed the guards as they moved around in real time. It was uncanny and it seemed like cheating. But war is war.

As Emily slept on the couch Calvin, Hobbes, Michael, Richard and Thomas watched on as four team members branched right. The other three branched off to the left amongst the dark jungle.

* * *

"All sections report in," said the voice over the walkie-talkie.

Sam watched though his NVG as one of the guards at the gate pulled a radio off his belt to reply.

"Gate secure."

"Tower One secure."

"Tower two secure."

"Tower three secure."

"Tower four secure."

"West courtyard secure."

"East courtyard secure."

"Nothing to report from the main house. All secure."

"Thirty minutes until the next check-in," the walkie squawked.

The two guards at the gate looked around one last time before they picked up their conversation again. One held his AK-47 in both hands while the other guard had his weapon slung over his shoulder. It was bad tradecraft, but they were obviously bored of guard work and overconfident.

Guarding Nikolay was nowhere near as rewarding as what they used to do for a living. But those days were over, and they knew it. The Soviet Union had collapsed under its own mismanagement. The people rose up and their voices were heard. Many of the Special Forces Spetsnaz, not to mention members of the KGB, had fled the Soviet Union while they had the opportunity. Nikolay had provided such a lucrative opportunity.

"I wish I had some vodka to help pass the time."

"I know what you mean."

"Don't get me wrong. I appreciate everything Nikolay's done for me, but I'm so bored of this shit."

The other guard shrugged. "The money's good. What else do you see yourself doing?"

"I don't know. Maybe go into the mercenary business."

"Really?"

"Or maybe visit Hollywood and get a part in a movie."

Both guards laughed at the thought. At least their lives ended on a high note.

* * *

Alpha One and Two had each inched their way along the side of the east wall towards the main entrance to the compound. They had their silence pistols at the ready. Sam and Bill knelt just inside the edge of the jungle next to the road to provide a flanking angle. They had their weapons up and both guards were in their weapon sights.

"I don't know. Maybe go into the mercenary business."

"Really?"

"Or maybe visit Hollywood and get a part in a movie." They both laughed.

"You're clear," said Calvin.

Alpha One and Two silently pushed away from the outer compound wall at the same time. Alpha One knelt down while Alpha Two stood directly behind him. Both of their suppressed pistols were up and fired milliseconds apart.

Pfft.

Pfft.

The two ex-Spetsnaz dropped where they stood with minimal noise.

"You're still clear. No activity."

Sam and Bill immediately rushed forward and dragged the two bodies back towards the jungle while Alpha One and Two picked up the fallen AK-47's and pretended to play guard duty. Sam and Bill, once they were done, moved to the wall and hugged it.

Calvin spoke up again. "You're still good. Wait. The east roamer looks like he's walking over."

"Fuck," Sam breathed out. "This could get ugly sooner rather than later."

Alpha One raised his right arm and waved at the approaching guard. He made a motion as if he wanted a drink. The roamer stopped walking towards the entrance, waved back and continued on his way. In the dark the only thing the guard made out was the outline of the AK-47's and assumed everything was fine.

"Hold it. Yes. He's leaving and heading back to his route."

"Nice," whispered Bill.

Sam spoke up. "Bravo. Charlie. Sitrep." *Situational report.*

"We're ready to gain access."

"Do it and let me know when you're in."

"Wilco." *Will comply.*

On the west side of the outer compound wall, directly in the middle of two guard towers, Bravo One swung a black rope over the wall. Attached to the end was a grappling hook made out of a composite plastic. It was very strong. But more importantly it didn't clang when it hit the stone wall and slid into position.

"You're good," confirmed Calvin. "Guard towers and both roamers haven't differentiated in their activities."

Alpha One pulled on the rope to verify its integrity and then pulled himself up and over the wall. He dropped silently on the other side and brought up his MP5SD as he blended in to the dark wall he was pressed against. Thirty seconds later Charlie One and Two had joined him on the inside. They quickly laid down as the west roamer passed within forty feet of their position without detecting them. They all tracked him through their NVG's, something they noticed none of the guards were wearing.

Alpha One pressed his transmit key twice to confirm they were inside rather than speaking out loud.

Sam acknowledged. "Roger that. Move to next position and hold."

Bill whispered in Sam's ear. "Good luck brother. See you on the inside."

"You too. Be careful."

"Are you kidding? This is what we live for."

Sam swore he saw Bill's shit eating grin as he snuck away to the north along the inside wall.

Just like old times.

He crossed by Alpha One and Two, playing guard, and made his way south along the inside wall.

Bravo One remained prone on the ground while Charlie One and Two split in separate directions as they headed towards their own guard towers. Overwatch, in this case, was the duty of Bravo One as well as the Alpha team. If the shit hit the fan they already owned multiple fields of fire that would keep the Spetsnaz soldiers heads down.

Two very specific flaws allowed the team's plan to work better than intended. The first was that the interior of the compound had very little light on at night. The second was that none of the guards wore night vision goggles. Apparently they had become somewhat complacent over the years; at whatever location they had been guarding Nikolay, because they'd never been attacked. Complacency and boredom travel hand in hand.

With the team's limited numbers they had devised this plan to simultaneously attack the outside threats all at once, as long as surprise remained on their side. If they were discovered then they would be outnumbered and potentially overwhelmed if the remaining Spetsnaz emerged from the barracks and joined the fight.

The guards in each of the four towers were tasked to look outwards for threats, rather than inwards. Combine that with the darkness and the four operators were able to hug the inner walls all the way to the base of each guard tower entrance. The towers were, like the walls, constructed out of stone and rose five feet above the existing ten foot walls. The entrance to each was identical and consisted of a stone archway with stone steps that spiraled up to the covered towers above.

Sam, Bill, Charlie One and Two paused right outside their designated tower, hugged the wall and drew their suppressed pistol. Each one, once in position, double tapped their mike to let the rest of the team know they were ready. Sam heard three separate double taps in his ear.

"Looks good Sam," said Calvin. Roamers are towards the center of the courtyard. Clear for twenty seconds."

Sam keyed his mike three times. That was the go signal and the four operators immediately executed their plan.

Bill, just like Sam and Charlie team, stealthed into the tower base. His pistol was extended out in front of him. The base was clear. Bill moved quickly, but quietly step by step up the stone stairs with his barrel pointed up and ahead of him. He heard voices and kept moving. He knew that he had the element of surprise and needed to match that with speed and violence of action. He had a job to do.

As the stairwell crested so did Bill's head. Black face paint covered his white and reflective skin. It was as if the darkness was alive.

The two guards barely registered his movement as Bill put a silenced round into each of their heads. The guards slumped over. Bill shot each of them twice more in the back on his way down the stairs.

"Eagle Two secure." *Tough luck suckers.*

"Eagle One secure."

"Charlie One secure."

Suddenly the alarm blared across the compound's grounds and all hell broke loose.

* * *

Charlie Two crept up his designated stairwell until one of the guards, out of nowhere, appeared at the top of the steps. The guard fumbled for his weapon as Charlie Two drilled him twice. Unfortunately the momentum of the guard's movements carried him down the stairwell and crashed into him. The second guard, having witnessed his partner's death slammed his fist on the alarm pad and readied his AK-47. He moved to the stairs, stuck his assault rifle out and blind fired down them.

The first two bursts tore chucks out of the dead guard's corpse and literally saved Charlie Two's life. He fired at the exposed arm that held the AK-47 and watched in satisfaction as one of his rounds struck the guard's shoulder. The impact spun the guard's body just enough so that his head came into view. That's all Charlie Two needed as he depressed his trigger. He pushed the dead guard off him and headed outside.

* * *

Nikolay jolted out of his desk chair when he heard the alarm followed by AK bursts.

What the hell is going on!?

* * *

When the alarm blared the two roamers whipped their rifles up and looked around. They focused their attention on the gunfire that emanated from the northwest tower.

* * *

Oh fuck!

"Converge and deny! Converge and deny!" yelled Sam as he rushed out of the southeast tower.

* * *

Bravo Two, had kept the west roamer in his sights the moment he laid prone in the darkness. As soon as he heard the alarm, and the burst of AK rounds, he fired his silenced weapon.

"Converge and deny! Converge and deny!"

* * *

Alpha One and Two cringed when the alarm went off. One of the speakers was directly overhead and it was incredibly loud. They dropped their AK's, shouldered their MP5SD's and dispatched the east roamer as the guard finished his turn towards the northwest tower.

"Converge and deny! Converge and deny!"

* * *

Two guards, in the main house, burst out of the front door and saw their comrade's fall dead in the middle of the courtyard.

* * *

Bill checked for threats as he exited the guard tower. He witnessed Alpha team drop someone so he holstered his pistol and changed over to his submachine gun as he made his way along the east side of the main house.

* * *

Charlie One raced out of the southwest guard tower as Bravo One dispatched the closest roamer. He holstered his sidearm and readied his main weapon as he ran over to Bravo One.

* * *

In the barracks ten guards were jolted awake by the alarm. They heard Bursts of AK fire.

"WE'RE UNDER ATTACK!"

They grabbed for weapons.

"GET UP!"

One of them mistakenly turned on the light switch when he couldn't find his weapon in the dark.

* * *

Alpha One and Two, after he dropped the east roamer, sprinted towards the barracks.

Bravo One stood up and was joined by Charlie One. The two of them ran towards the barracks together.

* * *

Charlie Two, having disentangled himself from the corpse, emerged and made his way around the west side of the main house. He switched to this MP5SD along the way.

* * *

Sam ran straight through the middle of the compound and past the two dead guards he'd seen taken out. Two guards appeared out the front door of the main house. They ran out with their weapons up and ready.

* * *

The two Spetsnaz, from the main house, saw two black shapes cross the open lawn and opened up on them. Chunks of dirt and lawn kicked up all around Alpha One and Two as they headed to the barracks. They kept running and didn't have a chance to return fire.

* * *

Bill turned the corner and the front of the house came into view. Two guards had just started to shoot. Bill aimed and fired.

* * *

Nikolay picked up his Makarov, went to his office door and locked it. Just then someone began to bang on the other side of it.
"Please sir! Open up! It's me, Sasha! Let me in!"
Nikolay chose not to unlock the door.

* * *

Charlie Two was a little late to the party but as he turned the corner he took aim at the closest guard that was shooting into the courtyard.

* * *

The barracks door opened and three guards advanced out the doorway. Their night vision had been ruined by the sudden light that had illuminated the room. They began to fire at the moving shadows.

* * *

Alpha One and Two felt the bullets kick up all around them. They ran, made it to the corner of the barracks and dove past the enemy's line of sight to safety.

* * *

Bill and Charlie Two's aim was dead on the money. The two house guards fell and were dead before they hit the ground.

* * *

Charlie One and Bravo One nearly got in the way of Alpha team's dive to safety. Two guards from the barracks rounded the corner after them and Bravo One cut them down.

* * *

Bill watched his target go down and shifted his aim left to the barracks where three guards had just emerged from. The guards fired at Alpha team just as the two dived to safety. Bill traversed his weapon as two of the guards that followed were cut down. He fired his MP5SD at the remaining guard and was satisfied when the man crumbled.

* * *

Charlie One stepped past the two dead men that Bravo One had killed and was delighted to see another guard topple in front of the barracks doorway. He pointed his weapon at the doorway and emptied his entire thirty round magazine to keep their heads down. He quickly pulled two fragmentation grenades off his tactical vest, pulled the pins and rolled them inside.

"FIRE IN THE HOLE!"

* * *

Sam could do nothing but watch as his team took care of business. Three men poured out of the barracks, as the two guards from the main house, and went down. Of the three that exited two were dispatched while the third taking a burst from behind. Sam reached his team just as Charlie One emptied his weapon and tossed his grenades.

"FIRE IN THE HOLE!"

Sam immediately hit the dirt.

* * *

Bill saw his next target drop and observed a team member actively engage the barracks. Bill traversed back to his right to cover the entrance to the main house.

"FIRE IN THE HOLE!"

The two explosions that followed were deafening.

Movement!

* * *

Charlie Two moved forward to cover the front part of the house.

"FIRE IN THE HOLE!"

The explosions were loud but contained within the barracks. He kept his eyes locked on the house entrance.

* * *

Bill nearly depressed his trigger before he realized the movement near him was a fellow team member.

* * *

"FIRE IN THE HOLE!"

Bravo One hit the grass as the two explosions rocked the interior of the barracks. The compound alarm abruptly went silent.

* * *

Sam got up, ran and kicked in the broken door to the barracks. He immediately moved right. Alpha team and Bravo One followed a second later. Charlie One replaced his empty magazine outside.

There was blood and bodies everywhere. The carnage was absolute and finite. Sam counted off seven corpses.

He keyed his mike. "What'ya got for me?"

"Holy fucking shit, that was fast!" Calvin replied.

"Calvin, is there any other movement!"

"No. No. Not that I can see. All seven of you are accounted for. Initial body count is two per tower, two roaming…"

"Faster Calvin."

"Twenty two. I count twenty two."

"And no additional movement outside?"

"Nothing Sam, nothing."

"Great. All teams, this is Eagle One. Friendlies coming out of the barracks."

"Charlie Two and I have the front covered," said Bill. "Move up."

* * *

The explosions shook and surprised Nikolay. After that it became deadly quiet.

Where are my men? Where are all my men?

* * *

Sam emerged from the slaughterhouse and the five men moved up towards Nikolay's house. The team paused and individually each of them executed a tactical reload of his weapon. Once Sam was satisfied he gave the signal. Alpha took the left side of the doorway while Charlie took the right side. Bravo covered their rear just in case.

"Moving inside." Sam tested the front door and found it unlocked. He nodded to Bill and they each prepped a flash bang. Sam kicked in the door and they hurled their grenades inside.

BANG!

BANG!

Sam and Bill entered right after the explosions. Alpha and Charlie were right behind them.

Immediately they discovered an elderly man crawling on the floor. He'd temporarily lost his sight and hearing from the flash bangs.

A large door was to their right but it was closed. The rest of the house opened up in front of the team.

Sam and Bill stacked up next to the closed door and then he pointed at the man. Alpha One subdued and patted him down.

"What's your name?" Bravo One asked the man.

"Sa…Sasha. My name is Sasha. I am the butler."

"He's clean."

Sam nodded as he turned to his team. "Clear the house. Bill and I have this room."

Charlie and Alpha teams moved out together while Bravo One remained at the front door to cover the entrance as well as their prisoner.

*　*　*

"He's clean."

"Clear the house. Bill and I have this room."

Nikolay raised his Makarov and fired five rounds into the door.

*　*　*

BLAMBLAMBLAMBLAMBLAM!

Sam and Bill hugged the wall. The bullets had struck the door they were stacked up by but they hadn't penetrated it.

"Looks like we have a winner behind door number one," said Bill.

"Continue to clear," said Sam. "Bill and I have this."

"Acknowledged."

"Same shit different door," said Bill. "I've got it." He pulled the last flash bang off his vest, prepped it and nodded.

Sam kicked in the door as Bill overhanded the grenade into the room.

BLAMBLAMBLAM!

Three rounds missed their mark.

BANG!

Sam rushed in with Bill on his heels and found another elderly man on the ground with his hands over his ears. An empty Makarov lay on the floor. Sam kicked the pistol away as Bill cleared the office of any additional threats.

"Clear!"

"One additional in custody," Sam said into his mike. He propped the man up and secured his wrists in front. Bill took the chair from behind the desk and moved it to the center of the room. Sam forcibly pulled the man up and sat him down. The effects of the flash bang began to wear off.

"The house is clear," reported Charlie One through the headset.

"Roger that," Sam replied. "Start tearing this place apart."

"You're too late," said the man.

Bill looked over at Sam. "Sounds like we found our guy."

Sam bent down and looked the man right in the face. "What's your name?"

"My name is Nikolay Dmitriev," he replied proudly.

Sam stood up and keyed his mike. "Target confirmed. We have Nikolay in custody. Requesting extract."

* * *

"Target confirmed. We have Nikolay in custody. Requesting extract."

Richard and Michael couldn't believe what they'd just heard over the intercom. They'd been listening to the communications as they watched the entire operation unfold on the overhead screen via satellite.

Calvin replied. "They're ecstatic back here Sam. I need to patch in the DCI. Gimme a second."

Michael sat down. *It's over. I can't believe it's really over.*

Richard put his hand on Michael's shoulder. He looked up at his old mentor. "How's it feel Michael?"

"I just don't know. Relieved. Anxious. Worried."

"Give it time. It's a lot to process."

Michael glanced around and lowered his voice. "We need to get out of here."

Richard nodded. "I know. I'm working on that."

* * *

"They're ecstatic back here Sam. I need to patch in the DCI. Gimme a second."

"Holding." He turned back to Nikolay. "What did you mean when you said we're too late?"

Nikolay smiled. "Just that. There's nothing you can do."

"See if you can find anything useful in his desk."

"On it," Bill replied as he began to rifle through Nikolay's desk.

Sam focused on Nikolay. "Then you might as well tell me what's going to happen if there's nothing we can do about it."

"Perhaps," he replied with a grin. "But first I'd like to tell you a story."

Sam ignored Nikolay and stood up. "What'd you find?"

"Just a satellite phone, a couple of vodka bottles and a bunch of files."

"I'm on the line now Sam," said the DCI over the comm channel. "You've got him?"

"Yes sir. Where's our extraction?"

"It's on its way."

Calvin spoke up suddenly. "I'm sorry to interrupt. I'm picking up military vehicles in route to your position."

Goddammit. "ETA?" said Sam.

"Ten to fifteen minutes."

"I want intelligence gathered," ordered the DCI.

"This is Eagle One. Evac. I say again. Evac. Rally point is the main house entrance." He pointed at Nikolay. "He's yours."

"Roger that," replied Bill. He stuffed the satellite phone in a vest pocket, slung his MP5SD, stood Nikolay up and hoisted him over his shoulder.

"Did you hear me!?" cried the DCI.

Sam finally replied. "There's no time sir. We're not supposed to be here. I will not compromise my team or my country." The DCI didn't respond. Sam and Bill headed out of the office as Alpha and Charlie teams arrived.

"What about him?" said Bravo One as he motioned towards Sasha.

"Leave him. We've got the Cuban military bearing down on us. We can't afford the additional weight. Move out. Back to the beach."

"You're too late," Nikolay repeated and began to laugh.

"Someone shut this fucker up," said Bill. Bravo One pulled out some cloth and gagged Nikolay.

* * *

The three thousand foot trek back to the beach went much smoother for two reasons. The first was that it was all downhill. The second was that the team wasn't concerned about any noise they made. They made good time through the jungle and arrived at the beach ten minutes later. Bill lowered Nikolay off his shoulder and sat him down on a fallen log.

Bill pointed at Alpha team. "Watch him." They moved to take up positions behind Nikolay.

Sam hit his mike. "Status?"

"Your immediate area is clear Sam. The military is two minutes away from the compound."

"Director? Where's our ride?"

"Like I said, it's coming. Let me speak with Nikolay."

Sam turned to Bravo One and motioned for his headset. He took it, walked over to Nikolay, removed his gag and adjusted the headset on him.

"He's on the line now sir."

"Nikolay Dmitriev. Can you hear me?" said the DCI.

Nikolay cocked his head. "Da. Who am I speaking to?"

"This is Victor Bannon…"

Nikolay interrupted. "The Director of Central Intelligence."

"That's correct. You've made quite a mess for us to clean up."

Nikolay couldn't help but smile. "And why do you say that Director? Does your country not enjoy children's bodies as they're removed from water parks? Do your citizen's not quiver and cry as their lifeless eyes stare back at them through the television?"

"You're a monster."

Nikolay spat the words out. "No more than what your country has done. The United States of America is the real monster. And monsters need to be destroyed."

"Well, that's quite an interesting sediment Nikolay, but as you're well aware, it's all over now. We've caught you."

Nikolay shook his head. "Even now you continue to believe your own lies, much like I did when I first came into power. My father held a coveted position on the Central Committee. When he was assassinated the Committee nominated me to take his place."

"I don't see how this has anyth.."

Nikolay persisted. "At first I did what was asked of me, proud to be part of the Soviet Union's backbone and leadership. But as the years passed I came to realize that I wanted more than they could offer. I began to consolidate my own power; my own plans. However, one thing remained constant and that was the United States was our enemy. With that foundational thought in mind I successfully infiltrated the CIA. I made arms deals around the world and skimmed millions. I even created a school for orphan children; to train them; to train them to become Americans yet retain the heart of a Russian. You might recognize some of their work in the past weeks." He chuckled. "You might have caught me but you can never stop me. I am immortal and will live on forever in the hearts of my children whose only wish is to harm your precious United States."

"Are you quite finished?"

"Be quiet fool. Your voice grates in my head." Nikolay changed gears. "Oh, by any chance would you be so kind as to put my old friend Michael Clark on the line?"

* * *

"Be quiet fool. Your voice grates in my head. Oh, by any chance would you be so kind as to put my old friend Michael Clark on the line?"

Everyone back at the TOC listened in on the conversation as Nikolay made his request.

"Why do you need to speak with him?" asked the DCI.

"Director, I told you to be quiet. I will only converse to Michael Clark from now on."

407

Michael stood up from the table and walked over.

"You know the drill," said Hobbes.

Michael bristled. "You don't have to remind me. I know my family's safety rests in my hands."

Hobbes handed over a headset and Michael put it on.

"This is Michael Clark. It's been ages Nikolay."

"Prove to me that you're Michael Clark."

"Fine. I personally stopped your assassination attempt of JFK at the Children's Hospital."

"But not the second one did you? Vasiliy and Oswald did their job that day in Dallas. But what you say doesn't prove anything. Continue Michael."

The group couldn't believe what they'd just heard. Nikolay had admitted to assassinating a United States President.

"I shot Vasiliy when he came to kill Kevin and me. I took the microfilm that contained all the information that Kevin had collected on Yuri, and you, Nikolay."

Nikolay chuckled. "My men never located that film. When you supposedly died you took that to your grave along with something else that belonged to me. What was that Michael?"

Shit. "Money."

"Who's money?" Nikolay insisted.

"I took a shitload of your blood money and it felt fucking great to stick it to you when I did."

* * *

Nikolay smiled. "I bet it felt good Michael, now that I know who I'm actually talking to. I have to admit that you really got under my skin, not only for stealing my money but for going after and exposing Yuri."

"I was doing my job. You're the one that made it personal you sonofabitch."

"You wouldn't be referring to the time that I had your lovely wife killed, would it? I'm an old man now and my memory isn't as good as it used to be. What was her name again?"

"Don't!"

"Betty? No. Your wife's name was Betsy."

* * *

Thomas shuddered as he sat at the table. Flashbacks of his fifth birthday began to play in his head.

Michael screamed. "YOU DON'T GET TO SAY HER NAME!"

"Awh. Come now Michael. All's fair in love and war. And you declared war on me long ago."

"I'll kill you. I've waited years to kill you and that's what I'm going to do. Then we'll see if you're laughing then."

"I admire your bravado Michael, I really do. But the truth of the matter is that I'm dead already."

Michael yelled. "Check his mouth for a cyanide capsule!"

Sam and Bill moved on Nikolay at once as he doubled over laughing. They paused.

"Oh my God, what era are you still living in Michael? That's a good idea though. I should have thought of that."

Sam and Bill held their ground next to Nikolay.

"I'm afraid my death is inevitable and far less dramatic that biting down on a cyanide capsule. The cancer, in my body, has spread too far. My doctor insisted I start treatments but at my age I wasn't going to put myself through any of that. It's funny. Power and money can get you anything but immortality, which brings our conversation full circle. You're too late."

Michael tried to compose himself. "I heard you say that earlier. What the hell do you mean?"

Nikolay chuckled. "If you only knew. My immortality will live on in the history books."

"There's going to be another bombing, isn't there? That's what you mean."

"And why would you come to that conclusion Michael?"

"Stop playing games Nikolay. People's lives are at stake goddammit."

"I don't care about the people I deem my enemy. I giggled, like a school girl, each time a body bag was removed on television. You think I'm going to tell you a fucking thing? You're not thinking very clearly. Why is that I wonder?" Nikolay laughed again.

Back at the TOC Michael ripped off his headset and threw it across the room.

"Mr. Dmitriev," said the DCI.

"I told you I don't want you speaking."

"That hardly matters at this moment. I'm going to take a stab at what you're referring to."

Nikolay looked around the beach and at the soldiers who stood around him. "Well, it's not like I'm going anywhere."

"And when I meant stab, I actually meant that I'm going to tell you exactly what you're talking about."

Nikolay sat up a little straighter. "You're too late."

"On the contrary. We now have all the time in the world. The NSA tracked a call you made late last night from Cuba. You're in Cuba, isn't that right Mr. Dmitriev?" The DCI continued without waiting for an answer. "That call, the one that you made, led to a house just outside the city of Washington D.C."

Nikolay didn't like where this was going and his smile faltered.

"The FBI swarmed that location a little while ago."

Nikolay's faced went slack. "Impossible."

"And do you know what they found? I'll tell you what they found. They found two men and one woman who are US citizens, and members of the United States Air Force."

Impossible.

"These citizens have worked for the Air Force for over twenty years. They passed their SSBI security checks, or single scope background check, in case you didn't know what that was. And they passed their Yankee White security checks; the very one that allows you to get close to the President. They each rose in the ranks and now hold very coveted positions in our government that maintain helicopters, specifically Marine One, the President's helicopter."

"No. Impossible." Nikolay's shoulders slumped.

The DCI was very pleased with himself. "It's over Nikolay. Schematics recovered at the scene clearly indicate that they were going to switch out components from Marine One with custom machined parts. Those machined parts would have failed and made Marine One spin uncontrollably out of the sky."

"No. My legacy."

"You don't have to believe me. In a few hours it'll be all over the news. My guess is that you're nowhere near a television at the moment."

Nikolay couldn't' believe what he'd just heard. But he also knew it was the truth. Killing two US Presidents, in his lifetime, would not be on his list of accomplishments. He lifted his head up.

"You're still too late. There are others. Many others who will take up the fight."

"You don't get it Nikolay," said the DCI. "I'll get you to talk one way or another. It's over. I'm going to roll up your entire organization."

No. Decades of planning, preparing and implementation will be exposed. Nikolay abruptly stood up. "You're too late."

"You're a broken record Nikolay," said the DCI. "It's over."

Nikolay allowed himself a small smile. "Are you sure? Are you sure you can protect your friends and family? How are Nick, Susan and little Lisa holding up after their encounter at the zoo?"

* * *

Thomas sprang up out of his chair. "What the hell is he talking about? I need a headset." He ran over and picked up the one that his father had thrown across the room. "This is Thomas Clark…"

"Remove him from the call," the DCI ordered.

"Don't touch a damn button! What are you talking about Nikolay?"

"Thomas, it's Sam. They told me they were going to tell you about the attack on Nick's family."

"They haven't told me a goddamn thing. We're being held hostage Sam. They want Emily."

"What!? Say that again?"

Curtis ripped the headset off Thomas' head and gut punched him. Thomas doubled over and fell to the floor.

"Thomas!? Thomas!?" Sam repeated.

* * *

The DCI spoke up again. "It appears we have a situation on our hands."

"How cute. A squabble," said Nikolay.

Bill pushed Nikolay back down on the log. "You're done talking." Bill removed Nikolay's headset and tossed it back to Bravo One.

"What the hell do you think you're doing Director?" Sam demanded.

"Bring Nikolay back home and we'll open discussions."

"Not good enough."

"You don't have a choice Sam. You need me to get off that island. I have something you want and you have something I want."

Sam's voice was cold and deadly. "This isn't over, not by a long shot. I'm coming for you."

The DCI wasn't listening. "You'll need to swim out to meet the submarine. Punch these coordinates in. There isn't much time." He relayed the information. "Get it done."

Goddammit!

"Fuck you sir," as he and his team made the adjustments to their GPS equipment. Sam turned to Charlie team. "Go get our flippers and respirators."

"Roger that." They ran down the beach to their hidden cache.

Nikolay stood up again. "This has been very interesting. Sounds like you were betrayed by your own country."

"Shut up Nikolay before I make you shut up," said Sam.

"Temper temper. I'll just say one more thing? I swear it's important."

"What you piece of shit?"

"You need to let me go."

Sam just stared back at him. "That's all you've got? Just let me go?"

"No actually. The reality is that if you don't let me go then I can't make one very important phone call."

"And what call is that motherfucker?" Bill asked.

"The call to wave off the impending attack on your families of course."

"You're full of shit."

"You all live in Kailua on the southeast side of Oahu. Your houses are on North Kalaheo Ave. Does any of that ring a bell?"

"Fuck you!"

"I can get to your family, right here, right now. Let me go or they're dead."

<u>53</u>

Saturday November 15, 1997 4:30am

"I can get to your family, right here, right now. Let me go or they're dead."

Thomas caught his breath and rose to his feet. He'd heard what Nikolay had just said over the speakers, just like everyone else in the TOC. Curtis eyed him warily.

"I have to warn our families."

"That's not happening Mr. Clark," Curtis replied. "I have my orders."

"I need to make sure they're okay. Please." Thomas took a step forward.

"Back away." Curtis raised his weapon and pointed it Thomas' chest. "I won't warn you again."

Thomas saw determination and righteousness in Curtis' eyes. He froze.

He'll actually shoot me.

Thomas turned and took two steps towards Hobbes. Curtis pivoted to follow his movement.

"You've got to help us."

"Step away!"

Out of nowhere Curtis suddenly was sent sprawling to the floor. Richard dropped the table chair he'd used on Curtis and stepped out of reach. His rifle skidded and came to an abrupt halt when it hit Thomas' feet. He wasted no time in picking it up and immediately aimed it at Curtis who had just recovered.

"Holy shit!" Hobbes exclaimed.

"Oh fuck me," added Calvin.

"What's going on dammit?" the DCI demanded.

"Hand over the weapon Thomas before I take it from you," Curtis growled.

Thomas stood his ground. "You might have been just following orders but you must know goddamn right from wrong. What the Director is doing, keeping us prisoner here, is wrong."

"Place the rifle on the ground and step away from it. Now!"

Thomas continued as if he hadn't heard him. "You're an idiot Curtis. I'm going to give you two choices. We can do this the easy way or the hard way. Frankly, at this point, I don't give a shit which one you choose. My family's safety comes first."

Curtis lunged and Thomas didn't hesitate.

BRRAAAAAPPPP!

A three round burst stitched across Curtis' chest as he came at Thomas. His face displayed shock as the bullets tore through him and he was dead before he hit the floor.

Michael, Richard, Calvin and Hobbes remained motionless.

Emily stirred in her feverish sleep and then rolled over.

"What the hell was that!" yelled Sam over the intercom. "Was that gunfire!?"

"What just happened? What's going on?" exclaimed the Director.

Thomas spoke up as he retrieved the headset Curtis had ripped off his head. "If one of you assholes makes a wrong move I'll kill you too. Tell me you understand!" he yelled.

"I got it. No problem," said Calvin.

"Don't shoot man. You're the boss," Hobbes added.

"Someone talk to me!" Sam persisted.

Thomas put his headset back on. "Sam."

"Thomas? What the fuck?"

"We're back in control. I don't have time to go into it. I need to call and warn our families."

"Do it! The sat phone we took off of Nikolay has an access code and the bastard won't tell us what it is."

"Stand by Sam, I'm on it."

"Don't do anything he tells you," warned the Director.

Calvin replied. "Sir, you're not the one with a gun pointed at you."

"Godammit!" The DCI was furious.

* * *

Early Saturday morning the phone began to ring at the Clark's residence. It rang three times before Laura picked it up.

"Hellllo?" she said sleepily.

"Laura!"

"Thomas, is that you? Where have you been? What time is it?"

"There's no time to go into any of that right now. You have to get everyone out of there. You have hostiles inbound. Nikolay has sent people. They know where we live. They're coming after you. You have to get out of there!"

Laura immediately woke up as the adrenaline of Thomas' panicked voice hit her system.

"Oh fuck! I'm on it. I love you!"

"I love you too. Now go!"

Laura threw the covers off the bed and yelled as she began to get dressed. "REBECCA! REBECCA!"

Rebecca shot up the stairs and appeared in the master bedroom's doorway, weapon out. She scanned for threats and didn't see any.

"What's going on?" She saw Laura's shaking.

"Thomas just called. He told me that there's an impending attack on all of our families. We're out of here right now!"

Rebecca didn't ask any more questions as she yelled into her radio. "All teams! Code Red! Code Red! We have hostiles inbound. Imminent threat. Get the families up and dressed. Gear up and get the vehicles prepped. We're leaving in three minutes! How copy?"

"Delta copies."

"Foxtrot copies."

"Hotel copies."

"Oscar copies."

"Whiskey copies."

"Yankee copies."

* * *

"Sam."

"We're still here Thomas."

"They've been notified."

"Roger that."

Thomas turned to Hobbes. "Are we going to have a problem?"

Hobbes was sweating. "No sir. No problem whatsoever."

"Good. Bring up satellite coverage of the east side of Oahu."

"You got it. It'll take a few minutes."

Thomas nodded and then looked over at Richard. "Thank you."

"You're welcome, but we're not out of this quite yet. You know there's got to be reinforcements on their way here right now."

"Yeah. Tell me something I don't know."

* * *

Shadows of the Past

Alexei's group had disembarked the plane the evening before and rented three vans. They took the H1 southeast to the 61 and then headed northeast on Pali Highway that led to the east side of the island. They parked the three vehicles at the Kalama Beach Park which was less than half a mile from where their targets lived.

The six men, two in each van, got out and scanned the area. Alexei pulled out his phone and made a local call.

"Yes, we've arrived. How soon can you deliver? Fine, that will work. Bring food with you."

He hung up and addressed the other five men.

"Four additional men will be joining us for this operation. They will be here in two to three hours with weapons and food. Until then I'm going to take one van and take a look at our targets. Remain here."

* * *

"Okay, I've got it. It's coming up on the main screen now," said Hobbes.

The top down view of Oahu appeared on the overhead screen. Hobbes punched some keys and the view zoomed in and focused on the east side. It continued to zoom in until the view hovered over Bill, Sam and Thomas' houses.

"Sam."

"What've you got?"

"I'm looking at the satellite feed. Nothing to report. Wait a minute."

"What? What is it?"

Everyone in the TOC watched as illuminated human forms rushed out of homes. They got into the three Suburban's, backed them out of the driveways and pointed north.

"Sam, it looks like your men are prepping the Suburban's."

419

"Good. They're two things I need you to do."

"Tell me," replied Thomas.

* * *

"Hello? Who the hell is this?" His voice was very gruff.

"Is this Gunny Malloy?"

"Speaking. Identify yourself."

"Gunny, it's Sam Paige." Thomas had Calvin patch Sam into the phone line. "There's no time to explain. I need your immediate assistance."

That got the gunny's attention. "What's the passphrase?"

"It's Oscar-Mike-One-One-Delta-Zulu. Our families are in danger."

"I know you live four miles away. Tell me exactly what you need."

* * *

While Sam interfaced with the Marine base Thomas dialed up another number.

A female answered. "I don't know who this is but now's not a good time."

"Rebecca, it's Thomas. Sam gave me this direct number."

"We're evacuating as fast as we can Thomas. I don't have time to give you a play-by-play update."

"You don't have to. I've got an eye in the sky above you right now."

"What? You have us on satellite."

"Keep this line open. You're providing our family's security and we trust you. That doesn't mean I can't help you out on our end."

"That's great news actually. How are we looking from up there?"

"No contacts. Nothing to report. Just get them to the Marine base. Sam is trying to get a Marine convoy moving to your position now to help you out."

"Roger that," replied Rebecca.

* * *

"Thomas? You there?"

Thomas had Calvin conference call Rebecca in on the fly.

"Yeah Sam. Rebecca's on the line now."

"Excellent. Rebecca. Sitrep."

"We're about to head out. The kids are scared along with your wives."

"Get it done Rebecca. I've got a convoy that should be leaving anytime. They'll meet up and escort you in. Once you're on the base you'll all be safe."

"Roger that Sam," she replied. "We'll get them there safe and sound."

* * *

Four vans left the Kalama Beach Park parking lot in the dead of night and turned left on North Kalaheo Ave heading south. The ten men were split in two groups of two and two groups of three. Alexei's contact brought ten AK-47's with him and six thirty round magazines for each man. The weapons had been smuggled in to Oahu years before in case they were ever needed. The four men who brought them lived and worked on the Hawaiian Islands as sleepers. It had taken them a few hours to fly from the other islands and gather together on Oahu.

Alexei made one final phone call as they departed.

* * *

On the beach in Cuba Nikolay's satellite phone began to chirp. Bill held it in his hand. There wasn't a way to answer it without punching in Nikolay's code.

Nikolay smiled as he spoke. "Last chance Sam. I can still call this off but you have to let me go right now. Otherwise the next few minutes are going to be very entertaining."

The DCI's voice boomed in Sam's headset. "You will not let him go. Confirm that you understand me goddammit."

Sam didn't reply and continued to stare at the phone until it stopped ringing.

* * *

Rebecca gave the word. Each of three Suburban's pulled out into North Kalaheo Ave, one behind the other. The first Suburban held Kim, her two kids and two of the security detail. In the second vehicle were Julie, her two children plus two men. Taking up the rear were Laura, Gavin, Rebecca and the remaining two men. Each of the wives nervously gripped their Glock 17's in one hand while they attempted to soothe their children's fears.

* * *

"Oh shit. This can't be good," said Hobbes.

"What?" Thomas asked.

Hobbes pointed at the screen as he pulled the satellite image back to a higher elevation. Four large vehicles, most likely vans, were headed south in a caravan together directly towards the Suburban's.

"Rebecca! Possible contacts closing in from the north!" Thomas yelled.

Rebecca lifted up her radio and began to speak. "Incoming!" Headlights loomed in the distance.

* * *

Alexei rode in the primary van with two of the other men. Nikolay hadn't answered his phone. He put it back in his jacket pocket, racked a round into this AK and looked up at the oncoming headlights.

He yelled his orders to the other three vans through his radio.

"Block the road! They're coming to us!"

The three vans behind his peeled off and completely filled the two lanes as well as the soft edge of the road.

"Get me containment!"

* * *

The road in front of the Suburban's suddenly filled with blinding light as all four vans completely filled the road and turned on their high beams.

The first Suburban yanked his wheel, braked and came to a halting stop perpendicular to the road.

Two of the vans screeched to a halt, fishtailed and effectively blocked the north bound road.

The second and third Suburban's had little choice but to follow suit.

The other two vans shot by all three Suburban's, screeched and blocked them in from behind.

Van doors popped open. Alexei and his men piled out, took aim and opened up on all the Suburban's.

* * *

"We're taking fire!" Rebecca yelled into her hands free headset.

Bullets thumped into each armored Suburban and peppered the glass.

The children couldn't stop crying.

"What do we do!? What do we do!?" Julie and Kim screamed out together.

* * *

Thomas was frantic. "Sam, our families are under attack!"

The overhead screen was like watching an action movie unfold. They couldn't do anything but watch as the four vans maneuvered to block both ends of the road. The Suburban's were effectively blocked. That's when they saw human shapes disperse from each van and open fire. They could even make out the hot shell casings as they ejected from the weapons. The sound of gunfire could distinctly be heard through Rebecca's headset.

"Holy shit! No no no!" Thomas felt helpless.

* * *

Sam tried to remain calm. Charlie Team returned with the gear they'd stashed.

"Gear up and head out. Bill and I will be along with the package."

Alpha, Bravo and Charlie teams donned their respirators, flippers and entered the water to swim to the coordinates.

"Sam, our families are under attack!"

"Holy shit! No no no!"

"Rebecca! Stay in the Suburban's! They're armored. The Marines are inbound!"

Nikolay spoke up again. "Seems like you two can't protect your women." His smile was pure evil.

Bill un-holstered his pistol and placed the silenced barrel against Nikolay's temple. "Shut the fuck up."

* * *

"Rebecca! Stay in the Suburban's! They're armored. The Marines are inbound!"

Rebecca relayed the order. "All teams…sit tight! Help is on the way! We're armored!"

Bullets tore into the armor plating as hundreds of rounds ate away at the each Suburban's exterior.

* * *

Alexei jumped out of one of the vans that had shot past their targets and blocked their escape. He and his men immediately began to fire their fully automatic AK-47's into the sides of the Suburban's. The heavy 7.62x39 rounds rapidly ate away at the stationary target's armor. Their targets had not exited their vehicles.

Alexei replaced his empty magazine for the third time. He pulled open a side compartment of his ammo satchel he'd strung around his neck, and removed a baseball like device. He threw it at the closet Suburban.

425

* * *

"We're sitting targets! We're dead if we stay in here any longer!" yelled Hotel from the first vehicle that held Kim and her kids.

"No shit! Let's bring the fight to these motherfuckers!" Oscar yelled from the front passenger seat.

"Don't leave us!" screamed Kim as she held on tightly to Sarah and Edward.

Hotel opened his door and rolled out. He brought up his MP5 as he rose over the hood of the Suburban and emptied his entire magazine towards the northern attackers. One man with an AK took a round to the neck and toppled backward onto the road. The rest scrambled to take cover behind their vans.

"Stay in the vehicle!" Oscar then turned and moved over the middle console to join Hotel on the safe side of the Suburban.

A loud explosion detonated behind them.

* * *

"Oh fuck! GRENADE! COVER!" yelled Whiskey as he watched a man toss a grenade at their vehicle. There was nothing Rebecca could do.

The grenade bounced and skittered under the front of the Suburban. The force of the detonation violently lifted the front of the vehicle up in the air and it crashed back down. Huge flames shot out from under the hood as it caught on fire.

* * *

"Where's the goddamn backup!" Sam yelled.

"It looks like they're about a minute out."

"Fuck!"

"Problem?" teased Nikolay.

Bill pressed the barrel harder into his temple and Nikolay shut his mouth.

* * *

Thomas watched as someone exited the first Suburban, opened fire and was rewarded with a kill. The other four attackers immediately moved back to cover.

However, suddenly an explosion under the rear Suburban briefly lifted it in the air. It caught on fire. The sound of the explosion was relayed a split second later over the speaker.

* * *

"Follow suit. Move!" yelled Delta from the middle Suburban that held Julie, Amanda and Craig. Their vehicle hadn't taken that many hits.

Foxtrot bailed out of the passenger seat and Delta did the same from the driver's. Foxtrot immediately ran to the side of the northern Suburban and yanked the rear door open.

"Get out!"

He practically pulled Kim and her kids out the back and pushed them on the ground.

"Stay low! Take your kids and get in the center vehicle. Do it!"

Foxtrot didn't look back as he began to engage the northern group of attackers alongside Hotel and Oscar.

* * *

"Is anyone hurt!?" Rebecca yelled.

Flames were coming through the front console.

"I WANNA GO HOME!" Gavin screamed from the back seat.

Whiskey had been dazed from the explosion and he opened his driver door and flopped out into the street. A second later he was cut down by three separate AK's.

Yankee kicked the front passenger door open, got out and moved to the rear door. He yanked it open and pulled Rebecca, Laura and Gavin out.

"Stay low and wait for my signal!"

Yankee took his MP5, poked it out from behind the rear of the burning Suburban and depressed the trigger. He swept his gun back and forth as he did. Two of the five southern attackers took rounds to their chests and slumped to the ground. Alexei, and the other two, moved to take cover behind their vans. Delta joined up with Yankee and began to fire over the roof because the hood was engulfed in flames.

"GO!" Yankee yelled as he replaced his spent magazine.

Rebecca pushed Laura and Gavin ahead of her towards the middle Suburban.

* * *

Thomas watched the attack unfold quickly in front of his eyes. There was little he could do from thousands of miles away. He did not like the impotent feeling that washed over him.

On the screen one of their men exited the burning Suburban and was instantly cut down. A second man pulled two adults and a child from the back seat after he took two attackers down. That

428

trio made its way to the middle vehicle. One adult and the child got in the front as Rebecca's voice was heard over the speaker.

"We've got at least one man down! Taking fire from multiple directions! Where's that backup!"

"Thirty seconds out," said Calvin. He hadn't realized he'd been holding his breath.

* * *

The four northern attackers kept up their barrage as they poked their AK's out from behind the cover of their vans. Bullets sprayed everywhere.

Hotel, Oscar and Foxtrot held their positions over the hood of the first Suburban. The three of them managed to keep the four men from effectively aiming at them. They each owned a zone and, with select fire, kept the northern group pinned down.

* * *

Kim, and her kids, piled into the rear of the center Suburban. She pulled the back door closed behind her just as a stray bullet ricocheted off the bullet proof glass and left a gash in the window.

"Fuck me!"

All four kids were past the point of crying. They had tucked themselves into tight balls on the floor and just whimpered.

"What the hell do we do?" she asked her sister.

"I don't know," Julie replied. "I don't fucking know what's going on. Who are these people?"

A couple more bullets thumped hard into each side of the Suburban. The pitch of their kids whimpers rose.

They both heard a long burst of automatic gunfire close by and then Laura and Gavin appeared in the front seats as if by magic.

"Oh Christ! Are you two okay!?" Julie yelled over the gunfire. "The explos.."

"I WANNA GO HOME!" Gavin screamed.

Laura tried to console her son as she stroked his hair. "It's going to be okay honey. You're okay. You're okay."

Gavin violently shook his head from side to side. "NO!…it's not okay! Bad men are trying to get us!"

* * *

Alexei saw two of his men take rounds and fall, their weapons clattered on the ground. He, and the other two that remained, took cover and engaged in a sustained firefight.

There isn't any more time.

He pulled another grenade out of his satchel, pulled the pin and heaved it over the van.

* * *

Rebecca caught the movement as the object sailed over her head and landed between the two Suburban's.

Shit!

"GRENADE!"

There wasn't any cover. The grenade exploded and rocked both vehicles.

* * *

A second explosion appeared on the overhead from Rebecca's relay. Three of their own no longer engaged the enemy and lay motionless on the road.

"Rebecca? Rebecca, come in goddammit," Sam said from a world away.

Thomas spoke up. "I…I think she's dead."

* * *

Everyone in the middle Suburban screamed when the grenade went off against the side of their vehicle.

Gavin saw Rebecca's unmoving body lying on the road and began to scream.

"BECCA! BECCA!"

The other four children's moans and whimpers became even louder.

* * *

The gunfire abruptly stopped in Alexei's direction. The two men that were with him noticed the same thing, peaked out and didn't see anyone. They stepped out from behind cover and quickly advanced on the burning Suburban. Alexei held back.

* * *

Gunny Malloy had immediately called for support. Marines on duty didn't question him when he ordered twelve of them into three Humvees and drove their convoy away as quickly as possible.

Four miles isn't that far but it felt like an eternity as Gunny gripped his M16A1 rifle in the front passenger seat of the primary Humvee. All he knew was that a fellow soldier family was in danger and he'd been asked to help. No soldier can ever refuse that request.

The convoy turned left on North Kalaheo Ave and punched the accelerator as the sounds of gunfire were heard through their open windows.

"Fuck! Move it Marine!"

"You got it Gunny!"

Up ahead the heavy automatic fire filled the early Hawaiian morning.

Two of the four remaining northern attackers turned around as the headlights bore down on them. The three Humvees stopped fifty feet from the vans. Doors opened and Marines emptied into the street.

"UNITED STATES MARINES! DROP YOUR WEAPONS!"

The two, that had turned, immediately opened up on the twelve Marines. The other two men turned to join in the fight just as twelve M16A1 rifles lit up the night. The four men never stood a chance. With nowhere to hide the Marine's combined three hundred and sixty rounds traveled fifty feet and blotted them out of existence.

* * *

"I can't take this anymore!" Julie opened her door and got out. She looked down and saw that she still had her Glock 17 in her hand.

"Julie! No!" Laura pushed open the front door.

"BECCA!" Gavin scrambled over his mother and fell out of the Suburban.

"Gavin!" She tried to grab him and missed.

Julie brought her weapon up.

Gavin ran out of Laura's reach towards Rebecca.

To the north a barrage of gunfire erupted out of nowhere.

* * *

"They're there!" Calvin said excitedly. "The Marines just showed up."

They watched as the four northern attackers were obliterated.

"Thomas! You've got to tell me what's going on?"

"The Marines just arrived and tore the shit out of four bad guys!"

"Are all the bad guys down?"

"No. It looks like there are three more. Two are walking past the burning Suburban while the third is staying back. Wait. Someone just got out of the middle vehicles. Shit! One of our kids fell out the front door and just ran to someone on the ground!"

* * *

"Julie! Get back in here!" yelled Kim. "What are you doing!?"

Laura exited the front seat and concentrated on retrieving Gavin.

Julie brought her weapon up. Her world felt like it was in slow motion. The flames that licked across the burning Suburban, in front of her, seemed to dance.

Movement to my left.

Julie traversed her weapon and now a man holding an AK came into focus at the back of the burning Suburban. He brought his weapon up just as Julie fired twice. She could practically see each bullet exit her pistol, take the ten foot flight and embed in his chest. He fell on his back on the pavement.

"YOU FUCKER!" she screamed as she advanced on the man.

"MARINES!"

Laura made it to Gavin's side, crouched down and tried to pull him away from Rebecca's body as she heard Julie fire her weapon. Laura looked up and saw the barrel of an AK-47 protrude from around the front of the vehicle towards her. With her left hand she pushed Gavin down as she raised her own sidearm up. The man came into view and began to take aim at the interior of the middle Suburban. Laura continued to squeeze her trigger as fast as she could.

* * *

Gunny reloaded his weapon on a dead run past the vans. The other Marines were on his heels.

POPPOP!

Handgun fire.

"YOU FUCKER!"

"MARINES!" Gunny yelled as he reached the dead bodies.

"Friendlies!" Oscar replied.

POPPOPPOPPOPPOPPOPPOPPOPPOP

* * *

The man with the AK came around the Suburban and on the screen they watched as the female shot him twice. POPPOP.

"YOU FUCKER!" came over the speaker as well. It sounded like Julie.

At the same time the second man approached from the right and took aim. The woman who'd gone after the child shot that sonofabitch and didn't stop. POPPOPPOPPOPPOPPOPPOPPOPPOP. The man's body took all nine rounds before collapsing where he'd stood.

434

* * *

"Talk to me Thomas!"

"Holy shit! I think our wives just took out two bad guys. There's only one left."

* * *

POPPOP.

"YOU FUCKER!"

Alexei watched one man fall on his back.

POPPOPPOPPOPPOPPOPPOPPOPPOP. His other man took every round and collapsed out of view.

Fuck! Wait.

A human form barely came into view at the back of the Suburban. Alexei raised his AK and fired.

* * *

"NOOOOOO!" Gavin screamed.

Stir appeared next to him amidst the flickering flames. The shadows from the fire danced over his small form on the pavement.

"STOP IT!"

Stir took off like a shot underneath the burning Suburban.

* * *

"Oh fuck me. Fuck meeee. Nonononononono."

"Tell me what's going on dammit! What happened!?"

"NOOOOOO!" *That was Gavin.*

"STOP IT!"

On the screen something fast jetted underneath the Suburban and launched itself at the last man.

* * *

Alexei smiled.

That's a kill.

"NOOOOOO! STOP IT!"

His smiled faltered when something fast and small suddenly appeared from under the vehicle.

Wha…

Stir lunged right at Alexei's throat and tore at it before he could react.

* * *

"What's going on goddammit!?" Sam was beside himself.

On the screen the head of the last man flew off of his body. The body itself stood for a couple more seconds before it toppled over.

"I…I don't know what's going on yet Sam."

"What the hell was that?" said Hobbes when the small but fast object attacked the last man. He and Calvin shared a glance.

* * *

Hotel, Oscar and Foxtrot lowered their weapons as the twelve Marines swarmed around both sides of the vans.

Gunny looked around. "Call it in. We're going to need a shitload of ambulances."

The Marines advanced forward.

* * *

Laura watched the man she'd repeatedly shot finally die. She dropped her gun and pulled Gavin close to her as Stir did his thing.

* * *

Kim and the kids screamed as the doors were pulled open by the Marines.

"It's okay ma'am. You're all okay now."

Six Marines moved forward to clear, three on each side, they passed the middle Suburban there were bodies everywhere. Two Marines began to check for survivors while the other four cleared forward to the southern vans. They discovered a man without a head.

* * *

The Marines passed by Laura and Gavin. She let her son go and rolled Rebecca's body over. There was blood all over her.

"Is Becca going to be okay?"

"I don't know yet sweetie." She checked for a pulse on Rebecca's wrist and couldn't find one. Laura tried her neck and was rewarded with a weak pulse.

"I need a medic over here!" She turned to her son. "She's alive but she's hurt."

Without all the shooting Laura actually heard something emanating from Rebecca. She realized it was the hands free earpiece and gently pulled it out of Rebecca's ear along with the phone it was attached to.

"Hello?"

"Laura?"

"Thomas?"

"Oh for Christ's sake, it's good to hear your voice. Are you okay?"

"I..I don't know. Everyone.....so many…"

"What happened? Somebody fucking talk to me."

"Sam?"

"What happened Laura?"

"I...I…there was so much shooting…"

"What about Julie, Kim and the kids? Tell me they're okay?"

Laura grabbed Gavin by the hand and slowly stood up. She saw the Marines extract Kim and the four children out of the Suburban.

Where's Julie?

She remembered that Julie got out of the vehicle right before Gavin got away from her.

"Julie? Julie, where are you?"

Laura walked over to the other side of the burning Suburban just as a Marine stopped her.

"Ma'am. I don't think you want to come over here."

"Why? What…" Laura saw Julie's legs protruding just out of view. "Get out of my way! Julie!"

* * *

Sam cringed as he listened to Laura call out his wife's name in desperation.

"Oh my God Sam." He barely understood her through her tears. "Julie's down. She's…oh fuck…she's dead Sam."

A single tear rolled down Sam's face from a world away. He'd never felt as helpless as he did at this moment.

Bill was stunned. He couldn't believe it.

Nikolay, on the other hand, just smiled as he watched Sam's demeanor change. "You could have prevented this by letting me go."

"Shut up," Sam hissed between clenched teeth.

"I'm guessing something tragic has happened to someone close to you."

"Shut up."

"Maybe you're a widower now?"

Sam punched Nikolay in the face. Nikolay fell over the log and landed on his back.

"Get up you piece of shit! Get up so I can kill you!"

"Godammit Sam," said the DCI in his ear. "I order you to return him alive.

"Fuck you sir. I don't take orders from you. You've already proven yourself to be a traitor in my eyes. Watch your fucking back, I'm coming for you!" Sam disengaged the comm channel and ripped his throat mike off.

* * *

"Oh my God Sam." Everyone at the TOC barely understood her through her tears. "Julie's down. She's…oh fuck…she's dead Sam."

They were stunned as they watched Laura kneel over Julie's body. Gavin was right there with her.

They heard Nikolay in the background. "You could have prevented this by letting me go."

"Shut up," Sam said.

"I'm guessing something tragic has happened to someone close to you."

"Shut up."

"Maybe you're a widower now?"

They heard a scuffle before Sam spoke again. "Get up you piece of shit! Get up so I can kill you!"

"Godammit Sam," the DCI said over the loudspeaker. "I order you to return him alive.

"Fuck you sir. I don't take orders from you. You've already proven yourself to be a traitor in my eyes. Watch your fucking back, I'm coming for you!" The signal from the team in Cuba terminated.

"GODDAMMIT!" The DCI turned his attention back to the group at the TOC. "My men will be there momentarily to take you into custody. I recommend that you surrender upon their arrival."

He ended the call.

* * *

Laura couldn't help but stare at Julie's still body on the ground. Gavin stared too before Laura noticed and turned his head away. She hadn't been really listening to the loud conversation in her ear.

"My men will be there momentarily to take you into custody. I recommend that you surrender upon their arrival."

What the fuck?

"Thomas. Did I just hear that right? You're being arrested?"

He sighed. "It's bigger than that now. The DCI's been holding us hostage."

"What?"

"He knows…or he thinks he knows something. He wants Emily and he's prepared to take her by force."

"Oh my God!"

"I had to shoot the man holding us just so I could talk to you. He was going to kill me. Laura…listen to me. You have to get everyone out of there. You're not safe. None of you are safe."

*   *   *

"I NEED to get home right now."

"Easy brother," replied Bill. "Take it easy."

"Fuck easy! Everyone wants a piece of our family. I'm through. This motherfucker dies right now."

Sam pulled Nikolay up off the sand and stood him up.

"Going to kill me Sam? Shame. Well, at least I can say I'm the one responsible for your empty life now."

Sam pulled out his pistol and pointed it at Nikolay's forehead. His hatred burned through his veins.

"You sure you want to do this?"

"Don't fucking get in my way Bill."

"Wasn't planning on it brother. If anyone deserves to die it's him."

Nikolay stared at the end of the barrel. "I often wondered what my father's last thoughts were when I had my gun to his head."

Sam tightened his grip. "What the fuck are you babbling about?"

"My father didn't see it coming. I wanted his power; his influence. When I assassinated him in that alley I always wondered what the last thing that went through his mind."

Bill stepped back as Sam pressed the barrel deeper into Nikoaly's forehead.

"You know what asshole. I actually met my dead father recently. It was one hell of a shock to my system. I have a strong suspicion that your father has been waiting a lifetime for this moment and will be very pleased to see you."

Nikolay's smile faded. He didn't understand.

"This is for Julie."

Sam's suppressed handgun ejected a single spent casing. It landed in the sand. A moment later Nikolay's corpse joined it.

* * *

Nikolay opened his eyes and watched as the two operators donned their own equipment and headed out into the ocean to meet up with the submarine.

What happened?

What the hell is going on?

Is that my body lying on the sand?

"Hello Nikki," said a familiar voice from behind him.

Nikolay turned and came face to face with his father.

"We're going on a trip, just you and I." His father's smile frightened him.

"Noooooo."

* * *

The early morning light began to creep up out of the ocean. The aftermath of the attack, that they'd just survived, was all around them. Shell casings, scorch marks and bodies from both sides still littered the road. Rebecca needed an ambulance.

Laura knelt over Julie's body and cried. She saw that her friend had two entry wounds to her upper chest. One of the bullets had torn through her heart. Due to that injury there wasn't a terrible amount of blood around her body because her heart had stopped pumping.

Kim had mostly collected herself until she realized that she didn't know where her sister was.

"Where's Julie?" she asked Oscar. "Where's my sister?"

He shook his head and didn't answer.

Kim looked over and made sure the kids were being looked after. She began to walk around and it didn't take her long to find Laura and Gavin. Kim rushed over and before she could say anything she saw her sister's outline on the ground.

"Julie?"

"Kim...I'm...I'm so sorry."

"No! I don't believe it!" She crashed to her knees next to her sister. "Julie's fine." She began to shake her sister. "Come on Jules...stop faking it. It's not funny anymore."

Laura tried to pull Kim away but she resisted.

"She's fine. You'll see. Come on Jules. Time to wake up."

"NOOOOO!"

Everyone jumped as Gavin screamed.

"Honey..." Laura started.

"NOOOOO! Get away from her!"

Kim backed off. Partly from shock and partly because she was scared of him.

Some of the Marines, as well as the security personnel, came over to see what the new commotion was all about.

Gavin knelt next to Julie's body. He placed his hands over her wounds, closed his eyes and concentrated.

The bird had been easy. This time is different. This time there is something new to cross.

Reviving Stir had given him hope and new strength; strength and depth he didn't know he had or even what it meant.

A thin line of sweat appeared on his brow.

Gavin grunted and concentrated harder.

Out of the ground rose a shimmering doorway right next to him and Julie.

Laura and Kim fell over in shock. Everyone else took a step back. They had no idea what the hell was happening. No one had ever seen something like this.

Gavin opened his eyes and stood up. Without even glancing at his mother he stepped through the portal and disappeared from the face of the Earth.

"Gavin!" she screamed.

* * *

Gavin stepped through and appeared in a different place of existence.

"Why hello dear."

Gavin turned and saw his grandmother Betsy.

"What are you doing here?"

"I'm looking for someone," he explained.

"Oh, I see. You know that you're not supposed to be here."

"I'm not?" he responded. "How come?"

"It's complicated dear."

"Can you help me find her?"

"Maybe. I think I know just where to find who you're looking for. Come with me."

Gavin took Betsy's hand and they flew. In no time at all she took them to a large arena. Below them a swarm of people aimlessly sat around. Betsy landed and looked at her grandson.

"Be quick."

"I will grandma. Thank you. I'm...I'm sorry I can't stay."

She laughed. "There will be plenty of time for that later."

Gavin turned and walked up a few of the arena steps. He saw her immediately and approached.

"Come with me."

"Where am I? Who are you?"

"Take my hand."

"Okay." She placed her hand in Gavin's.

There was even more confusion and disbelief as Gavin reappeared. However, in his hand he held onto a corporeal form. Laura and Kim stared, mouths wide open as Julie, very translucent, stood over her unmoving body. The portal lowered into the ground and disappeared.

Gavin looked up at her. "Here you go."

"Oh. Is this for me?"

Gavin nodded and let go of her hand.

Julie's form lay down over her body and faded away.

Julie coughed and abruptly sat up.

What the hell? What did my son just do?

Kim immediately moved forward and hugged her sister. "Jules! I knew you were okay."

Julie stopped coughing and opened her eyes. They were no longer brown. They were now black.

Laura spoke up. "Are...are you alright?"

"I don't know."

Laura pulled Gavin to her. "Do you know what your name is?"

"What are you talking about," said Kim. "Of course she knows what her name is."

Julie looked at both of them. "I have no idea. Who are you?"

* * *

Michael, Richard, Thomas, Calvin and Hobbes all watched the overhead, transfixed at what they'd just witnessed. With the early morning light Calvin had switched the satellite view off of infrared thermal while they continued to observe the aftermath of the attack on their family.

Out of nowhere they saw Gavin flip out and then, what looked like a portal, rise out of the ground. Calvin and Hobbes continued to talk to each other through their private chat window through the entire ordeal.

What the fuck?

No shit dude.

They watched as Gavin disappeared through the portal and instantaneously reemerged with what looked like a ghost not a second later. That ghost lay down over Julie's dead body and they watched as Julie sat up.

What the fuck! Did you just see that?

I've got it recorded. The Director has GOT to see this shit.

Thomas was awestruck. "Uh..Laura? Are you still there?"

"I'm here."

"What the hell is going on?"

"I literally have no fricking idea. I can't begin to describe what just happened."

"Neither can we. But you need to do me a favor. Run and hide. I'll find you. I love you Laura."

"I love you too."

Thomas killed the link and removed his headset.

"Um," said Hobbes. "I'm sorry to tell you this Mr. Clark but there are visitors outside. They're coming in right now."

Thomas nodded and walked over to his father and Richard. Michael placed his hand on his son's shoulder.

"I'm sorry son but I can't stay anymore."

"What? I don't understand," Thomas replied. "What are you talking about?"

Michael disappeared along with the weight on his shoulder from his father's hand.

What the fuck pop?

The door to the TOC opened and a number of tough looking men rushed in. They pointed their weapons at Thomas.

"Drop the weapon or die where you stand!"

Thomas was thoroughly exhausted from the entire ordeal. He let the rifle slip from his hands and it clattered as it hit the floor. His raised his arms.

"I'm going to walk slowly to the couch now. My daughter is sick and I don't know what the hell is going on."

As the men covered him Thomas walked over to the couch, sat down and pulled Emily close to him. It was at that moment he finally started to cry. His tears bore down his face and a few droplets fell on Emily's cheek. He whispered in her unconscious ear.

"Everything's going to change Em. I'm so sorry. I'm so very, very sorry."

Visit my website at

http://www.dwneuman.com

If you enjoyed this novel please consider taking a moment and writing a quick review about it (on Amazon). It helps me out more than you know and fuels my motivation! Of course, word of mouth works wonders too! ;)

Thank you!

And you can look forward to book five,
Shadows of the Heart,
in the future.

www.ingramcontent.com/pod-product-compliance
Lightning Source LLC
Chambersburg PA
CBHW071635260626
47170CB00001B/105